MEET JOHN TROW

FORGE LAKE

the Store

Wentworth

School

TO PARADE GROUND

Post Office

Farm

BRIDGE

WHEEL

BELLOWS

Rossiter

Cemetery

FURNACE

Slag Heap

REFINING
FORGE

House

Boarding
House

parking

GREAT
FORGE

BABY ROCK

MOUNT RIGA
DISTRICT No. 13

Mt Riga
National Historic Park
Salisbury
Litchfield Co. Connecticut

Map prepared by
Simon M. Sullivan & Sons.
New York, New York.

MEET JOHN TROW

✦ A NOVEL ✦

THOMAS DYJA

VIKING

VIKING
Published by the Penguin Group
Penguin Putnam Inc., 375 Hudson Street,
New York, New York 10014, U.S.A.
Penguin Books Ltd, 80 Strand,
London WC2R 0RL, England
Penguin Books Australia Ltd, 250 Camberwell Road, Camberwell,
Victoria 3124, Australia
Penguin Books Canada Ltd, 10 Alcorn Avenue,
Toronto, Ontario, Canada M4V 3B2
Penguin Books (N.Z.) Ltd, Cnr Rosedale and Airborne Roads, Albany,
Auckland, New Zealand
Penguin Books Ltd, Registered Offices:
Harmondsworth, Middlesex, England

First published in 2002 by Viking Penguin,
a member of Penguin Putnam Inc.

1   3   5   7   9   10   8   6   4   2

PUBLISHER'S NOTE
This is a work of fiction. Names, characters, places and incidents either
are the product of the author's imagination or are used fictitiously, and any
resemblance to actual persons, living or dead, business establishments,
events, or locales is entirely coincidental.

LIBRARY OF CONGRESS CATALOGING IN PUBLICATION DATA
Dyja, Thomas.
Meet John Trow / Thomas Dyja.
p. cm.
ISBN 0-670-03099-6
1. Cold Harbor (Va.), Battle of, 1864—Fiction   2. Historical reenactments—Fiction.
3. Fathers and sons—Fiction.   4. Connecticut—Fiction.   I. Title.
PS3554.Y48 M44 2002
813'.54—dc21   2001055905

This book is printed on acid-free paper. ∞

Printed in the United States of America
Set in Perpetua
Designed by Ginger Legato

For my wife,
Suzanne,
who is more wonderful than
anyone I could have imagined

AUTHOR'S NOTE

This book is a work of fiction. Names, characters, places, and incidents either are the product of my imagination or are used fictitiously.

While the historical circumstances of the Riga Village described here are true, and many of the places mentioned do indeed exist, the few scattered markers and old cabins that remain atop Mt. Riga have not, and hopefully never will be, transformed into the kind of national park I write about.

The 2nd Connecticut, serving under Colonel Elisha Kellogg, was indeed slaughtered at the battle of Cold Harbor, but without the services of John Trow, who is entirely fictitious. Except as described above, any resemblance to actual persons, living or dead, businesses, companies, events, or locales is entirely coincidental.

The thought of the future torments us,
and the past is holding us back.
That is why the present is slipping from our grasp.

—Gustave Flaubert,
in a letter to Louis Bouilhet, December 19, 1850

PART ONE

CHAPTER

I

WWW.CHOCOLATEPUDDING.COM

www.chocopud.com

"$76.71."

www.pud.com

"Dad."

www.Americaspudding.com

"Dad!"

It wasn't the voice that snapped him back; it was the shopping cart butting into his stomach, pushed by his indignant twelve-year-old son, Nate, who was currently more indignant than usual. The boy's eyes rolled. Steven Armour turned to the cashier, an acne-scarred teenager named Bobby Osselin, who often showed up at the town lake alone, just as the families left, to smoke cigarettes and stare at Hotchkiss on the other shore. "Sorry. How much?"

Bobby nodded to the register read-out, a disdainful move that seemed to put him in Nate's camp, "$76.71." Lines bulged back from every register on this summer Saturday morning. The man behind Steven coughed to signal his impatience. Bobby bounced a little on his toes. "Cash?"

"Yeah." Steven reached into his right pocket and found lint. A dismal week was becoming a dismal weekend. "Aw, *shit*. I forgot money." He looked up at Bobby for some understanding of the harried dad's lot, but instead the boy glared. "You guys take bank cards?" Bobby stuck out his hand. "*Excellent*. Listen, sorry, man." Steven fumbled through his wallet. "I totally spaced when I was running out, you know?" Just past forty, he occasionally lapsed into his own version of teen-speak when faced with youth, as if producing papers to prove his right to freely move among them. Steven handed over the card. "Thanks, man."

Bobby shrugged. "Whatever."

As he loaded the cart, a nameless yet very specific unease lodged in Steven's mind; he had forgotten something, something for Patty that, if missing when he got home, would destroy the balance of the day. He rolled out of the busy checkout traffic to consider whether it was a dairy product, detergent, or wheat bread. Plums and corn and tomatoes he'd gotten after culling through bins of overripe produce, all deep in color and stretched by late summer into what appeared to be perfection, yet bruised, bursting, or wooden when turned over, only a moment from rot. He doubted she would appreciate the effort, but her ability to surprise on occasion kept him trying, even though the object of his search remained just out of reach. Where had his memory gone? He ruled out cereal, was positive he'd mailed both the mortgage check and the satellite bill, though he'd had to transfer from savings to do it. Thoughts grew, divided, then grew again, faster than Steven's normally elastic sense of calm could accommodate: birthday presents to buy, repairs long delayed, squeezing in the lake for Patty, the nagging concern that Emily wasn't where a five-year-old should be. Work called out as well; the new domain had to be in place by Tuesday. He was ashamed to be so awash in minutiae. Whatever Patty had wanted was lost to him now.

www.silkypudding.com

www.puddingsilk.com

Two days ago the legal department at Dilly-Perkins had discovered that the URLs of some of the promotional Web sites Steven oversaw—www.chocolatesilk.com, www.vanillasilk.com, even www.butterscotch silk.com—had already been registered by an entrepreneurial pornographer willing to sell the names (except, intriguingly enough, www.tapiocasilk.com) for an amount deemed by DP's head counsel extortionate. Steven had seen this coming during the product naming, but it was years since he'd sat in on a meeting that important; these days people floated or, if in a hurry, ran things by him. They got a reading from him, lined up his support. What Steven did not do anymore was make the call, give the go-ahead, or look at all the options and green-light if appropriate. He'd slid into the vast sea of middle management, joining waves when roiled, becalming under sunny corporate skies.

Steven pictured his pending promotion sailing by. Since Thursday he had desperately blue-skied for new domains, even once brain-dumping with a colleague of long acquaintance. It was between him and one other person, said Dylan Petro, DP's king of dotcom, beloved contrarian corporate guru, his former assistant. If he could nail pudding and get Meal Solutions on its way, Steven would likely be the next director of Special New Media Projects under Petro, who had always seemed like his boss, even back then, indulging him by doing the filing as he met people infinitely more important than Armour, that lifer, in marketing. If not, Steven would end up as an odd bit of space junk, the last Japanese soldier on a remote Pacific island, a man who thinks he telecommutes but simply doesn't know he's been exiled. A new domain was more than a name; it was the hinge of Steven's future.

With a studied country weekend shabbiness—ancient purple Northwestern T-shirt, paint-spattered khakis, expensive throwback baseball cap, all of which happened to be his daily wear—he stopped in the breezeway and squinted into the glare coming off car hoods in the parking lot in search of Nate, who'd dashed out at the appearance of Cool Dad. Gone were the years when his son had to be pried off his leg. Steven had found him adorable then; an advancing case of adolescence had since whacked Nate out of normal human form, his arms growing ahead of his body, long and oversized when compared with the rest. This spring, Nate had begun to make the mistake, painful to Steven, of showing them off with basketball jerseys and T-shirts with cutaway sleeves, in particular the black KISS T-shirt he was wearing today; Nate's statement shirt, the first T-shirt that he'd bought for himself. Steven hadn't had the heart to tell him that KISS had been his favorite band too when he was that age. Steven had seen drummer Peter Criss on cable recently, double-chinned and ludicrous, singing "Beth" in his cat makeup. He remembered starting to call Nate in when a slight twinge of shame in Gene Simmons's face, tongue still flicking away over a now-jiggly stomach, made him think better.

The heat was punishing. Off near the end of the supermarket's brick porch a bit of black flashed and Steven aimed toward it, past the bulletin board filled with notices for county fairs, lobster sales, and firehouse barbecues, quiet signs of the country bacchanalia that marked summer's end. Over and between the daytrippers milling from shop to shop on Salisbury's main drag, the year-round residents had reached the point that comes every summer when they exchange the pleasant glances and patient smiles of a couple whose guests are leaving soon. And yet, as tired as they are, they dread the clean-up, the emptiness, the being alone together, and so there is another drink, and another town fair, before the fall. Steven stopped in front of a poster displaying a mandala of German sausages, faded after seasons of exposure, wieners, knockwurst, and braunschweiger unaware they'd lost their color, lolling as they did on the plate, all sickly tans and ochers—Alte Zeit brand, DP's main competition. A long ghostly face hovered in front of it, reflected in the glass.

Steven twirled the two shockingly long hairs he'd discovered this morning inside his ears—the start of the same bountiful tufts that an old boss once had, blooms of hair that must have impaired his hearing. He tested the wattles growing under his neck and briefly stuck out his tongue for a mock examination before noticing Bobby Osselin and almost everyone else at the checkout watching him through the window. Soon after moving here full-time a year ago, he had realized that only his grandchildren would have the chance to be considered true residents of this old and gently twisted corner of Connecticut, and this kind of thing would, he thought, probably set them all back a generation. He moved on and after a few steps made out the picture of Simmons and the drooping tongue. Nate stood safe amid a benign crowd of a few dozen people, five or six of whom wore heavy costumes despite the heat.

www.chocosilk.com? Steven mulled a few impact words—*creamy, luscious, smooth, rich.*

Two shrill sinews of sound suddenly writhed up from a fiddler over by the crowd. Protesting at first, long and whining, as if pulled up by the roots, the notes twined around each other and finally became one tune that skipped about the Audis and pickup trucks in the parking lot, around the small clutch of shoppers who circled the three pairs of dancers, men in military uniforms—Steven assumed Civil War—and women in extremely bright, extremely large dresses, one salmon, one sky blue, and the last emerald, all with wide hoop skirts. The lilt played adequately by the unseen fiddler moved with the energetic hop of a geriatric dancer, and its charm was similar—execution didn't matter. Unable to place its style exactly, Steven guessed the music to be some bit of folk exhumed from the nineteenth century; a reel, maybe, given the line dancing of the three couples. As he got closer he could see the fiddler, a gaunt man, tall, in rough brown high-water trousers, standing next to the bank of recycling machines. He expressed no joy as he sawed away at the violin. The harmlessness of the music, its reassurance that Nate was in safe hands, that easier lives were once had, soothed Steven's nervous soul, and for a moment he found stillness in the Grand Union parking lot. He closed his eyes and sank deeper into the mood, imagining the mountains around him and the trees as they were a hundred and fifty years ago. The dancers would be townspeople, probably the ancestors of these seven.

"Dad. Look at this stupid thing." Steven's eyes popped open, and at first he didn't recognize Nate, whose head moved gently to the music despite a throwaway sneer toward the fiddler. Who was this gangly kid, arms crossed in front, now tapping randomly on an oversized bicep? It wasn't his Little Nat. That boy was eager to please, funny, curious. This one eked out Cs, was growing hair in places other than his ears, places Steven preferred not to think about. This Nate left him alone when he wanted company, found him when he wanted to hide. Steven could detect a thickening fuzz on the boy's upper lip. "I don't get this. What is this?"

"Shhhh." Then Steven whispered, "It's some kind of Civil War dance."

The couples clopped for a moment across the asphalt in a polka-like skip, caught new partners in the crook of the arm, and twirled. Steven had always found the firm bodices and booted ankles of the nineteenth century erotic in the most primal way, the whole tightly bound package offering total control. Early in his marriage, he had learned not to dwell on his sexual imaginings; Patty's demands were limited, enjoyable, and increasingly infrequent. Most of the time Steven felt he was taking a pleasant vacation in a country he was not all that interested in visiting. As the dancers whirled by, he lingered on the women's waists, that place of meeting where the straight line of bodice blooms into the skirt, the place where his hands would go if allowed. Steven's shoulders and arms tingled nervously, and he felt an almost rhythmic pushing at his lower back.

Without a change in expression, the fiddler stepped up the pace. Laboring on beneath layers of velvet and wool, the dancers forced smiles as they worked at their reel, compelled, it seemed, by something more than pride and certainly other than enjoyment. The new, tauter rhythm tightened around Steven's chest. He could hear himself breathing. Summer couldn't stay this hot; the music couldn't keep on at this speed. He could not pull one of these women away for a Victorian debauch. Still, the pressure at his back and the high collars of the dresses made strange things feel possible. Steven looked into the bag full of bulbous, overgrown fruit—obscene, like everything else around him at the season's climax: the fairs, the parties, the late summer bikinis, monstrous purple zucchini. On the fringes of the lot, loosestrife swayed through patches of goldenrod, drooped over bull thistles, and a sudden enervating wave of cricket song—the sound of heat shimmering over a dry field—rose up to meet the music. *www.pudding.com. www.pudding.com.* Steven caught Nate sneaking a look at him from the corner of his eye, so he returned a reassuring nod, wiped his brow with a show of nonchalance.

"Oh, see, that's what this is." As if Steven hadn't just told him. "That's Manskart. See?" Nate pointed excitedly with an elbow at the thickest, most decorated soldier dancing, a saber bouncing off his left haunch. Sweat rolled off Manskart's flushed face and into his pointed black beard. The boy showed no interest in leaving, still randomly tapped away on his arms. "I get him for history and home room this year. Mister *Walter* Manskart." The act of saying a teacher's first name retained a sense of danger or privilege to Nate. "He dresses up like that for class sometimes. Everybody says he's pretty nuts." Mr. Manskart was the least winded of the six, despite his beer belly and Ruthian profile. He switched between the long-haired blonde in a blue dress, the chunky woman in the salmon dress, and the redhead.

A redhead. Whatever happened to her, he wondered. The woman he didn't marry. He wondered that often. The knot of this woman's hair was slipping out, and Steven positioned himself to get a better look as she joined arms with Manskart and skipped down between the other couples.

As the woman in green promenaded closer toward him, a blast of recognition froze Steven amid the heat. The back of the long neck and the hair were certainly right; the small space between her upper lip and nose was exact. But he hadn't seen her in fifteen years, and she'd never worn an emerald hoop skirt, not, that is, for him. Then she smiled and caught the eye of her partner, Manskart, pulled her chin back a bit, and fixed him, fixed the big, sweaty grammar school teacher as she had Steven at moments when something he'd said or done managed to fill her immense hunger. Steven held his breath.

The two times we see our lives pass before us, the two great moments of judgment, happen before we die and when we run into an old love by chance. Steven had long had a speech prepared for this exact moment, judicious and mature, outlining, with a legal precision unseen anywhere else in his life, the causes of their parting, distributing the blame fairly, but mostly on himself, expressing, then generously forgiving, her role in it, and explaining why he had done what he had done, why he had had to. Practiced largely in front of mirrors following more than four drinks, it was a masterpiece of *l'esprit de l'escalier*, a collection of everything he'd ever wished to say over their sublime and finally torturous coupling. And it was completely forgotten here amid the Audis and the dancers.

Using his cart as a wedge, Steven pushed between two hefty women, both wearing stretch shorts. One had a T-shirt embroidered with a chihuahua in a beret; the other's was red with the slogan "Mt. Riga Furnace National Park—The Forge of History" circling a cannon.

"Where're you going, Dad?"

"Just getting a better look."

And so the inventory. Steven stood outside himself to take stock, as he was sure every person he walked by, sat beside, or drove past, did of him. He was Steven Armour, forty-one years old, one of five associate vice presidents of communications slash new media, albeit largely ceremonial, at the major food conglomerate Dilly-Perkins. Springline Dairy milk and cheeses, Happy Gerda's Old Style Deli Meats, baked and canned goods, cereals, frozen foods, Your Life Healthy Meal Choices, which included the Silk Pudding line—all staples of the family kitchen and all the bounty of Dilly-Perkins, but no one Steven had ever spoken with socially had heard of DP, no matter how huge it actually was. In short, he made a reasonable salary working in a meaningless corner of a new world.

His wife, Patty, the same age, was a triumph of style; her attractiveness to him a matter of certain continually remembered angles of beauty. Tied to her unwarranted sense of entitlement—hard earned after charming herself into Northwestern's better North Shore circles—was a social arrogance that amused and annoyed him, given that he knew they had nothing to be arrogant about; in fact, he had come with better names to drop than she had, and those at best went back only a single generation to his father's fleeting success in television during its early years in Chicago; yet her lifted chin gave her and, by extension, the family an air of importance from which they all benefited. Her fair but hardly sustaining wages as an attorney of counsel at a middling New York firm specializing in real estate law could not be the source of her unshakable sense of self-worth, yet she loved to opine, to take positions as a lawyer should, whether or not the opinion was foolish, ill-informed, or gauche. He assumed she felt it stylish and smart to pass summary judgment, though it pained him when she did so, inviting as it did others to pass judgment on her, others who too often now included Steven, as her once smooth and elegant tastes began to sprout odd mistakes. She had taken to reading serial mysteries by women writers one after an-other, for example, and bought and actively defended a CD by Shania Twain. Patty's greatest gift, though, was that when she looked in the mirror, she saw a different person from the one seen by the rest of the world.

The woman—Becky was her name—came closer again. Steven imagined the softness of the velvet as it rounded her breasts, cupped un-derneath them, still soft as it ran down her side to the scoop of her waist to just so, then riding over her bottom like torrents over a fall, and pool-ing down below. "Bottom"—it sounded straight out of Victorian pornography. What would it be like if they slept together now? Steven squeezed the grocery cart handle so that he could secretly test his bi-ceps, his pecs, his back. It would be better now that they were adults. He was breathless again, more nervous than aroused, until he remembered all that he had become—a responsible man with a family and job on his back; what he had chosen to become when he married a girl as desperate to get ahead as he had been.

He sagged. Even thinking of the consummation burned its pleasure away. He felt a bit nauseated and foolish. Sex wasn't the point. Is this what she would look like after fifteen years? Deep lines in the face, an ef-fort even more desperate at forty to be winsome, to be perfect and beautiful and the center of all things? She steered another Union sol-dier—this one a reedy private in period glasses, probably just out of col-lege, chinless—gave him enough fire to own his gaze even after he'd gotten the plump lady in salmon. She hadn't changed, even with the sharper features, rounder cheeks. What reasons could there possibly be for her to envy him, still want him in her bed, still love him, after these many years? He considered his children, Nate and Emily, twelve and five, his three acres and old farmhouse on Route 41 toward Massachu-setts. But still the words flashed in his mind in a clear statement of the thought he constantly shook away—"I should be better than what I am." Most days he didn't know what to make of himself, but today he was certain that he'd failed, failed her, in so many ways. He'd sold his soul for snack cakes and security. The dance stopped.

He pondered what the next move should be. Go up and say hello? Touch her? The viewers applauded. As tenuous as Steven's life was, he had the consolation of wondering why she would be a Civil War re-enactor performing in a grocery store parking lot; it was, to him, such a stupid blue-collar thing.

"Dad."

Steven took a step closer to the knot of dancers.

"Dad?" Nate was right at his shoulder, in the KISS T-shirt, his big arms hanging down. "Manskart looks like he's gonna puke. Look at him." The woman turned toward him, and in a second Steven realized that the sharp features were not a function of age; it was definitely not Becky. Relief nearly bowled him over. Then the look between them lasted just that one extra beat. This woman was beautiful—and didn't know the long list of things he was not. Adding the quickest hint of a smile, she turned away for good, snapping back a stray lock.

The plump woman in salmon, shiny with sweat, strode over to Steven and Nate to hand them flyers, forcing Steven to lose the red-haired woman in the crowd. Nate began to read aloud, tentatively: "Mt. Riga Furnace National Park. The Forge of History. Labor Day! Come to our fourth annual encampment. Tactical demonstration by the Second Connecticut—one P.M. Full sutler alley all day. Enjoy the olden days with us. Come visit old Salisbury!"

Nate edged closer to Manskart, wearing a shy look, as if he were standing next to a celebrity, starstruck by an eighth-grade teacher who fielded questions with his chest thrown out in what Steven hoped was only dramatic pomposity. Manskart groomed his mustache and goatee with his thumb and forefinger, posing with one leg straight and columnar, and the other bent, free hand atop the saber. Steven guessed he was probably the same age he was, but rounder, damper, louder, more eager to rule a room.

"Come on. We have a million things to do." Steven pointed at the cart. "Here. You drive."

Nate looked back as they walked toward the Navigator, leased back in happier financial days. "That's Manskart."

"Yeah, you told me."

CHAPTER

2

THE DRIVE HOME BEGAN IN SILENCE, as both Steven and Nate watched a few minutes of New York State pass before the Connecticut line. This was borderland, a place of confluence between those two states and Massachusetts and, centuries ago, between nations. Since the establishment of the first white settlements in the 1720s, built by New York Dutch who came up the Hudson River and headed east, and by intrepid, greedy members of the Connecticut colony advancing from the other direction, the borders had often been redrawn. To a driver passing through them for the first time they appeared utterly arbitrary, but whether the lines affected one's vision of the land or the land had made the borders clear, each state, though so close, had its own character. Plump and rolling like a Dutch burgher, the low farm hills and round curves of Dutchess County, New York, gave way in the east to Connecticut's sharper edges, as if in New England an older, pricklier, puritan earth took over just past the governor's signature. In New York, overgrown vines swallowed abandoned cars, softened time with such worn barns and constant acres of green as put Rip Van Winkle to sleep not far to the west, while in the Mountain County of Connecticut, waterfalls hid behind jutting rocks and stands of old pine; one-lane roads twisted up mountains with only a single cable to preserve against the momentary lack of concentration, the sweaty palm slipping off the wheel. Connecticut had never been fully conquered, or, if it had, the conquerers had not been as insistent on civilization as in the neighboring states. To the north sat Massachusetts, reserved and superior, readying the hardy for their Berkshire bed-and-breakfasts, their dance performances and theater colloquia, with hundreds of middling, wind-chimed antique shoppes amid the foothills of Sheffield and Great Barrington.

Steven was glad they had chosen Connecticut. Until you'd lived here for a while, you couldn't relax, couldn't count on your expectations. For a small state, it held secrets well. To the left now as they drove was a small lake—a pond, really—that Steven had passed for the better part of a year before he noticed it one spring day while on the way to Millerton, New York, stuck behind one of the many elderly, sedan-driving inhabitants of the area.

"Dad? Can you drive me to Paul's house?"

"Now? No. I thought you hated Paul."

Nate's classsmate Paul had buck teeth and lived in the sort of tiny ranch home close to the road that often signified centuries of hand-me-down clothes, hunted meat, and service to generations of rich neighbors. Although he had been pleasant to Steven and Patty both times they met him, they kept Paul on small animal torture watch. He'd be a likely suspect if harmless Nate was drawn down that twisted road toward being a shitty kid.

"He's cool." Steven looked over at Nate, who was not smirking or posing. Nate's hands rested large in his lap, like dead sea birds or fish, splayed palms up and useless. One fumbled at the Seek button on the radio, then flopped back down. Nate's ears and teeth seemed huge to Steven. "Dad, watch out."

Steven blinked and realized he was halfway over the line. Gently swerving back in his lane, he said, "Well, I don't see how you can go. We gotta get home." No reaction from Nate save for pursed lips. The fact that Nate didn't continue the rally, had accepted the shot as a winner, made Steven nervous. Nate pushed the Seek button again, producing another bad song. "Listen, why don't you help me with this domain thing I've been working on? If I get this shit done, maybe I can take you over later." Light swearing, an offer to cut a deal; all the marks of Cool Dad. Of Friendly Dad. As genuine as Steven tried to be, he heard his words echo between condescension and desperation.

The boy shrugged a little when Steven snapped off the radio. "So far we've got www.silkypudding.com, www.silkytaste.com, and www.silk chocolate.com but with all the flavors and not just chocolate. What do you think? Any of them make you hungry for the silky smooth taste of Chocolate Silk Pudding?" Steven glanced at his son's bland face. "Any of them make you want to visit a Web site about pudding?" Steven wondered if Nate's oblivion was intentional or beyond the boy's control. Any of them make you want to blow your fucking head off with a Magnum, he imagined asking. That would scare the kid more than even Steven felt necessary. "This is Web stuff, Nate. Cutting-edge stuff."

After a few seconds, Nate shrugged. "It's like TV, Dad. It's not such a big deal anymore." That Steven worked on the Internet bought him a few minutes of interest from adults, most of whom wondered if he had options, but kids Nate's age, who felt no shock of the new at seeing a Doppler weather map updated on their computer, couldn't care less. The boy's hands fluttered about an imaginary drum set as Nate made juicy sounds of impact, nearly the same sound he'd used for playing guns a year ago. He bucked the seat back and forth, just enough to annoy, listening to his own song in his own head.

Coming up over a small hill beside Lakeville Lake and heading down, Steven felt his stomach drop out as if he were on a roller coaster. Ahead, through the canopy of green swaying trees and the flowering borders of orange and yellow and blue, under the sunny, milky melting sky, was a day that Steven dreaded for no other reason than that it would be spent with his family, locked to their whining, their needs, and their total lack of interest in what he wanted, in what he had to do. He could escape none of it—not the family, not the work, not the responsibility, nor the need to appear happy.

The whining of a mountain fiddle came back to Steven; he could hear it as they passed the old library and the white church of Salisbury, then veered left up Route 41 at the White Hart Inn and the Civil War Monument to ride along the base of the Taconics toward their home, toward the rest of the day. The fiddler rose again—the same song from the lot, or was he hearing something new? The Civil War uniforms of the dancers had had the clear, handsome power of knowing exactly what they were for; the dresses more substantial and more erotic than a thong bikini. What may have seemed chaotic in that parking lot had melody and steps, while all he had now was random drumming.

You should be someone better, the fiddle reminded him. She had not been in the parking lot, dancing; she was still out there, still a tiger in the jungle, waiting to surprise him someday, a cobweb in his mind that he'd never be able to reach.

The music stopped. "This is NPR."

Nate had turned the radio back on. The boy sighed heavily and dramatically. He had learned this piece of stagecraft from his mother, who liked to wake Steven with it during her restless nights. "Maybe Mom will take me."

A sour silence clabbered in the car. They drove past one of Salisbury's cemeteries on the right, past old and gracious homes and new ones coated with metal siding to where the truly beautiful homes were hidden from view; past a stretch of white horse barns on the right and a pond with a lone pony nibbling at its banks on the left. How had this happened, Steven wondered. How had he gotten here? He had done the right thing those years before with Becky, he reminded himself, and doing the right thing was paramount, or at least not doing the wrong thing. He may not have been the man to run into a burning building to save people he didn't know, but he did believe in a gentle step, justice, politeness, and paying the price if you ever did do the wrong thing. *He* certainly had. He'd made the mature choice back then, he told himself; taken his future into account. And that was what had brought him here, to this road, on this day. Who gave out second chances? he wondered. Maybe Dylan Petro.

Steven felt the need to do something he did at least once every time he drove—to close his eyes and let go of the wheel. The first times he did it, many years ago, he had closed his eyes for a count of two while stretching his hands right above the steering wheel, and he'd been surprised to see, when he opened his eyes and regained control of the wheel, that he was on the same line as before, as if he had been expecting to spin out and collide with a guardrail just on principle. If he'd learned anything from his suicidal tic it was that he'd have to try harder than just not steering to destroy everything in his life. Since then he'd done it hundreds of times, and by now it reminded Steven not of Russian roulette but of riding a bike with no hands, something he'd been able to do for a very long distance as a boy. It was a toll paid, a simple tribute to fate. Even with the family along he'd close his eyes and let go, sneaking a quick obligatory squeeze of the eyelids down some straightaway in the same spirit as he once dropped change into the collection plate on Sundays.

Steven came around a curve, closed his eyes and let go. The redhead at the dance immediately popped against the black, with the look she'd given him. She was not merely an image, though. She moved. Her mouth opened a little and she ran a finger along her lower lip. The tight bustier forced up her breasts, which rose and fell as she breathed deeply.

Heavily. The palm of her other hand slid up the flat of her stomach until it met her breasts, which curved out into—

"Holy fuck, Dad! Dad!"

A horn bellowed, and Steven's eyes jolted open to see a truck coming directly at them in the left lane. His hands grabbed the wheel, spun it to the right by reflex as the red-and-black truck ripped past and the car bounced onto the shoulder as he braked too quickly, squealing tires, the driver behind leaning on his horn forming a brief harmony as the car swerved back onto the road, tailed to the left then spun out right, slipping off to the shoulder again and stopping facing the oncoming traffic and the cars slowing to look at them.

Dust settled around the car, its motor panting. Steven turned off the ignition. Huddled in the corner, hiding behind arms that now seemed thin and pale, was a little boy staring past an elbow, amazed at what he'd just lived through. Steven burst into tears and reached out to Nate, embracing him as he wept, the boy's head pulled in under his chin and Steven's face deep into the boy's hair, smelling through Patty's papaya shampoo the sour puppy smell Nate's head had always had. He combed Nate's brown, bristly hair with his fingers and, expecting him to pull away, instead found his boy pushing in closer. They breathed together as they used to a decade ago when they'd nap beside each other on Sunday afternoons. He wanted to take one of those Sunday naps right now with his son. Fall asleep for more time than the day had. Wake up and be too tired to wake up; arms and legs too heavy to move. Steven's tears slowed. "Are you okay, Nat?"

"Yeah. Dad, what happened? What's wrong?"

"Everything's okay." Some firmness returned to Steven's bones. "Are you okay? Are you sure?" He was thinking, I'm so lonely, Nate. Please stay exactly this way. "Listen, don't tell Mom. All right? Nate. Please don't tell Mom. I'm fine. We're fine. I'm just wiped from work, and I zoned for a second. Okay?"

Nate nodded and edged over to the far door.

No other drivers had pulled over, despite the dust and the burning tires. Alone on the shoulder, Steven started the car and drove home.

In her black swimsuit with white piping, Patty stood in the kitchen they'd borrowed against their 401(k)s to rebuild, arms crossed, legs crossed, impatiently waiting, leaning against a counter of green slate, with Emily saying "Mommy" over and over to no response. Long-limbed, long-legged, long-torsoed; Patty was a little too long all over the place, but when mustered for uses other than attraction, her height could be dominating. Patty made a show of sighing and looking at her watch when they walked in, though her sunglasses probably prevented her from seeing much of anything.

Steven dropped two bags on the counter, and Nate followed with two more. "What?" said Steven. He was not in the mood for one of Patty's grand reactions, though he'd half-expected it. After the hoop skirts and bustles, she seemed to him naked in a most obvious fashion.

"Well, forget it."

"What?"

"Well, I wanted to go to the lake and now it's already noon."

"And?"

"It's boiling out." She sighed again, as if all were so tragically lost.

Nate stepped in. "We're late because a truck almost hit us and ran Dad off the road."

Patty held her ground for a few beats, then deigned to slide silently from her towering height and touch Steven's brow. "Well. Are you all right? Nate? Steven, you look flushed." She was warming to the task.

He closed his eyes, grateful for such a son. Grateful for covering, but also for restoring to him even for a few seconds the softer woman he had married. "Yeah, but I'd like to lie down for a few minutes. I know you want to go to the beach and I'll go after . . ."

Prepared, sober, and solicitous, Patty's emergency response rivaled that of a nurse during the London blitz. She pointed him off toward the bedroom. "Go and lay down. I'll put this stuff away. We can go after lunch." Patty sighed again once, quickly, as if steeling herself, and Steven heard the rattle of grocery bags being emptied as he walked up the stairs to their room.

After slipping off his deck shoes, he stretched out across the freshly made bed, the pillow cool from the air conditioning. He closed his eyes, but as tired as he was, he couldn't find a shore to rest on, no single emotion to use for cover. Both angry and anxious, he was also happy, even giddy, at being alive, yet none of it seemed substantial enough to base the rest of the day on. He felt as if he were floating atop the sea as the currents pull and the wind blows. *www.vanillasilk.com.* He opened his eyes. Around the room, tight vegetal patterns vibrated off the walls. This is home, he thought. This is my home. A doll on the top of his bureau. My home. He closed his eyes and began floating again.

Patty yelled from the kitchen, "Did you get raisins?" All Steven could do was groan, first to himself, then once more, loudly, as an answer. "Great. Just great." A paper bag was violently crumpled and a cabinet door slammed shut as she hissed a *shit* meant for general appreciation. "Well, pick them up after you take Nate over to Paul's." The emergency over, real life was soon to resume. A few minutes of weightlessness passed in which Steven nibbled at sleep before a folded piece of white paper landed on his chest.

He stared at the paper for a few seconds, then opened it: RAISINS printed in block letters at the top and some kind of ad on the back. He turned it over. "Relive the olden days. Visit Old Riga Village!"

He closed his eyes, but sleep had gone.

CHAPTER

3

AND SO THE PORNOGRAPHER WAS PAID and Dilly-Perkins launched its Web sites into the deep silence of cyberspace, where hundreds of thousands of lite-pudding fans commented on their favorite flavors, signed up for free merchandise, like water-bottle fanny pouches, and learned many facts about nutrition that they probably knew already and, if not, could have found more easily on the back of a cereal box. Steven was disappointed in what he had created, though the response was as strong as Dylan Petro had hoped.

It was Thursday afternoon, almost Labor Day weekend, two weeks after the accident (Steven considered it that, even though no one had been hurt); a threatening day of low clouds occasionally swollen dark blue with rain. Without a firm knowledge of the day's exact nature, the world seemed unsettled, fidgety. Cows bunched close together near their barns, and people trotted through errands, scooting from store to store trying to beat rain that hadn't begun to fall and maybe never would.

Steven sat in his small, messy office, a converted closet that resembled a workplace about as much as a bachelor apartment resembles a home, waiting for a conference call with Dylan Petro. He had calmed down since that confusing August day, stilled by a thick morning-after feeling. These weeks he tended to move slowly and gently, to be wary of loud noises, and kept his eyes open at all times while driving, having been as close to death as he needed for now.

Leaning back in his ergonomically correct Aeron chair, an expensive comfort he'd afforded himself among the pine shelves and giveaway phone in his home office, Steven heard the sounds of departure from the second floor. The tense, techno theme of *The Powerpuff Girls* provided the score to Patty's pre-liftoff scramble, ten minutes Steven had learned to fear. She jiggled keys, and her heels snapped crisply across the wooden floor, became muffled by a rug, then snapped again. He could tell she had a purpose, most likely looking for something without revealing what it was she wanted, growing more annoyed at each step, building pressure throughout the house. Steven predicted heavy weather ahead, especially with Emily and his father, Phil, obviously sitting on the couch watching cartoons and not helping her find whatever mystery item she was after. Only Phil's presence was preventing an immediate Force Five blow here; his father was in for the long weekend and Patty was working extremely hard to appear in complete control of every situation she had anything to do with. Despite their long-standing mutual dislike—Patty's pretense of hypercompetence clashed with Phil's natural drive toward chaos—they had, Tito-like, managed to hold their places within the family for thirteen years without an overt blood feud. Of course, this sort of thing doesn't always last, and after one evening Steven was near exhaustion from monitoring conversations and maintaining a constant readiness to jump into the ring and separate Phil's round self from the lanky Patty if they ended up in a polite but deadly clinch. They were well matched, which explained in part the détente. He heard his father's voice—kindly, as always—say, "Emmy, come on, little girl. Let's get ready to go. Turn off the boob tube before your dear mommy kills us."

The steps fell harder downstairs, a closet door slammed, the growling thunder of a storm that still might pass. Years before, he would have laughed indulgently at Hurricane Patty, but he'd learned to keep his laughter to himself. As he flipped through a five-inch-thick folder of random papers, all ostensibly related to marketing single-slice, wrapped pizza cheese, but who could tell by this point, Steven willed Patty out the door and on her way to her errands with the rest of them. He squeezed his eyes shut at the sound of her voice. "Where's Nate?" "Where's the list?" "How exactly do I get to Winsted?"—sharp, anxious questions that begged for comfort beyond their simple answers.

The television roared away. Steven imagined Emily huddled between his dad and the arm of the couch, concentrating on *The Powerpuff Girls*. TV seemed to be a matter of sustenance to Emily, or defense. Two hours without it counted as sensory deprivation to her, though it was, to be fair, a family addiction. Phillip Armour, once upon the fifties, had been a rising young face on the Chicago television landscape, often seen trading tales with Studs Terkel and cracking up the crew by making Kukla tell foul jokes when Burr Tillstrom left the studio, all en route to *Taffy's Time*, a groundbreaking television series about the ups and downs of a Korean War widow and her young son, a cross between *The Andy Griffith Show* and *Julia*, except that it was on years before either one. The Armours liked television, right up until *Taffy* was canceled in 1962, when Steven was four. Life had never been the same. Even just saying "Taffy" stirred great feelings in all the Armours save for Steven, to whom the reverent whispering about "when *Taffy* was around" and "in *Taffy's* days" served as a reminder of all that he'd missed, as though the show were a favorite aunt who'd loved him best but had died before he could remember anything about her. Emily carried on the family's video tradition with her name, stolen by Steven from *The Bob Newhart Show* and Suzanne Pleshette's character, Emily Hartley, the perfect wife—a smart, sexy woman who clearly took a crazy salad with her meat. As precious and lacy as his Emily was, her maniacal streak and two bite victims in preschool spoke to darker thoughts underneath her pigtails. The words *counseling* and *Ritalin* had yet to be mentioned, but the school year would begin in two weeks.

"Did you get gas?"

The question was for Steven, the moment he'd been dreading. "I said, did you get gas? Steven?"—in a tone that insinuated he somehow carried his own name falsely. "Hello! Can you hear me? Gas!" Her mutterings came closer as she made it up two stairs. He set down the file atop a shelf full of books, large, and largely unread, histories and biographies of men like Disraeli and Grant. "I got it last night when I got Nate."

She paused on the steps, slightly deflated. "All right." Now brightly, the clouds parting, "Good. We're going." She aimed a final warning toward his office: "We'll be back in a few hours. Then the kids are all yours." She did not have to mention that "the kids" included, foremost, his father.

The front door creaked open. Phil's voice, " 'Bye, Steven." Then crusty, as he could be now on occasion, "Emmy, turn that off, for chrissakes." The television finally stopped. He imagined Emily in her pink sundress and pink sandals, hopping over the threshold, his father waddling behind her in a terry cloth shirt, too-long khakis crumpling over his Nikes, a Roman haircut sitting on his head, and a trim salt-and-pepper beard: altogether, the look of a mogul gone to seed. Gone to seed he had—or had become a nut—immediately after *Taffy* was gone. The Armours post-*Taffy* lived mainly off savings, selling the houses in Door County, in Scotland, and in Nice, trading in the Lincoln for a more sensible Buick. Rather than take a serious office job in advertising or skip to one of the networks, Phil leaned into get-rich-quick deals and the establishment of PhiRob Productions, a needlessly shoestring operation that made schlocky local ads seen mostly on Sunday mornings and during Cubs games. As Steven grew up, his older sister Barbara moved to Europe and his brother Jerry moved into therapy and he watched the good stuff go with them, his parents spending all their time and money on building their piddling company and the bizarre collection of junk that lay in heaps around their house. Given his tender age when the show was canceled, he had never known Phillip to be anything but a nut and a good, if increasingly dependent, father. The martini-sipping *Playboy* keyholder who had sent his brother to the couch and his sister to another continent had left with *Taffy*; Steven got Captain Kangaroo in bedroom slippers.

The door slammed shut. Steven listened for the start of the engine, the gravel crunch, the car going down the driveway. The storm had passed; the house still stood. He took a deep breath, closed his eyes, and sank into the warm bath of a silence offered by a suddenly empty house.

After a few minutes of dizzying quiet, Steven looked out the window. A real storm would wash all the plants along the dirt road, silvered from the dust kicked up by weeks of passing cars and no rain. His one remaining duty for the day was the conference call with Petro and a few other folks from the Happy Gerda's Meal Solution team, the last act before Labor Day kicked in and, he hoped, a big step toward getting a firmer corporate hand-hold once again. Clicking around his homepage, tapping his fingers on the mouse, anxious for the phone to ring, he watched a large red bar with the phrase "Ram It Up! Only $49 for more power where you need it!" throbbing on the screen before him. He checked his stocks, reread the top news stories, bit his nails. Before he got too nervous, he reminded himself of the drill he and Dylan had cooked up yesterday—Steven would do the heavy lifting, present their concept for the Meal Solution site, and Dylan would ride shotgun, knocking off any other Meal Solution "Team Leader" who had the gall to put up a fight on this. Their little plan boded well, it seemed, for his promotion.

Steven skipped through a few of the photo personals offered on his homepage. Pasty rurban types found at the WalMart gave back sloe looks in fancy tube tops; Russian rent-a-brides desperate to escape tried not to appear too desperate. One South Carolina fresh-out-of-high-school mother of toddler twins advertised for "Fun Without Hubby." He shuddered. The Web could be a foul thing at times. He recalled the day Dylan and his sharp-cornered Fleet Street collars were moved up. His mentor, as much as he had ever had one, the gnomish Darius Shariya, senior vice president of marketing, he of the hairy ears, had called Steven into his office and, squinting under heavy black brows, his chin barely clearing the desktop, explained that Dylan's Web skills were needed elsewhere and thanked him for training young Petro in the DP ways. All the while he'd smiled in the disarming, friendly-old-man way that he reserved for those outside his immediate working circle, a clear sign that Steven was no longer under his protection. Afterward, Steven had walked calmly to the men's room and sat in a stall for an hour as his new permanent floater waited patiently in Dylan's old cubicle. Was there one moment when dark satori struck his superiors and he was deemed unfit, too old, or possessed of whatever flaw it was that damned him to the middle circles of middle management? Or, he wondered almost every afternoon at around this time, as commuters across the country began their journeys home, was it just evolution in action? He'd had his chances, but too often he'd mucked them up. Steven played back the regrettable Phoenix conference, when he knew he spoke for two garbled, blathering sentences too long at the managers' round table, reviewed the obvious weak points in the Alte Zeit competitive report he'd finished the night Emily came down with the measles.

A breeze from the small window fluttered the Post-its stuck around his screen, reminders whose constant presence no longer reminded him of anything. Outside, a few wild turkeys slowly pecked and gobbled their way across the lawn. He stared at the phone for a few seconds; then he could pretend no longer. He'd been waiting to do this since the night before. He dragged to his desk a large box his dad had brought last night and cleared a spot on the surface, a wilderness of paper he could only occasionally trim back. Wiping his hands on his torn Clapton T-shirt, he sliced through the duct tape with a key.

A smell of old paper rose from inside the box; happily no must or water or rot. This was Steven's time capsule, sealed by him forever in the sixth grade and opened since then for occasional contributions. Like his father, he was a collector, though Steven had tried to put his life in a box rather than let it take over his home. This was also Phil's main purpose in coming, to deliver Steven's past. A year had gone by since his mother, Roberta (the "Rob" in PhiRob Productions), had died suddenly of heart failure while visiting family in Michigan, and his father had done nothing; literally, it turned out. While everyone assumed that he would eventually empty the closets and clear the drawers if for no other reason than to make room for his own ever-expanding collection of historical flotsam, Steven's father had showered, shaved, laundered, and talked of the office, giving everyone reason to believe he was functioning. A collection agency had, in April, hunted down Steven—not, he thought with annoyance, Barbara in Paris, married to a French stockbroker, or Jerry, in and out of a daze as doctors continued to tinker with his dosage of Prozac—to share the news that Phillip hadn't paid a bill since the funeral—not the phone, not the electric, not the car, not the Visa. Happily, the house in Evanston was paid off. Rather than cleaning, Phillip had spent a year simply cramming in more treasures—a set of chairs made from bulls' horns, a neon sign that said HERE'S YOUR HAM BURGER!, mint copies of *Sport* magazine. After much coaxing from Steven and the cancellation of his first purchase on eBay, his father sold the family house, paid off his debts, and signed a lease on a small apartment in a newly fashionable Chicago neighborhood once known for its Polish immigrants and Latin gangs. This visit was a distribution of Steven's effects before he finally moved out.

Before allowing himself this wallow in the past, he stared at the phone, counted down from ten, counted down once more. No Petro. Shoving aside a level of surface debris—ticket stubs from Dyche Stadium, a "Daley for Mayor" button, two postcards from the King Tut exhibit—and a layer of momentous front pages and special commemorative editions, Steven pulled out a rubber-banded stack of letters which he rifled through until he found the two he'd been thinking of since Phillip pulled the box out of the trunk of his beloved vintage Mustang last night.

The first was from his father, many pages written on narrow white paper probably better suited for grocery lists than for what he had to say.

Dear Stevie,

I can't stop you from doing what you're planning to do, but I can tell you how sad it makes me. Patty is a fine girl. She seems intelligent and supportive of you and I can understand why you would want her as your friend, and even as a girlfriend. Your mother says she is elegant, and I agree that she is in ways. But from long experience of the institution I can tell you how complicated a thing marriage is. This is such a hasty move, and you've never mentioned a word about what happened to Becky. Some-

*thing doesn't feel right here, Steve, and I wish you could tell me what the
real story is . . .*

Steven folded up the letter and shoved it back into the box, far away
from where Patty could find it.

A photo of a girl fell out of the second envelope. Leaning against a
railing, sea lions behind her, Becky peeked through the ribbons of red
hair thrown forward by the wind off Lake Michigan. They'd gone to the
Lincoln Park Zoo that day, her twenty-first birthday. A few hours after
he took the picture, he'd sneaked his hand down the front of those jeans,
and she'd rocked against his fingers. She wore a terrific lacy bra underneath the cable sweater.

Dear Steve,

*I woke up early today to see the cranes. Mom and I set the alarms for
four (Ugh!), perked coffee, and drove out to the Flats, about 30 miles
away. The roads were darker than you could imagine and empty (Mom
never broke 55. Pokey!). We didn't even put on the radio.*

The long letters of Becky's handwriting splayed across the page with
confidence and sensuality, descenders easily crossing and uncrossing on
her words. The paper was good heavy stationery, light blue, with her
mother's name—Louisa Padden—crossed out with one firm stroke.

*We just drove along, being quiet, looking for the first signs of the sun
ahead of us, and I thought mostly about you. I never thought "Oh, I love
Steven so much, and I wish he was here so we could share it together."
(Don't make a face—it gets better!) What I was thinking was how much
that first glow in the east reminded me of you waking up, getting warmer
and happier with your coffee. I never missed you all the rest of the day because you just seemed to be everywhere.*

That's all!

Good night dear Steven, says Becky P.

Steven felt weary, the silly sweetness of her words fresh after all these
years and, at his age, tiring, too. He had loved that bra, and that shy and
smoldering look she could have. Still, there'd be no Nate and Emily if
things had gone the other way, if he'd chosen a less certain life. If he
hadn't thought everything was being handed to him all at once.

The phone rang, cutting through the heavy air and surging Steven up as if he'd been prodded. He dropped Becky's letter. "Steven Armour." His standard answer, with a slight inflection at the end that implied, "And what do you want?"

"I have Dylan Petro for Steven Armour."

"Hi, Dorothy. It's Steven." A silence, as if she didn't talk to him every day. "Armour."

"Umm." Said suspiciously. "I'll put him through." Petro's secretary always greeted Steven's attempts at civility with the disdain of an Edwardian butler. Steven had been unnerved on his last visit to the city to see Dorothy, a hard old woman with gray hair bobbed into a girlish chop not nearly as stylish or youthful as she imagined, standing outside in the breezeway of their Madison Avenue building in a howling rainstorm, desperately sneaking a Kool while making no sign that she recognized him. The fine lattice of lines on her lips and mouth were a natural wonder possible only through years of such bitter and solitary chain smoking.

"And how are you, Mr. Armour?" Petro offered his traditional little joke, a sign—supposedly—that he remembered all that Steven had done for him, a fresh-faced, Marmite-eating Australian lad not long out of the University of Brisbane, his Australian accent, by now, Steven guessed, practiced to maintain its Murdochian echo.

"I'm well, Dylan. About to rain up here."

"Yes. Dreary here as well. Nothing to do, though. Listen, Steven, let me conference in a pair of Meal Solutions people and a few other management folks."

Concerns filliped in Steven's thought. This was supposed to be just the MS team leaders. "Who else is . . ." But he heard his voice floating out into blackness as he retreated to the dark side of the moon while the call was assembled. First in the call could be flattering, as in the first stop, the bedrock, you're always there; or else it meant it didn't matter if you were the one who had to sit through endless minutes of silence while more important people made the conference call wait so that they could deal with their lunch reservations.

Dylan again. "Amanda? Jay? Are you here?"

The bland voice of the always bland Jay Porter—"Yes, Dylan"—and Amanda Telestratta, whose sheaves of brown hair curled in the precise, regular waves of a child's cartoon of curly hair. She and Jay were from Meal Solutions out of Omaha, the home office. Unless you considered the Bern, Switzerland, headquarters of the multinational that owned DP the home office. At their one meeting at the Phoenix conference, Amanda had given off a perfunctory sexual allure, as if she felt it was expected of her, though it bored her and was beneath her, which it probably was, but then, he often wondered, why had she bothered? She was very hot right now, in house, and the only question was whether she'd stay hot or burn out. Steven was not much taken with Amanda Telestratta. "Hi, Amanda. Hi, Jay. Steven Armour."

Hellos around the imaginary table. It never hurt to be nice. About to rain here. How was your weekend. We're jazzed about the new site.

Dylan broke in. "Excuse me, gentlemen and lady. Dale Anders from Group Sales and Mark Solotow of Brand Marketing have joined me in my office, and I'd love to get started talking about Meal Solutions."

Steven took a deep breath; Dale and Mark. Dylan might as well have said Romulus and Remus. One of these two would probably become CEO within the next three years. As friendly as his conversations had been with each over the years, he'd never shared a drink or a confidence or a joke with either.

Amanda dove in before Steven could even think not to. "Big Dale!"

Dale's rumbling voice tore through the usual fuzz of a conference call. "Mandy, how's that pool of yours? Did you finally get it cleaned?"

Amanda had a pool? Steven grabbed for a pen to chew. And Dale had visited her house to see it. Even better. He took a deep drag of the pen as Amanda and Dale chatted about pool-cleaning arcana.

Dylan stepped in. "If I may. I would like to bring us to the matter at hand, which is the new Meal Solutions Web site. Steven has cooked up something awfully terrific, I think, and we're keen to run it past all of you."

Disembodied *greats* and *supers* floated by, and Steven waited a moment for more preface until he realized he was on and already seeming a bit slow on the uptake. He pinched himself—hard—and sat up straight.

"Thanks, Dylan. What we've been playing with is an opening screen the exact size of a Happy Gerda Mixed Meat Luncheon Hero Wrap Set. The user enters by clicking on the particular elements of the sandwich as they lie in their bins within the packaging. So you'll have across the top row: Salami, Provolone, Olive Loaf, then American Cheese, Bologna, and Braunschweiger—"

Amanda, always full of fun, said, "That's liver sausage to you, pilgrim." Laughs all around. Steven was glad no one could see him rest his forehead on his desk and tap lightly three times to regain control. This call had nothing to do with brainstorming and everything to do with looking good.

"Whatever you call it, Amanda, I love it. Always have. Send me a truckload and I'll eat my way through by Christmas." A properly cheerful retort. Impossible to insult the product with Dale and Mark there. Some little random snorts at the very little joke. "Anyhow. You click on each slice of lunch meat, a condiment packet, the roll, to learn more about each: how it's made, nutrition—"

Mark Solotow broke in with a mealy voice, slightly damp. "Do people really want to know how we make salami? Have you ever seen how salami's made? We'll get parental advisories, for chrissakes."

General laughter. Steven fielded the chance cleanly. "This isn't about going into the slaughterhouse. It's about showing great cuts of meat. Archival imagery of salami labels; some story about the priceless recipe brought over the Atlantic more than a hundred years ago by the original Gerda, the mother of us all, the mother of all sausage and lunchmeats." More laughs, though Steven listened for Amanda's and didn't hear it. "Recipes for each product, and—I think of extreme importance—the recess bar, where those lovable young users can click on a space featuring banners for whatever movie tie-in we're doing at the moment. This may be opening up a can of worms, but we sense a real opportunity here for starting up a kids' club like the ones the franchises have. We can collect millions of names of kids and direct push mail for every promotion we do for years." Had he gotten it all in? Steven took a deep breath and waited for the huzzahs.

Jay this time, not Amanda. "This sounds a lot like the Pudding Silk site. You've got that six-cup Workout-Mate Takealong Pak with each flavor, the trip back to the farm in Grenada where the bananas were grown and all that, and here you're just doing it again with the Lunch Solution."

Steven pictured himself on top of the Empire State Building, swatting away at a Sopwith Camel. "Well, Jay, we did it before, and it worked. The hits on the Pudding Silk site are tremendous. Dylan, what sort of numbers do we have there?" A little behind the back pass to Dylan; could he dunk?

"We're waiting for yesterday's hits. Suffice it to say the numbers are extremely promising." Petro had stepped back and bounced a seven-foot jumper off the glass. Promising? Dylan had been wetting himself only three days ago about the hits.

"It still strikes me as old hat."

Steven sensed something odd in the air, as if he were out on point alone. He quickly ducked for cover and returned fire. "One man's old hat is another man's consistency. What's wrong with good old-fashioned brand loyalty?" Magic words: *brand loyalty* and *good old-fashioned* weren't bad, either. The speaker could only be held blameless; at worst, it was a cliché. It was like coming out against wife beating. Who would argue?

"I guess I'm just thick. I don't see it. We need something more conceptual for Solutions. We see Meal Solutions as the sum of their parts; not just for the specialty-meat buyers, but the entire lunchmeat demographic, especially the six-to-elevens. To me, this is all about fun. I don't know if touching meat is fun."

Hmmm. He would leave the meat touching alone and let the silence on all the other lines do the talking. Steven assumed that the rest of what Jay Porter said had something to do with kids. "We threw around a lot of things, and we felt this wasn't the place for something like a Lunch Circus, with three rings and lion tamers, and I doubt if something on-the-go is going to work here, either. I mean, we're basically trying to get kids to play with lunchmeat." Oops. That sounded bad. "I think we're on the same page as you, Jay. We want kids enjoying the concept of eating, and in particular eating Happy Gerda's whole line of Meal Solutions. The only difference is that we're seeing kids, especially kids on the Web, as being savvier, even the six-to-elevens." Where was Dylan? Having a shoe shine? Feel free to chime in at any time, thought Steven.

Instead, Amanda chimed in. Steven felt as if a fresh opponent had taken the tag from her partner and cleared the ropes, looking for a pin. "Have you thought about something that centers on Happy Gerda?"

Mark's nasal voice rose out of the distance in a spectral fashion. "Let's not go there. We're having some Gerda problems." Gerda was a former college German instructor from the St. Louis area, discovered fifteen years ago by Allan Bristine, current CEO of DP. Her likeness on millions, even billions, of Happy Gerda products belied one very unhappy refugee from World War II.

Dale laughed a deep, lacrosse-playing, Jack Daniel's–drinking, contract-signing laugh. "Gerda's been hitting the schnapps pretty hard. I hear that on the last two spots she's shot, she spent all her time between takes talking about eating potato beetles after the war because there was no food. I honestly don't need to know any more about Gerda's wartime experiences."

There was silence across all lines until Mark finally said, "I don't know" in a somewhat doubtful way.

Steven slumped in his chair. Using the last of his ammunition, he offered their second idea. "Well, what about a sandwich that the user can take apart?"

Jay clucked. "You're still touching meat."

Amanda sounded sincerely annoyed. "Jay, I keep telling you it's a cursor, a meta-hand. Besides, people do not have an instinctual dislike of touching lunchmeat." The call was dissolving into chatter. He had failed to put them over, and in front of Dale and Mark, no less. Steven's eye caught a plastic Union soldier poking a rifle from behind a copy of *Jonathan Livingston Seagull* down in the box.

"I beg to differ," said Jay. "The Beef and Pork R and D people have numbers on popular attitudes toward incidental contact with raw meat that will have you going into the garment business." Silent now, Steven reached down into the time capsule and plucked out the soldier, a lonely survivor of many tabletop battles. He put him on top of his computer.

"This meat isn't raw. Oh, Jay. Imagine you're wearing a glove. And at most you're using one finger. It's like a poke; no one's rubbing raw lamb chops on your arms or something."

That image sank in around the call. Finally Dylan spoke. "I think we're focusing far too hard on the Lunch Solution at the expense of Dinner Solutions and Breakfast Solutions." *Umms* and *yeses* all around. The cavalry had arrived, just in time to bury the dead. "Let's reorganize our thinking, shall we?"

And reorganize they did, around Dylan's own description of Steven's conception, delivered this time, though, with an alluring Australian burr, as tangy, exotic, and ultimately friendly as a freshly sliced kiwi fruit. Petro tipped his cap occasionally and with great ceremony to Steven, but with a generosity that quickly took the appearance of largess rather than self-effacement.

Within minutes after hanging up, Dylan e-mailed in the cool, molecular type of the Web that he thought it had gone off rather poorly, considering. "We're facing real obstacles now" was Dylan's phrase. "Lacked a bit in presentation" and "utter let down" were two more. The good news was that Dale saw where they were going and would talk to Mark, who could probably corral Amanda, but there'd likely be resistance from Milt

Konig over in International and Clayton in whatever the hell Clayton was in, and they'd have questions from someone Steven had never heard of in ten years at DP but was obviously very important. Dylan also hoped to have word on the promotion in a few days.

Steven read it all on his screen, a screen like every other computer screen in America, tabula rasa after tabula rasa. Whatever happened to stationery, to handwriting, he wondered, to something that gave the sense of thought and decorum and grace to one's words and thoughts? He hated the Internet. There was no kidding himself any longer. Trivial, inhuman, a step back toward pictograms, but delivered at high speed, and he was desperate for it to give him a second chance at success in life. Yet even this second chance was for "Special Projects," the kind of position, as he'd been told by the one less-than-encouraging headhunter he'd spoken with after Dylan had vaulted by, that meant you'd been "neutered." As he thought the word, it filled every corner of his body, perfectly describing how he felt after the call. Neutered. A corporate gelding.

The edge of the next mortgage bill peeked out from beneath Becky's letter. Running his finger back and forth over Louisa Padden's engraved name, Steven stared at the plastic soldier taking aim at ghost Rebels from the monitor.

CHAPTER

4

UNCERTAINTY ALWAYS CLOUDS THE TOP of Mt. Riga, even though its rounded presence looming over the perennial borders of Salisbury gives the town a solidness beyond its wealth and a wildness that seeds mystery among the rows of Congregationalist roots set three hundred years before. To start, there is no "Mt. Riga" in the sense of a single summit to be mastered, a Mt. Everest or Matterhorn to climb. When speaking of Mt. Riga, a Salisbury resident may be referring to Riga Village, the area around the old furnace and ghost town that once overlooked Salisbury from two thousand feet above, since turned into a national park; or the whole Taconic Range, which stretches from Bird Peak near Lakeville through to New York's Monument Mountain to the west and Bear Mountain, pushed up against Massachusetts, to the north. Or he may mean the broad and tillable plateau that rides the mostly gentle roll of these peaks, including two cold and quiet lakes that spill into Wachastinook Creek and then on down the mountain; or any of the summits and outcroppings, such as Ball's Peak or Lion's Head, that draw those looking for moderately stressful conquests achieveable in a day. Therefore, no one truly knows what you mean when you say you're going to Mt. Riga.

Even the name is unknowable, both in pronounciation and derivation; a curious fact, given the importance of Mt. Riga in the history of Salisbury. Some pronounce it *Rye-ga,* after the Latvian capital, from which, supposedly, laborers emigrated to work in the iron explosion of the early nineteenth century; others say *Ree-ga,* after Mt. Rhiga in Switzerland, from which, supposedly, other laborers emigrated. A small, quiet faction supports the former pronunciation, but holds that it is another word for the spruce pine that probably stood among the chestnuts felled and burned to make charcoal, while a final group says *Ragga,* in honor of the Raggies, a now-lost breed of mountainfolk created when the furnace atop Mt. Riga went cold in 1847 and left the residents with little aside from subsistence farming, freely prescribed opium, and a lore rich in ghost stories likely developed under its influence.

The very location of Mt. Riga has been in question too, as it sprawls across three states and over once-disputed bits of land known as the Oblong and the Northwest Triangle. The former was a long strip claimed by both New York and Connecticut; the latter, a rugged chunk unwanted by any of the three bordering states. Avowedly unpoliced by any government in the mid-nineteenth century, the Triangle sheltered crooks, counterfeiters, and unlicensed boxing, as if it were an island of exile; Massachusetts and New York have since assumed responsibility. On days of fog or rain, the top of Mt. Riga disappears into the clouds with its secrets, its ghosts, and its town.

To those who live here, and the New Yorkers who have been spending weekends here for a hundred years, the degree of specificity you can apply to Mt. Riga begins to define your position within the town. No one has to know anything about Mt. Riga, but to do so is to learn about Salisbury and its people. A popular bit of town legend holds that anyone who drinks from the fountain next to Town Hall, at the base of Washinee Street, the one road that leads to the top of Mt. Riga, must someday return to Salisbury. Steven Armour, though, knew very little about the Northwest Corner of Connecticut; he had never planned on laying such a foundation, had never stopped at the fountain, especially not during the last year. When the farmhouse had been his baronial country manor, small handbooks to area hikes, guides to the Appalachian Trail and New England wildlife piled up on the bedside table, but once he'd bought into Dylan's telecommuting scheme, convinced Patty to relinquish the now-decontrolled apartment near Lincoln Center, and made this his one and only home, the idea of touristy wanderings caused his lip to twitch with the same sneer of residence Steven had once caught himself wearing while waiting in line with visiting relatives at the World Trade Center. Even more, trapped as he was now in a nonchalant, WASPy battle for survival between the chuck hunters and the rich, such diversions as touring the living history program and working forges of the newly created Mt. Riga Furnace National Park bordered, to him, on the irresponsible.

*   *   *

History major Steven Armour remained ignorant of Salisbury's past only until that Saturday, the day history began to claim him. Stunned and angered by Thursday's conference call, Steven had squandered Friday, a perfectly sharp day of sun and breezes, on a handful of calls that he elevated to urgency in order to appear more on top of things to Petro, as well as having reason to hide away in his office from Patty and the rest of them. Saturdays, though, flushed even the most mole-like parents out of their tunnels and into the light of their families, Steven included. Phillip woke before everyone else, measured, stirred, and grilled up breakfast, waking the other Armours with the smell of pancakes, and then presented his plan for the day—a trip up to Mt. Riga to see the Civil War encampment and the historic village—with such brio, displaying the flyer–turned–shopping list he'd found within a stack of magazines, that even Patty agreed without complaint. Emily liked the possibility of livestock.

Steven finished his coffee, relieved that he did not have to come up with an idea of his own for the day. His father had always been the king of guilty pleasures on vacations, dragging stick-in-the-mud Steven more than once in his childhood aboard a roller coaster that he'd secretly wanted to go on, into a gift shop that he'd been thinking about all afternoon.

A few hours later all five were scaling the steep road to Riga Village in a small bus, listening intently to the recorded voice of Meryl Streep narrate points of interest along the three-mile journey: the falls to the right, the tree where Tory spies were once hanged, Wachastinook Creek bubbling away alongside, at one time a mighty run that powered the forges of Riga Village. The way was smooth at first, but the second and third miles became a pitted dirt road with only a pair of thin cables between it and an increasingly steep dropoff visible through the trunks of thick pines and hemlocks, their exposed roots like massive fingers gripping the side of the mountain. Only minutes from Salisbury's boutiques and wine store, Steven felt the press of something wild, though smaller and more personal than the usual indifference of nature, as if a testy household deity ruled these boughs and rocks rather than a life force. He leaned forward into the small circle of civilization shaped by the two-time Oscar winner's warm, teacherly voice. A bearded hiker taking a day off from the Appalachian Trail and gorp to sightsee like an average American also listened intently, while an Australian couple—massive, shark-wrestling husband in a Greg Norman hat spread out across the backseats with his Matilda snuggled under his furry arm like a koala among the branches—looked out the window with the same smug "what else was there to do around here" expression that Patty had as she alternated between Streep and a copy of *New York*. These days, Steven now officially hated all things Australian: marsupials, Foster's, Peter Weir, even Judy Davis, and especially this couple, who seemed, like Patty, to have it all figured out, unaffected by either the world of nature or the world of man.

They neared the crest and turned off into a clearing. Meryl Streep's sunny goodbye—"Enjoy this very special journey into our nation's past; you may never want to leave!"—did nothing to lighten Steven's thickening mood. Stepping from the bus into a staging area bounded by a low stone wall, he could sense them gathering, beetles gnawing on whatever small blooms a day out with his family forced. He needed air, and distance, so he moved toward an opening where a wooden arrow saying RIGA VILLAGE pointed through a gap in the trees. Though unseen, the town made its presence known. Small sounds and smells he could make no sense of reached him as he stuck his head into the opening: a spicy taste of wood smoke; water trickling, growing into a rush, setting wood to creak and starting a chuffing burst of air, all on the slow rhythm of waves. To the left, among the trees, billows of heavy smoke boiled up as a sharp point of white fire, always at the same place, stabbed into the sky. The blacksmith clang of metal on metal spoke of man somewhere in the forest.

Emily sprinted past Steven, all legs like her mother, black hair pigtailed for an effect that he placed somewhere between clueless Japanese teenager and Bjork. Patty called after her, but Emily ran on, so Patty, in her Jackie O sunglasses, Laura Petrie capri pants, and thick-soled black platform sandals—a look reliant on the past to be sure, if not what one would call historical—gave chase. Behind them, the doors of the bus closed in a gust, and the sound of the engine, the wheels crushing dirt beneath, receded down the mountain road. The metal hammered in a clean beat four or five times, then five or six rapid finishing blows. Silence—and the regular beating of the hammer resumed.

"You are about to leave the twentieth century," said a sign beneath a narrow shingle roof. "Please keep in mind that the residents of Riga Village know nothing beyond the Civil War, the final period of ironmaking on the mountain. World Wars, professional sports, telephones, movies, the Internet, cars and airplanes, just to start, mean nothing to them and, worse, may make them apprehensive. Instead, we suggest that you ask them questions about their lives and let them tell their own stories. The people of Riga Village welcome you warmly to their homes, their work, their school, and store. Please accord them the same respect you your- self would expect of a guest. And refrain from cell phone usage."

Ignoring the rest of the text—a description of the boarding house that once stood on this site, soon to be rebuilt—Steven turned to smirk with his father, but instead of an accomplice, he saw Phillip and Nate nodding seriously. A bell began to toll.

"Excellent," said Nate, grinning. "It's like we're really going back in time or something." He patted some imaginary drums and made a sort of Indian dance sound as he went through the trees.

Phillip, in a shockingly purple jogging suit, and Steven, in frayed jeans, strode forward along a short, steep path through dense brush and arm-thick trees to emerge into a clearing. Only its slope, the green and wildflowers streaming down to the trees, gave an indication that this was a mountaintop; all else was essentially level. A gauzy haze of smoke ob- scured the patch of whitewashed wood-and-stone buildings before him and to his left; the effect—a distancing, a screening-back—made Steven's first full look at the town come as a mirage might, a mysterious city on a hill, wreathed in clouds, appearing only at the whim of its resi- dents; a dream village. The bell, still ringing, seemed to have called away all the townspeople for some purpose. The intersection visible from the clearing and the two streets feeding it were empty, save for a small girl, Emily's size, in a long dress and ankle boots, holding a hoop and waving to Emily. When presented with new faces, Emily, skittish as a lap dog, would either yap or retreat, but this morning she ran ahead and allowed the girl to show her how to roll the hoop, her pink Barbie print pants nicely matching the girl's purple gingham.

Steven exchanged an amazed glance with Patty, then found where he was on the map he'd been given by the bus driver. Straight ahead, Washinee Street continued up to its end, intersecting with a north-south road that ran along the ridge of the Taconics. At the intersection, a berm held back Forge Lake, save for an opening at the bottom where a small run began. This was the head of Wachocastinook Creek. It slid under a footbridge on the ridge road ahead, and continued down, parallel to Washinee Street. Along the way, it ran through a stone housing, three stories high, off to his left. According to the map this was the water wheel, the source of the creaking wood and rushing water. Through windows in the stone, he could see the wheel, as well as a massive piece of wood rising and falling in time with the water. This was the bellows, feeding air into an even taller, barnlike wooden structure that held the furnace. Reddish brown for one story, it tapered up in white on three sides for two more toward a central shaft that sheathed the flame darting in and out amid the smoke. On the fourth side, the one facing down the hill, a door large enough for a wagon opened under a peaked roof, and atop that sat a cupola and the bell that just now went silent. Its ring had been no call to worship; Riga Village had no church. The water wheel and furnace, the largest structures up here, clearly supplanted God for those living on Mt. Riga. Past the wheel, the creek went down the mountain along the road they'd just come up. Stacks of what Steven figured were rocks as well as a long shed—the charcoal shed, said the map—rose on a hill behind and parallel to the furnace, linked to it by an overpass that fed directly into its top. A few stores with signs over the doors, the others buildings unmarked, crowded around the road and the left side of the lake. Only a handful of oaks and rounded maples stood among them.

Patty tore through the still air. "Tell her your name, honey! Emmy, tell her your name!"

As if called, townspeople emerged—a woman in a long maroon dress and white apron out of a store, a bearded man wearing a blousy white shirt from the side of the furnace building. Emily, who had turned back at the sound of Patty's voice, ran on with her friend toward a sign pointing over the bridge and up the hill, where the encampment and the one o'clock drill exhibition would be held. The Armours, trailed by the hiker and the Australians, who had all lagged behind, made for the road.

A hand slipped into the crook of Steven's elbow as he walked. "I can't believe Emily did that."

The touch surprised him, though even as he felt the energy between them draining into a broad pool of common interest, Patty continued, when happy, to insist on public affection. Steven responded with varying degrees of enthusiasm, their views of happiness coinciding less and less these days. It wouldn't take much to wreck her mood—a small change in temperature or a bad sandwich. News that he'd blown the promotion. Today Steven put a covering hand over hers. "I know. But isn't that girl in her class? Her parents own that restaurant on 112 we never go to."

He hadn't told her about the dismal conference call, though she had continued to dole out advice this weekend on how best to corner Dylan and force his hand with power plays seemingly culled out of Michael Douglas corporate-intrigue movies. Had she that little sense of what he did, where he stood in the general DP scheme of things? Though dismayed by her ignorance of his life, Steven pressed her hand tighter, hungry for a forgiving touch, for some reassurance that this woman whom he wasn't sure he loved anymore wasn't completely out of love with him. She'd resisted the full-time move to Salisbury at first, but he'd sold it as a combination cutting-edge strategy and lifelong dream, a chance to spend more time with the kids and avoid paying another crushing private school tuition, until Patty had finally agreed. As uninvolved in the town as she was, he often assumed guiltily that she'd done so only so that he could get his act together out of the public eye.

She returned the pressure. "I don't think so."

He, on the other hand, was nearly positive. The restaurant was called The Sage, one of those fancy-for-out-here sort of places that probably ran out of gin-and-tonic fixings on Saturday nights. But why argue? The dream of a reasonable day, tantrum-free, unforced, drifted among the tufts of smoke rolling through the town, blurring corners as it went, filling spaces, hiding things; an occurrence as surprising and welcome as the little girl with the hoop. Steven proudly walked across the footbridge and entered Riga Village as a married man with two normal children ahead and a dotty but kind-hearted father. He was determined to relish these precious moments of family happiness as hard as he tried to consider eating at Burger King a satisfying and true version of dining. He would tell Patty about the failed promotion after his father left, he decided, once he was sure it was failed. Once there was nothing he could do about it. Steven immediately put his arm around her, and she did not edge away, as she sometimes did.

Rocking on the waves of his emotions, the rise and fall of his own mood concerned him as much as Patty's. Steven wondered about Prozac, what it would feel like. His brother, Jerry, said it made him feel in that happy mood you have right before you wake up. His father, now chatting with a man in a leather apron, had slogged through years of strict Freudian therapy with a doctor on the North State Parkway who claimed, though obliquely, to have secretly treated the sisters Ann Landers and Abigail Van Buren. Now, stomach pushed out by a straight back, one hand tucked into the small, Phillip grazed his fingers and thumb along his trim beard as he spoke like a Viennese therapist himself.

"And what do you know of this so-called telephone this fellow Bell is working on?"

The man in the apron looked desperate for escape, wholly uninterested in enlightening them on the details of life in the nineteenth century. "I haven't heard of him. Nope." His eyes cast about for release, landed on Steven for a long few seconds, then cast about some more. "I pretty much know just stuff about eighteen sixty or thereabouts." The man, bearded and burly, seemed familiar to Steven, but he couldn't place him.

"What about electricity? Franklin invented that in—what? Seventeen eighty-something."

"Dad, the sign said . . ."

The man gritted his teeth. "Just the mid-nineteenth century. That's it. I was born in eighteen thirty-five. Don't know anything that happens after that. You folks are free to . . ."

Phillip poked his index finger into the sky, inspired. "Aha! Then you know about . . ."

"Really, eighteen sixty-five. That's it. All this stuff sounds just dandy, but—" A deep voice called out a biblical name—Japheth or Jonah—and the man quickly shoved through the Armours. "Pardon. I gotta get over to the forge. Work and, you know, other stuff. To do. Good day to you." He put a finger to his brow in salute and limped off.

Steven folded his arms. "Why'd you do that, Dad? They ask you not to. It's like feeding the animals at the zoo."

"I'm just planting the seeds of the future, Steverino. Everything about computers came out of cheesy science fiction novels, you know? Maybe if we get the telephone a little sooner, we can avoid World War Two. And when, by the way, have you ever known me to feed the animals?"

"Dad, it's not real."

Phillip looked wounded; rolled his eyes. "I *know* that. Jesus, can't we have *any* fun?" He grabbed Nate's big arm. "Come on. Let's find us some women who never heard of Betty Friedan."

Patty scowled, "Phil . . ." rising at the end in distinct warning.

Nate asked, "Who's Betty Friedan?"

"A friend of your mother's." Phillip steered the boy into the saloon for one of the sarsaparillas advertised on a blackboard beside the door, then popped his head back out the doorway. "We'll find you for the drill show at one. This place reminds me of a movie we saw once." For a beat, he groped for the title, then ducked back in.

Steven and Patty walked up the hill with Emily, whose friend was called away with what sounded to Steven an angry tone, and after that their interactions with the locals were like his father's. As understandable as his annoyance was, the man had, to Steven's mind, shown very little patience for a harmless visitor. Who *was* he? Steven was sure he'd seen the man in the apron somewhere before, as he had many of the people around him, familiar faces, who appeared as busy and harried up here on Mt. Riga as they did at the video store, the chiropractor's, or the pharmacy. And why shouldn't they? Often toting heavy baskets or tools, smudged with the smoke that continued to pour out of the furnace, the people of Mt. Riga worked at tasks more challenging than shaking hands at the gates of the Magic Kingdom. When pressed, they addressed Steven and Patty and the aggressively genial Australians, who were becoming a bit perturbed with the attitude, as if they were speaking to the spirit world. When Patty asked the price of a brooch at the town shop— hair jewelry, it was called, supposedly made of human hair—the woman tending the counter looked past and around Patty, as if trying to locate the source of the question, then finally locked on her and answered. Passing on the dusty streets, the townspeople never looked at them; never offered angry looks or happy ones, instead saving, when possible, all communication for one another. If the residents were play-acting, they did so with great skill and application.

The same held true for the buildings; they were not sets. Stained by smoke and dust, dim within and smelling of damp wood even in the rising September heat, the shop, the saloon, and homes they peeked into appeared entirely genuine, though with no indication of whether they had been built a hundred and fifty years ago or last summer, down to an absence of signs or explanations as to what was going on or where you were. That which was, was, and it was so for reasons a visitor had to care enough about to disturb a serious person working hard at his task. Riga Village, though ostensibly a national park, seemed to exist not for the sake of the visitors, but for those who lived there.

As they dragged Emily away from a pen where a large pig eagerly tried to blot its snout on the inviting Barbie pattern of her pants, Steven began to enjoy the conceit. Patty, who had most certainly not bought the brooch after such sorry service, said, "What a pain in the ass. If they don't want to sell anything, fine with me." She handed Emily a Kleenex.

"Wipe off your pants." Innocuous as it was, the incident had clearly dented her mood.

Past the small working farm at the top of the rise and the piles of rocks, two rows of canvas tents formed an alley in a clearing that opened onto a field where a clutch of Union soldiers stood talking with some visitors. The noon sun was as unwelcoming as the town, blasting an early autumn heat directly on one's face and arms. Still, no trees had admitted the inevitable and begun their swoon into color; this was the last hot moment of dark green before it all started to unravel. A sign before the tents said SUTLER ALLEY. Women in period dresses, a few in hoop skirts, hair tied back into buns or held in nets atop their heads, swooped from tent to tent, bags in hand.

"Let's get some shade," said Patty, and ducked under the open canvas flap of Miss Sarah's French Emporium and Millinery. Behind a card table edged with pink bunting sat a plump woman in a huge dress festooned with flesh-colored flowers and green leaves. A white collar trimmed with lace came around her neck, scooped down and back up to her throat in the shape of a split eggplant. Where the ends met, dozens of small buttons fastened the front all the way to where her waist would have been, had she had one. A pink bonnet seemed to force out her face, beaming with pride and a sheen of perspiration. "Please let me know if I can help you with anything." They thanked her, and could not possibly imagine anything she could help them with in this teenaged girl's dream of Victoriana. Frilly, fussy things piled on the tables rimming the whole tent. Off four or five racks, massive nineteenth-century dresses hung in rich, overripe colors, magentas and loud florals. Cloying, densely illustrated postcards lay scattered about, a few glass cases of intricate and undistinguished silver *objets* stood by the counter, near where Miss Sarah presented a selection of blunt-toed leather boots for women. Some battered books on costume design and women in the nineteenth century flopped on a shelf by the door, their plastic wrappings grimy and torn. Scatterings of straw represented the floor.

"Look at this," whispered Patty. "They've even got a fitting room."

A pair of ankle boots, clearly attached to someone trying something on, and the lacy bottom of bloomers could be seen below a canvas panel in the far corner of the tent. As garish and dress-up as the French Emporium was, Steven found himself incredibly aroused, as if he had been allowed into a boudoir of French postcard vintage, lights dimmed, sounds muffled. On a table he spied a light stack of loose chemises, rolls of stockings, and there, the Grail of Naughtiness, a beautiful black corset. Was the woman trying one on right now? Although they had escaped the sun, they had not escaped the heat, held in here by the canvas. His breath grew ragged. Miss Sarah gave Steven a kindly smile, deferent, but a little wry, very sure about certain aspects of the male mind. He imagined it the look of a madam, or more particularly the look of a madam who sees you on the street with your wife. Had she seen him eyeing the corset?

"At least she's friendly." Patty held up a blue velvet jacket to Emily, the front panels trimmed with ornate weaves of gold braid. "Maybe we should get this for Halloween." Miss Sarah's face froze. Holding the price tag, Patty whistled. "No, we shouldn't." Silk and cotton rustled in the fitting area; Miss Sarah met Steven's eyes. Patty continued, "All these lovely costumes. Aren't they pretty, Emmy?" The girl nodded and picked up a fan, which she waved around her face in broad strokes, Scarlett O'Hara in spasms. "These are all so *pretty*," Patty articulated slowly to Miss Sarah, as if *pretty* were a new word for Miss Sarah, or she was mentally infirm.

"Why, thank you," Miss Sarah replied, her gratitude as genuine as her wares.

Emily spread the fan open once or twice. "I want this. Mommy, I want this." It was simply a matter of time before Emily, in any retail environment, locked onto some piece of crap and sent out the magnetic pull that tenaciously, and often with great crying, drew all manner of plastic figurines, pretend cosmetics, and other random kiddie junk into her possession. The running cost, though never calculated, was tremendous.

"Mommy, I *said* I *really* want this!"

"No," Steven snapped. There was no end to Emily's wants; they'd segued directly from a bottle and a clean diaper into dresses and videos and American Girl dining room sets, with no distinction between them. Steven watched as a panicked expression formed on her face at the prospect of not getting, and she crumbled into psychic overdrive, the tears starting to flow as part of her push to victory. He imagined her years from now hiding under a blanket in an empty college dorm room, tearing chunks off a log of frozen cookie dough, eyes darting from side to side, an image that made him profoundly sad. What fine tissue in her soul hadn't grown to cover this hunger? What had they done so wrong?

"I want the fan!"

Or was she just normal?

"Oh my God, look at that," exclaimed Patty, pointing at a hooped red dress over a black-and-red blocky tartan underskirt with broad sleeves as broad as Christmas hams. "Who would ever wear that?"

The canvas door of the fitting area snapped open, and there stood a homely woman in thick glasses, her eyes wobbling about but clearly thrilled to be wearing the exact dress Patty was pointing to. The woman's face fell, her lips not able to fully cover her sizable teeth. Patty grabbed Steven and pulled him toward the door as he ripped the fan out of Emily's hands, said an apologetic thank-you to Miss Sarah, and pulled Emily along in Patty's wake.

Emily began screaming.

"We don't have the money, dear," Patty explained a few steps away from Miss Sarah's door. This line was a standard dodge he and Patty had often used on the children during the late toddler years, but the full impact of that very large statement was beginning to mean something more to their daughter. To Steven, even knowing that it was a parenting move akin to the half-nelson, it sounded accusatory. "Daddy and I work very hard, and we can't spend our money on everything we want. When Daddy gets his promotion, he'll buy it for you." Steven walked to the next tent.

A few moments later Nate and Phillip caught up with them inside Fittmann's Rifles, where a weathered man in a dingy kepi glared from behind his makeshift counter surrounded by many, many Confederate flags. Goaded by racks of well-oiled muskets and smoothly clicking pistols, Patty the real estate lawyer transformed into Patty the expert in constitutional law and loudly asked some rhetorical questions as to whether such things should be allowed in a free society. While Steven agreed, he hardly felt inclined to second her thoughts right here in this traveling arsenal of the New South.

Fittmann was not amused. "Every *man's* titled to his opinion," he said in a high, greasy drawl that bore no resemblance to a waxed and polished Southern accent, stressing the word *man* to make his meaning clear. Steven imagined he spoke this way every day back at the war surplus store, wolfing terrible Chinese food out of a tin even as the day's few customers wandered in, a cow bell tied to the doorknob clanging at the disturbance. Politics aside, Steven did not blame Fittmann for his sour mood.

They left without incident, but the spirit driving them had died.

After the last tent, another women's wear shop well-stocked with widow's black crepe accoutrements, Patty planted her feet and said, "All right, this is a big waste. Let's go." She was bored; so was Emily. They'd clicked through all the levels, run through all the channels, consumed what they wanted, and were ready to move on, locusts in how they devoured life and nearly as unstoppable.

But Emily had some unfinished business. "Mommy, I want the fan."

"Honey, I told you. When Daddy gets his new job . . ."

"Don't hold your breath," said Steven, too tired to pretend anymore.

Patty turned away from Emily. "What does *that* mean?"

"It means the call on Thursday didn't go well."

Patty extended to her full height, chin tilting back; a prosecuting attorney, the principal. "When were you planning to tell me this?"

"It's not final. I mean, he hasn't told me, but . . ."

"Well, what are you going to do?"

"What is there to do?" Steven held up his palms. "He's gonna do what he's gonna do."

"Can you e-mail him? Can you call Darius? How exactly did you screw this up?"

A line had been crossed; he saw Emily wince and Nate stare at the grass, scratching the back of his neck. "Let's do this later, all right?"

Emily tugged at her arm. "Mommy, I want the fan!"

Patty crouched down to her level, pointedly excluding Steven from the conversation. "No, you definitely can't have it. We don't have the money." He felt the skin being ripped off his back and sides in long sheets. Phil pulled Emily away and disappeared with the two children into Miss Sarah's tent. "Well, let's go home so you can do something about this."

"Why don't we eat lunch up here at least?"

"Why?"

"Because I want to look around, all right? I want to see the drill exhibition. All right?" Because we were all having fun, he thought. Because we were holding hands for a while.

CHAPTER

5

"So, FINALLY GOT YOU, BOY-O." Unable to hide his pleasure at having his son to himself, Phillip guaranteed Steven's attention with a brief jig in the grass à la Jackie Gleason in *Riverdance*, then pointed casually toward the small crowd growing near the soldiers. "Still want to go?"

The oscillations of time and tide, of happy and sad, no longer operated on a leisurely seasonal schedule for Steven. In recent months he'd gone from two-week blocks of anxiety and normality to weekly alternations to day-by-day shifts. Now he feared he'd slid right past the hour-to-hour into a minute-by-minute basis, slapped back and forth by any passing psychic breeze or event, vibrating so quickly he seemed to be frozen in place. In twenty minutes he had hated her, loved her, then hated her again. Patty had marched off with the children in search of food. Steven's eyes began to mist. He pursed his lips and nodded, blinking as if he'd been struck by a sudden attack of hay fever. Phil slipped his hand up to Steven's neck and squeezed. "There's a lot to be allergic to around here. All this smoke."

Edging their way to the center of the audience, a mixture of visitors and village residents, the two found themselves blocked by a taut line of twine rubbing against their shins, the border of a small clearing where a group of men had gathered. It was a broad and puzzling mixture that included two men who looked too old to wage war for anything more than a mug of Postum. Two others had clearly spent time at the Dilly-Perkins trough of fine snack cakes and frozen comestibles, though in defense of the one wearing the bright red turban, he *was* an enormous man, nearly six feet nine, by Steven's guess, and in need of reserves. The others were nondescript and naggingly familiar, except for three whom Steven knew for sure. One, Joe Swan, was the man from whom he'd bought his house; the other was Bobby Osselin, Grand Union's dreaded checkout teen. At the front stood Walter Manskart, beard freshly trimmed to eye-poking sharpness for the grand event, swiping his gloved hand at the swarm of no-see-ums swirling around his head.

Once Manskart delivered the first command in a deep, firm voice and eight guns cracked to eight shoulders, Steven's points of reference blurred. Osselin, Swan, and Manskart, straight and rugged in their 2nd Connecticut uniforms, suddenly existed outside Steven's use for them as characters in the daily show of his life. From the side, a fat wife and three fat kids, all dressed in nineteenth-century garb, watched their fat father sweat through Manskart's orders, beaming all the while as did he. Still, the seriousness of the men, especially with a turbaned giant in their midst, amused Steven. Firm-jawed and staring straight at their leader, they had the look of altar boys piously serving an unfathomable mystery, but as they toed crisp lines, squared into perfectly timed movements at the sound of Manskart's voice, he stopped chuckling. At a certain point, the innocent devotion of altar boys becomes as beautiful as the mystery they serve. Steven stared down at his old jeans, toed the hole in his sock, and realized he had no right to pass judgment, no matter how goofy the scene was, and it *was* goofy—the costumes, the accents, the eight intense backyard sol-diers representing a company of one hundred. Manskart sent the line into a wheeling maneuver, creating a circle around the sprightlier of the two old fellows, who vigorously bit his lip to maintain the right beat, while the others, especially Bobby Osselin on the end, kept up a brisk pace for him to match.

Pinched and thin, Joe Swan's wife—her name escaped him—had a spot next to the fat family. At the closing she had nearly broken down crying, as they sold the house they'd dreamt their whole lives of owning and then, like so many locals, had to sell when their employment failed to keep up with their mortgage. Yet today she glowed, maybe not with the purity and simplicity of the family beside her, but with pride in a man still standing.

Chin held high, Manskart called the men back into one line with a se-ries of barked commands. Eight rifles held at eight shoulders, perfectly level. Steven wondered where he could find such order, wished he'd been born with this ability instead of inheriting his family's bent for sim-mering chaos.

"Load! Handle cartridge!" The rifles snapped down to the ground and each man opened a box on his belt, pulled out a small paper packet, and lifted it near his mouth. Steven hated his job, had surely been passed over for a token promotion that would have made him hate his tenuous position less.

"Tear cartridge! Charge cartridge!" The men tore open the cartridges and poured the contents down the muzzles of their rifles. His children were both in what Steven prayed were merely unattractive states of transition.

"Take rammer!" A thin rod was pulled out from along the shaft of each rifle. "Ram cartridge!" Rammers plunged into eight muzzles, pushing the bullets down. His father had nearly lost his mind, and instead of making bequests, he was quietly sucking money out of Steven's bank account.

"Return rammer!" The rods went back in place. His wife was driving him insane, and he hadn't wanted to marry her in the first place . . .

"Prime!" A charge was put on the cap, below the hammer. When the hammer struck, the resulting spark would light the powder. He'd only admitted it since he'd started thinking again about the woman whom he had loved in the first place.

"Ready! Aim!" The rifles went to their shoulders, fingers slipped to the triggers. Was he this much of a failure in every aspect of his life?

"Fire!"

The volley burst forth in a descending crackle that resolved in a most satisfying cumulative boom. Up to his ears a second before, Steven's shoulders released at the sound; his entire body stopped vibrating, the tightly wound energy gone to mingle with the sulfurous smoke of the rifles and the echo rattling among the low Taconic peaks. The sensation was like nothing so much as those nebulous, cottony moments after an orgasm.

Five more rounds of firing, and the smoke cleared. Silence fell over Steven and Phillip as they walked at a leisurely pace through the sutler alley toward town. The intrusions of radios, cars, motors, computers—the Web—all the electrical fog of life was gone on Mt. Riga. Not only was there no humming current; there was no expectation of it. No exaggerated problems, high-flying Internet stocks, asshole celebrities, or bathetic TV news. There was no need to get anywhere fast. A few low conversations bubbled at the pitch of a small running creek, but mostly this was a place of few words and no explanations. Simple things pressed forward, elevated and cleansed, rising in the quiet. Steven saw himself reading Browning under a tree, editing the town newspaper, doing basic, wholesome work that would connect him to the cycles of life. The thought of leaving his own time felt like strong, warm hands on his shoulders. He was envious of these men and women who had wiped the other world—the present, their future—completely out of existence, even if only for a while. Nor could he pretend that he wasn't turned on by all these corseted women, their slowness, their apparent submissiveness. Relief seemed possible among these trees.

Under the guise of looking for Patty and the kids, the two wandered in and out of tents, examining uniforms and guns. They spoke little, one moving ahead then being leapfrogged by the other, occasionally stopping together to trade a few words about a kepi or a display of buttons and buckles. Outside the Gettysburg Gallery, a long tent featuring prints of such historic moments as Christ welcoming Stonewall Jackson into Heaven, Phillip casually fell into step with his son. "Hi ho, Steverino," he said—Steve Allen's catch line. Family legend held that his father had coined it with Steverino's wife, Jayne Meadows, late one night at the Pump Room. "Remember that show where Steve and Jayne would have on Newton and Shakespeare and . . ."

"What the hell would Wayne Newton have to say to Shakespeare?"

"Funny. Well, Jayne and I used to talk about that show a very long time ago." Though he never overtly claimed ownership of an idea, Phillip made broad hints. "My idea was to re-enact things like all this; Roman times, orgies and all. Egypt. Hogarth's England with lusty barmaids addled by cheap gin. Like *Westworld*. Remember that movie, Stevie? That's the one I was trying to remember. Christ, I loved that movie. Remember that movie? We saw it together."

"Yeah."

"Richard Benjamin's in that, isn't he?"

"I don't remember, Dad."

"I think Richard Benjamin's in that."

"Yeah, I don't remember. I guess this is kind of like that, but, you know, with no machines and Yul Brynner. Nobody dies."

"Sounds great, Stevie. Think they need old men? I could go hide under some lady's skirt." Given that his father had squandered every penny he ever had and was now officially and legally bankrupt, Steven figured the idea of hiding under a woman's skirt had its attractions for Phillip Armour.

"Did you talk that way to Mom?"

Phillip seriously considered the question. "I did. Yes, I did. That's probably why we were so happy. I never had to think twice with her. She bought me down to the toes."

As they neared the small farm, occasionally craning their heads for a glimpse of Nate or Emily, Steven's search included the woman in the green dress. Why wasn't she here, he wondered. Three residents of Mt. Riga passed by, two aproned men, ironworkers, flanking a thin woman holding a tan chicken under one arm. The trio stared at him steadily, with looks that seemed to say that among all the shades passing through their town, they had seen one they recognized. Steven acknowledged the gaze; he felt something stir, as if moved by a memory from the farthest fringes of childhood.

He sensed other eyes on him. A clutch of four women at the post office, each of them bonneted and holding a basket, gave him approving nods. Like a gentleman, he nodded back. From behind a shop window, a teenaged boy seemed to light up at seeing him, and waved from the other side of the glass. Steven checked to see if there was anyone else he could be waving to; not Phillip, who was buying some authentic imitation stationery at the post office; not the Australians, whom he'd last seen chomping historically accurate pickles on their retreat back to the bus. The small bunches of other tourists milling about the streets of Riga Village elicited no similar greetings. Steven returned the wave with a toss of the hand and moved on, hoping he'd run into his family.

But there in front of him, taking a sarsaparilla offered by one of the reasonable-looking re-enactors in the company, stood Joe Swan. As much as Steven wanted to turn and run, he knew he had to face this. When the broker had first taken Steven and Patty to their home, the whole building ached with the Swans' striving, their self-improvement books—*10 Days to a Better Vocabulary, Super Memory Power*—all carefully displayed on the shelves, framed reproductions of Renoirs on the living room walls. The Armours had spent months, after taking possession, stripping away veneers and removing false fronts the Swans had proudly applied to put a good face on everything they couldn't afford to fix, a desperate sunniness reinforced by scrap wood kitchen objects painted in big Amish bursts and exhortative magnets on the fridge. He'd seen signs for Joe's electrical contracting business around the area, so he hoped that business had been good for him during the last few boom years, but Swan's color, the reddish burn of outdoor workers, and the gathering wrinkles at his eyes didn't come from St. Bart's.

Steven extended his hand. "How are you?" he asked, the tone sincere as he could muster, yet unsure whom he was addressing, a possibly still bitter ex-homeowner or a Civil War veteran.

Peering over small wire-rimmed glasses (not the aviators Steven remembered), Swan seemed to check first if he was playing the game, then said with conviction, protected and even blustering a little behind his uniform, "I am well, sir. Very well indeed. Sergeant Calamus Dawes is my name. Second Connecticut."

Steven relaxed and shook his hand. "This is a lovely town."

As a soldier, a man of pride in Riga Village, Private Swan felt free to swagger; a far cry from his submissive acceptance of Patty's hardball negotiating. He hooked a thumb into the waist of his pants and pushed out his chest. "Indeed, sir. Indeed."

A blast of winter suddenly wedged itself between Swan and Steven. Walter Manskart planted both over-the-knee cavalier boots in the grass, stuck his hands on his hips with exaggerated purpose, lowered his face into Steven's, and glowered. "I've seen you skulking about," said the colonel, who reminded Steven right now of a very large Puss in Boots. "Don't deny it. I've laid eyes on you outside the store." Manskart turned to the four or five soldiers and the growing cluster of people, local and visitors, stopping to watch. "Ladies and gentlemen, this is the face of a coward."

Feeling somehow found out by the accusation—though what he shrank from he could not say—Steven was left unsure of which world he was being attacked in. He froze, dislike boiling up for Manskart's inexplicably superior attitude.

"Sign up, boy. Sign up and fight this war! Make an example to your son."

Phillip nudged his arm. "Go on, boy. Sign up and fight the war." He nudged him again. "I mean it. You should."

"Ah, you've got the look of a Raggie about you," said Manskart, disdainful, but Steven knew enough about Mt. Riga to sense the compliment: it meant he looked like a native, a man who belonged here and nowhere else. A few of the soldiers stared him down, clucking and nodding in agreement with Manskart's appraisal, even Bobby Osselin, who appeared encouraging.

"What's a Raggie?" Phillip whispered.

"The mountain people who lived here," said Steven. "They're like the local hillbillies."

The wilted black curls creeping from under the band of Manskart's kepi were plastered to his temples. With a small, piggish nose and fleshy lips that his beard could not hide, the colonel would have had the thick face of a pure thug if not for a pair of dark eyes lit by a sense of command and wide black brows that struck various dramatic poses across his forehead, one compressing here at the nose, the other arching, then the two trading positions. He was a thug, but a complicated one. The paunch of his stomach pressed against his leather belt, but the vest was ample and so not tested—Manskart did not try to pretend he was a thin man. "So will you join, you pile of lumber?"

What a dick, thought Steven. He was fascinated by the act, though, the uniform, the courage of this grade-school teacher to bull about as if he were a war hero and not a grown man playing dress-up. With his promotion all but gone, maybe it was time for new things and new resolutions. The long rods of the soldiers' rifles leaned in toward Manskart. He wondered how heavy they were, what they'd be like to shoot. Still, being asked to dance felt different from asking. He had to think. "Maybe. What do I have to do?"

"What do you have to do, eh? What do you have to do? Father Abraham's bidding; that's what you have to do. Put your worthless blood in a bowl. Stand straight and hard like a man to save the mother country that gave you life. Whatever is asked of you. That's what you have to do, you Raggie bastard. Toting along your sorry tattered pa."

His father melted into a beggar's hunch. "Watch now. Pity for the aged, sir. Pity for the aged. 'Tis the only Christian thing."

The colonel swept off his hat and bowed. "Right you are. My humble apologies to one who's surely seen his share of life." He turned to Steven. "Unlike some I see."

"What the fuck have I ever . . . ?" Steven stopped. A bloom of red hair, like a swatch of blue when a jay swoops by or the gold of a finch in a field, flashed in the crowd. She turned to him as she had in the parking lot, in his imagination. Their glances locked. After a few seconds, Steven began to burn with a light guilt, as if he'd stayed out in the sun a bit too long, but he could not retreat. Manskart followed where Steven's eyes had gone. "That's Mrs. Kellogg. The pure soul of this dirty lot of sinning soldiers. Reason enough for you to enlist, to receive the benefit of her counsel. Her presence teaches many a man how to be a Christian."

Steven's thoughts about her were hardly Christian, but his reaction to her frightened him. It wasn't the rising lust that gave him the most concern. Lust, he knew, was uncontrollable, as unreasonable a thing to blame someone for as feeling hot on a summer day. Yet he pictured her doing needlework next to him as he read his Browning under a tree, saw her making a hearty meal for him after he'd finished his labors at the press or out in the field. She was an element of the way things somehow should be. We see many people every day whom we'd be happy to sleep with; some with whom we can picture a long-term affair; and very occasionally we see someone whose particular combination of eyes, nose, and lips opens something inside us, a person for whom we could change a life. Teased out of wisps of despair and desire, the colonel's wife became woven into the fantasy spinning in his head, wound and pulled into a thread of thought that could pull a man along.

A woman's leaden voice interrupted. "So there you are."

Patty.

Nate stood in front of him. "Didn't you see me in the store? You were looking right at me." The teenaged boy waving at the window had been his son. He'd looked his son in the eyes and not recognized him. Patty continued to bitch and look at her watch; Emily wept because she still didn't have that fan she wanted. Steven sighed. He would never be an English duke sipping whiskey and soda in a tuxedo. He would never hunt bison with the Sioux, explore the South Pole, tumble with selected handmaidens of Marie Antoinette. His history had been written. But on top of this mountain, hidden in the smoke, remained one chance to be someone different, someone else, or at least himself in a different way.

"I think a hobby would be good for me."

"What? This?" Patty winced as if at a sudden foul odor. "You're not serious, are you?" He made no response. "Well, I guess now with your diminished job demands"—she articulated the words precisely—"you'll have more free time. But so why don't you build houses with Jimmy Carter or something? Spend more time with your family."

I work at home, I'm already under house arrest, thought Steven. He shrugged. "I *was* a history major. I want to do it."

"We need to talk about this."

Steven gazed into the crowd and back at Patty. The colonel's wife had left. "Do we really?"

Patty looked at him with disgust. "Go ahead. Make an ass of yourself."

Somebody snickered. Patty stomped off.

Steven took a deep breath, then said, "Where do I sign up?"

The little assemblage, including his father and children, broke into a cheer. "Good man! Good man!" The colonel saluted him and pointed at the schoolhouse on the corner

Inside the shingled schoolhouse, the rebirth of Riga Village came to a stop. While the grain of the exterior wood, drawn out and exaggerated like wrinkles, displayed an old man's depth of character and provided a clear bridge to what once was, the interior had an arrested feeling, as if the room had been stripped of its past and no replacement yet found. The only light came through six small windows of sagging glass, a thin broth by which to see. Steven squinted into the sudden shade and the abrupt, unnerving silence, almost able to hear the last echo of a roomful of children just gone quiet. It was cool here and empty, except for two desks and three long tiers of legal bookshelves filled with binders and leatherbound books. A low narrow door anchored one end. The school-house offered space for ghosts to shamble about and step around the furniture that once was there. Steven, Phillip, and the two children huddled together near the door, motes of dust floating around them in the pale light.

The door opened. In two soundless steps an old woman was standing before Steven, hands behind her back, seemingly waiting for an explanation as to why he was here. Her age—early seventies—was only an assumption by Steven; unwrinkled, her skin was smooth and lightly downed, though spotted, and the more he looked at her, the less he was able to fix on any age. Her short hair, cut in the sensible style of many Connecticut women of means, was a brownish blond, tilting neither enough to brown or to blond to deem comment. Indeed, everything about her seemed designed to avoid comment, even her gender; if not for the skirt, modestly just past the knee, it would have been easy to imagine her mannish, unflappable bearing in a Brooks Brothers suit or the bonnet of a Shaker. She was a nun out of habit, married to New England, and her mastery of the precise movements of femininity, how she stood, how she held her arms, appeared the result of great practice.

"You finally made it." Holding out a firm, dry hand to him, she nodded to the others. "My name is Mrs. Melton. My family has been in this area since before King Philip's War." Like everything else about her, Mrs.

Melton's voice was unadorned, her sentences no more decorated than the inside of Salisbury's Congregationalist church.

Steven expected her to continue, but when she folded her arms across her chest and tilted her head in what appeared to be puzzlement at his presence, he began to speak. "I wanted to find out about becoming a re-enactor. The colonel outside, Manskart, he pointed me in here."

She pursed her lips, nodding and giving each of them a look that lasted a few beats longer than necessary. Without preamble, she said, "Every resident of Riga Village spends a good deal of time here. Some men join the Second Connecticut Regiment. It proudly serves the Union cause. Those men drill and participate at re-enactments under the guidance of Colonel Elisha Kellogg, of whom you speak." She paused and waited for Steven to nod his comprehension before she continued. "Each person selects an actual resident of Riga Village and does research on him. They learn the craft of ironmaking, of farming, of whatever trade their resident had." Nate gave his father a thumbs-up. Noticing, Mrs. Melton said, "Will you be coming as a family?"

Without looking at Nate, Steven said no. Mrs. Melton waited a few moments, then said, "We have many families here in Riga Village."

Steven shook his head. "I don't think they're much interested."

"All right." She straightened out the front of her skirt, as if crumbs had fallen during the conversation, and led him to a chair next to her desk. The family trailed behind. Outside, the fiddler from the Grand Union plucked out the first notes of an Appalachian tune.

Phillip hovered over Steven's head. "What's a Raggie?" he asked. "I heard that Kellogg say—"

"They are a people lost," said Mrs. Melton, dismissively. "No one truly knows where they came from. The mines and furnaces were worked by many types of people, many of whom intermarried. To the best of our knowledge they were those who made their living from the mountain. They died off when a living was no longer to be had here." She pulled a binder out of a drawer and placed it on the desk between herself and Steven. The subject was closed. Phillip retreated. Mrs. Melton opened the binder and ran a finger down a page. Finally, she tapped one name two or three times. "Here he is. Meet John Trow." She showed him the name. "I think he will suit you. He was a Raggie."

Steven's heart dropped a little at the prospect of being a poor woodsman; he wanted to be dashing. Seeing his expression change, Mrs. Melton offered consoling words. "From what I know of him, he led an interesting life. He was a private in the Second Connecticut." The uniform and gun were some consolation for not being a captain of industry. "You have much reading and research to do. Here's a reading list to start with. I also recommend that you subscribe to the *Fort Bluff Monthly* and *Civil War News*, re-enactor magazines; you'll learn much about the times and crafting your impression, as we call it." She handed him a few catalogues full of uniforms and hoop skirts. "You'll want to look sharp before you muster with Colonel Kellogg."

A great rustle of silk came from the doorway. Mrs. Melton looked up. "Mrs. Polly Kellogg, meet John Trow."

A new voice welled out of Steven, strong, with only enough edge to amuse. It was a voice he'd never heard. "A great honor to meet you, Mrs. Kellogg."

She extended her hand. Steven surrounded it with his. The touch lasted only one slow second; then they pulled apart, Mrs. Kellogg allowing her fingertips to slide across his palm as they disengaged. Her smile was completely innocent; her eyes were not.

"Welcome back, Mr. Trow."

Before Steven could think what that meant or where that voice came from, Manskart strode into the room. "Ah, made it here before I could warn Mrs. Melton. Good man. He's a new one, he is," Kellogg said to Mrs. Melton. He turned to Steven, who had been bent over slightly by his arousal. "Take care you don't stir the waters. I know your sort." The colonel's scowl brightened. "But this makes me happy. I'll see you in a few weeks. The fall meeting of the regiment. Big campaign coming, sir. Cold Harbor in the spring—a major re-enactment, twenty thousand men. We'll need as many bodies as we can get." He put a proprietary arm around his wife and guided her out the door, adding "Good day to all of you" halfway through.

Mrs. Melton allowed the dust to begin drifting down again before she spoke. "You are quite sure about this?" After a beat, Steven nodded. She seemed to consider for a few moments the sincerity of his response, staring at Steven and leaning forward to be certain she was catching his eyes as she slid the roster book toward him. "We are serious here. Especially the colonel. You are taking on the life of someone. You are going back in time. You must be totally accurate. You must live that person's life. Most volunteers spend their weekends here at the village. You must bring John Trow back to life, yes?"

Steven recalled the roster of duties he had every Saturday and Sunday, the repairs, the errands, the visits. He had no time for this, no time for Mrs. Kellogg. "I don't think it will be a problem."

"Good." She handed him a pen.

He looked at Phillip, who nodded reassuringly. Steven smiled as he hefted the fountain pen and signed in slow, looping letters that barely resembled his normal hand. He was now John Trow, whoever *he* was.

CHAPTER

6

THAT NIGHT, AS SALISBURY TRIED TO SLEEP, a line of storms rumbled through the Taconic hills and hollows with the malice of a biker gang, roaring packs of unruly travelers bent on rousing good solid citizens out of bed. The fringes of one gray bank of clouds cruised low through the backyard oaks and called Steven out with a bolt of lightning and a house-shaking thunderclap that jolted him upright, eyes open. Was he up, he wondered, or still asleep? Were the windows closed? At the next flash and volley, a sound Steven's sleepy mind briefly mistook for musket fire, he saw something pressed to the bathroom door, a roundish shape, taller than he was. A figure. Gripped suddenly by animal fear, a bit of small prey being watched by a large thing, he could not move, his eyes straining toward the gray hulk frozen against the door, waiting to make its move.

A massive gust rattled the windowpane. As Patty stirred, shapes around the room took form—his dresser, the rocking chair, her folded-up Nordic Trak leaning against the wall—all pulled away from the con-suming black and placed him squarely in his room. Steven's full bladder began to lend him courage as well, but before he could ponder his ability to fend off an alien or a hatchet-wielding drifter, he made out, in the next burst of lightning, the Black Watch plaid of Patty's robe and the white yoke of a Lanz nightgown hanging over the towel hooks. He took a deep breath, his eyelids fluttering with relief, and walked into the bathroom, where he knocked the clothes down onto the tiles for revenge. He did his business, then fell backward into his pillows, fairly certain he had closed the windows while locking up. Snuggling into a ball, Steven imagined the first scatterings of colored leaves, the puddles and cool air he would wake to hours later. Autumn was starting. He slept well the rest of the night.

*   *   *

Phillip had coffee waiting the next morning when Steven came down to the kitchen. "Quite a pissah, that stahm, eh?" said Phillip, affecting a Boston accent as he tore the crust off a piece of toast.

Steven peered over his mug, dim memories of the night's disruption burning off in the sunlight. "Cliffie from *Cheers?*"

"I was thinking the Gorton's Fisherman. Or maybe Oliver Wendell Holmes."

Steven nodded at the very moment he noticed his father's two bags standing next to the door for a quick getaway. "You're going to say good-bye to the kids, aren't you?"

"Of *course*. I'm not leaving until after lunch." Phillip looked wounded for a moment, then brightened. "Maybe I'll stop off at Gettysburg, now that my son's a Civil War veteran. Or casualty. Do you have to be a casualty sometimes, too?" Phillip popped a piece of crust into his mouth.

"I don't know," said Steven, annoyed at his father's glib tone, especially after the frosty evening he'd endured with Patty. Her sneering comments throughout the indifferently barbecued hamburgers, the mealy, undercooked corn, had made it quite clear that he'd pay a hefty price for both the lost promotion and his impetuous choice of hobby. Regrets had started to gnaw at his earlier resolve. Steven tore a paper towel off the roll and dabbed at the small patches of rainwater quivering beneath each kitchen window. "Just don't buy any overpriced Civil War shit," he warned his father. "No gen-u-wine relics, all right?" Since he'd be the one paying for them.

"Yeah, well, it was just a thought. Maybe I'll slap some Bob Wills or Yankovic in the deck and see if I can drive it in one shot." Phillip's words picked up speed. "Did it once before. This car. Remember? Nineteen seventy-five. Remember that? Picking up Jerry from Bennington." The thought stopped Phillip cold. He pursed his lips and ruefully shook his head. "He wasn't happy there."

Steven was about to say that Jerry wasn't happy anywhere, but instead bit into his toast. Watching Phillip pour himself another mug, he guessed that his father was on cup number two, or maybe even three, his mood alternating with each sip of the Starbucks French Roast they begged as house gifts from their very occasional guests. As far as Patty could tell, Litchfield County was Starbucks-free. Phillip sloshed the fresh coffee in his mug with exaggerated jauntiness. "Or maybe I could just live here."

"Oh, yeah. Right." Steven smiled at the joke, but Phillip continued to stare at him, taking distracted sips at his coffee, still sloshing the mug. Steven wondered what he was staring at, brushed some crumbs off his chest, thinking they were the reason for Phillip's attentions until it dawned on him that his father was not a victim of overcaffeination—he was serious about moving in. Steven groaned, as if something in his foundation had just shifted slightly and settled. He should have seen this coming, the inevitable last stop of parents who don't end up in Florida or Arizona.

"Go ahead and laugh, but there's something to it, you gotta admit, Stevie. Want more toast?" While Steven kicked himself for not predicting this, what most upset him was his father's nervousness. With the fidgety gabbing, white frost of whiskers on his jowls, and Snoopy sweatshirt, Phillip looked like someone you'd edge away from at a diner counter. What a terrible, embarrassing thing to have a parent at your mercy. Had there been actual practice for this moment? Steven imagined him setting the alarm for an early hour, summoning up courage in the kids' bathroom mirror above teddy bear soaps and Nate's fledgling Speed Stick. "Maybe I could just live *here*. Maybe I could just *live* here." And only yesterday Steven was nearly in tears with him, relying on him for strength.

"So, no, really, what do you think, Steverino? We could have a great time. You've got the playroom empty. I can do errands, straighten up, help out with the kids. Hell, I'll even put on one of those French maid get-ups for you. I'm sure they got some big gal maids over there. Like that one on *The Practice*."

Steven winced at Phillip's desperate joke, at the complicated brew of revulsion and guilt boiling in his own stomach. Though he knew he would soon have to say something, he chewed slowly and made various expressions intended to communicate the deep thought and due consideration he was giving the entire range of issues presented by this horrifying concept. In truth, he was mulling just how profoundly disturbed and tense his father's constant presence would make him, Patty aside. Yet when he ran through the specifics, Steven had to admit that he had no reasons beyond the simple one that he did not want him around. He'd left Phillip, left *Taffy's Time*, back with the time capsule that his father had brought here to Connecticut, apparently as a package deal. For thousands of years, parents had spent their last years with their children and grandchildren; part of the original ordering of the universe. But they'd lived in caves once, too. Separate lives struck him as a sign of human progress. To their credit, Patty's parents, Larry and Lois Bilmanet, had retired to a community of inexpensive shacks around a lake in Wisconsin, surrounded by other expatriated Chicagoans of a certain age. But hearing day after day about Jerry's breakdowns, the anniversary dinners with Mom at Café Bohemia, what they used to do at PhiRob when this or that happened, would be the psychic equivalent of displaying Hot Rod models around the house as *objets d'art*. He wanted his childhood to be a garden he escaped to, not a topic in his daily life. He didn't want to be a son all the time. He didn't want to be his father's parent. And Steven knew these were all unworthy, miserly thoughts, so he darted to the relative safety of Patty's long, thin shadow as if it were a telephone pole, convinced that he could hide behind it. "Listen, Dad. If it were up to me . . ." He shrugged, palms up. "But I really have to talk to Patty. It's a huge thing, you know? I mean, we can't do it right now. School's starting this week."

Phillip nodded knowingly, sat straighter, acted the father again. Steven remembered the day before when Phillip had put his hand on his shoulder and knew exactly what was wrong. "I'm not saying no. I'm just saying I have to talk with her. All right?" The Pokémon theme song throbbed into the kitchen from the living room TV. "Emily's up. Why don't you go play with her? We'll talk later."

Mistaking as a glimmer of hope Steven's inability to say no, Phillip smiled and winked. "*Oui, oui,* Steverino." He made a show of mincing out of the room, leaving Steven alone with his coffee.

Once Phillip drove away that afternoon, Patty attacked the back-to-school process with the vigor and drive of Eisenhower before D-day. With two sweeps through Ames in two days, she brought forth the required classroom materiel for both children, all stamped with socially acceptable logos, characters, and licensed brands sure to remind Emily and Nate of their individuality among the dozens of other children toting exactly the same Pikachu, teams of the NFL, and Anakin Skywalker backpacks into the comforting red brick Colonial that was Salisbury Central School. Emily displayed an inordinate amount of interest in her things, lining up the pencils, kiddie scissors, and folder in new combinations, then breaking most of the crayons, causing a tearful emergency third Ames trip prior to the big First Day.

Steven stood to the side amid all this excitement and the continued late summer heat, encased in what felt like cotton or some other soft, thick material that spared him life's full impact. That Tuesday, as Nate claimed his school supplies out of the big crispy Ames bags—sluggishly, to hide any real interest—Steven tried to guess how long it would take Nate to trash them. Two days, outside, on notebooks; one week on folders before names of bands unknown to him would appear beside intricate labyrinths. Steven had warily admired them last year as a form of outsider art, worrying all the while about what they revealed of his son's increasingly ingrown mind. Exactly two days later, though, when he spied Nate's pre-algebra notebook lying on the kitchen table among the bowls of cereal with the seed of a larger design already erased out on the cover, Steven realized with some shame that his interest in Nate's doodling habits didn't extend much past a betting one. What was there to do but monitor Nate's behavior? Spreading mustard across sandwich bread, laying out sliced turkey for school lunches as Patty showered, Steven reminded himself that the boy hadn't done anything to warrant such suspicions. He was simply growing up, a smelly, unattractive process for every male he'd ever met, and those who looked good while doing it usually ended up stocking shelves at Kmart. Save for occasionally steering him away from such bastards-in-training as Paul, he and Patty could do little to mold Nate at this point. He plopped the sandwich halves together, licked the knife clean. Let that maniac Manskart give it a try. And when Emily wept for three hours each morning of the first two days of school, what could he do about it? Nothing, he thought, as he slipped overripe bananas into the brown bags. Wait and see; stay the course until she become acclimated. She had to grow up sooner or later. Emily's pre-departure tears barely penetrated, and all he felt of Patty's frenzied reaction was the breeze she created as she darted through the house, searching for answers. Nowadays he ate to eat, napped to escape, and did not need a pop quiz in *Men's Health* to tell him he was due to pay a visit soon to Jerry in Prozacland.

The one name, the one phrase that sifted with any clarity through the mounting drifts of blurry thought was *John Trow*, and it popped again into his mind as he kissed the kids goodbye and dispensed lunches, stuffed Nate's notebook in his bag, and listened to Patty's pep talk to Emily, even though the afternoon on the mountain seemed years away and the religious fervor of his experience there, its baptismal residue, had receded. Emptying coffee grounds into Patty's composting project, the name *John Trow* flashed once more in Steven's thoughts, and the memory of being liberated and becalmed on Mt. Riga washed over him.

Bracing his arm against the sink, he closed his eyes and wandered happily into the sense of well-being that Trow's name conjured up: images of Polly Kellogg, her sharp waist and surrendering eyes, the sulfurous clouds of gunsmoke blending with masses of rain-filled air. Men full of purpose at peace with themselves. Steven had hidden away Mrs. Melton's costume and re-enactor catalogs following that morning-after dose of regret, but he scheduled a few hours with them now in his mental calendar.

A leaf blower down the road blew apart his thoughts. Next, the phone rang. "I have Dylan Petro," said Dorothy, in a tone more suited for "I have rabies."

Here it was, the other shoe about to drop right on top of him.

"Steven?" Dylan sounded rushed. "Look, bad news for you." No blindfolds for lame horses. "But I think you'll agree that it's good news, really. The person who's most standing out right now around here for New Media is . . ." Amanda. Fucking Amanda Telestratta starfucking her way up. ". . . Jay. We've looked at this long and hard"—Dylan slathered Aussie all over the "lahhng and hahhd" for sincerity and emphasis—"and Jay brings an unusual amount of creativity to the whole endeavor."

The blatant untruth of the statement took an edge off Dylan's announcement that Steven had been passed over for a bland, corporate no-man, a type much more prevalent and useful than yes-men. Petro had set the conversation in that surreal world where reality is twisted to fit expedience and the politics of business, and Steven stepped into the fun house himself. "Absolutely. He's just great. If it was going to be someone else, I'm really glad it's him." The only consolation to Steven was imagining how pissed Amanda must be at that very moment.

"Super to hear that from you. *Sow* important. *Really*. The other news is that Dale's restructuring his office, and Amanda's going over there. It's a new thing, some marketing, some strategy. Really *exciting* stuff."

"Oh, terrific. Yeah, that sounds perfect for her. Wow. Great." Steven stepped away from the sink and sat down at the kitchen table.

"I know you're disappointed, Steve. *Sow* am I. I must say we were really hoping for more from you on Meal Solutions. You've got some good things to offer DP, and I know you're going to find the way to add them to the mix. We'll need your input. *Really*."

How breathtaking. Well, at least he still had a job, thought Steven, someplace to send his output. And Jay Porter could be neutered instead of him. Steven gleaned what grains of consolation he could from among

the burned stalks—"It would have sucked"; "I hate the Internet"; and all
the other negative halves of the chipper half-truths he'd told himself
while hoping he'd get the promotion—as Mr. Australian Fucking Rules
Football, under the guise of enlightened management, described some
of the many flaws in Steven's recent performance. Listening to Dylan's
velvet putdowns, head on the table between bowls of crusting Grape-
Nuts, Steven had another thought, one he'd had before but so unusually
stated this time that it sounded like a new voice in his head. *Tell him to
kiss your arse*, it said. *Say it. Kiss my arse.* As many times as he'd contemplated similar phrases involving other humid parts of the body, the
words had remained locked deep in his brain, along with propositions to
women on the subway and other imagined unspeakables. But today they
actually formed on his lips. Luckily, he caught himself just before they
popped out, and instead of swearing at his boss, he promised to buy
some Stephen Covey books right away. Steven hung up with grateful
noises, wondering where he'd come up with *arse*.

In a burst of manic energy, Steven slammed through his three calls of
the day, left three messages, and collapsed into the big chair in the living
room for something between a midmorning nap and a breakdown.
When he woke up an hour or so later, he grabbed a peach and shuffled
out to the road for the mail: Two Pottery Barns, a Williams-Sonoma, and
some old ladies' shoe company in North Carolina. Also, a credit card offering low, low 2.5 percent APR financing, his frequent flyer statement,
which he didn't have to open, given that he hadn't flown anywhere in a
year, and a fat manila envelope addressed to him in a hand crabbed and
immature. On the label, two cannon barrels crossed beneath crossed
Union and Confederate flags, with an ornate number "2" tucked underneath the cannons. The motto "In Their Honor and the Honor of the Nation" circled it all.

Steven noticed an odd smell wafting up, something like rotting or-
ganic matter. He sniffed the air, houndlike, until he realized that he
hadn't showered, that he was wearing the same tennis shorts and polo
shirt he'd worn yesterday and had slept in. He thumbed the edges of
three or four colorful magazines poking through the corners of the envelope mixed in with sheaves of papers. Chucking his peach pit into the
trees, he trotted back inside.

Upstairs in his office, Steven tore open the envelope and spread the
contents across his desk just as he'd once poured the contents of the
thick packet from Northwestern across his parents' dining room table.

Freedom had arrived that day, along with the pages of rules and class lists and requirements. After repeated browsings, he had fixated on one photo in the "Welcome to Northwestern" pamphlet—a girl with long blond hair and a boy holding their books, the two obviously flirting in front of the library en route, Steven had assumed, back to their coed dorm. At the time, it represented to him all things sophisticated and adult, and he'd steered Becky there once four years later to live out that scene and what he'd always imagined happening afterward, an extremely satisfying experience he could still recall.

At first glance, though, he found nothing so inspiring here. A piece of stationary with the same emblem and motto in fake Gothic type up top, but now all in the washed-out blues and golds of a color Xerox, had been clipped to the top of sundry catalogs and papers. The same unconsidered hand that had addressed the envelope had written the letter:

Dear Mr. Armour,

We are pleased to welcome you to Company C of the 2nd Connecticut Heavy Artillery. We are a group of men dedicated to honoring the memory of those who gave their lives in most sacred sacrifice for the cause of freedom. Our goal is to educate and honor by re-enacting the lives of the "Heavies" and the men who once devoted themselves to proud and dedicated service to the Nutmeg State. I will be sending you more information very soon about the "Heavies" and about Riga Village National Historical Site. Please report to the schoolhouse in Riga Village next Saturday for your orientation with Mrs. Melton. In the meantime, I ask you to familiarize yourself with the materials I have enclosed and begin reading the books on the reading list. Do not consider this the extent of your research. If you are like most re-enactors, this will only be the start! Researching the history of the time is important in the creation of a strong impression. Our standards are very high, so we expect your full commitment.

I understand that you may be eager to purchase a firearm at this juncture, but by no means should you do so. I will issue you one when you are adequately trained and prepared for the right to carry a weapon. (I will bill you for the weapon at cost.) As I have mentioned, as we are a group of progressive re-enactors, our level of authenticity is high. Your uniform and materials should be purchased only from the approved sutlers, whose catalogs I have enclosed. Please order as much as possible from the list of required materials as soon as you can so that you can be trained in its usage. Shoes should be ordered first. You have fourteen (14) months to acquire all *the objects on the enclosed list. Please accord your materials the respect that the 2nd accorded theirs, and regularly shine, polish, and clean your uniform and accessories.*

We expect to have a good deal of fun this autumn, especially as we look toward re-enacting the 2nd's heroic stand at Cold Harbor next spring. We need more men such as yourself, and we are counting on your complete participation. From this point forward, since we try as much as possible to employ first person in our historical impressions, I shall refer to you as Private John Trow.

Huzzah!

Yours most sincerely,

Colonel Elisha Singer Kellogg

(a.k.a. Walter Manskart)

Manskart's tone hardly brought fun to mind. Wincing, Steven leaned back in his chair. He pictured the colonel—the big Puss in Boots, the Mikado—and suddenly the basic dorkiness of the whole endeavor exploded in his mind, as though he had just woken up from a bender and remembered he'd done something bizarre; married a stripper or traded houses. What, he wondered, had he been thinking? Whatever his idea of fun or relaxation was nowadays, it did not involve being yelled at while marching around in a wool uniform.

Yet here he sat, enrolled in a costume version of ROTC. The regimental rules, the reading lists, the primers on drill to accompany the manuals that Steven was supposed to order and memorize—none of these cheered him up, either. After the first rule—"#1. Obey all officers ranked higher than yourself"—the regimental orders did calm down, he was happy to see, into a litany of dues, meetings, weapon maintenance, and hydration. Drinking water and avoiding sunstroke seemed to have an importance in this world that Steven had associated with the French Foreign Legion. He assumed that "#24. No farbiness" would be explained in due course. Short hair required; jewelry, wristwatches, and modern eyewear prohibited, though contacts, big concession, were okay. Since he had not been in the Army, Steven could only imagine that this hyperseriousness and sense of actual enlistment went toward achieving the martial effect. A flip through the catalogs and magazines only made him feel more uneasy; the self-important white guys in uniform, impossibly chubby for men they were supposed to be portraying, the general reduction of history to trivia.

No less forbidding were the digests of *Hardee's Tactics* and the *School of the Company*, the two manuals that laid out the commands and basic maneuvers for nineteenth-century American soldiers. After reading, "Turn the piece with the right hand, the barrel to the front; carry the piece to the left shoulder and pass the forearm extended on the breast between the right hand and the cock; support the cock against the left forearm, the left hand resting on the right breast," Steven skimmed to the pages of diagrams purporting to illustrate the orders. Boxes, circles, and arrows formed lines, split into multiple lines, twirled around, re-formed. As much as he quietly admired the precision of those men at drill, looking at these diagrams sucked the air out of him like the assembly instructions for some long-lusted-for present under the Christmas tree. He could make no sense of any of it and hid the pages under the pile.

The reading list, heavy with popular names such as Foote, Catton, and McPherson, and first-person accounts like *Hardtack and Coffee* and *"Co. Aytch,"* Steven deemed a reasonable survey class curriculum at a none-too-challenging college, save for the complete absence of any mention of slavery. Hydration definitely beat that out as a topic for discussion. As to the history of the 2nd Connecticut itself, the story was brief. Consisting largely of men from the mountains of Litchfield County, the 19th Connecticut Infantry stood around Washington, D.C., pulling guard duty and shining their shoes for most of the war until 1864, when they were turned into the 2nd Connecticut Heavy Artillery, were called to the front, and were decimated at Cold Harbor before ever shooting a cannon. Not exactly *Glory*. The *Civil War News* only made him more glum. He flipped through the chunky, earnest little newspaper full of battlefield preservation updates, reports from re-enactments, book reviews, and whatever else might be of interest to Civil War buffs, and concluded that it was the school paper of re-enacting, complete with shots of bearded men grinning at the camera as they received awards for Best Infantryman Impression of the Event (Confederate) and of dowdy, bonneted women ladling out questionable stews at living-history programs.

So far none of this promised freedom from the weighty pressures of pointless jobs and wives in Lanz nightgowns. Instead, the walls of his office seemed slightly closer. The long list of expensive items to buy, almost $2000 worth, stipulated the lining the jacket was to have, the size of the sweatband on the forage cap, and on and on, with page references to *Echoes of Glory*, a Time-Life Civil War book he had left unopened on his shelf since it was sent to him as an enticement to rejoin the History Book Club. Steven heard Patty's voice ringing in his head, her snide comments. He hated when she was right, at least in her blithe criticisms, but what if, God forbid, someone he knew saw him? Did that delicious sensation of total escape, like a tiny sip of some exquisite liqueur, demand that he become an obsessive loser? Where was Polly Kellogg in all these pages? Where was that rush of John Trow he'd had that morning at the sink? Was there really no way to escape? Steven picked up Manskart's letter again and read it over, desperate for some hint that he and the 2nd were somehow different, more palatable; that it was a cool regiment, if such a thing could exist; but his eyes kept returning to one word: *commitment*. He'd committed to them. Atop his monitor, the old Union soldier he'd retrieved from the time capsule thrust forward his rifle, knees bent, teeth gritted beneath the plastic lips. "Gung ho," whispered Steven, lightly impaling his index finger on the bayonet.

With a sigh, he moved on to *Fort Bluff Monthly*, "The Organ of Civil War Re-enacting," a seemingly homemade magazine with a cardstock cover featuring a photo of two Rebels lounging in the grass, pre-battle. Inside, the articles largely replayed experiences at re-enactments past or discussed, with a crusty brio, the intricacies of such subjects as removing the lockplate of your musket. Clearly, the folks who contributed didn't care all that much what anyone thought of them; they weren't looking to be extras in History Channel programs or to lecture fifth-graders for a living, and the editors had a sense of humor in measure equal to their commitment. The letters, pages of cantankerous re-enactors recounting wrongs done at various events, offered a glimpse of what really went went on in re-enacting: shoving matches between Blue and Gray at one place, "casualties" being stripped by historically correct graverobbers at another; bruised egos, egregious examples of that mysterious and apparently horrible quality called "farbiness" (which Steven finally understood to mean not staying in period), and poor water availability (hydration issues again). Some of the letters, though, let loose a particularly frightening sound:

Dear Fort Bluff Monthly:

    In response to Jim Crozier's deluded letter last month (June 1999), I have to say that he's right about one thing—he can't speak for the millions of us who have suffered the deprivations of Northern occupation. For the last 134 years we have lived under a "government" not of our choosing, and if Crozier wants to come down here and tear out the roads his federal "government" put down, he can damn well try it. He should read his history again, if he was ever taught it in Michigan. The South exercised its God-given constitutional right to leave a corrupted union it no longer wanted to participate in. I will fly my battle flag anywhere and anytime I please in honor of my ancestors who died trying to uphold the values and culture they held dear. Let him try or anyone try and stop me.

All that said, I wish there were more Federal re-enactors like Crozier in our hobby, because then there'd be more of them to "kill."

Long live Southern Heritage!
Yours truly,
Pvt. Larry Mannis
18th Mississippi Infantry
Gusto, MS

Rather than scaring him off, though, Private Mannis's bouyant missive drew him in. Before last Sunday, he and Private Mannis had shared only the most general ties: gender, nationality (at least by law), race, possibly even species. Now they had the same hobby, something to chat about if they ever sat together at a Hank Williams, Jr., concert or a lynching. Rippled by a minor frisson of danger, Steven had to admit that the motivations of most Civil War re-enactors operated far beyond the Renaissance Fayre types in snoods and kohl who munched ye olde meat on a stick as they waited for Goth to happen. There was at least complexity here, and emotion about something that still had resonance in the world.

The phone rang. A woman's voice that blended some Southern tones with a lot of deep Midwest said, "Mr. Armour? I have Jay Porter. Please hold the line . . ." without offering the option of refusal.

Steven gritted his teeth and breathed heavily. Jay had probably already ordered a litter and bearers. When the new senior VP finally spoke, it was with the busy go-go of someone suddenly thrust into meeting after meeting, forced to accomplish everything on the fly. "Steven, how are you? Dylan told me you're my right hand on this, right? So I wanted to let you know I'm sending over an e-mail that outlines the new direction I want to take on Meal Solutions. Since we hadn't committed to your idea, we wanted to fly something else. Use yours as a backup. Plus, we need a digest of the annual Canadian taste profile ASAP."

He said *a-sap,* not *a-es-a-pee.* "You'll be getting the e-mail in a day or two."

Steven slumped in his chair. He hadn't done a digest of a Taste Profile in years. That was shit work, the province of kids just out of school. He was a fucking vice president. "Great. Listen, congratu—"

"Thanks. I'm on my way to the airport, so e-mail me as soon as you have something to show me. Talk to you soon." And that was that for Mr. Jay Porter, factotum turned god.

Steven hung up the phone. Little ferret bastard, he thought as he picked up the letter again. So what did "commitment" mean? To Jay it at best expressed agreement, yet the word had a different weight coming from Manskart, a personal meaning that couldn't hide behind department heads and focus groups. "Purpose"? That word definitely did not exist anymore. "Mission" did. "Quarterly sales figures" did. One hundred years ago, Myer Dilly used to make dinner every other night for five indigents in the backroom of his Omaha butchershop. Sometimes he catered parties for free just because he enjoyed feeding people. At least that was the legend. DP didn't feed people anymore; it made money off food.

Paging through *Fort Bluff Monthly* some more, Steven came across a photo that pulled him up short. Two lines of Union re-enactors stood at attention, guns on their shoulders, the flags seeming to snap in the breeze on a sunny day. All toes, all hands, all guns lined up straight and sharp. COME ALONG BOYS! FOLLOW THE FLAG! said the caption, an ad for a major re-enactment that fall in Georgia. At first he blinked at the corny phrase, yet, he thought, if he had been alive for the Civil War it wouldn't have sounded corny at all. Even to pretend he had a purpose now would be wonderful. And what was wrong with liking the symmetries and patterns of drill? Though minutes before he had been positive that learning close-order drill and drinking beer with his "pards" were not his idea of fun, considering the last phone call and the realities of his life, he had to admit that he no longer had an "idea of fun." Years ago, it was playing with the kids maybe, or sports. The few times he'd been on a yacht, he'd enjoyed it. He closed his eyes and tried to remember what fun felt like, an effort more involved than he'd expected. His life had collapsed into itself, and what passed for fun now tended to be those moments not consumed by anxiety. These re-enactors making a conscious effort to enjoy themselves were part of something, whereas he got dressed every morning in order to be flung deeper and deeper into space.

He had another look at the drill pages. How hard could it be? Soldiers did it, and they weren't known for being the brightest bulbs in the room. The indecipherable diagrams looked like a cross between football and synchronized swimming. It would take a long time to get it right, but it would be all up to him to get it right, and he surely needed to get *something* right about now. Manskart's preferred sutler catalog had a Post-it on the page with the uniform. There, a man stood alone in a field, radiating a mournful resolve even as he modeled a Federal Enlisted Man's Shell, available for $75 (chevrons $15 extra). Steven could hear the birds, someone playing the "Battle Hymn of the Republic" on a violin.

So what if it was stupid? So what if the reality probably featured plumber-slash-history buffs spilling liter bottles of Gatorade down their chins and farting in sleeping bags? At the end of the day, it was all theatrics, one small remove from summer stock. He'd been a history major, so this made sense. He would take the role of a historical figure named John Trow. In the end it was just a hobby, for God's sake, somewhere else to aim at for a while instead of over the cliff. And he'd be away from the house.

A spread on corsets, all pink flowers and modesty, greeted Steven when he turned the page. Not the cheesy *Penthouse* type in firehouse red with little flowers, these sturdy numbers did the work of a lifestyle. Manskart himself must have signed off on the corsets, products as they were of an approved sutler, meaning that Polly Manskart probably owned one of these very styles. Was it the obviously named Victoria, with its firm whalebone stays? Or the Marietta, teasingly chaste trimmed in white lace? Deep passions *had* to run beneath costumes like these. You had to be committed.

CHAPTER

7

IT WAS TWENTY MINUTES TO FIVE ON MONDAY, and Steven crouched behind the sofa, Super Soaker in his left hand, pirate sword in his right. The UPS man had just brought his uniform, or enough of it for Steven to play with, so he sat in ambush, camouflaged by the gaudy magnolias and watery yellows of the fabric Patty had bought from the Colonial Williamsburg catalog. Ten minutes earlier, while scampering about like a kid home sick from school, this lying in wait had struck him as a hysterical idea, but it hadn't fallen together in quite the way he had hoped. Immediately after trading shorts and a yellow T-shirt that said "Dilly-Perkins Mustard: Slather It On Me!" for the same dark blue woolen artillery uniform he'd ordered four days earlier, every inch of Steven had begun to itch in the 86-degree heat. Sweat beaded and skiied down his shins; the hydration obsession finally made sense.

He emerged slowly over the back of the sofa, at first peeking above the rim of the trench, then rising tall and exposed to fire. Aside from standing straighter, a function, he decided, of the stiffness of the fabric rather than the strengthening of his character, the experience of wearing the uniform had so far been closer to re-enacting his childhood than bringing to life the long gone and forgotten John Trow. The plastic pirate's scimitar, the no-socks and deck shoes, did not help the effect. At first he'd felt a pulse of national pride, a serious concern for what it stood for, followed by a bit of intellectual curiosity as to how true it was to the period, though he had no way to judge beyond Manskart and *Echoes of Glory*. The thoughts that had melted into a rush of guilty pleasure now faded into mostly guilt and puzzlement. The heavy wool of the shell—and there was a lot of it, since it came in only one huge size—felt at once totally strange and utterly familiar, a sensation born, he concluded, from man's natural need to conform. Uniforms make you a mob of one, and wasn't that part of what he wanted?

The guilt came from not working, though he'd done Jay's bidding for the day, finished skimming the endless Taste Profile report that highlighted some new and surprising differences in Canadian and American spice sensibilities. He scouted the room for a new spot. He considered darting into the dining room and taking cover under the table, but, about to get on all fours, Steven stopped himself. Being under the table had an undignified, groveling, hiding aspect, and the more he thought about it, the more he knew that even the simple surprise would be too short-lived. He checked his watch: 4:45. Right on time, a car rolled into the driveway. Whatever his plan, it would have to happen now and be suitably ironic, or they'd have him committed.

Tossing aside the sword and gun, Steven sat down on the couch, crossed his sky blue legs, and tilted the kepi, its front crunched down for a rakish effect, silliness without aggressive stupidity. With all the normalcy he could summon, he picked up the report, eyes focused on the subhead, "Destroying Preconceptions—Canadians and the No-Garlic Myth," and tried to appear nonchalant as the door swung open.

Paper bags crinkled, feet shuffled, then came Patty's voice. "Go ahead, honey."

As Steven kept pretending to read under the leather brim of his kepi, waiting for the laugh from Patty that would signal the grudging acceptance he hoped for, his wife and daughter walked past him into the kitchen without a word. At least he had appeared to be working hard. Sensing her silent presence off to the left, he looked up from a bar graph entitled "Rosemary, Sage, and Fennel: Usage by Province" and smiled warmly. "Oh, hello, dear. How was your day?"

"Pasta Pomodoro. Come help." Lit from behind and billowing like a sail on a mast, her flimsy cotton sundress, already short, revealed much through its bold floral print, and both bra straps had slid off her shoulders. She was very tan; imperious and waiting to be conquered. An urge familiar to every fighting man returned from the front swept over him, and he imagined himself pulling her down onto the couch. Then he imagined her swatting at his head with great violence.

"All right. Let me just finish this one page, and I'm done for the day."

"Good." She made only a doubtful *hmmph* as she walked away, to be replaced by Emily, who twirled a pre-dinner Charms Blo-Pop in her mouth, one short pigtail pointing up and the other down.

"Are you a soldier, Daddy? Did you join the Army?"

Well, the outfit worked on *her*. Before he could say anything, though, Patty called out from the kitchen, cabinet doors slamming, "No, darling. Daddy didn't join the *real* Army. It's grownups *playing* Army. Like those boys in your play group, remember? Who were always playing guns? Billy and Ivan?"

"Yeah." Emily wrinkled her nose, as if they had smelled bad, to boot. Billy and Ivan lived back in New York; Emily had had few play dates after the biting incident in preschool, though Steven and Patty were trying to stay bullish on her prospects for more dates this year. The long transition from weekender to full-fledged local didn't help, nor did Steven and Patty's lack of involvement in the daily politics that constitutes acceptance. Emily stared at Steven with what he took as admiration. "But Daddy looks real." He made a move to kiss her, but she stepped back.

The commuter hour had kicked in, and the house snapped awake; plates clattered, the TV popped on, and Nate straggled in from parts unknown, wearing a Limp Bizkit T-shirt. Steven puffed out his chest for full effect. His son rewarded the effort with a nod and a muttered but sincere "Cool" before disappearing upstairs to his room with the plodding tread of a burnout.

Emily tugged at Steven's jacket. "Daddy, I want a *de-de*." Quid pro quo, it seemed, for the compliment. Amelia, their old Dominican babysitter back in New York, used to call a bottle a *de-de*. Emily's secret bottle use was to him the five-year-old's version of alcoholism, but no one in the house was prepared to sit through the five-year-old's version of DTs, so into the kitchen they went. Steven fished in one of the oak drawers and produced a bottle, pulled a nipple out of the German dishwasher. After listening to the proper warning that it was her only one for the day, Emily skipped back into the living room, nipple clamped between her teeth, bottle dangling, for another episode of *The Wild Thornberries* on Nickelodeon.

"Listen," Patty said, after a silent moment of shared embarrassment at the sight. She was standing at the counter, stroking long peels of green off a cucumber. "Emily's teacher is concerned." Steven filled a pot of water for the angel hair pasta. "She says she's not focusing on tasks. Her mind wanders."

"Jesus, it's only the second week of school. What's her name again? Ma Rainey?"

"Ha, ha. Miss Trainey. She says sometimes Emily stops what she's doing and stares into space for a minute or two."

"Emily's always done that. She's a spacy kid. We know that. Christ, she just stopped crying yesterday."

"I'm just telling you." Patty moved on to tomatoes, energetically whacking them into oversized wedges with a cleaver. "Miss Trainey also says that while she seems to be very creative and she tells some fascinating stories, they all happen to be episodes from old television shows." Steven smirked; an Armour through and through, already confusing TV shows and real life. Up to second grade, he'd believed that the late minor bombshell Cynthia Costang, who'd played Taffy, really was his aunt. "She thought it was cute, too, but when she asked the kids to draw their families, Emily drew three girls, three boys, a mom, a dad, and a housekeeper."

Steven put a lid on the pot. "So?"

"It was the Brady Bunch. She asked her to do it again, and she drew the Jetsons."

He smiled. "Wel-l-l-l, I mean it's only——"

Patty stopped and leveled the cleaver at him. "It's not a good thing, Steven. Her letter recognition is apparently dismal for a child her age. I think we seriously have to look into doing something."

None of what Miss Trainey said surprised him, nor did he have any idea what to do about it. He tugged off his cap, wiped his brow, now dripping sweat from the rising heat in the kitchen.

"You really do look like an asshole," she said.

At dinner, Steven sat at the head of a quiet table, still in his uniform, the brass buttons on his shell glimmering in the light of the clunky arts-and-crafts chandelier. Chin forced up by the stiff collar, he looked as if he were surveying his domain even as he asked for more parmesan cheese. It had gone lost somewhere amid the butter containers and soda cans cluttering the farm-style antique that they seemed to have all fallen on at that moment for nothing more than convenience, an unoccupied table at life's banquet. After much coaxing, Emily handed over the shaker, and drifted into one of her zones while the other three silently ate on like a family biding time at an airport gate, waiting patiently for her return. Since for once no one was clamoring for attention, Steven decided to do what *he* wanted to do after dinner—maybe read. He'd bought *The Killer*

Angels over the weekend. Emily's eyes refocused, and she resumed twirling pasta without comment. In the corner of the dining room, the Super Soaker and sword lay where he had tossed them, crossed in dramatic fashion. Steven caught Nate's eyes going back and forth between him and the toy weapons. It occurred to Steven that he didn't give a shit what Nate thought right now. In fact, he didn't give a shit what any of them thought. He liked his uniform. And for whatever reason, he felt more like the man of the house tonight than he had for years. "So how was your day, my dear Patricia?"

"I can't talk to you dressed like that," said Patty.

Steven decided he might never take it off.

CHAPTER

8

From: Steven Armour@dillyperkinsfood.com
To: Jay Porter@dillyperkinsfood.com
Subject: Food Wizard

Jay:
I think you've hit the ground running with this! The Food Wizard
sounds to me like the right thing at the right time. Everybody is
talking Wizards, especially in my family—even my wife has read the
Harry Potter books! What's so perfect is that this site works for the
whole family, the Magic Wand with instant answers for busy
homemakers, the Tournament page for kids, and so on. The sooner we
get this up the better, since the movie is in the works and a new book
is coming out soon. Therefore we can ride the wave without needing
the license, or having Legal worry about look and feel. What a great
way to launch Meal Solutions.
Just a few thoughts from my (many!) years here:
1) Make sure the designers steer clear of anything that looks
   "magical" and count all the elements, i.e., stars, wizards, toads, so
   that nothing adds up to 7, 9, 13, or, of course, 666. You may recall
   the troubles P&G has had over the years with their logo. Some
   people still believe they are in league with the Devil.
2) Similarly, I recommend you keep any actual wizards Smurfy in
   appearance . . .

JUST AS STEVEN ASKED HIMSELF WHETHER Jay Porter would have any clue
as to what a Smurf was, the phone rang. Miss Trainey, her voice all Tin-
kerbell and the wonder of childhood, explained that Emily had just

thrown, with apparently shocking malice, an entire basketful of plastic food at another child, and then taken up a spot in the block corner, where she'd been sitting, silently staring at the wall, ever since. Apologetic but firm, Miss Trainey insisted that he come to the school immediately for a brief conference.

Luckily he'd taken up regular showering again. What he'd written so far of his dung-eating memo to Jay had temporarily sapped his will to work, so, happy to stop justifying his existence, no matter the reason, Steven saved and braced himself for family drama. As he bent himself into the Navigator in the driveway, he patted the dashboard and said, "Let's go pick up Emily." Since moving to a car culture, Steven had taken to addressing his vehicle as a semi-sentient being and assigned it a benign, horselike personality useful for urging it up hills, though he'd stopped short of giving it a name. Poking away at the radio for something soulful from one of the three stations they got out here, he steered out onto Route 41.

The mist and foggy patches clotting the roads called for an occasional pass of the wipers, while inside, the windows steamed up with Steven's breath. When he switched on the defroster, nothing happened. "Come on, baby." Steven tried it again, cursed, cursed again, the second time at himself for forgetting to have it fixed. Driving slowly, he cleared a hole in the windshield with his hand, the car's interior now clammy and damp like the day.

As radiant as dying maple leaves could make Salisbury on a sunny autumn afternoon, dismal days like these brought out its true personality. Colors faded into the blacks and whites of the stark woodcuts done by the area's first settlers, stern, mercenary types who set into motion the continuing tension between the saved and the damned, the haves and the have-nots, that had consumed so many Salisbury residents over the centuries. The cemeteries, like the one on his left as he neared town, leaped forward in the pallid light. Blank, grayish skies passed the kind of unemotional final judgment on the land that Connecticut ministers like the dour Reverend Jonathan Lee, Salisbury's first spiritual leader, had pronounced on generations of its people.

With a brief nod to the Civil War memorial also to his left, a robed woman brandishing a small shield, Steven bore right onto Route 44 and the two or three blocks that constituted downtown Salisbury. As usual on a weekday afternoon, only a few cars with local plates were parked in front of the town's stores—a handful of crafts and antique shops, a liquor store, pharmacy, bank, post office, and a few boutiques, all housed in old or old-looking buildings, mostly of white wood or weathered red brick. Not a cutesy town, not a buy-an-ice-cream-and-stroll town, pleasant and consummately New England as it was, people tended to drive up to Salisbury, do their business, and move on; leaf peepers hoping to browse the outlets rolled through to points north for that sense of doglike affability and dependence exuded by most Berkshire villages. Salisbury, instead, held back from offering itself to every passerby and so maintained a pointy integrity all its own. Its two lovely inns—the Ragamont and the White Hart—had the studied beauty and measured welcome of guest rooms in a fine home, open, it seemed, more out of necessity than desire. Upon the Reverend Lee's arrival in 1744, at the town's behest, one must add, he was forced to live with his wife for two months in a corner of the blacksmith's shop before anyone could find time in their busy schedule to provide him and his young bride with lodgings of their own. Once in place, the reverend adapted to local priorities and built a fortune in earthly real estate while simultaneously leading his flock toward the hoped-for pastures above. Money—making it and having it—had always come first in Salisbury.

Only one crosswalk cuts through Route 44 in Salisbury. Bridging the liquor store and the pharmacy, it compels cars to stop for anyone who so much as thinks about crossing there, and Steven had the luck of hitting it as an older gentleman in a big yellow slicker and matching hat shuffled across with his walker. Steven's impatient sigh again fogged the windows. As he reached to wipe clear another hole in the windshield, a broad motion ahead and to the right caught his eye. Next to Town Hall, by the veterans' monument, something moved wildly back and forth.

Figuring it for a branch caught in a sudden gust of wind, Steven pulled slowly through the crosswalk, still wiping as he looked. What the clearing revealed, though, was not a tree but a man dressed in a Union Army uniform identical to his, engulfed in the mist pouring down the cemetery hill and pooling around the sides of Town Hall here at the base of Mt. Riga. As the soldier emerged farther into the light, away from the monument and the hedge beside it, Steven saw that he was waving directly at him. The man was tall and bearded, handsome in a rough sort of way, hair longish, but not unkempt, with a uniform cut a little short at the arms and ankles, proudly bearing the well-worn look of having survived many campaigns.

"Who the hell is that?" he asked his car. In his brief full-time here, Steven had developed an acquaintance with a modest collection of Salisbury residents, locals he saw and even chatted with at the pharmacy, the grove at the Lakeville lake, and a few restaurants, and he recognized dozens more. He had placed most of the faces that had haunted him during his first visit to Mt. Riga among them. This man he could not. Yet he was somehow familiar. Very much so. Not angry, not laughing, the man's face bore a stern, slightly mournful cast, a reasonable expression for someone standing near a cemetery on a wet September day as he tried to flag down a ride. The windows clouded again, rapidly, as his breathing sped up. "Who is this guy?" asked Steven, squinting. He wiped at the passenger window.

A car honked behind him. The guy was clearly a member of the 2nd, thumbing a lift up to Riga Village, a guy he'd seen on Labor Day or in the Grand Union parking lot, his face merely one of the thousands of things he'd seen and stored in his brain during the past month without thinking about it. This time the driver behind leaned on his horn. With a glance at his watch and a memory of the little scene he was driving to at the Salisbury Central School, tiny Miss Trainey in her Indian print skirt doling out parenting tips, Steven decided that a short detour wouldn't make that much difference, especially for a "pard." He gestured to the man that he would meet him in the lot, mouthed, "Hold on," then turned right at Washinee Street to park.

Shoulders hunched into his jacket, Steven trotted past Town Hall, a two-story white barnlike structure meant ostensibly as an updated Colonial. The building seemed embarrassed rather than proud of the six columns stuck on the front. That his research so far had consisted of finishing *The Killer Angels* and searching for the rest of the list on Amazon.com nudged Steven's conscience, and he mulled over whether he deserved to identify himself as a member of the unit. When he reached the monument, though, the question became moot. The man had disappeared. Steven craned his head around the monument's panels, hunted behind the hedge and the side of the building, but turned up no one.

Next to the veterans' monument, flush with a five-foot hedge, Salisbury had put the old forge hammer and anvil from Mt. Riga on permanent display. Steven ran a hand over the bumpy surfaces, each piece about the size of a small TV, a rusty, reddish brown. Then he looked back into the graveyard. Maybe half a football field long and about as wide, it climbed up the first small rise of the mountain, plateaued for a stretch in the middle, and tabled under a wall of sixty-foot pines at its highest, westernmost edge. Massive boughs, bluish-green, redolent of Victorian death fixations and sick, romantic excess, drooped low through the young maples and honey locusts growing among the ancient trees and framed bowers in the corners. A massive sarcophagus surrounded by three obelisks owned this top shelf of the cemetery, towering over the worn limestone stumps left to the lesser names of Salisbury's past. The obelisks echoed the stark verticals of the bare pine trunks behind.

As often as he'd driven past the cemetery and tossed it a curious look, Steven had never had the time to visit, and in truth he didn't today, but he'd allotted fifteen minutes for giving the re-enactor a lift up to Mt. Riga. He opened the gate and walked over to a few of the skewed tombstones bleached white by the years. Miniature American flags marked veterans of the Revolution. Steven tried to make out some names— Nathaniel Everts, Hezekiah Eldradge—and strode on to where the steepness of the land became evident, about halfway up. Folding his arms in an appraising way, he turned and took in the view. With the hemlock and the pines behind him, the cemetery looked like an empty set for *Our Town*. Below him, all of Salisbury became visible, bordered in front by the white walls and slate roof of Town Hall, punctuated by the tall steeple of the Congregationalist Church across the street topped with its whale weathervane, and the lower cupola atop the hall, which flew a metal "1741." Behind the town, clouds swept through the minor peaks of Barack Matiff and Wetauwanchu Mountain, blurring their tops. The dead, names as blurred as the tops of the mountains, looked over the town they had built, guarding it, supervising it, one might say, from their posts on the hill. All that took place on the main drag of Salisbury, all business done, all prayers said, took place before them. A gravity reigned in this cemetery, as if all of Salisbury leaned toward it, the unseen heart of the town.

Steven made his way up to the large sarcophagus, his socks getting damp through his Rockports. Up close, it looked like a stone bathtub stuck atop a base, one word and a stray period—COFFING.—engraved on both sides. Two of the obelisks flanking it also belonged to Coffings, as did a striking granite pedestal topped with an iron urn labeled "Our Mother." Children's heads adorned the rim, likenesses of the deceased's offspring staring blankly off into eternity. Ghost faces. Cobwebs more than blood connected the children now. Who, Steven wondered, were these people, with their creepy, absurd memorials to themselves? Whoever they'd been, it appeared no one cared much anymore; unchecked lichen had softened the gray marble and granite of their monuments with patches of pale green. Already a dim day, the light thickened in the back of the graveyard where pine needles covered the dirt as the old trees had long ago defeated the grass for control. Cars rolling past on the slick road sounded like waves on a beach. The only other noise came from his shoes, squeaking in a mash of grass cuttings.

Suddenly, from his right, he heard the tinkle of what had to be a tiny bell. He turned in its direction, over to the most remote corner of the cemetery, where mist had yet to reach the bare dirt. Expecting a cat, he started when he saw another person: a woman, head bowed, kneeling before two thin slabs as white as alabaster. The magenta wide-wale corduroy pants and hunter green smock immediately proved that it was not his disappeared soldier. By squinting, Steven could make out her face, the small space between the prominent nose and lips, the plaited cord of red hair down her back. Indeed, the woman did hold a resemblance to Polly, yet with none of her elegance, none of the pride and sly delicacy that so distinguished Mrs. Kellogg. It was Mrs. Manskart.

Eyes closed, head bowed in prayer, she had not seen him. Rather than introduce himself, though, Steven did something he'd never expected to do—he played spy. Edging closer, he ducked behind Mr. Coffing's sarcophagus to watch, and with more intent now that he knew this was Polly. But was it? While his recollection of Mrs. Kellogg fairly glowed with straightness and light, Nancy Manskart stooped as she prayed, her head edging forward into what would surely someday be a widow's hump. A yellow patch that read "Diane's Amenia Hallmark" decorated one side of the smock's front, and a silver, angel-shaped bell hung from a big plastic nametag blurting "Nancy!" and rang weakly as she moved. Circles made of yarn and small sticks—dreamcatchers—dangled from her ears.

Accustomed to picturing himself in the act with every half-attractive woman he saw, Steven found nothing in Nancy with which to build a fantasy. Risking detection, he pressed forward slightly for a better look, his fingers gripping the damp stone. Patty may not have been the most beautiful woman in the world, but he had to admire her ability to float along on the currents of fashion, jumping from style to passing style and never drowning, always finding herself anew in what she wore. Nancy, on the other hand, was clearly flailing, her effort at seventies retro possibly not even an effort, but standard issue from her wardrobe. On her way to another day of cards and figurines, she wore no makeup; freckles and lines clear, eyes no longer smoldering but glazed, she looked tired, one more person bobbing in the waves, an unconsidered twin of the carefully assembled Polly. Could Polly be the real person and this woman the imitation?

Still without seeing him, she crossed herself with the slow, deliberate motions of a true believer and rose to her feet. After dusting off her knees, Nancy clumped past him, the bell ringing lightly. Even her gait lacked Polly's smooth glide. Steven continued to crouch behind the sarcophagus, curling around it to remain undetected and feeling more and more like a stalker. Who was she visiting? he wondered. Time and fortune can play brutal tricks in old towns like Salisbury; businesses die, blood lines run thin, leaving descendants of a past century's power to satisfy themselves with only their names. Was she a Coffing?

Once Nancy had made it down the hill, slid into her generic red car, and pulled out, Steven stole over to the two graves where she'd been kneeling. Both were the same size and shape, but time had worn down the letters in the stone on the right. The epitaph read:

> *Daniel Trow*
> *Dear Son*
> *18 yrs. 4 mos.*

The other read:

> *John Trow*
> *at 70 years*
> *May We All Be Forgiven*

Steven stood there in wonder until a quick burst of rain sent him running down the hill and into the Navigator. Unnerved, he stared out the windshield, out toward the pair of lonely tombstones in the corner; once unnoticed, now they shone at him, blanched white like the tips of exposed bones among all the slate tablets. John Trow, *his* John Trow, was buried there. In some way, he was buried there. And Mrs. Kellogg was visiting him.

His mind as fogged as the windows, he was halfway home before he remembered that he had to pick up Emily.

"The more I think about it, she feels a little warm to me," Miss Trainey said as she handed over Emily, already in her windbreaker and ready to go. She had less interest in lecturing Steven than in packing his daughter off and out of her hair for the rest of the day. "Let's write this off to not feeling well and try again tomorrow, shall we?"

Steven jumped on the excuse, happy not to discuss counseling or drug therapies yet. "I'm glad you said that, because this is s-o-o-o unlike her." He stroked Emily's head. "You're just not yourself today, huh, sweetie?" he said in a gloppy tone more for Miss Trainey than his daughter, who stirred from her extended sulk in order to nod.

Miss Trainey tilted her head indulgently and said, "Awwww." Holding it for a beat, she smiled hard and said, "All right. See you tomorrow" and strode back to the class, crepe soles squeaking on the tiles. Inquiries in the car as to what had happened in the classroom proved worthless. Though the facts were incontrovertible, the illness line gave Emily an alibi, and beyond saying she didn't know why she'd done it, she made no further comment. Not in the mood for interrogation, Steven sentenced her to her room for a nap and drove the rest of the way in silence.

By the time they got home, the mail had arrived. Emily headed directly to the television and sat down in front of the *Animaniacs* without taking off her jacket. Steven sorted the mail: two PCMalls, two Pottery Barn for Kids, a Sharper Image, and a Lillian Vernon. A dental bill for Patty, a note from The Foot Soldiers of Moncrieff, North Carolina— "Replica footwear specialists since 1989"—saying that his shoes were on back order, and a large manila envelope the same size as the one he'd gotten from Manskart, but postmarked Riga Village. Steven assumed this was the further correspondence Manskart had referred to in his first letter, but the label, a simple white press-on with his name typed by a typewriter, had no 2nd Connecticut insignia or official Riga Village National Historical Site markings. Steven went into the kitchen, closed the door halfway, and opened the packet. Reaching inside, he found two small and clearly quite old envelopes.

Intricate engravings adorned the first, a small sky blue envelope not much larger than his wallet, addressed to *Mrs. Celia Trow, Riga Village, Conn* in a tight, self-assured handwriting that, upon closer examination, melted away into a scrawl. The engravings did, however, hold up to scrutiny; ornate depictions of Columbia in her gown bearing up huge shields of Stars and Stripes bedecked with woven laurel, all executed with the detail and triumphant sensibility of stock certificates or paper money. When he opened the top flap, he discovered that the other three flaps were not sealed and in fact opened into one sheet of stationery, a modest sample of Civil War ingenuity and service to the fighting man. To make the most of the space, the writer had tilted the diamond sideways into a square. Steven had to guess at much of the script as he began reading.

> *September 23, 1862*
> *One mile West of Alexandria, Virg.*
> *Dearest Celia and Daniel,*
>   *The trip was long & I have slept all possible hours since arriving—I have taken too long to write, I know. I have now seen Philadelphia, which is a bully town, & the traitor's nest Baltimore & I am now in Alexandria, which is across the Potomac from Washington. Our duty is to guard the capital from invasion by the Rebs—Gen. Lee's recent visit to Maryland makes the entire city fretful about this possibility & so we shall be part of the blue wall that protects them. We have as many rumors as bad meals, but there may be some truth to one that says we shall be sent to Gen. Mc-Clellan in replacement for troops lost at Antietam.*

As he forged on, Steven found he could understand if not exactly make out every word, and the writing became clearer to him.

>   *I think of you both often & of Mt. Riga. Please remember me to all that you see. Tell Barbara her Calamus weeps for her—which is not true but will be of comfort. Daniel—you must remember to keep the woodpile full and neatly stacked. We have felt mostly heat here, but last year by now we had already bore a hard frost. I would send you warmth from the sunny South, but there is little for us here. I dream of having news to tell you, but in truth my days in this place bring less to do than at any day on Mt. Riga. We drill—we guard—we shine our shoes & buttons—we go on parade. Some boys are eager to see action. If you guessed Helton, James Truby, & the other hotheads you are right. You may guess where I stand. We are all patriots, yet those who have lived a bit longer prefer to stay alive—Manning the gates is fine service & no mean feat when the Rebels are just across the river and when an imbecile such as Kellogg is your commmander.*
>   *I have seen the President once from a great distance—I regret to say that the effect on my spirit was small. Peter Frote claims to have seen "Father Abraham" at a lesser remove two nights ago. He snuck out of camp & was strolling through one of Washington's disreputable districts—there are many. He placed the meeting between Stanton's house & the White House, so it is possible, although few believe him. Lizzie would start howl-*

ing if she knew her husband went "strolling" there. If you believe him, Frote
says he (if it was him) was as tall as they say & bent.

I will write again soon.

Believe me your

John

The other letter was written not on a serviceman's form, but on a clean sheet of thin white vellum tucked into a simple white envelope. Outside, the same dense hand had scribbled only *Mrs. Kellogg*. Steven had to nearly pry open the letter, creased for a hundred and forty years, and though the blue ink had faded and brown stains nearly obscured the lines that had the misfortune of running along the folds, he could still make out the contents.

September 23, 1862

Dear Polly,

Today my heart rebels. I have been silent in the face of this torture & now must speak.

To leave that dead town atop the mountain & my pain, I enlisted. Even all these years later I wanted to depart the places you & I shared—the trees I watched grow & harvested into acres of unshaded grass—the lake deep & unchanged like the space my heart holds for you. When you left I filled that space with hatred & bitterness. Now I finally escape from the mountain, "have hoisted sail to all the winds Which should transport me furthest from your sight"—yet I see you again. I see you standing next to him—using his name—Mrs. Polly Kellogg—& I beg God to know if I am damned. But as much as my mind begs to hate you, my heart cannot. I can only wonder why you ran away.

I have watched you since August & asked myself if you watch me too. You stand on the side as he runs us like pet dogs. Do you remember who I am? Do you think that I do not know—that I do not recognize the way you turn your head—the green of your eyes—how you twirl a parasol & where you first used those deadly talents? Your eyes fuel me. I lift my chin higher. I hold my chest up & strain to catch their glance. Your husband may think I am an improving soldier, but in truth I wait your sign. For months now I have waited & I can wait no longer. Tell me that you do not know me & I shall take my bounty & run back home. Know me & I shall stay.

I am assigned patrol in Alexandria tomorrow night. A note or a person would find me alone at 10 pm guarding the theater.

I have never stopped being your
John

So the little tingle between him and Polly Kellogg had historical value after all, and Mrs. Melton had not exaggerated Trow's interesting past—the dawg had a secret life. Prepared to play a minor spear carrier, Steven now caught the whiff of romantic lead in his Mr. Trow, or at least a good tragic role, what with the wife and son back on Mt. Riga. He immediately wanted to know more, yet he had no clue where or how to start. Trow obviously had survived the war; the tombstone said he was seventy years old when he died. But where was Celia's grave? Did Trow and Polly reunite? If she had sent these letters, as Steven had to assume, Nancy Manskart may also have paid her graveside visit for his benefit. He had a sudden chill.

The mysteries only grew. Steven grinned as he skipped up the steps to his office, where he grabbed an empty file folder and labeled it JOHN TROW. What had Trow looked like? Steven flipped through a few Civil War books hoping to find a handsome, world-weary face staring out at him from a Mathew Brady photograph, a face willing to stand in for John Trow, but no one volunteered; every blank expression seemed too busy contemplating its own fate. He tried to create his own John Trow, as if he were describing him to a cop—a little taller than average, maybe six feet; short brown hair combed to the left; deep-set brown eyes; full lips, aquiline nose—but the details remained only words, and the face never came to life. Then he saw the plastic soldier standing on his monitor, the perfectly regular features, the set jaw; a generic Union Army man hunting for an identity. Steven pictured the toy six feet tall, brandishing his bayonet from the other side of the room. "Kiss my arse," the soldier said, in the crisp, new voice Steven had been hearing lately. He looked at his uniform, brushed and hanging from the hook he'd nailed behind his office door; at the imaginary soldier; at the letters. Meet John Trow, thought Steven.

He closed his eyes. Out of the mist appeared Polly, very much alive, daintily opening the envelope almost 150 years ago, biting her lip as she read the words, pain and hunger for her former lover both rising. He imagined a corset pinned to a satin hanger, hiding behind her door. Whoever sent the letters, Steven wanted more.

❧ PART TWO ❧

CHAPTER

9

WHILE STEVEN WAITED IN VAIN FOR MORE communication from the past, the world took a gentle curve into autumn. Lease expired, summer preened for a last few boiling days, then packed its Speedos and moved on, accompanied by all the bugs and final much-too-fat tomatoes left to rot by even their most avid fans. Cooler every day now, the area gave in to the ups and mostly downs of the Housatonic Valley Regional High School football team and the challenging question of what to do with all the apples dangling from the thousands of apple trees. Baked up, bobbed for, or sold to passing cars, the bracing Macs and mellow Goldens each offered a handful of the different types of early fall day available in New England. Yellow leaves began to fleck the poppels and sometimes lone trees blazed dramatically into orange or red, deciduous Camilles swooning for attention, but mostly the trees held green, giving Salisbury a moment to catch its breath before the onslaught of beauty and people that foliage season brings.

Halfway up Mt. Riga, Steven pointed out to Patty a prematurely reddish-orange maple glowing in a ravine. She had insisted on driving him up to the village for his first day, as much as anything to torture him, he decided. Since his close encounter with Nancy Manskart and the arrival of the letters, Steven's preparations for citizenship in Riga Village—reading Shelby Foote, one pass through *Hardee's*, and trying on the uniform—had drawn Patty's notice with predictably negative result. Her subsequent pop quizzes on various facets of the Civil War, usually sprung in front of others, and his generally poor performance on them had left him shaky and concerned that the daunting Mrs. Melton might have a similar form of hazing in mind. He had majored in European history. Did it really matter if the *Monitor* was Union or Confederate? Steven thought not, but who knew what was important to these people?

Fiddling with the shiny buttons of his uniform, he reassured himself that the entire process of joining Riga Village would be gradual. A vestigial feeling of embarrassment at the prospect of spending a day in mock Civil War garb returned even as he imagined himself cracking into different drill positions, in perfect synch with the rest of the regiment. Patty glanced briefly at the tree and pointed it out to Emily, strapped in the back seat of the second-hand Saab. This brisk Saturday morning had arrived dotted with clouds and no firm promise that there wouldn't be more as the day went on. Steven's wooly uniform felt good against his skin, and between the crisp breeze flowing in the windows, the promise of an encounter with Polly Kellogg, and his nervous edge, he had trouble sitting still despite Patty's current mood, as sharp as one of the ubiquitous baking apples.

"Don't miss us too much, now," she said as he bounced a bit in his seat.

He ignored the comment, though he did stop moving around. "What time is Nate's soccer game?"

"He's not doing soccer, remember? Hated the coach?" She let his ignorance of the situation sink in, then said, "He's going to Great Barrington with friends."

"Oh, great. Hackysack on the corner and annoying tourists."

She turned to Steven. "Well, you're not doing anything with him, are you?" Steven had to cede the point, though he believed that Nate would surely enjoy hackysack more than anything he'd have come up with as a father-son event. Nearing the parking lot, she spoke again. "So what time are you done?"

"Five, I think. I'll call you."

"Are you sure they have phones up there?"

"They have to."

"Did you check?"

"I mean, they *have* to. What if there was a fire or something?"

She pushed her sunglasses onto her forehead to emphasize the importance of the question. "But did you *check*?"

Time to lie. "I thought I saw one in the schoolhouse, in the office there."

With a doubtful glance, she pulled into the parking lot to let him out. "Try the cell first. Maybe it'll work if you call me from a mountain." Emily, who had busied herself with a WNBA Barbie all the way up, climbed into the front seat and said goodbye with a dismaying lack of concern.

Steven leaned into Patty's window, backpack dangling off his shoulder. Should he tell her that he was a little scared? That he never would have done this when he'd had an actual future. That if she smiled, pulled him into the window, and told him how much she loved him no matter what happened in their lives, he would leave with her this moment? Instead, he gave her a light kiss, which she received with passive though extended lips. "Thanks for driving me up here."

Another skeptical *hmmm*. She flipped her sunglasses back down. "We'll be waiting for you back in the twentieth century when you're done." As she rolled away, she stuck her head out the window and yelled, "Hey soldier boy! *Monitor* North, *Merrimac* South!"

Steven stepped through the small thicket between the parking lot and the first large field of Riga Village expecting Mrs. Melton and her Victorian inquisition, but in the distance, on the bridge over Wachocastinook Creek, stood Walter Manskart holding a cup of Salisbury Pharmacy coffee as he stared off toward the waterwheel. Instead of the fuss and epaulets of his uniform, he wore a red flannel shirt of large plaid, khakis a size too tight and a size too short, and brown Wallabys. Steven approached with caution and intuitive dislike. Their strange Labor Day encounter on the mountain had continued to rankle; for all of Manskart's later peppy banter with Mrs. Melton, the teacher's abrasive pomposity still nagged at Steven, disdainful, yet nervous, as well. Would this be the second moronic authority figure he'd have to buckle under to this week? Jay Porter was quite enough. Walking on, he reminded himself that Manskart was only a grammar school teacher, a pearlike colonel manqué who looked more like a donut-munching cop on break than any Civil War hero he'd ever read about.

Before Steven reached the bridge, Manskart acknowledged him with a nod and began biting at a fingernail under the edges of his walrus moustache, spitting it over the railing and into the creek. Steven put him at roughly his age. Unsure as to whether he should salute and certainly not thrilled about embracing Manskart's just-nibbled hand, Steven stopped and said, "Colonel Kellogg, how are you?" He used the affable, manly tone usually reserved for meeting corporate types, its low, hail-fellow resonance meant to send out the message "Let's be businessmen together" to the other guy's melon.

Manskart extended his hand with a bluff smile, his heavy eyebrows and plastic face held in check while dealing with a person of this century. "Welcome, Mr. Armour. Thank you for coming so early." Steven had anticipated a firmer grip; the short, conical fingers, incomplete somehow, underdeveloped despite Manskart's size, explained the big white gloves he'd worn on Labor Day. Nate had only good things to say about Manskart, and ordinarily Steven would have factored that into his opinion, but he couldn't get past his gut feeling of profound dislike, his illogical, almost animal distrust. He'd only met the man once. "Mrs. Melton usually does these orientations, but she called me early this morning and said she couldn't be here. I didn't have a chance to . . ." Manskart waved his hand down the length of his body and back up again, like a magician's assistant.

"Well, don't worry about . . ."

"I usually prefer dealing with members of the Second as soldiers, not as . . ." Manskart searched for the right words. "Not as real, how shall I say, *people*. Helps us build the impression. Do you see? The reality." The contrast between today's off-the-sale-rack look and the colonel's impeccably tailored uniform clearly suggested that the Manskarts' annual clothing budget could support only one wardrobe for each of them. Steven imagined the couple standing in Penney's trying to decide between a new pair of jeans for Walter and some odd bit of war junk they'd seen in a catalog, doing quick math on small numbers.

"Sure, that sounds—"

Manskart cut him off again, a teacher laying down the law. "I'll start here at the furnace, show you around the rest of the village, give you a brief history, let you see a few other points of interest. It won't take more than half an hour." He paused a beat. "Will it substitute for your own research?" Lifting one brow, the teacher gave a stare that bored into Steven.

Steven waited for more, wondered if maybe life was too short for this. Then he realized that Manskart was calling on him. "Uh. No?"

"Correct. No, of course it won't. There's *no* substitute for your own research. Every person working here in the village or in the Second is a historian. Accuracy is very important here. It's how we teach; it's how we have fun . . ."

Manskart crumpled the empty coffee cup and hitched his pants up into a self-inflicted wedgie, revealing a few more inches of sock. "Please stay in first person while you're here," Manskart went on. "Always *be* the person whose impression you're performing. If you need help on first person, what should you do?"

Manskart apparently didn't deal with adults all that often. He raised his chin as he waited again for Steven. "Uh, practice?"

"Well, yes, yes. In a way. But what do you need to become a *true* citizen of Riga Village?"

"A uniform?"

Manskart shook his head vigorously, unable to hide his exasperation. "*No.* Yes, you do need that. But you must do research. *Ree*-search. Do more research. Talk to me or to Mrs. Melton. The more you *know*, the more you can *do*."

The fact suddenly struck Steven with a great relaxing power that nothing Manskart said, be it silly, boorish, or brutal, had a direct bearing on his life. He reminded himself that he was John Trow here, not Steven Armour, and as Manskart continued explaining the finer points of first-person impression, Steven stashed away the everyday Steven Armour somewhere behind the dark blue shell and sky blue pants, giving him a much deserved day off from caring about things like the fact that his elastic suspenders were pulling his trousers up into a kind of codpiece. "If you have any questions, ask them. By then, the rest of the men should have arrived, and we'll muster."

"Sounds good," said Steven in a chipper, what-choice-do-I-have tone.

"Let's get a look-see at you." Calling on his years of watching *Gomer Pyle*, Steven stood at what he assumed to be attention—knees locked, chin up, chest out, elbows back. No haversack, no cartridge or cap box, no blanket. Only the canteen, smooth and covered in blue wool, hanging at his hip, in addition to the jacket, pants, and cap. Woolen hiking socks and a pair of battered Rockports served as footgear. In truth, he represented a soldier more than he resembled one. Manskart checked hems and linings, rubbed fabric. No one since rush week had inspected Steven with quite this intensity, and from Manskart's squint and occasional tongue cluck, he could tell it was not going well. The colonel flipped the canteen so that it bounced off Steven's hip. "Nobody wore it this way. Cut the strap and wear it high. And get rid of the chain on the stopper— they used string." He folded his arms over his stomach and locked his knees, the posture of an aggressive hall monitor. "What's next?"

Though he'd told himself he was safely hidden behind his uniform, Steven couldn't help taking Manskart's brusque manner personally. Giving well-considered thought to the Colonel's inclination to avoid dealing with his men in real life, Steven fought back a strange and, for him, unusual urge to throw a punch. He decided that laughing at Manskart's pants, which turned out to be a pair of severely pilling double knits, would be more in character for him. "Well, I can't buy it all at once, so . . ."

"What's next, Mr. Armour . . ." Manskart drew out the correct answer for dramatic effect. ". . . are the belt and the shirt. Those come next."

The teacher gave Steven's jacket a few final tailor-like tugs to settle it into a better fit, then stepped back. Smoothing his mustache with index finger and thumb, he finally shook his head, disappointed, and, to judge from the slightly raised corner of his mouth, maybe even disgusted. "Casey makes the best coat, but this'll have to do for now. For godsakes, though, don't wait to start working on the buttonholes." Steven nodded. Somebody else would know what that meant. "All right then. Let's move out."

Manskart burst into full waddle toward the furnace, further grinding away the outer sole of each Wallaby, and Steven followed, a half-step behind. After a couple of paces, the teacher halted abruptly in front of the thirty-foot-high waterwheel, planted his feet, and clasped his hands behind his back. "The story of the Mt. Riga Furnace goes back to the mid-eighteenth century, when Thomas Lamb, a land speculator, bought up large portions of real estate in the Salisbury area, including in seventeen forty-one, three hundred sixty-five and one-half acres here at the top of Mt. Riga, seventy-five of which were held with one Thomas Norton and include the water rights to the pond, its outlet, and the stream." Manskart took a deep breath and launched into a detailed and bloodless recounting of the mountain's provenance, raising his voice a little to overcome the sound of rushing water.

Steven let his eyes wander around the outside of the furnace, the white walls and the chimney, in search of Trow's motivation. Having so little to work with to create this character, Steven fell back on his gross understanding of method acting and transferred some of the emotional energy he had used for his actual elementary school, his childhood penny candy store, to the local landmarks of Riga Village, telling himself that he had gone to that school at the crossroads as a child, bought candies at that store by the lake, fallen asleep beside this rushing water. To his amazement, it worked. How different was it, really, from pretending, and as he gathered small details and invested them with meaning—his friend Calamus had been hit in the head with the horseshoe lying over there in the grass; his son, Daniel, sat on that rock at the creek's bank to scoop tadpoles—his assemblage of things that meant John Trow, letters, uniform, even the plastic soldier, began to slowly merge into one vision of a man.

". . . King and Kelsey began this furnace in eighteen oh-two, but soon went bankrupt. The consortium of James Coffing . . ."

So that's who the Coffings were. Though he could imagine the money running out, he couldn't picture New England industrial scions ending up at a Hallmark store. Steven wondered when he'd see Polly.

". . . Luther Holley and Joseph Pettee finished the work in eighteen ten, and Pettee became the ironmaster. For the next seventeen years, the Riga Furnace was the most important iron-production facility in America."

How Manskart prevented a class full of hormonal preteens from rioting was beyond Steven. Unable to resist a tweak, he said, "*Most* important? Is that really true?"

The teacher's lips pursed and froze; he was not accustomed to having his facts questioned. "Yes, in fact it was. Anything else?" He waited for an answer. "No? Then let's go on to the furnace."

As they moved on, Manskart displayed, Carol Merrill–style, the water-wheel and the huge leather bellows that fueled the fire inside the furnace with blasts of cold air; hence the term "blast furnace." He went on delivering facts and numbers and details in crushing volume and magnitude. They saw the tunnel head, a hole in the furnace chimney on the same level as the rise with all the piles of rock, connected to it by a covered ramp. Here the fillers poured ore, limestone, and charcoal into the furnace; thirty to forty pounds of limestone per four or five hundred pounds of iron ore, fifteen bushels of charcoal. The flame and gaseous impurities shot out the top of the chimney.

One ear on Manskart, Steven's eyes continued to acquaint themselves with the world as John Trow saw it. He imagined his father—James Trow, that was—hauling tons of rock and flinging them down the hole, one slip away from a fiery death. At night, a heroic workingman trudging home black and grimy to eat the small but satisfying supper Mother had waiting. A rough man doing rough work, he managed to raise John and his—two brothers? No, one brother and one sister—with love and guidance. A hard life, but it built character in young John.

Manskart led him down to a dark, cool two-story room built around the stone casing of the furnace. A few windows high up on the sloping roof let in columns of light; bugs and dust swirled around and through them. Inside a receding arch on the stone wall was a small iron plate, the door to the hearth. "A gate to hell in those days," said the teacher. "This whole room would be 120, 130 degrees when the fire was going." The hot, molten iron came through the door and flowed into a main trough that branched into smaller troughs, like a sow suckling pigs; hence the term "pig iron." The process was called tapping the furnace, and Riga Village's head founder, Japhet Beck, offered small demonstrations three times daily.

Steven tested his fingertips on the sharp edges of a chunk of slag, a jagged rocky substance similar to hardened lava, the by-product of the whole process. He, John Trow, had sifted through this stuff, played on the piles with the other children of the town. Here he'd met Polly, the girl who broke his heart, and the devoted Celia. "When exactly did the furnace close?"

"The furnace went cold in eighteen forty-seven. Some work was done into the eighteen fifties, but eighteen forty-seven was really the end of it."

"I feel weird asking this, but why are we dressed in Civil War clothes?"

Mr. Manskart paused, his manner frosty. "We do not re-create a certain day here. Riga Village re-creates an era. A time. I hope that's not a problem for you," the last sentence faintly sarcastic.

"Uh, no. I was just wondering."

"Good. Then let's look at the post office." Manskart had more history to get off his chest when they got to the small frame building. "The post office was founded in eighteen forty-one, originally with just the name 'Riga.' This is the first instance of the use of the name Riga in relation to this settlement and this mountain. Approximately 940 pieces of mail were moved . . ." Steven peered around corners, and as he did, more human details pulled away from the facts: jugs left next to doors, one on its side; dusty handprints on a leather yoke; forge tools laid out in a precise order meaningful only to the person who had created it. He imagined the cranky old woman who'd set out the jugs, the massive hands of the blacksmith. As Manskart droned on with crop statistics, population figures, the inventory of the store, Steven ran a hand up and down a sleeve of his uniform. The more he imagined for John Trow, the more he filled it out, the more it changed from costume to clothing. "Mr. Armour, what was the population of Riga Village at its peak?"

Steven cocked his head, and said, "I'm sorry; I must have missed that."

"I told you an estimated 250. The facts *do* matter here, Mr. Armour." Manskart scowled. "Accuracy is the point of everything we do." Steven nodded repentently and the two stood there while the teacher considered whether to continue. Finally, he hitched up his pants again and said, "All right, come along. One more thing to see."

A five-minute walk north out of town, in the woods maybe twenty yards off the dirt road, a four-foot-high rock jutted from the leaf litter, out of place, almost a little obscene. Steven hesitated to get close, but Manskart slapped its side as if it were a faithful old horse, and Steven ventured an imitative pat with an extended arm.

"This is Baby Rock. One of the haunted places on Mt. Riga," said Manskart, making finger quotes around "haunted." "The story told is that one rainy night, one of the mountain's opium addicts couldn't stand the cries of his two infant daughters, so he brought them out here and staved their heads in against this rock." Steven pulled his hand off as though the rock's temperature had suddenly shot through the top of the thermometer. Manskart laughed.

"Some old woodcutter claimed he saw two babies here once, holding on to each other and crying. Others said they'd heard the cries, too. Became known as Baby Rock." Manskart gave the boulder a sympathetic rub. "I don't know if it's true, but it is a heavy burden for one rock to carry, don't you think?"

Steven had nothing to say to that and was grateful when they turned south toward the center of town. The figures of its pretend civilization bustled from building to building, the citizens of Riga Village assuming their other, older identities, taking their places among the ghosts. He wondered where Polly was among them.

Back at the small farm on the other side of the furnace, Manskart pointed out the locker where Steven could store his backpack and any personal effects; no jewelry or electronic equipment carried while in the village, please. Then he gestured toward the field where they'd mustered on Labor Day. "That's enough. The rest is up to your own research and learning from the others. You'll start your job in town in a few weeks. Mrs. Melton will talk to you about that. Report to First Sergeant Dawes now. I'll arrive presently." Manskart took some quick, chopping steps away, then stopped and called back, "Your son's a fine boy. I see where he gets his inquisitive nature."

A fine boy? Inquisitive nature? Steven hadn't heard phrases like that in years. It was entirely possible that Manskart wasn't as much evil as he was a social misfit. "Well, thank you. I think. He's, uh, he's been saying how much he's been looking forward to having you." Happy to chat about his children, as fathers often are when said children are nowhere around, Steven was about to ask him if he had kids of his own when the colonel turned and walked away.

CHAPTER

10

OVER THE RISE, A BRACE OF EIGHT MEN in uniforms chatted, some smoking, all but two standing, a few leaning on their rifles. Their uniforms approximated the consummate Union soldier look of Steven's plastic ideal—dark blue jacket, light blue pants, forage cap. Far from his own skimpy version of soldiering, though, cups, canteens, bayonets, and a variety of sacks, pouches, and boxes in leather and fabric hung off each man, along with a knapsack and bedroll. Every outfit appeared new, buttons and brass gleaming, colors rich and unstained.

Underdressed for the party, Steven hung back for a moment to case the scene. The fat guy and the turbaned giant he'd noticed on Labor Day both sat cross-legged, facing each other as they shared a package of Hostess Cupcakes. He might not be happy at DP anymore, but it was still *his* company, so Steven had to wonder with some envy why no one ever bought Creamy Dingles. More sugar and a dime less had always struck him as a good deal, even if the red dye stained a little. As he got closer, Steven heard the turbaned man say, "They can put you out, you know." The off-white band of cotton wound its way a good nine inches above his forehead. Had there been a ghurka in the ranks of the Heavies, Steven wondered, or did it signify a medical condition or hair plugs? The man had an undershot jaw and a huge, bulbous nose that ranged in color from a florid red to burgundy. Steven pictured him slurping bargain merlots in his recliner every night as he watched the History Channel get fuzzier and fuzzier.

"Really?" asked the fat guy.

"Yeah, you don't have to watch. I didn't."

"They said the thing is really small, like a thread." He was trying to be brave.

A lanky man, early forties probably, stubbed out his cigarette in the grass. He had gray hair mixed with black, cut in the longish Prince Valiant style popular with mid-1970s folk singers, and his kepi was tilted down, the brim hiding his black, Dondi eyes. His small features crowded into the center of his face, and though the haircut made him appear harmless, the sneer peeking through his black mustache did not. "Who the fuck wants to stay up while you're getting your ass snaked?"

They all made queasy faces. Once Dockers proved you were over forty; now an active interest in colonoscopy separated men of a certain age from those who hadn't yet considered their wasting mortality. The smoker plucked a piece of tobacco off the tip of his tongue; this, Steven concluded, was the unfiltered hardass of the group.

"I mean, you'd have to be fucking crazy. Or like it or something."

Everyone sniggered. Having just gone for the local on his, Steven, a tested veteran of the battle for renal health, could afford to swagger as he approached.

Joe Swan said, "That's cold," with an authority that closed the subject. He made directly for Steven, an apparently genuine smile on his face. "Hey, Steve! Does your mother know you're here?"

The others rolled their eyes at the period jocularity. First Sergeant Dawes appeared very pleased to have a new subordinate, especially one who now lived in his dream house, and Steven registered this possible landmine while Swan introduced him around as "that son of a bitch who bought my house."

He traded consciously solid handshakes with the rest of the men, each of whom clanked as they shook. Tubby Oren Scobeck had the colon issues; his beturbaned friend was David Burney. Though Steven recognized Bobby Osselin and his father, Hube, from the Grand Union, they, much to his relief, did not seem to remember him, nor did the son exude anything other than good will toward a new face and immense pleasure at being able to call an adult a "fresh fish." After shaking Steven's hand, he returned to his pastime, which involved dashing about in a half-trot, ducking occasionally as if dodging bullets. He looked like a sparrow darting among a herd of old bulls. His father had dimples and sparkling eyes that classed him as an unusually attractive man of late middle age, but they did not help the sense Steven had that Hube was not a bright man.

The two seniors—wiry Jerry Sears and the pasty Murray Lummer—represented opposite approaches to aging. Wrinkled dark and lean as a strip of beef jerky, Sears put some strength into his handshake and probably would have pinned Steven if Lummer hadn't stepped in to offer his own doughy greeting, a two-hander full of the superior beneficence of a church usher. The hardass, Gary Kucharsky, took a reluctant break from lighting another Pall Mall to say hello; he was clearly reserving judgment until Steven wiped out a nest of Cub Scouts or displayed whatever else passed for admirable action in the world of re-enacting.

"Is that everybody?" asked Steven.

Swan gave him an odd look. "Yeah. Why?"

"Isn't there one more guy. Tall? Dark beard?" They shook their heads. "I saw a guy last week in a Second Connecticut uniform in front of Town Hall. Thought he'd be up here."

Swan shrugged. "I heard some guys in Litchfield want to start up a company of the First. Maybe he was with them. They want to do something a little easier than what we got going. We're pretty serious progressives here. You know that, right?"

"Yeah." The most hardcore, realistic re-enactors called themselves progressives, but Steven had trouble connecting the word *progressive* with those people trying the hardest to go back to the past. Swan unsnapped a pouch and stuffed some tobacco into a short wooden pipe with his knobby fingers. In his crisp blues and sergeant's stripes, Swan had an easy confidence that had never appeared during the house-buying process. His thin, tanned face looked more comfortable, more considerable under a high kepi, as if he belonged back in the nineteenth century.

Snack finished, Scobeck stood a bit too close to Steven, hovering over his right shoulder as he sniffed at the new meat. Though the big man had used a lot of soap that morning, the sour tang coming off Scobeck was already winning that battle. He stared down at Steven's Rockports and in a prissy, sniping way said, "No farbs here, thank you very much. Keep your coolers at home."

Steven stopped himself from asking whether they'd had Hostess Cupcakes in the Civil War, or colonoscopy tubes; instead, he just nodded. While most hardcore re-enactors looked as if they spent time wrecking their uniforms in the hope of developing a patina of real use, the men of the 2nd apparently took pride in being bandbox soldiers. If they weren't smoking or talking with someone about what they'd just bought for their uniforms or what they were going to buy next, they were shining their buttons, dusting grass off their pants, or dabbing at their glossy shoes. These men worshipped their uniforms.

Fond as he was becoming of his own, it felt slight beside these full-blown rigs. Steven leaned over to Swan and said apologetically, "I really don't have enough stuff yet, do I? I mean, should I even be out here?"

Swan looked surprised. "Hey, you look great for a fresh fish!" He put a consoling hand on Steven's shoulder. "C'mon, you'll get there. It takes time."

Like a large-pawed puppy, Bobby Osselin sidled up to Steven and said, "Watch this!"

Trotting forward again, gun in hand, the boy set his acne-scarred battle face; heartbreaking in a way. Steven could instantly imagine young silly boys like Bobby fighting this war, something quite different from simply knowing that it had happened. Bobby called to his father, "Dad, shoot me!" Without turning away from Murray and a discussion of Civil War pension records in the Connecticut State Archives, Hube aimed his finger at his son, cocked and then dropped his big thumb like a pistol hammer, and said, "Bang!" Bobby crumpled in a most alarming fashion, arms and legs akimbo as he made a heap, eyes open. After a final twitch, he went still.

Steven didn't know what to do. Swan, like the rest of the company, hadn't even turned his head in Bobby's direction, but he said, "Nice hit, Bobby." Kucharsky and Scobeck appeared annoyed by Bobby's antics. Swan shrugged. "The kid loves taking hits. He's one of the best bloaters I've ever seen. Bloat, Bobby." Bobby's body suddenly swelled into the awkward position of a casualty caught in a Brady photograph, his jaw slack, eyes no longer glassy, just empty and cold, as if he'd been dead a week. "See?" Bobby sprang up, dusted off his uniform, and bounded over to Kucharsky to bum a cigarette.

"Okay, he's gonna be here soon," said Swan. "Here's the rundown. You'll never remember this now, but there's gotta be a first time, right? I'm First Sergeant Calamus Dawes. Scobeck is Corporal Dexter Colley . . ."

Bobby Osselin woofed, then said "Lassie come home!" in a mocking falsetto.

". . . Burney's Private Chauncey Richardson. Jerry and Murray, believe it or not"—many snorted at the aside—"are brothers, Jabez and Peter Frote. Bobby is Private James Truby and Hube is Private Munson Qualls. They're not related back then. Gary is Corporal Sylvester Hyte. Who are you again?"

"John Trow."

"Trow. Right. You and I are friends." Swan, puzzled, squinted before he could stop himself. "Then, I mean. I mean we are now, but Trow and Dawes were *really* friends. I mean not that . . ."

Steven held up his palms to stop him. "No, I get it. I get it." As unlikely as he would have thought it after the Swans had nearly backed out at the closing, today Steven felt at ease around Joe.

"The more you get into it, the easier it is." Swan took another drag. "Sometimes you might feel more like him than yourself."

That would be nice, Steven thought. He tried to get back into his John Trow character, but it wasn't as crucial here, with these men. Another "bang" and Bobby went sprawling again a few feet away. David Burney related some fact about car transmissions to Jerry Sears as he downed a pint of Nestlé's Quik. That he wasn't surrounded by people who'd bought Cisco five years ago pleased Steven; no should-haves or sticky wonderings as to the other men's portfolio sizes. No one cared what anyone did or did not do for a living. The coin they trafficked in was historical perfection; ownership of Civil War material and an infinite store of related ephemeral knowledge decided who was boss.

Kucharsky let smoke dribble out his nostrils as he spoke. "Is that what you got so far?" Corporal Hyte, the challenger to Swan's seat beside Manskart's throne, struck a pose, hooking the nonsmoking thumb over his waistband and bending one knee. The blue of his spotless uniform set off the lightness of his hair. With his permanently dissatisfied look, Kucharsky clearly craved obedience. Steven picked up the glint of gold on his ring finger and pitied the wife, hoped they had no children.

"Yeah. Everything's on order, so I should have . . ."

"Has Kellogg seen you?"

"Yeah, he took me around. Mrs. Melton was . . ."

Kucharsky shook his head and grinned a little grin. "No. I mean did *Kellogg* see you?"

Uncertain as to just how subtle a point Kucharsky was making, Steven began to understand when he looked up and saw Manksart leaving the shade of a doorway, splendid in his regalia of frock coat, saber, sash, and knee-high boots, a long wooden rifle in one hand. With each step the colonel took into the sun, his body transformed. His stomach tightened, his chest swelled, chin rose, and eyes widened, suddenly taking in a far wider prospect than the officious little teacher Manskart could ever hope to see. The band of turkeys that roamed occasionally across his front lawn immediately came to Steven's mind, the drab little toms that inflated themselves and shook their tail feathers to scare off rival suitors and draw in their mates. Yet even as the colonel—for Kucharsky was right; this was surely Kellogg now, not Manskart—strutted toward them like one of those massive, gobbling fowl, Steven had to admit that a kinder comparison would also apply: a tarnished bowl, maybe, found in a back drawer, polished, and put on display. This was the man he'd met on Labor Day, not Manskart. As unlikable and annoying as the teacher was, Kellogg added an element of military fear.

Cigarettes were stubbed against the soles of shoes. Burney edged over to Steven and asked, in a low voice, "So, how crack are you on drill?"

"I looked it over," Steven whispered back. "I'm definitely no expert."

"Did you practice?"

"No, not really." What exactly did he have under that turban?

Whispering too by now, Burney said, "Oh, fuck," and did a charade of laughing. "Really?"

"No."

"Oh, shit." He shared the news sotto voce with the rest of the company.

Some closed their eyes as if pained; others smirked. Scobeck burst away from Steven's side like a bird flushed from a bush, unwilling to stand near him. All of a sudden, Steven felt nauseated. He gestured to Burney that he had some chocolate milk on his mustache. The big man smiled and wiped his lip, surprised, it seemed, at his concern.

Silence fell over the men, formed in a single line, as Kellogg, now all twisting eyebrows and squinting eyes, took his place before them. After a haughty sniff, the colonel snapped straight and bellowed, "Attention!" Immediately, he began shaking his head. "By size order! You should damn well know that by now!"

The line melted apart and the men re-formed, Steven squeezing between Hube Osselin and Scobeck as the men checked their positions, touching elbows to get the correct spacing. As roll was called, each put his rifle to his side, and then Kellogg tucked his hands into the small of his back and walked up the line, starting at Lummer, the shortest, toward Burney, making a rolling stop at each man for a brief inspection. How bad can this be, Steven reassured himself. He wasn't in prison. He could walk out if he wanted to. The man had already seen him, understood that he didn't have everything yet.

Kellogg pulled up in front of Steven, who had the good sense not to stare him in the eye. Long, then longer, the pause portended comment.

Steven steeled himself under the colonel's slow gaze, tried to recall Manskart's jumbo wedgie to stay loose. Like Scobeck, Kellogg finally settled his eyes on Steven's shoes. Steven could feel his leg jiggling. He clamped it still. "Exactly what *are* those, Private," Kellogg asked reasonably, sweet honey before the rock.

"My shoes, uh. Sir." Respect couldn't hurt. "I haven't yet been issued my brogans," said Steven, satisfied with his initial stab at first person impression.

Kellogg's voice rose word by word from a whisper to a scream. "So until you get your goddamned shoes, you will wear nothing!" A fleck of foam caught on the edge of his mustache and his face flamed as red as a terrible sunburn. "Take those idiotic things off! You'll march barefoot like one of Jackson's men until you have the proper shoes."

Was he kidding? Kellogg didn't budge, so Steven began to slowly bend toward his Rockports. "Move! Move! Move! Move!"

Obscenities poured into his mind, all in the voice he'd assigned to John Trow, and he had to squeeze his jaw shut in order to keep them in, so great was the impulse behind them. Flustered, Steven slowly tugged at his laces, buying time to decide whether to stay or to bolt at this first obstacle.

"Come on, missy. If you can't do *this*, what *can* you do?"

Steven went still. That was the question, wasn't it? Being a good driver, making a tasty omelette—these achievements provided little comfort late at night. Riga Village was looking like the last stop on this train.

Fuck it.

Steven ripped off his shoes and socks and tossed them off to the side of the field. Immediately, a sense of being naked rose in him. Beyond the cursing, Steven tried to bring forth the John Trow he was building in his head, but there wasn't enough there to fend off Kellogg. Standing in the sun, he didn't want to be Steven Armour, but he wasn't yet John Trow.

The colonel handed him the pretend rifle with great care. "Here's your Quaker gun. If you earn it, you'll get a Springfield. Learn to love it as these other good men have."

The gun felt stupidly light, like a popgun. Swan called out the next orders. "Attention! Company! Support arms!"

All the guns went to shoulders in three quick moves. Each man clamped his gun between his left arm and his chest by holding his hand on his breast as if pledging allegiance. Steven, though, was frozen. He had given *Hardee's* only the most cursory read, had never practiced, yet he'd expected this all to snap into place. He had no clue about what to do. What had he been thinking?

Kellogg boomed, "Company! Support arms!"

And suddenly the gun went to the right place, albeit noticeably later than everyone else's, and it had nearly flipped over his shoulder because of its lightness, but when he peeked around at the other men to make sure he'd gotten it right, he saw his feet were turned out at just less than a right angle, heels touching; his right hand held palm forward at his side, pinky behind the seam of his trousers, elbows in. He'd done it. Somehow. Bobby gave him a quick once-over and nodded approval. Steven mentally patted himself on the back for remembering that much of the book, though he didn't remember reading the order support arms.

"In two ranks, form company! Company, left face!"

Leaning over slightly, Bobby whispered, "Watch me."

Kellogg howled, "How's that?" Everything in the field went still. "There will be silence in the ranks!" Over by the farm a cow mooed and a clinking hammer echoed in the trees by the forge. The waterwheel filled and rushed empty before Kellogg spoke again. "Private Trow!" The colonel looked at him for something to criticize, but there was nothing. Knees bent, eyes forward, Steven stood at perfect attention, not the cartoon version he'd executed before. Kellogg's voice dropped. "Good." Then it ratcheted up again. "Company. Left face!" All the men turned to their left, a simple enough move that Steven at first thought he was fudging with little stolen glances at the men around him, but he performed it with competence. "March!"

Every second man held his place while the other hooked around. Though Hube bounced off him and had to make a little circle to regroup, the error had been Hube's. Steven was again in exactly the right place. Burney winked at him. Now the men counted off in twos. Kellogg called for "Shoulder! Arms!" Each man grabbed his rifle with his right hand and put it on his right shoulder, index finger on the underside of the trigger and thumb around the stock.

"Private Trow!" Kellogg strode over to see the new recruit in correct position. He may not have been the unit's most graceful or most crisp, but Steven was hardly the least capable; at worst, he seemed rusty. He could only figure that *Hardee's* had somehow stuck in his brain, but, if asked, he could not have described what precisely he was doing. While his earlier conjuring up of John Trow had been an entirely conscious act of imagination, this felt as if hands were guiding him into place and, once there, his body remembered the action, as if it were something he had done long ago and forgotten until this reminder. "Company! Present! Arms!" The guns went forward in front of each man; then Kellogg ordered shoulder arms again. "Company, forward! Common time! March!"

Overture completed, Kellogg led the men into a run of movement and rhythm as choreographed as a ballet, and Steven found himself thrust on stage with only the slightest clue as to the steps or the music but somehow able to perform. His everyday mind switched off; he stopped wondering how it was happening and let his body assume the responsibility for producing the precise action of each maneuver—lifting his right foot and turning on his left heel on right face, keeping his knees bent and chest forward, stepping the exact twenty-eight inches demanded of each step in common time march. He never once wondered what Dylan Petro would say if he saw him at that instant. It was Bobby Osselin who dropped his rifle on Kucharsky's foot, not Steven; it was Murray Lummer, not Steven, whom Scobeck called a shitbag for bouncing off his stomach. Even as Kellogg ordered complex combinations, Steven kept up, increasingly elated at the proof that he might finally be good at something, as relatively inane and inexplicable as this something was.

After an hour Steven smelled like a sheep, the wool heavy and darkening with his sweat, and he itched everywhere. Though they were fraying in the heat, Kellogg pushed them even further. Men bunched or else spread too far, nipped heels or had to scamper to keep up, especially Scobeck, who couldn't maintain the double-time pace. After the third failed attempt at a complicated sequence of wheels and oblique marching, Kellogg got into Scobeck's face, stuffing his fists into his own fleshy hips.

"You stupid side of beef!" It looked for a moment as if Kellogg might strike him. Near tears, Scobeck held his chin high, doing his best to maintain a soldier's composure. "This unit WILL NOT embarrass me at Cold Harbor! This unit WILL NOT embarrass *itself* at Cold Harbor."

When it came time for bayonet drill, Steven thought he should opt out, since he had no bayonet, but at the command "Fix bayonets," Kellogg screamed for him to join the action. Steven bent his knees and mimed the perfect angles at which to repulse infantry and cavalry. It all felt right.

Kellogg then called the men back to order. Even though he had no powder or cartridges, or even anything to put them in, Steven played along with the rest of the men as they prepared their weapons for firing. He imitated all the loading and priming moves, but when it came time to fire, something odd happened. Rather than moving in synch with everyone else, Steven, following whatever it was that guided him—be it superior reading comprehension or Jungian subconscious—pulled the gun away to his left shoulder, his left hand on the trigger. He never did anything left-handed, but as soon as the butt of the rifle hit his shoulder, Steven knew that it was in the correct place.

"What the hell are you doing, man?" Kellogg knocked the rifle barrel so that it aimed down and then pointed to Hube on Steven's left. "You'll blow his ear off! The right side! The right side!"

"But, sir, this works better for . . ."

Manskart wagged an imperious finger off toward the side. "Get the good hell off this field, soldier! I'll not hear another word from you!"

In a few steps Steven was on the margin of the field, his head spinning as if he'd been removed from a loud place and then plunged into silence. A dozen or so visitors had gathered to watch the performance, among them a little boy with an odd haircut: crew cut and black on top, long and dyed blond from ear level. The boy held an American flag in one hand and pointed at him, not kindly, with the other. Steven recognized him; he'd shown up once at the Grove wearing tattered pajama bottoms for swim trunks. This morning his biker dad sported a Stone Cold T-shirt over his vast stomach and little white anklets on his stout legs. To complete his Hell's Elves look, he had chained his wallet to his belt, and a wispy red beard flicked off his chin. Steven wondered what they thought of him as he played soldier in his half-assed uniform, and thanked God no one he knew was around. He took another look at the kid digging around in his nose and imagined the many hours biker dad must spend watching professional wrestling; from even the most jaundiced viewpoint, re-enacting didn't feel quite so asinine. At least this pastime honored lives sacrificed to the nation, the flag, all sorts of things that once seemed peripheral to him but were gaining value in his life. Steven considered flipping the kid a bird or a dirty look but decided it would dishonor the uniform. That, and he'd get his ass kicked by the dad.

Instead of sitting, Steven stood straight and watched his company. He was already feeling one of them despite his skimpy uniform. With the sun high in the sky and the clouds broken apart, the colonel ordered the men through another few volleys then dismissed them for lunch, to the applause of the spectators. Steven sat down in the grass, his ears ringing with what reminded him of a strong buzz. As he looked at his uniform and his bare feet, twentieth-century life, laden with concerns and fears that didn't exist for John Trow and the story that Steven had created for him, felt unreal, or at least optional. Now that the shooting was finished, the sounds of farm and forge took over again, the water and the sporadic eddies of leaves gathered together before being expelled in gusts. Against it all, streams of human voices murmured in their own ways. His daily life pulled hard at him; names and thoughts started to take form. Before they shattered this moment, Steven slowly opened his fist and let the self he knew slip away like a released balloon.

A heavy swat on his shoulder made him blink and shake his head. Swan grinned. "Nice morning's work, huh? You did great, Steve. Really great."

Steven thanked Swan as he reeled himself back in.

CHAPTER

11

AFTER A COLD CHICKEN LEG THAT HE HAD JUDGED progressive at seven A.M. and a handful of saltines to stand in for hardtack, Steven began to scout for the telephone he'd guaranteed Patty the village possessed. Riga Village had come fully to life while he'd been in the field with his wooden gun; the smell of wood smoke and the furnace surrounded him as he strolled among the buildings, his still-dazed post-Kellogg expression drawing smiles and gracious nods from the civilians of the town. An elderly woman in a rough brown dress and a blacked-out front tooth let out a *pssst* as he passed.

Seeing that he was the only person she could be addressing, he went over. She stopped sweeping her doorway, checked both ways with shifty eyes to see if anyone was spying, and whispered, "Want some uh the hard stuff?" With her finely plucked brows and French manicure, she was apparently Riga's version of the Ladies Who Lunch. Steven had seen her below once or twice in her pearls on Sunday mornings when she led an equally dapper octegenarian out of a Lexus and into the Congregationalist church. Curious as to whether she'd produce a bottle of ginger ale or a tiny envelope of heroin, he kindly accepted her offer. The cloudy brown liquid she came back with, probably from a plastic jug bought yesterday at the Grand Union, puckered his mouth with its sweetness, and though he could barely detect a spike of rum, he tipped his kepi and thanked her all the same.

Through the town, Heritage travelers milled from schoolhouse to furnace to farm in clutches of threes and fours. Seniors in sun visors blurred their memories of the New Deal with life in the mid-nineteenth century, dads juggled cups of apple cider with brand-new digital cameras, and hundreds of people with nothing better to do roamed about, sweeping up factoids and immediate impressions like conventioneers filling bags with mini note squares and foam-rubber footballs. Soon, the meaning of both *telephone* and *Patty* had to him the otherness of words repeated over and over into nonsense.

Walking along the dirt paths, he could see why the villagers had kept to themselves on his first trip up. These people plastered in Disney characters and corporate logos wanted nothing so much as to pull you back into their time, their age of leisure and horror, the empty hours no longer devoted to the necessities of growing and making. The visitors sniggered at the handmade clothes, marveled at life without telephones, sneered at the absence of Diet Coke, and asked questions designed to boggle the minds of the rustics or, better yet, make them break out of character. As drab as they seemed, though, the consciously pre-Technicolor citizens of Riga Village had the more colorful visions. While those in the present imagined the future out of all possibilities, those who lived in the past had to imagine away the specifics of the world, had to imagine what they did not know. And so they hid from Elvis and the hydrogen bomb and the Holocaust behind ox teams and other basic, time-consuming jobs, filling their minds with tasks and facts from an age when innocence still seemed possible, before humanity had proven itself so tragically flawed. A world without Hitler, without AIDS, grew that much closer to the Garden, and with the weight of a hundred and fifty years of history beginning to lift off Steven's shoulders, he found himself walking taller, judging his uniform an uncommonly fine shade of blue. Everyone, not just him, could be a better person here; Joe Swan, for example. These Riga faces bore no burdens beyond virtue and hard work. Steven closed his eyes and let the smoke of the furnace sweep over him.

Encouraged by the curiosity of the tourists and the supportive greetings from the other villagers, Steven ventured forward into his new life. He doffed his cap politely to an elderly couple sharing a large pickle, by far the most popular snack in the Village, and got trapped in a one-sided conversation on the Korean War, the particulars of which he did not have to feign ignorance. He patted the haunch of a gray ox bearing two large bags of rocks to the furnace, made a show of inquiring after the postmaster's health at the post office, and explained to an overbundled four-year-old adoptive Chinese girl that he wasn't wearing shoes because he'd worn them out marching.

Lackadaisically, Steven checked out the schoolhouse, the farm buildings, and the houses nearest the shore. While heading to the store, only paces from the lake and a reasonable place for a link to the outside world, he heard a strange music floating into the still air and wavering like a softly shining ribbon of crepe caught in the boughs of the trees. Drawn by the music, he stepped off the path and went five or six paces toward the large oak whence this weird beauty came.

There, under the tree, sat Polly on a rock big enough for two, a few wisps of her red hair hanging around her temples and framing her face, the rest captured by a black net, as she stared in concentration at her instrument. Only the tips of black boots peeked out from the yards of black skirt pooling before her. Thick strips of black velvet ran up from waist to yoke on the off-white muslin of her blouse, boasting the fullness of her breasts, and a diamond-shaped red panel on the skirt's front waist emphasized its tight fit over her corseted body. Polly was all texture, from the soft shirred blouse and lace around the high neck and cuffs to the velvet of her skirt and the firmness of her waist. Steven could feel her in his hands. In her lap, her left hand supported the source of the music, a long box, two inches deep, made of dark wood and stringed somewhat like a zither. Intricate fretwork decorated its sharp angle and metronome face. With the bow in her right, the colonel's wife took precise strokes on the strings. The sound produced, an ethereal, almost mystical hum similar to that of crystal goblets or a bowed saw, surrounded them with the placid shimmering Steven imagined angels make, and easy traffic with the dead somehow seemed possible. Fate had called his bluff. He stood still, unable to decide what to do, what was proper.

He whisked off his cap. "So it is true that beauty is born of beauty." The words seemed to come straight from John Trow. She smiled but continued playing without looking up, making no sign of recognition. "We—" He stopped. "You and I were . . ."

"Were. Are. May." Her hands fluttered out of her lap, away from her instrument, fingers waving. Polly looked at him, pinning him with purposeful green eyes in a way that similar eyes had pinned him once before. Though he'd always recalled Becky with fiery eyes, as strong as these were, they held an equal amount of softness, a sad sympathy for the labors of anyone living and especially so for the one she loved. What wildness she had was not coltish but mature. "Our moments together will be short, and poorly spent on the past. Those thoughts are for letters written late in the night. Sit here, next to me." She patted the rock.

"Will Walter . . . ?" She made a cross look. "I mean, the Colonel . . . ?"

"Do you not remember this place? How often we would sit here? How I would play the psaltery for you in just this manner?"

He nodded as he lowered himself, though he had no idea what she was talking about beyond the certainty that they were once a couple. "Of course. Those were beautiful times."

Given that she was bowing the first bars of "Rock of Ages," he decided that any naughtier flirting would be out of place. The glimmering notes of the song gave a reason to the silence, though the truth was that Steven had nothing to say, knew nothing about the place or the time or the person he was supposed to be.

Her song ended suddenly. "You don't know who you are, do you?"

He looked at his bare feet, could not remember what he'd been looking for when he found her under the tree. As much as he wanted to be John Trow, he knew nothing of him besides the two short letters. "No. In fact I do not." It felt as if the only thing holding him up was the stiff wool of his uniform. A slow breeze pushed the stray locks of hair across her face, and for a moment she was Becky, standing in front of the seals at the Lincoln Park Zoo.

"Well . . ." She considered the problem. "I shall help you." She put aside the psaltery. "Let's start small, shall we? Do you like autumn? All the final flashings of life drifting at our feet? Hmm?"

"I do. Yes."

"Good. And lemonade. Do you take lemonade?"

"Yes. I do."

"Sugar?"

"Yes." Warming to the game, he pushed himself further. "Indeed, a surprising amount."

"Ah, see how much you know already! Dickens?"

"I read *The Mystery of Edwin Drood* in college and—"

She looked stricken. "Mr. Dickens has written a book called *Drood*? In eighteen sixty-four? *Droooood*? What a silly name. I do not know it. When last we met, you had not gone farther than our one-room schoolhouse. You speak so queerly." Steven winced and looked out toward the audience, who had surely caught his gaffe, but there was no audience. No one but the two of them. They were doing this for themselves. "Now speak to me of flowers, of tastes and smells and touch, of things that have always been. Do you enjoy the rain? You once did."

It took all his strength not to lay his head in her lap. From her eyes came interest without judgment, comfort and a longing to be comforted, desire and desire gratified. She would stroke his hair, forgive him everything. His troubles wouldn't exist. He imagined his hands on her breasts. Touching her would not be a consumer issue; it would be a connection to the wholeness of things, to that truth one can reach in the act of love, which he had not had with Patty in years. As it was, Steven contained himself, sat bound next to her in fear of what one touch could bring. How could this be the same woman he'd seen in the cemetery? Having watched Manskart transform into Kellogg, Steven closed his eyes as she played a Bach hymn and pictured her metamorphosis. Did it happen when she put the dress on? Or earlier? Was it when she slipped the corset around her waist? When the strings were pulled tight and even tighter and she gasped in surprise at the sensation even as she knew it was coming and wanted it? He hunched over to hide his trousers as scenes of happy modern family life reflexively popped into his head, his usual response to stolen glances on a bus or at a restaurant. After reviewing in his mind Emily's third birthday party, Steven rose at the song's end, the need for a cap in front of his crotch long gone at the thought of the wildly expensive Barbie cake. "Mrs. Kellogg, I must thank you for the concert, but I must also beg your pardon and attend to business."

To anyone else, at any other time, her smile would have appeared completely innocent. " 'Tis a pity. I shall often be here under this tree"—she struck a note—"waiting for you." The sound of the psaltery shimmered in his ears as he walked away.

After another hour of drill in the field, the men of the 2nd melted off into Riga Village to perform their duties as citizens. Steven, as ever uncertain of his station, had looked around for direction until Mrs. Melton appeared and led him to the post office, where he now restocked a spinner rack with postcard views of Mt. Riga, the village, and the general Salisbury area. As he worked, she sat atop the postmaster's high stool, eyes closed, pressing one finger to the bridge of her nose. Occasionally she took a sharp sniff that made her wince with pain.

"I most regret not introducing you to Riga Village, Mr. Trow," she said. The postmaster, a long and saurian man named Mr. Guston, slowly handed her a glass of water and resumed his place behind the desk, arms crossed, regarding her from beneath hooded lids. Steven recognized him as the owner of Mr. Fay's Fine Dry Cleaning, an imperious man known to comment sourly upon elements of his customers' wardrobe. "But this sinus." She pressed her nose with a renewed firmness. "I woke quite late today." Mr. Guston *tsked* in commiseration but did not move, nor would he look at Steven, whose incomplete uniform had at first sight forced an impatient little burst of air from the postmaster's nose.

Steven opened a box of souvenir pencils. "Well, the colonel did a tremendous job."

"Did he?" Mrs. Melton seemed genuinely surprised.

Before Steven had to feign further enthusiasm, two townspeople walked in. Though Mr. Guston moved only his eyeballs, conserving his energy, it seemed, for predators, Mrs. Melton roused herself at their greeting and came to the counter where Steven stood. "Ah, good. Mr. Trow, I would like you to meet Mr. Japhet Beck, our founder, the man in charge of running the furnace, and Mrs. Bella Kurlander."

Both were familiar faces to Steven. Beck was the burly, clubfooted man whom his father had waylaid that first day, and Mrs. Kurlander was the cider lady.

"Mrs. Kurlander is one of our leading townswomen. An expert candlemaker and the most devoted voice of temperance on this mountain." Mrs. Kurlander smiled slightly and raised one thin eyebrow as she shook Steven's hand. "We have some planning to do for the fall Harvest Festival on Halloween weekend. Mrs. Kurlander organizes the lovely spread of food you'll enjoy that day." Bella nodded her gracious thanks. "I wanted you to meet them. Please ask them for any help you may need."

By now Mr. Guston had receded into the shadows of the post office to loudly thump his postal stamper on the day's mail.

"You are a collier, Mr. Trow." Steven nodded as if he knew what that meant, which he did not, though the word had a solid feel and clearly named a trade respected enough to deserve a special term. "You make charcoal." Mrs. Melton handed him several pamphlets about Riga Village and a booklet entitled *From Wood to Coal: Historical Charcoal-Making in America*. A massive pile of wood smoked heartily on the cover. Steven tried to appear sporting.

Mr. Beck addressed Mrs. Melton. "We'll need a good half-ton for the festival. Can you do it this year?"

"Mr. Trow will read his materials and the other colliers are returning." Beck rolled his eyes. "We'll be fine," Mrs. Melton said, with some defiance.

For a moment the only sound came from Mr. Guston's stamper. Steven bit the inside of his lip, unable to fathom how he would produce a thousand pounds of charcoal by the end of October. He had forgotten to call Patty. "Is there a phone anywhere up here?"

The thumping stopped. The three at the counter stared at him.

"What am I thinking? Of course not, right?"

Mrs. Melton cocked her head slightly. "For emergencies." Guston coughed. "Is there an emergency?"

Steven thought for a moment. For once, there was none. "I'm sorry. Of course not." He looked at his watchless wrist. "I should be going, though."

Armed with his wooden rifle, Steven cracked open the front door of his house.

Laughter exploded, as if timed to his entrance.

He slammed it shut. Murray Lummer had happily driven him home, asking all the while if he wanted the air conditioner on, whether he minded the Three Tenors tape, and telling him how much he liked the air on and how much he enjoyed the Three Tenors. Still floating in the world of Riga Village, Steven had kept his answers short and Murray had seemed to understand as he turned off the music and opened the windows. Steven wasn't ready for this. Taking a deep, bracing breath, he forced open the door of the house against the blast of normal premillennial life.

"He's cute. But he's not that cute." Another roar from the television. "I mean, he can't even surf!"

Emily sat benumbed by the syndicated perkiness of the hula-skirted Olsen Twins as they weighed the qualities of their new Hawaiian friends. She did not greet him as he staggered past. Upstairs, Patty's modem twanged away to prove it had made a screaming 49,333 bps connection and Nate's CD player, bass on ten, throbbed a big, deep, dope-smoking throb through the floor of his room. With little interest in breaking into the intimate connections his family had made with their electronic appliances, he stumbled into the kitchen, sick to his stomach and trembling.

In search of a glass of water, Steven opened the refrigerator. The light popped on and a thousand colors leaped out at him; cans and bottles and jars filled with unnaturally tinted condiments milled about in no particular order, like a crowd on the verge of riot. Slamming the door shut, he closed his eyes and ducked his head under the faucet for his drink.

"Hi, Daddy!" Steven hit his face on the fixture. A commercial, if possible even a few decibels louder than the show, had sent Emily dashing into the kitchen to grab a cookie. Before he could say anything, or even pull his head out of the sink, she was jabbering on. "Is it gonna be the end of the world this year? A boy at school said so. Ephraim. I don't like him." Steven began to offer a reassuring denial, but she raced out of the room.

Sonic garbage piling up, he tried to remember the quivering tone of the psaltery, Polly's music. He searched his mind, but the memory of the sound escaped him. It was all slipping away, he realized. Angry, even panicked, Steven dug a utility candle out of the junk drawer and took measured but brisk steps up to the second floor, where, instead of announcing himself, he slipped into his office. Candle in one hand, wooden rifle in the other, he pressed his back against the door like a man pursued. How could this be the real world when so much of it was intentionally unreal? Dylan had urged him to use the word *virtual* as often as possible; it was where the consumer wanted to be, he always said, part of the new, perfectible, possibly ending world. Right now Steven felt like a man who'd died on the operating table and been yanked back from the light by some do-good resident. *This* world, the world he had re-entered, the one that could implode because of the movement of a clock, felt like the strange place, not Riga Village.

He closed his blinds and lit the candle as the sun began to set, dark clouds edged at the bottom in a reddish pink, burning from within. Steven revisited everything he could recall about the day, hoping to preserve a little flame of the sensation that *this* was the house he was visiting, *this* was the foreign time, a sensation being quickly worn down by the mindless drumming coming from Nate's room. Downstairs, plates clanked with the inevitability of the present. Steven would have to take off his uniform soon. He opened his backpack, and there on the top sat two more small envelopes. While not identical to the first two he'd received in the mail, the top one bore the same hand. The second, a crème color and smooth, was addressed to *Pvt. John Trow* in a florid feminine script. Polly's.

CHAPTER

12

September 30, 1862
Fort Worth, Vir.
Polly,
   Your letter, so short, does hold me to this place, & to you. Its one phrase—"I remember Mt. Riga"—rattles about my head but I cannot hear your voice. Would you speak them with the gloom of a past beyond retriev- ing? Or as a bright admission that something lost has been rediscovered? What is it you remember? Daniel knows only the mountain without trees. His memories will always be of a barren place even as he grows older & the young trees grow taller with him, & he begins to conceive of a world an other way. This prospect of a forest on Mt. Riga does still astound him after a boyhood without benefit of shade. I fear his unprotected youth in some ways burnt his soul.
   When we walk the past, do we two walk the same lands? The Riga you & I walked when young—the one I was born to—had both "sounding cataract" & "deep and gloomy wood." Salisbury's fathers climbed the mountain for those trees & that water. Though Indian torch had burnt much of the woods the Greenwoods promised, a beautiful forest stood on Riga, surely placed there by G—to fuel ironworks. This forest—& its darkness—brought me to life.

IT WAS A LONG LETTER, and both Trow's handwriting and his style defied casual reading, but Steven braved Trow's windiness and overgrown prose, thrilled by the writer's efforts to put a fine point on a moment of experi- ence instead of relying on a colon and the flip of a parenthesis to express the range of human emotion. Wading through the rhythms and odd usages sent another, older music through Steven's head which drowned out the graceless beat from Nate's room with trills and twists and turns around unexpected corners and soon he was drifting back to that calmer land, floating through things that once were.

> It is right that I sit now amid all this red clay & these white tents, not a tree in sight—a Trow damned to a treeless life for all that our name has done to them. I have been told that they cleared these hills by cutting each trunk halfway on the downhill side, then felling the trees at the very top onto them, thus producing an avalanche of timber. If we had had such intelligence, we most certainly would have similarly stripped the sides of Riga. Truly I smell death in this air, & finality for much of who I was, that & seeing your face which forces such memories that I must write them "in true plain words by thy true-telling friend." Tho I have tried to bury my youth & its betrayals, suddenly I do not wish to be forgotten. I shall remember for both of us if you will not, bring you back into being just as something better in me seems to live again with the sound of cannons.
>
> My name, as Grandmother Claire told, arrived by stealth, a windblown seed, not proudly. My grandfather, a Hessian mercenary captured at Saratoga, stole into the woods of Mt. Riga while camped outside Salisbury, on the way to a Virginia prison. He lived a fugitive the next score & ten, feeding off berries & rabbit until he took up with a widow named Claire in 1810 & moved into the town then growing around the mountaintop furnace. My father, James, was born later that year & the name "Trow" took hold in the rocky soil of Connecticut. James grew to be a collier, a trade he learned from his mother's brother & so I from him.

Here Trow laid out a precise description of how the mounds were made. He and his father had made charcoal from May to October in huge pits they maintained around the mountain. After stacking the wood in twelve-foot-high mounds around a central chimney, they covered each mound with leaves and dirt. His father lit it with a careful placement of coals dropped onto a small pile of kindling at the base of the chimney. For two weeks, they would steadily tend the mound. As if he'd wanted to preserve all this for future generations, he described his father's special way of spreading the dust and leaves and of reading the smoke. It was so vivid that Steven could imagine himself producing the half-ton of coal. When the pile had burned down into a heap of charcoal, they'd load it into big wagons and take it to the furnace in Riga Village.

The personal side of the story was bleak, though. James Trow Senior sounded like a nightmare. He once knocked out little seven-year-old John with a rock for admiring leaves instead of gathering them, and regularly terrorized him and whoever else was around. The grandfather showed up once in a while during the summer to make fun of his workaday son, whom he lived off in the winter months. It was a particularly brutal childhood, spent in the forest with only his grandmother's Bible for diversion. This new installment in Trow's real life made Steven feel foolish for his *An Actor Prepares* approach, how he had assigned false meanings and moments to someone whose true history had more color and strength and fascination than he could ever create. A more three-dimensional idea of Trow arose in his mind, a sense of person only more intriguing because it was real.

> *I saw other children there—surely you more than once—dressed in town clothes, carrying schoolbooks, buying candies at the store—& I would understand why my father was so hard. At night then I would take out into the thinning woods—never too dark, lit as they were by the flames of all the furnaces dotting the hills & lands below—& look for Riga Furnace, picking it out as one picks out a star or planet in the night sky. . . .*

In the spring of 1844, when John Trow was fourteen, his life changed forever.

> *Do you ever imagine James's dark face? You would have no reason to, but it comes at me now each time I look into a fire. I wished H— for him & the Lord granted my wish. Three days into a burn, a huge plume of white smoke erupted from the head of the mound. I had no words to describe it then but now know that it resembled most a volcano likely to explode. Given what little wood the mountain still held by then, the smoke & light seeping closer, the stands of trees engulfed by dark & empty air, we could ill afford to lose this mound, so Father climbed up on top to jump the pit. His actions did drive the wood closer & close the mull where fire had worked too fast, yet what he did proved that fire had worked too fast throughout. Flames licked up beneath him & as he came down from a jump, the pit collapsed & he was plunged into fire.*

His legs burned to stumps, James Trow could no longer work. As was the custom of the time, John was rented out to another family.

Which brings me so to you, for I have finished my journey to Lethe, at least for now. Write to me what your memory holds of that place. Until, I shall march the mindless paces of your husband. Shall Gen. McClellan use us when he moves the army forward? Have you rats as we do in our tents? I hope that you do not. They romp and terrorize us & come joined with Brothers Typhus and Quickstep. As the Lt. Colonel has taken over the regiment in Wessells's absence, I am left to imagine that you are left alone a great deal. I remain on guard at the theater until further notice & so believe me your,

John

Patty called up that dinner was almost ready; he hurried through the next one.

November 2, 1862
Dear John,

More than a month has passed since your letter, and you must know that every day for that month I have thought of it. How much I do remember is a constant cause of pain to me, if that holds any consolation, though I am frail and proud enough to hope it does not. I am bored here, dear friend, when I am not filled with terror and many une nuit blanche I have recently passed with Stuart riding so close to our gates. God save us if Washington falls. If nothing else (and there must not be) may we attend each other with these notes.

You ask what I remember, and so I will tell you, though I must admit here at the doorway that I am afraid of this stroll through gardens abandoned to the past and I shall stay within sight of my home. That said, I most remember a day in early summer the year I had turned fourteen. A strange boy came to our door. I would say his clothes were rags, but they appeared more like a skin being shed, a molting fur, for their open patches and how they hung about him waiting to drop off. You were a lean, almost wild boy that day, but how you hung next to Father! When introduced, you rolled his name—St. John Fenner—around your tongue a few times under your breath like a wonderful new taste. How do I know that? I was watching from the small oval window beside the door, Tilda above me, while Eleanor and the boys stared from the other. We scattered when the two of you approached the doors and reassembled as if fresh to the scene when Father called; a large family learns to break apart like that, you see, then flow together again like a flock of birds. . . .

St. John Fenner was Riga Village's schoolteacher, master of a dwindling herd of children for ten years. Once he had taught the Pettees and Coffings and other great names of the mountain, and raised his own children among them, but the dream of Riga as a town of culture and wealth was dying by the time of John's arrival in the Fenner home.

. . . And so you, the wild boy, hung next to Father as you stood in the parlor, although it was clear to me at first sight how deeply you wished to be tamed. A horrible accident had befallen your family, we were told. You would live downstairs in the old pantry, perform chores, and attend classes in the school when Father deemed you fit. As Father spoke, you ran your fingers through your mass of dark hair in a feeble attempt at grooming. Tilda, though, two years older, was never immune to your charms and I heard her sigh at that moment. Craftier, I held the expression of my heart inside, which left it nowhere to go but deeper.

"Thank you for having me," you said in a quiet voice, fear quite evident. And there was ever so much to fear! Three very pretty girls who found ways to be near you whenever possible (even sober Eleanor, the oldest, confessed to me later that she would catch herself musing as to what you would look like in four or five years!); George and Andrew, two young boys with a firm command of Latin grammar and an absolute desperation to learn how to fish with flies or whatever else you wanted to teach them; a woman who clothed you, scrubbed you clean, and performed more of your chores for you than you'll probably admit to even now; and a Pater in charge with no predilection to violence or strong drink, a man willing to pay for the privilege of opening the doors of his tidy, cozy home to you in exchange for only minor assistance around the school. I believed then, and still do, that you were afraid that day not of evil befalling you, but of so much good disappearing. Shall we ne pas reveiller le chat qui dort? Or shall we continue?

In those days, you were still filled with the forest, wild in ways you did not understand. You had a taste for swimming too far, climbing too high, for giving back whatever was thrown at you. You were dangerous, and what proper girl of fourteen does not love a dangerous boy? And yet you had wandered into our town to warm yourself beside our civilizing flame. The fires of the furnace cast a glow over Riga at all times, yet I did not think it unusual to live in a town always lit, as if we were all settled together around a hearth, watched by one great benevolent soul. I had no fear as a child. By day the flame hid, ceding authority to the sun, but at night the pale light crept into all corners, supplanting the moon in constancy and rivaling its silver with yellows and pinks that danced in window glass and iced colors onto standing water. We had no secrets and this was normal to me, just as the forest was to you and treeless Riga is to Daniel. But once you had arrived, I decided that Riga's power to keep night at bay bordered magic.

Magic was to me, that first summer, everywhere and because of you. The furnace flame reflected off the South Pond, gilded the caps of the low waves with light, and found the shadows on every face it touched. With no lessons to attend, the season seemed an endless morning to me; new things could be started at any time and I needed to be bribed into slumber with promises of new adventures after rest. I also tried to swim too far and climb too high. I noticed clouds massing over the mountain and my own shape. You devoured Shakespeare and wore new shoes. In that furnace, very disparate materials were burned together to create iron, one new and indivisible thing. It was that process which caused the light. Does that furnace yet stand?

I have wandered. As you must know, Daniel Lyman has succumbed to his fever. His is our first casualty. The increasing level of sickness gives me great concern, and although you may not wish to hear this, it is of even greater concern to the Lt. Colonel. Easy though it may be to find fault with his lumbering ways and cruelty, he is trying every moment of the day to teach all of you how to save your lives, or to give them with the most effect. Know that I do love him. Like you, he is a force of nature, and while you are a storm at sea, Elisha is a tornado, a gusting land-bound whirlwind that can do profound damage. A sailor in Japan, an adventurer who had chosen to take on the mundane yoke, he was thrilled to be called back into the life of action. Do not underestimate his power or the limits of his ambition.

I shall stop praising him to you. We shall continue to write, you and I, but I shall never know you otherwise, and I will deny any contact with full breath if you mention a word. And know that my word is better than yours in the court that matters. I am sorry to coat these last words with venom, but my hope is that they shine enough like any poisonous being and you will be warded away from the idea.

Until then, your
Polly

Emily's voice called to him from halfway up the stairs: dinner was ready now. So this is who I am, thought Steven as he wandered down in his uniform. A storm at sea. This is the script he and Polly were to follow, the true facts of his other life. A romantic hero, John Trow was passionate and courageous and kind, with an impulsive streak and a taste for Shakespeare, a polished rock from the mountain, and Polly was lush and just as smart as he was; their minds had met as surely as their bodies once must have.

Accustomed to his Union blues, no one commented during dinner, nor did anyone ask how his first day at Riga Village had gone. Steven's curiosity extended no farther than his tablemates', and once they completed their meal, all four went their own ways. Retreating to his office, he read the letters again by candlelight, until the house was still and he began to nod off. Though he knew he should take off his uniform, Steven paused every time he started to undo a button. Bruce Wayne must have sat around in the Batsuit once in a while, too, he told himself, burning in the afterglow of some amazing deed. Today Steven had gone back in time. After he finally stripped, he replaced the uniform, with some reverence, on its hanger behind the door, touching it with the soft hands one uses for something living.

Down to his Jockeys, Steven sat again, patted the head of his plastic soldier, and stared at the wall. The green light of the Zip drive flickered on the other side of his computer, a sort of digital bonfire reassuring him that the computer elves remained cheerfully on the job. At times the light lapped over onto the guttering gold given off by the candle. Steven checked his watch—after eleven—then remembered that daylight saving time ended that night. He pulled the plug on the Zip drive, checked all the clocks in the house to make sure they were set back, and went to bed.

CHAPTER

13

ONE DAY CAN CHANGE A MAN'S LIFE. That Saturday Steven had walked into Riga Village alone but had returned home with John Trow, a complicated mental construction that he discovered tagging along next to him now wherever he went. He treated Trow, the first new presence in Steven's life for many years, with care even as he continued to learn about him, continued to build him in his mind with small suppositions. Still, John Trow was not a being of pure idea; Steven could not separate him from the uniform; indeed, like any superhero, Trow relied on it for existence. Nor could he live without the plastic soldier whose image he shared, without the letters he wrote to Polly. Born of these objects, past years, and dead matter, Trow was beginning to take up space on the earth.

Yet while so much of his life had changed, much more had not, and no matter how deeply Steven craved escape to John Trow's life, he could not get there merely by sitting in his room and imagining, try as he did for many days behind the locked door of his office. The tasks put forth by the suddenly despotic Jay Porter sat untouched in the in-box as Steven attempted to satisfy the urge for that remarkable sense of losing himself that he'd had in the field. But closing his eyes and daydreaming, practicing drill, reading about the War and old Riga Village, none of these put him back on the rock next to Polly. Two wasted days and a snippy Jay call later, Steven hit on the idea of wearing his uniform jacket as a kind of mental methadone, a little chip to get him over until the big fix on Saturday.

Whatever secret existed behind the metamorphosis he'd seen in the Manskarts, Steven figured it rested in the clothes, so he treated the jacket and pants with a near worshipful gravity; as much as they were Trow himself in a way, they were Steven's vehicle of transport, his time

machine. And so they were for the time being, together with his brogans, which arrived that Wednesday, hard leather numbers that resembled the chukka boots he'd worn pre–Elvis Costello. Clomping about in
his heavy shoes and rereading his letters, Steven could see that although
research could educate him about the nineteenth century, only more letters and more objects would bring him closer to the reality of Trow and
facilitate his metamorphosis, help him summon Trow back from history.
Steven's wallet would have to heal before he could order up a round of
accessories to further speed the journey back.

Outside his front door, Mt. Riga pushed up into the clouds as something more than scenery now and Steven noticed it constantly in his daily
travels to school and store, felt its presence as well, neither benevolent
nor evil, hanging over his life. By night, his preference for candles grew,
and he didn't notice at first when all the lights on the second floor blew,
cosseted as he was in the warm glow of his beeswax attempts to recapture
Saturday's no-tech euphoria. On Thursday evening, as Patty was showering, the second-floor lights blew again. Wishing the problem away—
candlelight was so much prettier—Steven had tucked into Shelby Foote
somewhere around the siege of Vicksburg, when he heard a woman
scream. He opened the door to total darkness and Patty's voice: "Call that
idiot Joe Swan right now!"

Steven hesitated, despite the pitch black, as he did whenever he had
to ask for practical help, concerned that his helplessness would provide
fodder for around-the-back-panel-of-the-pickup-truck jokes. His relative newness to the area did not add to his confidence; the work they'd
had done on the house seemed suspiciously expensive, due, he was sure,
to the same halo of naïveté that he felt hovering over him whenever he
entered the Millerton hardware store. The slap of Patty's wet feet on the
tile warned him that he'd better act, though. Searching his desk for
Swan's number, what came to mind for all his white-collar paranoia was
not the local striver hoping to trade work boots for tassel loafers, nor
the man who'd left two hundred pounds of newspapers and derelict
tools in the basement, but the nineteenth-century man at home in his
uniform, John Trow's friend. *His* friend. It also occurred to him that a
visit from Swan would bridge the remaining days until he returned to
Riga Village. Despite the late hour, nearly ten o'clock, he dialed.

If what Swan said was true, he'd been doing reasonably well with his
contracting business. After Steven made his apologies for calling so late
and described the situation, Swan spooled off three or four possible

causes and then claimed that the earliest he could come out would be a week from Friday.

Steven made a wounded sound. "Lemme take a look at my calendar," said Swan. Steven listened for the shuffling of paper, but didn't hear it. Maybe Swan had a Palm Pilot. "Well, you know, I got a job at one of those antique places on 7 I can move around. They make a lot of that crap out of kits. Did you know that?" Before Steven could express dismay—sincere dismay, given how much he'd spent at antique places on Route 7—Swan said, "Yeah, I can do tomorrow around four. Work for you, pard?"

Steven accepted and hung up, smiling. Swan had called him "pard." He was a pard now. Having kids in the school went only part of the way toward becoming a true local; small breaks like these were the real test. Steven delivered the news of Swan's appointment to Patty, lying in bed, as if announcing that Bill Gates himself would be coming by to install the Barbie Dress Designer CD-ROM that had so far resisted a presence on their hard drive.

Patty did not look up from her fat *Vogue*, sucking in as much type as she could before the next blown circuit. "What's the big deal? That's what he does, right?"

That she had no sense of how little they belonged to this place grated on Steven. Without trying to explain this small crack in the stony social wall of everyday Salisbury life, he crawled into bed just as the lights went out again. "Do you want me to light a candle for you? I know where they are . . ."

The magazine hit the floor with a loud smack. "I'm just going to sleep."

Like a man who's run into an ex with her new boyfriend, Swan looked mournfully at the house when he rolled up the driveway in his shiny green Ford pickup the next day, but his upper lip remained stiff. Entering the foyer, he gazed slowly around the hall with his old aviators, then pointed to the ceiling. "Oh, you took down the molding. That was original. Did you know that? Original eighteen fifty-three molding." Swan wore tan corduroys and a long-sleeved rugby shirt appropriate for the host of *This Old House*, a boyish look that passed for dressed-up in some area circles.

"No, of course we knew," Steven said defensively, remembering all the times Swan had pointed out that and other rotting, hazardous, and otherwise unusable—but original—aspects of the house during the sale. "But when our painter got up there—"

"Who'd you use?"

"Guy named Henderson. Falls Village."

"He steals old wood. Go on."

"He said it was shot, all cracked and everything." Swan shook his head as Steven spoke. "He put up a new one. I don't know . . ." He shrugged and glanced at the ceiling. "Looks good to me."

"He stripped it. Sold it to somebody in Sharon probably. Maybe that Frank McCourt guy. He was buying a new place out there. Maybe he got the molding."

"I don't know. It was in pretty bad shape. I saw it. It was crumbling apart."

Swan let his expression convey his doubt. This was not Calamus Dawes, the Swan he'd actually liked on Saturday. The two stood there for a moment, Swan looking toward the kitchen and the basement door, too polite to take liberties with an old flame and proceed unescorted. Steven finally caught on. "Oh! I figured you knew where . . ." He took his hands out of his jeans pockets to gesture vaguely toward the kitchen. "Yeah, let's go down."

No longer waiting for invitations, Swan headed straight to the circuit box, Steven stomping behind him in his brogans. After monkeying around for a few minutes, Swan pulled a pair of pliers out of the back pocket of his corduroys. "So you got your shoes, huh?"

"Finally. They feel pretty good, though."

"You recovered from Saturday?"

"Yeah. I had a great time." Steven held open the little door of the box to justify his presence as Swan worked the screws on the panel.

"Yeah? Whaddya think of Kellogg? Did he arouse your, uh, con-ster-na-tion?"

Steven caved inward a little, embarrassed at the reminder that while Trow and Dawes were from the same world, he and Joe were not. "He's tough. Knows what he's doing."

"He's a fuck." Swan tugged once, and the panel came free. "We love him. Kinda. But he's a fuck." Steven did not disagree. "But the real Kellogg was supposed to be exactly like that, so whaddya gonna do? Wally won't even talk to you about the regiment unless he's doing Kellogg. Your tour was something to tell the kids about." He smiled, the sarcasm evident, but he was still hiding his position. "The guy who started the regiment? His name was Fred Borg. Good guy, pretty laid back. Mostly wanted to hide from his wife and drink beers. Which is okay, too. You just having trouble upstairs, right?"

"Yeah, the bedrooms, bathrooms, my office. The whole thing up there."

Swan pulled out a flashlight, pushed up his sleeves, and squinted into the wires. "So whaddya got going on in here?" He began poking around with the screwdriver.

You put the wiring in, asshole, so you should know, thought Steven. "What happened to Borg?"

"Oh. Well, Wally came in, and since the best part of Borg's impression of Kellogg was his beer belly, he took over pretty easy. Freddie was a good guy. I think he was just as happy to liberate himself of all the work. He quit when Wally took us hard core. Died a couple years ago. I think we gotta look upstairs. This is looking extremely fine down here."

They made their way back to the first floor, Steven toting an aluminum ladder. As they passed the coffee table, Swan pointed to the open copy of Foote and a video case from Ken Burns's *Civil War*. "There you go. That's the right stuff. Especially Burns. I think he nailed it. You ever watch the History Channel?"

"Sometimes," lied Steven, who was starting to breathe a little heavily.

"They do a good job most of the time. But they make their mistakes. I'm trying to understand what it was like for those men back then, you know? If that's something you're interested in, then you're not gonna be looking for a limit. I say B-I-R-D, you know? Because It's Right, Dammit." They clomped up the stairs to the second floor. "There are for sure some wacky fucks out there—Kellogg's one of 'em—but the bottom line is you don't want to be some farby dickhead with Cheeto dust all over your beard when you're charging the Rebel line. You know what I mean?"

Steven wasn't sure he did, but he nodded and held the ladder as Swan clambered up the rungs and began on the first light fixture in the hallway.

"You can definitely go nutsy," he called down. "I mean, I'm no stitch-nazi."

"Huh?"

"Some guys check out stitches on buttonholes to see if they're done by hand. They didn't do them by machine then, see? So a lot of guys rip 'em out of their clothes and restitch 'em themselves. Everybody wants

The Look, you know? Well, not everybody. I did mine, but to each his own, I say. Here, hold this." Swan handed down the glass bowl. "Look at Burney's turban."

With Swan's mind on the regiment, some of the awkwardness evaporated, and Steven felt free to ask questions. "Yeah, what's *with* that?"

Swan began unscrewing the plate on the ceiling. "Who knows? Maybe it's some religious thing. I think even Kellogg's scared to call him on it. He's a mechanic at Lime Rock. Owns part of a sprint car. Real maniac. Good guy, though. Says he's friendly with Paul Newman, but I think that's bullshit.

"Jerry and Murray?"

"Hate each other. That's why it's a joke that they're brothers up there. Jerry's wife is like thirty years old or something and Murray thinks it's immoral. Jerry's a reporter on the Litchfield paper. Pretty progressive for an old guy. Used to be a big union man. I don't think Murray likes that, either. And then Jerry thinks Murray is a pussy because he was in the Navy during Korea, and Murray always talks about the National Guard like it was fucking Iwo Jima. Nice bunch of ladies we got, huh? A real lovefest."

"They all seem to get along."

"Well, all the boys love the uniform, and that's the bottom line. The Second was a spit-and-polish regiment, and that's who *we* are." Swan went back to the last two screws. "Be careful with Scobeck and Kucharsky, though. They're the real hardcores in the bunch. I'm pretty progressive and I gotta say that having them is like having priests around sometimes or, what do they call those guys in Saudi Arabia? They chop your hands off if you don't have the right clothes on?"

"Mullahs?"

"I don't think so."

The wires sprang down in a mass. Confronted with the vast tangle of exposed wires, all meaningless to him, and infected with the smug air of so-called progress, Steven found himself repelled, as if he'd been shown someone's guts during an operation. "How do you feel about electricity?"

Swan stopped and slowly turned around, ready, it seemed, to brace himself for a few thousand volts. "Why do you ask?"

"I don't know." Steven hesitated, then confessed. "I feel weird sometimes using it now, after being in the village, you know? Like it's wrong, or something. I mean, I know it's what you do, but . . ."

"Oh, that. Well, yeah, I feel that way sometimes," said Swan. "After a weekend when you're trying to make the feeling last. Sure. You feel like everything else in your life has just totally. Fucking. Disappeared." The bluish whites of his eyes bulged slightly, giving him a look of awe. Swan sounded almost reverent as he recalled the experience. "Like the person you are deep down hopped into some other guy's body that lived a hundred and forty years ago." He looked down toward Steven. "You get that yet? Lotsa times it takes a while. Some people never . . ."

Steven leaped on their shared passion for the experience. "No, I did! Yeah, I definitely did." So much so that he'd begun to tally his days around that watershed experience, considered life in terms of pre-Riga and post-Riga.

"But the electricity? I just tell myself they would have loved to possess it. Oh, wait. Here's your problem." He indicated a thicket of blue and red wires bound together with black electrical tape. "See this? You're shorting here, and then everything else blows. Can you hand me those pliers?"

Steven passed him the tool. "Yeah, and they would have loved to have AK-forty-sevens and cruise missiles, too."

Swan shrugged as he pulled the tape off the copper bundles. "You're right, but what are you gonna do? Not many people make a living off this stuff, you know? Unless you look like Abe Lincoln or something. I have bills to pay." He reached over and touched the molding along the ceiling. "You should polish this wood once in a while; it looks thirsty." Steadying himself with one hand, Swan began stripping away the rubber coating of a wire. "Maybe if this Y2K thing happens you'll get your wish and we'll all be inhabiting in caves."

Steven looked up the ladder at Swan, the person he'd come closest to getting to know in the entire area for an entire year, someone else who knew how it felt to give yourself over to the past. In the same way that he'd felt sudden waves of anger at Kellogg, Steven felt a pulse of Trow's friendly affection for Dawes. Whether they'd become friends would depend on what he was about to ask. "Hey, Cal. Do me a favor?"

Swan kept his eyes on the wires. "What's that?"

"Stop with the vocabulary words. Okay? You're making me crazy with all the 'inhabiting in caves' business."

The electrician smiled down from the ladder. "That's a fucking relief. But if my wife's ever around, I gotta do it, okay?"

*   *   *

After rewiring the first fixture, Swan checked out a few more, then declared the job finished and delivered a brotherly pop to Steven's arm when offered money. Even as Swan lusted at his walls and low doorways, and made known his objections to the track lighting in the kitchen, Steven could find only fraternal feelings for him, his new pard. "So do you know anything else about John Trow?"

"Shit, I thought you had it all figured out after drill Saturday. A lot of the guys said they'd never seen anybody do so well on drill their first time out. You sure you never done this before?"

Steven wondered if he was blushing. "No, but somehow it just all makes sense to me. I guess I have a good short-term memory or something."

"Once you get your uniform together, you're gonna kick ass. Scobeck's already worried." Swan spied the wooden rifle by the kitchen door where Steven had been practicing earlier. He picked up the gun and stood at attention, his eyes focused far ahead. The pose looked silly in corduroys and a rugby shirt, like Steve from *Blues Clues* gone a-soldierin', but how silly was that really, thought Steven. Both armies had been full of men like him. A nice earnest guy, Steve from *Blues Clues* probably would have been a captain and gotten blown apart at Bull Run if he'd been alive. "On Trow, I mean, outside of him being pals with Dawes, I don't know much. Why don't you ask Mrs. Melton? She gets everybody started on their research with the pension records and the National Archives and everything."

"Is that her real name, or her name up there?"

Swan shrugged as if he'd never considered the question. "Don't know."

"So what are some of the hardcore things you do?" Steven said this in a tentative way, as if asking how to mainline or perform some act of perversion.

"I make my own salt pork. Usually before an event. It's pretty harsh. I've made hardtack, too, and essence of coffee. It's all disgusting, but, hey, that's what it was like, and that's what I'm after. Go on-line, too." Steven blanched. "What's wrong? There's all these great Web sites with good sources and instructions and tips. Listen, at the end of the day it's all about your mindset." Swan tapped his temple. "If you really want to go back there, you'll have an easier time with the right stuff on your back."

As Steven wondered whether he should mention the letters, the front door opened, and Patty's voice, wavering somewhere between tentative and threatening, reached them in back. "Hello? Who's here?" Swan's head ducked down as if he'd just heard an incoming shell scream overheard.

A cool veteran of this war, Steven hollered back, "Joe's here. He just finished." He waited to see whether she was coming in to check up, then turned back to Swan. "Does he have kids or anything?"

"Who?"

"You know . . . what's his name."

"Kellogg? He's got a son."

"Oh."

"Manskart doesn't. He's married to Nancy. You know—Polly. She works over in Amenia at the card store by the Ames."

"You want a beer or something? Water? I should have asked you before."

"Nah."

Steven decided to push a bit further. "Is she from here? I know he is."

"Yeah, no, she's not. I think she's from Pittsburgh. Worked at a public radio station, I heard her say once. Was something like a ballet dancer or taught ballet or something, but I may be wrong. That's about all I know. Listen, I gotta shove off."

They made their way down the hall to the front door, Steven scouting ahead to see if the coast was clear. Unbidden, Swan said, "You know that business on Saturday? That's about the high-water mark for Kellogg. He's done worse damage in his day, but that's as bad as he usually gets. And nobody else wants to be the colonel, so there you go." A few more silent paces. "I hope you stick with this. If you quit, all you're left with is . . ." He waved his hands in a vague way that represented everything on the planet below the peaks of Mt. Riga.

Patty's voice cut through the house, and through the heart of the legal secretary she was reaming at that moment. "How the fuck could you lose that contract? Are you *blind*? I'm serious. Do you have a vision problem? If you do, I'll pay to have it fixed. You've got insurance. How *the fuck* could you lose that?"

The two men stared at each other, Swan biting his lip. Steven kicked aside a tangle of three Barbies twined at the hair and nodded.

"And just wait until you get to shoot the gun." Swan ran his fingers along the hall chair rail the languid way a lover trails a finger down a naked spine and over a hip. "Wouldn't it be funny if I bought this place back from you?" he asked. "You think you're here for good?"

That evening Steven grilled hamburgers outside on the porch. For months he hadn't truly enjoyed a meal, despite the rote sounds he made at the dinner table. He'd been hungry, filled himself with whatever the world placed before him or required minimal effort to create, then forgot about food until the next refueling. A matter-of-fact barbecue chef, Steven had no science of proper temperature, never trafficked with spice rubs, but this night, darkness already on the Taconics, the smell of the meat roused whatever receptors his depression had numbed, and he found himself salivating in front of the grill as he watched drops of fat fall heavily into the propane. All of a sudden he had a taste for bread-and-butter pickles and gourmet kettle-cooked potato chips. He put another burger on for himself and ate both with gusto. It was a discerning hunger, too. For a late night snack, rather than a cold Pop-Tart or Pepperidge Farm cookies, Steven surprised himself with a bowl of freshly popped popcorn drizzled with a touch of butter and two hard shakes of salt. His breakfast the next morning, two pieces of french toast, featured a dozen nice rounds of banana, some powdered sugar, and a maple syrup design.

While he packed the lunches, Steven could feel the hunger growing, spreading out from his stomach, beyond even his desire to fade into the past, into a more general attitude. The kitchen curtains lifted in a breeze then dropped, but the heady smell of a changing season remained, full of anticipation and warning of the longer, less mutable months to follow. Standing in front of the open window, reluctantly putting yet another slice of turkey on yet another slice of white bread, he closed his eyes and sniffed in as much of the fresh air as he could. As he hunted through the refrigerator for mayonnaise, he wondered why his family ate so much white food: milk, pasta, cheese, apples (well, white on the inside), bread, chicken, fish, yogurt. Only a bag of baby carrots added color to the inside of the SubZero. No wonder he'd felt enervated.

Another breeze hit as he slipped a Ziploc of bonus cornichons into Patty's bag. The world seemed large again to Steven, filled with more than he could ever understand. In fact, faced with the mysteries of autumn winds and the causes of the Civil War, his ignorance astounded him. He'd figured that once he could tell Vicksburg from Fredericksburg and had read all however many thousands of pages of Shelby Foote, he'd have the War in hand, but now, confronted with letters involving a real life in that conflict and a sense of detail from the men of the 2nd that outstripped anything Foote would have bothered imagining, those three volumes were like a children's menu at a four-star restaurant, able only to hint at the war's fabulous complexities, the seemingly infinite number of stories that swirled together to create history. To march back onto that field in Riga Village, he'd have to arm himself with more than a wooden gun. He'd have to take the next step, learn more about Trow and his world if he wanted to talk to Polly about anything other than the psaltery, the early works of Dickens, and charcoal. He would have to read, and he would have to do things.

First, though, he had to organize the refrigerator. Finding the mayo had taken too much time, and he remembered the shock of its gross disorder Saturday evening. The firm belief that everything had its place made nineteenth-century life that much easier, so taking that as his creed, Steven attacked the shelves and bins, sniffing at suspicious Tupperwares, discarding old lemons, and creating separate lines on the shelves for milk, juices, and individual brands of soda. The kids were only a few minutes late for school.

CHAPTER

14

THAT EVENING, HALFWAY THROUGH HIS FIRST buttonhole, the door of
Steven's office creaked open. With great caution, Emily, in flannel Hello
Kitty p.j.s, her wet hair combed straight, craned her head around the
door and into the candlelight.

"Daddy?"

Steven looked up from the face-contorting effort of sewing by such
feeble illumination; his nose and upper lip pushed up to meet his squinting brow, rabbity front teeth showing. Emily flinched and stepped back.

"What? What's wrong?" His features dropped back to their normal
place and Emily crept forward again, this time with even more appre-
hension.

"Can you read me my stories?"

Steven sighed at his presently sad and sober little daughter. He'd hidden up here in search of privacy and quiet after hours of nonstop television and some effusive and uncoordinated ballet practice, but birthday
parties for two girls in her class had come and gone, and she hadn't been
invited to either one. There had been tears at dinner. Though in no
mood to read *Madeline and the Bad Hat*, Steven felt the responsibility of
parenting pull at his stomach, heard the words *And then there was the time
he wouldn't read me a story because he was too busy sewing* being said to a
shrink later on. He shoved the needle into the wool and put the shell
down. Miss Trainey thought they needed to do more of this. "Of course,
honey."

As he rose, Emily's eyes glazed over, her head leaned loosely to the
right, and she stared far, far beyond the wall behind him. No one had
ever timed them, but her dreamy spells lasted only a minute or two. At
first, her straying attentions had annoyed Steven and Patty to the point of

screaming, but since neither of them wanted to hear a therapist say something unpleasant and unsolvable, they'd resigned themselves to their daughter's dreaminess and focused on what were termed "aggression issues." Miss Trainey reported on Emily's progress in much-dreaded weekly phone calls, though today's had been highly positive, and there was talk of a corner being turned with her enthusiasm for the letter H. Emily's lower jaw drooped a little, opening her mouth into an expression that struck Steven, painfully, as something less than visionary.

Where was she, he asked himself. What was she thinking? She never woke up and dashed over to her journal to jot down big thoughts; she wasn't working on a unified field theory. Was she replaying episodes of *Hey Arnold* in her head? Imagining a personal relationship with Ken? Was she rising off into some astral plane, or just lost between point A and point B?

Emily's eyes focused again. "Where do you go when you go on the Internet? Do you really go someplace?" She yawned.

"Well, no, you really don't go anywhere. The Internet is a real thing, honey, but it doesn't really exist, you can't touch it. Like God." He stopped and held up his hand for emphasis. "No, not like God."

"Is it pretend?"

"Kind of, but it's . . ."

As Emily wandered away, she said, "I'm tired, so you can keep sewing. I'm going to sleep."

The temperature dropped that Friday night, and a colder wind drew a bulky mat of uneven clouds across Mt. Riga on Saturday morning, thick and dark in some places, thin in others, like a down comforter in need of shaking. Novelty past, Patty was happy for him to drive up alone, though his short ride felt anything but solitary to Steven. Every day that week he'd added something to the odd collection that made up John Trow—a new thought or fact, the buttonholes, which he'd restitched according to directions posted on a re-enacting Web site, the brogans— and that morning the passenger seat seemed occupied with hopes of seeing Polly and an eagerness to walk in Riga's simplicity next to others who lived as he did, people like Swan, who also knew how to become someone else. His sense of returning to a familiar place, though, tugged at Steven with more strength than he'd expected from one day's life there, those hopes and that eagerness strained forward up the mountain in a way fascinating to him, as if Trow indeed were taking form. Steven did not dawdle.

Still, for all of Swan's compliments and the growing reality of Trow, Steven felt acutely farby that morning as the others appeared in the field, their accoutrements banging like the chains on Marley's ghost. Even though he knew by now that metamorphosis clearly involved the patient accumulation of details, his envy of the others in their full kits made him want to bypass the collecting stage and just buy his enlightenment. The men around him talked about what they were buying next and where they'd bought what they'd bought and who they'd never buy from again; clearly the gradual nature of the hobby appealed to these men rather than depressed them. Most of them had probably spent their childhood years collecting complete sets of baseball cards or saving change to buy new boxcars for the HO layout down in the basement. Immediate gratification smacked a bit too much of the age they were trying to escape.

He wandered among them, asked around about who made the nicest shirts and who had the best prices on period underwear, facts that everyone, even Scobeck and Kucharsky, were happy to share. Swan had made it clear that not everyone got along, and maybe because of that, it seemed they'd all silently agreed long ago that issues of the 2nd were the primary topics for conversation on the mountain. This was what they thought about all week; why start bringing up the things that they were trying to get away from? The mutual illusion sustained by every man there created a bond stronger than personality traits and eliminated half measures. Either you wanted to be there or not.

Jerry Sears rolled in on his tough little bowlegs, a bantam among them, and headed straight to Steven. He handed him a small, snapped leather pouch, a cartridge pouch.

"Here," said Jerry. "This has been layin' around my apartment forever. You give me an excuse to get rid of it."

He also passed on a video about drill that he thought Steven might enjoy, and when Swan arrived, he gave Steven an old belt. As Steven slipped the pouch onto the belt and strapped it on, he choked up for a moment. He wouldn't have had anything to do with these people while he'd lived in New York, and today that struck him as disgusting. These were basically nice people who were being more than nice to him. Patty might pretend otherwise, but the Armours were neither hosting nor

attending genteel lawn parties with the landed and occasionally even famous Salisbury gentry. This Variety Pack of low-end locals represented
their closest brush with friendship here, and he was grateful for it.
Maybe Emily would get invited to a birthday party someday.

Bouyed by good spirits, armed with more practice and his fresh brogans, Steven again performed well through another brutal morning of
Kellogg's training, though the rawhide leather of the shoes left him limp-
ing after twenty minutes. Again, the greater hands that had led Steven
the first day guided him, and after a time Steven imagined a new form of
Trow, a kindly guardian angel with feathery wings who steered him away
from mischief and danger and onto the path of good in the form of
proper weapon maintenance and firing procedure. He didn't mind hand-
ing himself over to whatever impulse drove him. His first hour of drill
last week had put him in the mindset of every soldier who's ever lived,
namely, that drill was a grueling, soul-sucking exercise no matter how
good he was at it, and today Steven occasionally saw himself as part of an
all-male Rockette line, shiny and precise. Being stripped of choices,
though, left him no room to consider anything but the ordered tasks and
the hollow, rhythmic clanking of cups and canteens. It was as relaxing a
sensation as he'd had in years and as close as he'd ever come to understanding the lure of S & M. Only his mounting dislike for Kellogg, bel-
lowing and blowing spittle, marred the hours.

Identity stowed in his wallet at the farm, Steven strolled into Riga Village
at lunchtime as John Trow, his masquerade self, confidently greeting
faux neighbors with faux queries about children or their work, nodding
at tourists, until he came to the store, with the oak tree, he knew, not far
away. As he had the first time, Steven paused, and there he stood, tucked
into the wool of his uniform under a cutting breeze, curling his shoulders up to conserve what heat his still-modern undershirt could hold
while he wondered what to do. A gust of wind kicked up small caps on
the lake a dozen yards away, and though it bore no tempting dulcet
traces of the psaltery, he checked the tether to his normal life, imagined
his family, his home, before he went any farther. The last weeks had
passed quickly, and as benign as his actions and inquiries regarding Polly
had been to date, no more than a couple of flirty conversations and a
mutual glance or two, he reminded himself that they had been con-

certed. Susceptible as he was right now to another woman's interests, he sincerely wanted, as much of the time as he did not, to remain Patty's husband and the father of their children.

As the leaves of the oak tree near the store drifted down on the spot, *their* spot, where she was probably standing right now, Trow's voice sliced through with the imperative: Go to her. Bring John Trow back to life. Go to her.

The voice had an edge, and Steven tried to shake his head clear of this silly urge somehow put into words. Why should he screw up his life for a clerk at a card store? To be a hardcore progressive? The answer instantly came back. Because It's Right, Dammit—that was what John Trow really did. At worst it's a harmless flirtation.

He could understand now why movie stars slept with their co-stars. The passion of the parts, the blurring of identities, good costumes; even the smallest sparks would blaze quickly under such confusing conditions.

At this moment of uncharacteristic clarity, Steven heard a light sobbing in the direction of the tree. He bit his bottom lip, resolved to remain in his place until he'd given more thought to the porous walls between reality and his role. Yet before he'd taken a breath, he found himself standing under the oak tree, in front of her, stunned not only by the sight of the weeping Polly but by his inability to stop himself. The same hands that had guided him through drill had pushed him forward to the tree.

Polly's skirt was not hooped, nor were any of her colors as dramatic as the black, red, and white of her dress last week. She was a sparrow today, in a plain brown working skirt and beige blouse, ornamented only by her coppery hair, its full power visible as she leaned against a lower branch of the tree, face between her arms, the mane rising and falling with her sobs. Though he was a few feet away, he stretched out his hand as if to rest it on her back. Who was crying, he asked himself, Polly or Nancy? Becky had cried when he'd told her about Patty. Even then, sitting on a bench at Montrose Harbor, he knew he'd made a mistake, but it was too late. These tears seemed genuine, too. Polly had not peeked over her shoulder to check whether her scene had raised a crowd or a rescuer; as far as he could tell, she was oblivious of his presence. The words came from him without his thinking. "My dear, what's happened?"

She turned, startled by his presence. The sorrow of a damsel in distress, the tear streaks and helplessness, a woman thrown on Steven's passing mercy, charged the air around the tree. "I'm glad it's you." That said, she straightened, wiped her cheeks dry, and lifted her chin in the resolute fashion of a person who's had great practice at picking herself up, though sadness had left a vulnerable cast across her face. The corners of her lips, full and pink, were forced over into a pout even as they pushed forward into a greater softness, even though her chin appeared set. A cloud of indecision, of complicated emotion, blurred a beauty usually made from its clarity and turned her as overcast as the day. She closed her eyes.

How could he not want to kiss her? Steven's hand opened and his index finger strained forward, as if to gently touch her lids from a distance. What would they feel like? He looked at his hand, stretched forward, and the blue woolen cuff around it, the brass buttons gleaming even in the October gloom. Whose hand was that? he wondered. These last few weeks he'd stepped into an uncertain place, yet the edges of this lake, the fringes of this affair, all appeared to be lands he'd traveled through before, long ago. She knew him in a fundamental way that calmed as much as aroused him. The solutions of his everyday life felt thin up here, and he reeled a bit, as he had that first day in the field.

"What has he done?" As soon as he said it, Steven blinked at his gross assumption, though on further consideration he thought it a fine guess. Wherever she went, in whatever century she lived, Polly was indeed married to a buffoon. The thought sickened Steven; his anger at Kellogg flooded him. "Has he hurt you?"

Composed now, her spell of tears broken, she waved away his question. "Some simply must hurt others. It is their nature. And yet we love." She smiled and shrugged her shoulders, as if resigned to her lot. "So be it, I say." A speck of light had returned to her eyes. "Come. Relax your fists."

He looked down and saw that he'd balled both hands, had both arms flexed and ready to punch. Her voice opened them, and his face, which had also tensed, smoothed under it.

"Don't tell me—I am shocking to see. I must be." She rubbed some color back into her cheeks and took a few bracing, corset-filling deep breaths. "There. Come with me, will you? I want to walk." Polly pointed toward the lake. "Will you walk with me?"

He followed behind her on the dirt ribbon, only a foot wide, as it wove through brush and under fallen trees, staying always within arm's length of the bank of South Pond. A good quarter mile long and a few hundred yards wide, the lake was a sharp gouge into the mountaintop;

the blackness of the water close to the edge proved its deepness. He saw no beach, no usable shore save one grassy stretch across South Pond, maybe ten yards long, where canoes and rowboats could launch.

"Look!" Polly stopped abruptly and pointed toward the middle of the lake. A golden eagle skimmed across the surface, sending a small trail of spray to each side as he tore a trout out of the water. As they resumed walking in file along the path, Steven watched her heels kick up the hem of her skirt, noticed how her long fingers hung down like swaying willow branches. He imagined the young Polly as she had described herself in the letter, swimming too far, climbing too high, watching these same small waves flicker with the magical light of the furnace. After what Steven guessed was a city block, the trail widened enough for them to proceed side by side. Sneaking a look at her, he immediately saw Polly as the girl in the letters, as the woman who wrote them, could imagine her peering from behind the door at the intriguing new resident. Him. The wild boy. He was brave and adventurous, even dangerous, she had said. Courtly in a somewhat rough manner, and especially adored for it, considering his mountain background. A storm at sea.

"A pleasant day for swimming, don't you think?" He swaggered a little.

"You've swum in colder water, John. Shall you try?" She grinned at his slack face, then let him off the hook. "No, on second thought, I would not have it. I will not have you ill." Polly's next question came as suddenly as the eagle had sliced into the water. "And are *you* happy?"

Like many an unhappy husband or wife, he gagged at the answer. He stammered, tried to swallow, but then his mouth opened and Trow's voice, the voice he'd previously heard only in his mind, spoke forth on behalf of an identity deeper than either of the names he now answered to. "I would be, but there is little from which to graze. I must peck among the rocks."

"Is it starvation?" Polly's tone was light. Steven nodded, amazed that at the word *starvation,* he had pictured drawings of Irish potato famine refugees rather than the stock images of Ethiopia. "Dear friend, our hearts are both so poorly fed."

As she faced him, the wind tossed her hair forward over her face. She leaned toward him, pushed back the hair with a flip of her head and her hand, her gaze locked on his eyes as she did it so. With that motion, both necessary and sexual, Polly began rushing into the empty spaces of his life.

They walked together west, along the shore of the lake, never touching, yet speaking, in only the broadest terms, about their lives; the happiness, the frustrations they described could have been from any marriage from any time. What was there to hold him back? Those pleasant scenes of Life With The Armours he'd used last week to fend off his lust for Polly were as gilded and inaccurate as the impressions of these re-enactors, as imaginary as episodes of *Taffy's Time*. In truth, someone was usually crying or had just puked, and whenever the camera caught Patty in the background, where she believed herself hidden behind Emily's Christmas stocking or a smoking Weber grill, her smile gave way to a faraway stare that chilled him.

Steven went forward. "It is Celia's earthbound nature that wears me most. She is a constant thudding at times. The sunrise for her signifies nothing more than a revolution of the planet." As he said the words, he felt a weight lift off his shoulders. "For as much as I admire her civilizing impulse, we've not enjoyed a walk such as this one in years." The curves and filigree and complex Victorian rambles flowed from him easily, some thoughts never before considered, others he had never thought to utter aloud. Trow's words gave him something stronger to hide behind than the uniform or a character. Spoken by John Trow, they forced no treason on him even if they were drawn from a common pool of emotion. He was not a traitor here, with her. He was John Trow.

"My husband is no better. He is a servant to his pleasures, laboring at an enterprise until its attainment seems not so much a joy as an end to his dissatisfaction."

"Ah, but at least he *has* his passions. Celia lives every moment in immediate perils of the most mundane sort. And yet if there is none present, she complains of boredom."

Steven went on to bemoan his son Daniel's aborning wild streak, the boy's questionable future. What struck him even as they walked was how natural this was, to speak with another woman, this woman. To be friendly with her and not have to be actively a husband and father, though he was still surely both. They made each other laugh, the first act of foreplay, and complimented each other quickly and regularly, letting minor words of admiration for the other's thoughts and emotions speak in place of the intimate ones they refrained from saying. They tried different positions of being near each other—Steven stood behind her as they watched the sun pass toward the late afternoon; they faced each other to share a confidence about Sergeant Dawes, then walked side by side—and each had their own pleasures. Given the use of Steven's voice, Trow displayed his energy, and Steven had trouble fixing any face to him other than his own, couldn't imagine Trow's life as anyone's but his. Steven's mind soon had the bubbly sharpness of two glasses of champagne. Was this, he wondered, what having a mistress would be like? Was this how it would be to see Becky again? Or was he just remembering what it was like to have friends?

So close they walked, sometimes bumping arms, brushing hands, heads leaning near to listen well. They stopped after twenty minutes and turned around before they'd wandered too far into the woods. Before they went where they could not go. Before anyone noticed.

CHAPTER

15

PATTY NEARLY INTERCEPTED THE NEXT BATCH of letters. Passing by the
house that Wednesday between appointments, she scooped up the mail
from the box, a typical heap of junk that also happened to include another large brown envelope with a Riga Village postmark, addressed to
Steven. Either she hadn't focused on it, or else she had, because he unearthed it the next day beneath a stack of old *Peoples* and *Vanity Fairs* and
AOL CDs all ready to be bundled and left out for the man who picked
up their garbage. Steven noticed it while prepping a surprise dinner, the
first in years; a nice capon with a rosemary-and-garlic rub he'd seen in
the *Times* magazine.

Though his first impulse was to raise a considerable stink, Steven let
well enough alone. He'd missed a bullet, he told himself as he marched
up the stairs to his office, an Emily-made construction-paper apple in
hand; he'd nearly been found out. But found out for what? They'd done
nothing on their Saturday walk, committed no impeachable offense, unless flirting was grounds for divorce. Sinning required intent, and Steven
wasn't even sure that intent had come into play. He hadn't gone looking
for John Trow; the world of Riga Village and Polly had come for him,
drawn him in, and welcomed him. He hadn't wanted to go to the tree;
he'd found himself there. Would he have done that a month ago? That the
answer was *no* cheered him; he was doing things instead of just thinking
about them. Yet he hadn't made that decision, had he? The John Trow
impulse had sent him there, and his sense of guilt came from the fear
that he might be unable to control the small flames now burning between him and Polly, flames he planned to enjoy until they burned out or
became dangerous; he wanted to see her, no matter the risk.

The days since their meeting had passed quickly, with Steven fueled
by a jittery energy that sent him scurrying around the house like a wood-

chuck smelling winter in the air. He straightened drawers and made lists of things that had to be done around the house, all highly uncharacteristic of Steven Armour and all welcomed by him. Though he'd not heard it since Saturday, Trow's voice had clearly spoken through him, and with an eloquence he could not rationalize as his own, yet since it was not at all unpleasant, Steven felt no need to examine causes. The world was a wild, uncertain place, full of unexplained phenomena more bizarre than this small sign of Trow's independent existence. He also attributed to this solidifying Trow the sour impatience he now felt toward things like Nate's music and the mere thought of Walter Manskart or Elisha Kellogg. Trow did not simply do Steven's bidding, and Steven liked that.

With Trow's actual being undeniable to his host, though unprovable and undefined, Steven imagined the features of his generic Union soldier as Trow's mask until his identity, his true image, could be found. As it was, he played in Steven's mind like someone often spoken to on the phone but never seen. What, he wondered, would Trow look like if he ever met him in a photograph? At times he imagined or felt Trow standing next to him, keeping him company and offering opinions about life on the edge of the twenty-first century. Baked chicken with rosemary and garlic? Sounds tasty. Bradley or Gore? No, sir. Bush? No, sir, once more. If forced to choose, McCain. Trow was a Grape-Nuts kind of man. A Brokaw viewer. Mac, not PC. Even now, lights off, the timer ticking downstairs the only sound, Steven could swear that Trow was sitting immediately past his vision, there in the office with him.

Steven taped Emily's apple to the corner of his computer screen. The darkness had fallen before he was ready. As much as the time change triggered in him a need for warm fires and thick soups, it started the annual race to January 1 and, this year, the new millennium. Holidays would speed by with mounting anticipation and urgency, maybe even panic. Italian fishing boats would soon cover Emily's small stack of construction paper apples on the kitchen counter. Then pumpkins and witches, dozens of Pilgrim hats, Indian headdresses, and hand turkeys. Christmas-Hanukah-Kwanzaa would come and go before he'd have a chance to enjoy much more than the pine tree smell, and then it would be winter. If they were lucky—if everything didn't come to a halt at 12:01—the grueling cycle would start over again in the spring.

Emily's questions about the end of the world had continued, and he had explained the whole situation to her as best he could, wisely keeping out the mania he'd heard in the voices of tech guys he talked to and their harrowing pictures of a world made suddenly computer-free. As he lit his candle and placed it back in the saucer, Steven wondered whether he should be stockpiling anything. The town had had a few meetings about Y2K, none of which he'd attended. That Riga Village could continue in its nonelectrical, predigital, Luddite splendor encouraged him in his belief that he was in the right place at the right time, increasingly off to the side as the world made the same mistakes, over and over. He moved the apple an inch to the right so that it obscured more of the screen and provided some cover for the plastic soldier.

With an hour to read before the chicken was done, Steven opened the envelope. Six letters this time: five between John and Polly, some quite short, and one to Celia. Although Mrs. Melton had shared with him tales about Riga Village, fading copies of articles from the *Lakeville Journal*, and accounts of Raggie life from the town oral history project, she'd never given him anything about John Trow as important as these letters.

November 28, 1862
Dear Polly,

Our snow came unsuspected to me. Such a fall in Virginia—& in November, though "fine days are few" in that month, here as anywhere—did not seem possible. The boyish chaos that ensued sent me searching for you among the thousands throwing balls of snow & building forts. If chance could bring a blizzard South, I thought, it could as well bring you walking in it, & so it did. You did not see me—I was not trying to be found— but I bear my proof of your sighting. You wear a pine green dress & rabbit muff & bend down toward a drift with full hand of snow, in deep consideration of the propriety of your addition to the many hundreds of other flying missiles. You have the very face of mischief's triumph, & the one I've seen many times when you are tempted. I report to you that your victim— & I speak only of that snowy day—was not amused, sergeant that he was, though as always you escaped.

I add this to my other memories of you against white, to those of you against the green of leaves & all the colors of autumn. I have tried not to burden you with letters—they are suspicious & you are right & yet "What freezings have I felt, what dark days seen! What old December's bareness every where!" . . .

From what Steven could gather, with Jeb Stuart and Wade Hampton knocking on the doors of Washington, Trow and Polly saw each other during parades and the like, but they could not speak to each other. Still, she was there, her presence providing comfort amid the manmade evil their redoubts represented, a mechanical evil not all that different from that of Mt. Riga. Trow described more of the real Riga Village.

> . . . For all your girlish memories, you must admit we are children of a devilish place. Tho you loved that unnatural light, men stoked their flames under it with the constancy of the damned & hauled tons of rock for burning in a cauldron as hot as the sun, all half-naked despite the shame of it. Once, long before we met, I saw the tapping. Mr. Beck limped to the door and swung it open so that the white light could burst free. The molten white iron rolled into the channels, & for a moment I nearly wept, so certain was I that our star itself had been captured, so brilliant was the light, so dark was the sky outside, clouded with charcoal dust. Trains of ore-laden horses marching up & down in an endless stream, no longer fighting against their burdens or the absence of sweet grass; the wretched saloons that took root among the slag. The noise of hammers ringing on iron, the jabbering languages, grunts, the bellows chuffing. Chattel tho I was, I entered your home that day breathless & searching for peace . . .

The good-natured Fenners had saved him, taught him kindness and generosity. Steven thought Trow made them sound too good to be true, but he'd known families like that—palsy and smart and affectionate. If the Fenners lived now, they'd go on ski trips together, chip in to send Mom and Dad on a cruise, torture prospective in-laws with the exclusivity of their intimacy. Every night, the Fenner clan would gather around the hearth for the evening's entertainment, but Trow's sense of what constituted entertainment changed over the course of that first year.

> . . . Your brothers took turns slicing through my poor defenses at chess & your father began schooling me in the Ancients. I would haltingly push through the popular novels Tilda & Eleanor chose, as all of you nodded & mouthed difficult words. I could not understand why you regularly pulled us away from Ivanhoe in favor of Shakespeare's Sonnets, yet as the summer passed, I began to anticipate your turn. Tho I always saw Tilda and Eleanor as sisters, you became less and less so. Sisters do not pretend to sleep beside the fire with a sliver of their eyes open, watching to see if their brother watches them, & brothers do not urge sisters to take long, lonely

walks that require great assistance & much catching by the waist. For some-
one with such natural delicacy & sure-footedness, you stumbled into me so
often as to raise my concern. Your mother assured me that you would grow
better in time, that surely it was a passing condition. That I had listened
well to what she said. Instead, you & I took to reading the sonnets privately,
tho we understood but half, & had, if not a kiss, an understanding. "Thy
love is better than high birth to me," wrote the Bard, and I made his words
my own.

That winter, though, a servant girl accused John of stealing from the
larder, a claim that Polly could not bear to believe and that sent her to
follow John one January day as he went into the woods.

. . . What faith you had, & what kindness not to speak of your dis-
may or your revulsion when I opened the hut's door. You greeted the three
bodies in rags, lying on straw piles, gnawing stolen food, as if you were the
humble traveler & my parents and grandmother the royalty. A part of me
begs to know how every one in your family fares, but I cannot bring myself
to ask.

You must know that I had no part in the recent theft of that cow—a
shameful act most certainly perpetrated by my Riga comrades—& hardly
the instigator, as your husband so publicly announced. I saw your scowl as
he tied the sign around my neck. If you chose to "kill me outright with
looks" you came near. Know this, Polly—tho I have gone to harsh extremes
to feed my parents & grandparents, went to harsher ones for you & our
son—through all that happened since & any hardening of the soul it ef-
fected in me, such outright thuggery falls beyond the limits of my weakness
or my strength. I suffered that punishment out of fellowship, not guilt, & I
suffer a punishment to see him at your side.

Believe that I remain your
John

January 3, 1863
John,

Elisha is a dependent man, despite what you believe as you see him
strutting through camp. He needs me at his side for every decision, no mat-
ter how slight, and I have not been at liberty to answer your letter until

now. Colonel Wessells's illness has weighed heavily on him, both in the responsibility it has placed on him and in the absence of credit he believes should be his as he takes over the regiment. He worries, he fidgets, he harangues, he sulks, he pledges his undying devotion. I am often tired.

And you, dear friend, have taken us down a winding path, and this was not my hope in responding to your letter. Cela me fait mal au coeur. Indeed, I am fairly caught in my recent winter crime (although the colonel also exchanged snowballs), yet you catch me out for so much more. My memories of youth and all that were part of it are so shot through with light that often they alone bear me up through these weeks of muddy red ground and attendance to Elisha's needs. I have been felled by your letters, both their light and their dark. More has been restored to me by your words, and when I now see you, I am reminded of walking alongside the Forge Pond on a sun-filled afternoon. As you march or guard, I run races with you, climb Ball's Peak, remember making whatever use we could of our bodies together to express what was rising in them and in our hearts . . .

Reading Polly's words made him picture Becky, made him ache in time with Trow. Polly went on. She tries to see Daniel in John's face, and cannot miss the pain she sees instead, a pain she caused him, one beyond her ability to resolve. She reminds him of the great difference in the worlds they came from, even though he is right to say that Riga Village was a sooty, declining place. That was true, as was the way his aspirations pushed her into womanhood and love for him.

. . . But for a thing to be true, does that mean it must remain so? The seasons are true and yet they change, and never a tree turns in the same fashion. Happiness is not an object; it is a way things are. Those days were happy, but days change. If today we sat under the tree and once again exchanged readings of the Sonnets, your choices I hazard would be the gloomier passages, as would mine, when once we spoke of love and eternity. I must be as your true sister now, John. You have kept my secret. I am grateful, and I too am consoled to have such a friend . . .

The Fenners are all well. Tilda and Eleanor are both married with children, as is Andrew, a lieutenant in the 14th Connecticut. Bachelor George studies divinity at Yale. Her mother has died, but St. John remains spry and thin, a sapling with old bark. He continues to translate Ovid. In return she asks for news of Daniel.

> . . . *Though I have held many infants in my arms, I can still perfectly describe each aspect of him, from thick black hair to his squared-off toes, and I shall retain that ability until I die. It is a particular ability of a mother that God and nature provide. Mr. Darwin may say it is a matter of the propagation of the species, but my decade and more of torment tells me that such a connection has a greater purpose, and I have been unsuccessful in my attempts to form another. I think Elisha would envy you your son, such a proof of love. He is a man who demands both tangible reward and tangible punishment. (Of course you did not steal the cow; my scowl was for him, but your submission to him—right or wrong—helps all of you. You must understand that.)*
>
> *Please be happy. We have both gone on to others who love us and whom we love. I am happy for your good fortune; please be happy for mine, your wife,*
> *Polly*

His wife! That was a bombshell. Steven stood up and paced around the room, tense and thrumming. And Daniel was their son? Were they divorced or both bigamists? What did that mean for him and Polly? So far the letters' arm's-length tone did not match her forward actions at the village. Or did it? In truth, they'd done nothing more than what was in these letters. He pulled the next one, addressed to Polly, from its envelope and continued to pace as he read it.

January 15, 1863
Fort Worth, Virg.
Polly,

> *Here is your news of Daniel. Your son came to age wondering who you were. I have many memories of mornings when he entered the kitchen, red-eyed, to report the return of his mother in a dream. Back from Heaven, she would tell him—I had kindly told him you were long dead, and the good people left in Riga Village, those who care, confirm the fiction. If you are interested in preserving your fiction, I recommend you stay clear of Mr. Dawes, who has yet to place you but may do so, having little else to occupy him here. Daniel curses the stars for missing you & believes there is no*

G——, *for what G—— would be so cruel. His attitude can be equally con-
temptuous of those not divine. The happy news is that he has survived your
absence & my presence, & he has found his own ways to joy. This is what
Celia writes me.*

*Many days I do not wish to return in thought to that parlor & those days
& that mountain, but I have come to believe that an officer far more punishing than your husband commands my soul & I am unable to disobey when he
forces me down the "winding path" you seem less traveled of. Such memories
are as sweet as arsenic to me, for I know the roses——& their thorns——cannot
survive the journey back, tho I have at times believed they could.*

*You are right that I would select other Sonnets. Let me begin with
these lines——"For if you were by my unkindness shaken, As I by yours,
you've pass'd a hell of time; And I, a tyrant, have no leisure taken To weigh
how once I suffer'd in your crime."*

*And so we shall all be happy for you & your new life far from Mt.
Riga.*

John

The chicken had begun to send its aroma through the house. Steven
flipped through the remaining letters and figured that he had enough
time to finish before everyone got home.

February 2, 1863
Dear John,

*Do flowers speak of their beauty and their purpose? Does the rain ex-
plain in words how it is to be life itself? I speak no shame, for I am all
shame. As you have lived in pain, so have I, yet without the benefit of the
righteous anger that is properly yours, and my every day is Hell, for I wish
to confess yet can confess to none, and now that you are here the words are
thick in my pen and do not flow. I have no doubt you well know how your
words cut me. You intended pain, and you have caused it, sir. I am bent low
after your letter. Read sorrow and penitence in my every word.*

*But I beg you find pity, too, John. Pity for us both. We were children
then; babies who had stumbled upon gold in a field. We built a house in
which to play, but were too young to know its true purpose. "Love is too
young to know what conscience is." How those words sound different now,
written in this tent, not read beneath our tree. I, like you, have tried to best
live the life I have found since my leave, but nothing has surpassed the*

light of my morning. "In me thou see'st the twilight of such day As after sunset fadeth in the west." Choices have been made and cannot be undone, no matter what our wishes are. Please do not let your pain keep you from hearing my words. Read what cannot be spoken.

With affection,
Polly

The next letter in the batch was written in a near scrawl.

Feb. 5, 1864
Mrs. Kellogg,

Is not the unspeakable word Raggie? Tho the Fenner lights often shone to me at my father's hut & I sat at that table as I grew to manhood, neither words nor affection bridged those worlds. That is now clear. I was, & still am, a mountain rough; schooled at your father's hand, a reader at the Library, but always a collier's son. The burdens of survival keep me from happy hours in the Library or the Bible. I live as my grandfather did, a man who learned to lose his past in order to exist. Here I find contentment reading Shakespeare with some other men, tho forced to convince Cpt. Storrows, "good" Yale man, that I count reading as a skill, together with the assumed rustic facilities. Perhaps I am more like Mrs. Shelley's monster than any natural being.

So much cannot be said that I constantly read all that the world holds, yet I still find only one answer—"To me, fair friend, you never can be old, For as you were when first your eye I eye'd, Such seems your beauty still." I shall, if I survive this War & your husband's brutal attentions, melt back into the woods & my people.

John

April 3, 1863
Dear Celia,

I am sad to report that I did not receive a furlough as I had hoped & written in mine of last week, though Calamus did, & I have directed him to see you so that you may hear yourself how I miss you & Daniel. With little drill to occupy us, we have received new duties, along with clearing stumps & digging ditches. We have been learning the uses of artillery, an ear-splitting venture. Deafened, however, as we all are to an equivalent degree, we scream at each other at the same volume, & so it is a wash. When we do not work, we sing, clean our guns, play cards, & do whatever else bored men do, which is little.

There has been a drama in camp wholly unrelated to the readings of plays some of the men perform. Our brave & overblown Lt. Colonel yesterday mounted his horse and gone on his way to Connecticut with his wife because he had not been consulted as to who would receive the furloughs. What will happen we do not know, but this is a strange & better place without him, especially for me, his particular source of anger. The presence of Kellogg & his gadabout wife has proven distracting to all good men of this company, & most wish they remain safe & sound in the home state to bandage his wounded pride.

I hope you are feeling less alone. Much of the value a spouse provides is his mere presence & I have put other things in front of that, as valuable as they may be. I see why you are angry. As it is, the threat of my facing a Rebel minie is small & I will surely be home to your arms the day following our release. We are glorified policemen, in truth, but I will come home a man who has done what he had to do for his nation. Please dream of how the rest of our days will be. Try not to cry before Daniel. He is too young to be in the business of consolation, his childhood so meager that I want him to be saved of such things until truly necessary. Give him my love. I am afraid that I will never see my boy again, for when I return he will be a man. I ask as well that you or Daniel look in on James. I know it is not a rewarding task. He is a difficult man, but he is our blood & so I must give the one order I can as a husband & father, & that is to see if Daniel's grandfather needs supplies for the balance of the winter.

I think of you every moment, & wish that I were sitting next to you, twining violets through your cool fingers.

My love,

John

CHAPTER

16

STEVEN SAT FANNING HIMSELF AS PAIRS of feet spread through the house, little sneakers slapping straight to the television, Patty's heels clicking on the kitchen tiles. The oven door opened, then slammed shut. Half expecting to see John Trow standing behind him, he swiveled his chair around, but saw only the uniform hanging on the door, now seemingly a thing he'd borrowed from Trow. If he had read these letters in a novel, something halfway between Heathcliff and Harlequin for all their yearning passions, he would have politely closed the book and taken a stiff shot of Elmore Leonard, but real people had lived these real events, felt these surges of sadness and loss now coursing through the room, pouring into him.

He slipped the letters into the John Trow file, growing with the letters and notes he scribbled down in his reading. However much he gathered, now, though, he knew no newspaper clippings or factoid could tell him what he wanted to know about John Trow, the truths about who he'd been. The strange, painful reality of Trow's life suddenly took Steven beyond his ability to guess which cereal Trow would have liked and into a place where Steven could not make creative predictions. What he didn't know about Trow was not so much the gaps in the historical record, as the unknowingness we have about any living person, the necessary darkness of another man's mind. Trow was no superhero, yet he was a man whom Steven envied.

Time to fix the rice and broccoli. Trow had been a soldier, he reminded himself as he got up and walked down to the kitchen, a man of the land, not some cyberspace salaryman dreading panicky e-mails from Jay Porter. John Trow was a nineteenth-century man; for all his gothic past, he didn't go into analysis, didn't take Prozac, wasn't looking for a gene to explain his situation. He *knew* what the problem was. Did Polly and Trow ever see each other again, or was that it? Would things with Polly change? He had a quickened pulse of possessiveness, of fear that she would be taken away. Passing through the kitchen, Patty slowed for a second as he put chicken broth on for the rice. "What's wrong?" she asked. "You look scared." She offered a fast smile as she sorted through the mail, bracelets ringing on her still-tan arms. "How was your day? Smells good."

"Just some Molly O'Neill thing I . . ." Patty had already steamed on to the living room. Steven shrugged, tossed in some expensive French salt he'd bought in Great Barrington.

A soda can fizzed open behind him. Waiting to be noticed in a Slipknot T-shirt and below-the-knee skater shorts suspiciously low on his hips, Nate leaned against the counter. When had he upgraded from X-Men underpants to Calvin Klein briefs? "I'm getting a drum set," he announced. Was he going metalhead or white rapper? Either choice disgusted Steven, who'd ingested a fair amount of illegal substances and enjoyed a period of indiscriminate sex in his day. After a long sip, Nate let loose a belch that Steven would have considered cute when Nate was six but that came off as rude at twelve. This was one of Manskart's best students?

"Jesus. Nice belch."

Nate belched again. Steven glared at him. "Sorry." He scratched at his cheek, flush with a crop of young zits. "When's dinner?"

"Pretty soon. What's Slipknot?"

The boy plucked at the front of his T-shirt and looked down at it. "A band. I don't know if you'd like 'em," the last delivered a little under his breath. Nate looked up. At least he had a relatively normal haircut, short brown hair as yet undyed. "I've been playin', you know, Paul's brother's drums at Paul's house? Because we're startin' a band? So I gotta get my own set."

The broth had begun to boil. "And what's the plan on paying for it?"

Nate shrugged. "Get a job or something?"

"You're twelve."

The boy took a sip and smiled innocently. "You buy it for me?" This look once withered Steven and had resulted in many a big-ticket purchase over the years, but today, garnished with pimples, it turned Steven back to the rice.

"Yeah, right." Grunting, Nate slogged off, his unfinished can left on the counter. Steven had a memory of Little Nat walking on the balls of his feet, padding along with a bounce that sent him into constant action. He tossed some spices into the rice. This was all Ronald Reagan's fault. Becky had wanted to travel, have adventures with and without him, see where things would lead. A little too dicey for Steven, that plan. Somewhere along the trail, she would have met some Syrian financier or just grown tired of him. So there was Patty, searching for instant life and instant money in law school. All those yellow ties had worked on him like red on a bull. As the letter said, some choices couldn't be undone.

And where had it gotten him, he wondered as he searched for a lid. His contribution to the sum of knowledge, such as it was, skipped through space, and he did, too, never touching solid ground, never moving so much as one spoonful of earth, thrilled to find a lid for a pot. Steven imagined Trow taking Daniel hunting, making cornhusk dolls and little chairs from scrap wood for Emily, reading her books and teaching her things. Rather than pouting about his wife, he would wonder whether she was happy. *Those* were things a husband and father did, the things *he* didn't do. *He* was making a Tuscan chicken recipe from the *Times*. *He* put his daughter to sleep by trying to explain the Internet. She hadn't even said hello to him, what with *The Wild Thornberries* to watch. Once involved in directing the lives under his roof, he'd become merely a functional element, either operating around them or serving them.

A month ago such thoughts would have sent Steven sulking to his office, but today Trow's purposeful energy rushed through him. He did not want to live this way anymore, and it was up to him to change it. What would John Trow do, he asked himself as he chopped broccoli. No answer was immediately forthcoming, but once Steven had dinner under control, he felt an urge to call his father. Nickelodeon rang loudly in his ears now that he'd let it in. Phillip had polluted the family with all that television. Goddamned *Taffy's Time*. Steven had begun to feel as though he'd been raised a crack baby, large blocks of dialog from *The Dick Van Dyke Show* still working through his system, and that he had passed the addiction on to his daughter, who apparently had him confused with Mike Brady. Obviously, television was the cause of her problems; he and Patty both knew it and had done nothing. But why the urge to call his father, he asked himself as he dialed. Instead of the same purring mental stream of excuses and complaints that usually ran through his brain, Trow's voice spoke.

Because you should, it said. It's your duty to the man.

Though Steven hadn't used the word *duty* in a while, he liked its sound.

The phone rang three times before his father answered, surprised, from his tone, to hear from him. "How's everybody up there?"

"Oh, we're fine. Emily's having some trouble getting used to school. It's a long day, you know? Nate's Nate."

"You two?"

"Fine." Steven tried to make out what was blaring in the background at his father's house; someone yelling. "You know . . . we're fine."

"Good. How's that re-enacting business?"

There was the opening. "Oh, I've gone a couple times." Steven paused, suddenly unwilling to share the experience. "You know, it's fun."

Phillip waited for more, but Steven didn't go any further. "My neighbor bought a rottweiler. Big dog. Shits all over the yard. I think Reifenstahl had one." Whoever was yelling over there was still yelling. Phillip kept going. "Had a chance to talk to Patty about me moving in up there?"

The laugh track on his father's television was perfectly timed to the question. No one was yelling over there, it was a TV show. Concentrating, Steven could now make out Don Rickles's voice and the big blond stiff who played his underling on *CPO Sharkey*, arguably the worst sitcom ever made. "She's been swamped with a couple deals. She's got something going with a minimall over in Canaan." As soon as he heard the words "you hockey puck," Steven knew he had to get off the phone fast before the image of his father watching *Sharkey* and counting dog piles in the neighbor's yard took firm root. "I will definitely talk to her about it. You okay?"

"Yeah. Why?"

"Just wanted to check in. Listen, I have to go. Dinner's almost ready."

Steven hung up. He pictured his father freezing in a mountain shack and nearly called back, but the rice was boiling over.

After setting the table, silverware all lined up level at the bottom, Steven went hunting for his loved ones, inspired still by Trow's example. In the endgame of a phone call, Patty held up a finger and nodded when notified of dinner, but Emily howled as he snapped off *The Wild Thornberries*. Rather than his standard accommodation of waiting until a commercial, today he stuck to his guns and picked up his daughter, gone limp in her chair in Gandhian protest. Once placed at the table, she found her spine and sat quietly. For Nate, he had to reach down to the phone jack before the boy took his threat seriously and CONNMAN324 signed off. "Goodbye," said the nice AOL man, and soon all the Armours were assembled at the table, waiting for a sign to begin in the absence of grace.

Patty rubbed her hands together and looked genuinely pleased at the set table and steaming capon. "This is great. Do it more often." Even her compliments sounded like orders to Steven, who sat ramrod straight in his chair. She picked up a napkin. "We don't need the good linen."

"Why not? Once in a while it's nice to be a family." My God, that sounded horrible, Steven thought. He divvied up the chicken, scraped garlic off Emily's piece, and tried to pry information out of his children. "Emily, what did you do in school today?"

She shrugged. "Stuff with apples."

Nate smirked. "Like did you eat them, or what? What kind of stuff?"

"I don't know." She poked at the dark bits of parsley and oregano in her rice. "What's *this* stuff?"

"Spices," said Steven. "Like on pizza." Emily spooned some rice in her mouth and crawled back into her shell while Steven primly sliced his broccoli. "What about *you*, hondo? What kind of *stuff* did the amazing Manskart teach you today?"

Nate chewed some more before registering that a reply was expected. "I don't know. Like history. You know? *Stuff*. School stuff."

"Excellent. *School* stuff." Steven dabbed at his lips with his napkin. "Honey? Good day?"

Patty waved him off. "I don't even want to talk about it."

The three sank into silent chewing, each as much in their own world as solitary diners at separate tables. The inertia of such living, the downward gravity of doing, saying, thinking nothing pulled at Steven, and he too began slipping into silence, his military posture slumping, until the fire leaped awake again. What would John Trow do? I would take control of this family, Trow said, its chaos and its silence. I would make a family out of these four people bound only by a name.

Steven slammed down his fork and knife. The clatter snapped all three heads toward him. "Okay. There will be some changes in this house, effective tonight." No one moved. He made a little cough. "First off, Emily gets one hour of television a day." Chopping off his daughter's hands would not have produced a louder, more pained, or more immediate response. Since she was not likely to stop screaming soon, he forged ahead. "Nate gets an hour a day of TV or computer."

His son's voice joined Emily's, adding a lower register of groaning and barely disguised curse words to her keening. Patty shook her head. Dinner a shambles, Steven considered retreat, but the next words came out of his mouth before he could stop them. "This family will spend time together, *doing* things together. Like a family. The way families used to."

Patty nodded. "I would have liked to talk about this first," she said, sending a broad look to Steven. "But I totally agree. You guys watch too much television." She folded her napkin, and took another sip of Fresca. "And we definitely should do more things as a family. I have to go to that meeting about the minimall tonight, remember? So you three start."

Having cast her supporting vote, she plopped her elbows on the table and put her chin into her hands while the children bitched, that faraway look forming on her face like a coating of rime. For the first time in a while, Steven took a good look at Patty. He could see that her bland expression conveyed not the disgust with him that he constantly assumed, but exhaustion. She had colored slightly outside the lines while putting on her lipstick that morning, a stray curve of red over the crest of her lip so oddly sloppy and out of character for her that he felt embarrassed. Had it been that way all day? All her makeup became visible to him—the powder in her pores, where the base left off, where the blotchy skin began. Her effort at putting forth her look and personality every day was apparent to him this evening, and he could see a small, scared girl working the levers, afraid of being found out, afraid of failing. She picked around the chicken carcass with her fork, searching for slivers of white meat amid the bones. He had never pictured this for them. He'd dreamed of success, not this heavy lifting, not this constant responsibility. Not his own star dimming so quickly. Not the slow, steady stretching-apart of their marriage.

Like the urge to call his father, an urge to protect Patty welled up in him, to protect her as he had when she was just a Rogers Park girl trying hard to be as fancy as her friends. Steven reached over and wiped off the smudged lipstick; the touch woke her from whatever she was thinking. She pulled back in surprise, her eyes wide, and paused for a moment. With a confused expression, Patty thanked him for making dinner, stood up, and left for her meeting. The rest of the family left with her. Dinner was adjourned.

*   *   *

To his surprise, the televisions and computers stayed off after Patty left. Both children were in the living room as Steven walked in, a surly audience of two, Nate leaning his head over the top of the couch and staring up at the ceiling to make evident the depths of his boredom. Did he honestly believe that Steven had enjoyed every one of the nine thousand conversations they'd had about Thomas the Tank Engine? He'd spent years cramming Nate's life full of dull wooden learning toys and happy talk, been a regular song-and-dance man, all to produce the indolent little shit before him. But Nate had been a great kid then. Or, Steven asked himself, had he been a great kid because of the attention? Poor Emily had received only the revival tour, the late Sinatra for whose presence, not performance, you paid. "So, what do you guys want to do?"

Emily bounced off the couch. "Watch TV!"

"No, let's do something else." Steven ran through a dated roster of their interests, and they reached accord after a spirited and ultimately cooperative negotiation: Steven and Nate would teach Emily how to play rummy. Already a skilled amateur at Go Fish and War, Emily caught on to the basics of the game, drifting off only once or twice, and the three killed enough time for Steven to rate the evening a success. What did not succeed was the Cool Dad bit. Nate shot down every reference even slightly past its expiration date with a roll of his eyes, until Steven decided, once and for all, to acknowledge himself as an old guy in khakis, the look that he ultimately believed God sported on weekends anyway. He wrangled dreamy Emily into bath and bed while Nate finished his homework, and forty-five minutes later he pulled the headphone plug on his sleeping son. That was that: no tears, no *de-de*, and both were asleep by ten.

Full of congratulations on creating the kind of evening John Trow probably always had, Steven tiptoed into his office and lit a fresh candle. He'd planned to practice his drill with Jerry's video, but hesitated, not wanting to tear the tissue of silence they'd allowed to grow in the television-free evening. Instead, he sorted some papers on his desk, then pulled a book on Cold Harbor he'd borrowed from the library out from a stack rocking in the candlelight. Of all Civil War battles, Cold Harbor may stand as the most foolish and the most bloody. From June 1 through June 3, 1864, Ulysses S. Grant ordered wave after wave of Union soldiers against the lines of Lee's well-fortified Rebs. The resulting slaughter left mounds of dead and wounded, and Grant, unwilling to call a truce for more than a week, let the screaming, weeping casualties suffer and die and bloat in the hot summer sun within sight of their friends. Of all the future horrors the Civil War set into motion—machine guns, submarines, trench warfare, just to start—this pathetic waste of life best predicted the sick stupidity of the Somme coming fifty years later. And thousands of re-enactors and their families would assemble next March in Virginia to relive the experience. Something about that struck Steven as bizarre.

Skimming ahead in the book, he found the first mention of the 2nd. A regiment swelled with men who by that point never expected to see action, it was among the first to arrive at Cold Harbor. But no general had any intention of letting the men of the 2nd, officially an artillery unit, near a cannon. From what Steven could tell, they were fodder, bodies for others to hide behind once they'd been piled high enough. As he read, he tasted something bitter on his tongue. A stray bit of rosemary? Steven was certain he'd experienced the taste before. Smacking his lips, he tried to place it, find the childhood scene it belonged to, fished around his teeth, and finally got up for a glass of water. It did no good. His tongue was coated with the metallic taste. The room had become warm. A strange smell thickened around him, like dry, dusty leaves rotting on the ground. He began to feel tired, able to fall asleep at his desk, and yet he was edgy, too. Trow told him to wake up, wake up. Steven tried to rouse himself.

Putting aside Cold Harbor and this puzzling sort of déjà vu, Steven dug out the letters again. They looked real. Who would have kept them after the War—Trow's family or Kellogg's? How did Polly get her hands on them? He pulled out the last letter, the one to Celia, and examined the paper; very thin, the folds deep and sharp and long-pressed into permanence. Unlike the first letter to his wife, his *other* wife, this one had been in a regular envelope, though decorated, like the first, with those intricate Federal engravings. They *must* be real, he told himself. What happened next? Did Polly come back, or did she stay in Connecticut? What would happen next time he saw her in Riga Village?

Patty's car pulled into the driveway. As Steven stood up and tried to slip the letter back into the envelope, he felt resistance, something flat and cardlike he hadn't noticed before. He squeezed open the envelope and pulled out a small photograph, tinted blue and framed within a tiny cardboard edging.

As soon as he focused on the face, Steven sat down, his heart racing. He knew the man, knew the bearded, serious face, the thin, lanky body in a Union uniform. It was the man who had waved to him by the cemetery.

On the back, written in faded ink, was the one word: "Trow."

CHAPTER

17

HAD HE REALLY SEEN A GHOST that dreary September morning in front of Town Hall, John Trow's ghost slinking back toward its grave on the hill? A secret part of Steven had always wanted to see a ghost, but now that he may have seen one, he didn't know what to make of the experience. Both unsettled and entertained, Steven played back the scene all week: a waving motion near the short hedge by Town Hall; his driving up and seeing a bearded man in a uniform, gesturing to him. Steven remembered the face, the hooded, aggrieved eyes, the pressed lips, the unkempt hair, the pained and resolute expression that, from what he now knew of Trow's story, made great sense. Still, the car window had been fogged. The man wore a uniform from the 2nd, the same one in the picture. Had there been footsteps in the grass? On such a damp day, a man that sizable would surely have trampled down the wet grass and stirred up some mud, but Steven couldn't remember anything like that. Was he positive that the uniform was from the 2nd? Could he say for sure that the man had been waving at *him*? That he may have conjured up a nineteenth-century Hyde to his twentieth-century Dr. Jekyll, summoned a guiding spirit, amused Steven as long as he didn't think too hard about all the heretofore concrete facts of existence that would suddenly crumble if he did so. But even this had its attractive side. To spurn the purely rational meant that all the answers were not known, that endless and varied possibilities could extend to his life, and by regularly shuffling back and forth between reality and unreality, he could blur the line that separates them.

The ability to fully imagine Trow now animated everything Steven knew about him. He pictured Trow, long and wolfish, walking the paths of Riga Village, holding Polly's hand, pacing the walls of Fort Worth. And having seen him, Steven found Trow's words richer, could see the expressions behind them, could picture Trow scribbling away next to a campfire, biting the end of his stubby pencil as he considered a word. Often the sense that he'd created this character gave way to respect for a man much bigger than he was, a man coming into existence once again, and in ways free of him.

Early that Saturday Steven got up in the dark, showered, and shaved. Since Wednesday, he had many times felt the photo drawing him to it, and now, while putting on the set of rough worker's clothes Mrs. Melton had sent to him, he again gave in to the urge. Half-dressed, he stole to his desk and pulled the small image from the envelope, losing himself in Trow's persistent gaze. Back in the bedroom, he propped it against a French candle on the bureau and took inspiration. As he studied it, his shoulders slackened and his arms hung down longer now at his sides. Was that how Trow had looked? He furrowed his brow and ran a hand through his hair to match the image on the card. While he was checking his appearance in the mirror, Patty shifted around under the comforter and exhaled a long, sleepy breath. Steven left the bedroom and tucked the photo back on the desk.

Dew covered the windows of the Navigator, and as Steven laid his uniform and wooden gun on the backseat, sat down, and buckled up, a chill passed through him. The sun had done nothing yet to push aside the night's cold. He rubbed the top of the dashboard, an automotive scratch behind the ears, and asked the car nicely to warm up for him. As soon as he hit Route 41 he cranked some R.E.M. to ward off the demons. It was only six A.M. Driving up Mt. Riga, a slow and tricky task in the dark, Steven focused on Polly. No matter where the story of Trow and Polly went, he would see her today, the very alive Polly, and that bright fact forced back his disquiet more than the music did.

What he did not sense in the car was Trow. The passenger seat felt empty, and though Steven was not actively in search of another sighting, he had to wonder where his companion had gone, now that he was coming to completion. One other car, a beefy red SUV, sat in the parking lot when Steven, feeling totally alone, pulled into a space. He assumed the car belonged to Mrs. Melton. The Saturday before, she had reviewed with each man his job: Kucharsky, Scobeck, and Hube Osselin would work at the furnace with the club-footed Japhet Beck; Bobby, Burney, and Jerry got the farm, and Steven, Swan, and Murray Lummer would start a charcoal pit under her eye. The goal, after a fortnight of tending, was a fresh half-ton of charcoal for the furnace. Steven had reread his pamphlets, the book, and the letters and felt mildly optimistic. Still, given the amount of work to be done that day, the men on the charcoal team had all agreed to come early. Comforted by the massive Durango indicating at least one other corporeal being walking the streets of Riga Village, Steven made his way through the hedge and entered the field.

Riga Village sat dark and silent in the mist ahead, the buildings hulking close to the ground. If he was not by himself, any company he had was not making its presence known. As he drew closer and began to walk, wooden gun on his shoulder, over the bridge, he had an odd sense that Riga Village was not entirely still. He looked to the furnace, behind to the Rossiter house, to the Wentworth house at the corner, the store behind it by the lake, and the post office. The town seemed to be holding its breath, as if he'd walked into a room in which he had been the major topic of discussion; as if things in motion had frozen at his approach. The shuttered windows and weathered wood of Riga Village appeared not asleep for the night but dormant in this time, tolerating the outsiders manning the stores and wandering the paths so that it could exist again without them after they drove away and left the mountain to the stars. And he had disturbed that.

Steven took careful steps into the town. He turned around to look north up the road to where the Fenners' house had once stood, just past the Rossiters'. Without closing his eyes, he imagined a fine, tight little house and saw six children—three sisters, two twin boys, and a rough-cut young man—romping around on the porch. Lulled by the regular splash of the waterwheel, he put down his rifle and leaned on it as the pinkish light of the furnace flame settled over the town; long lines of horses roped together snorted behind him, passing next to bunches of children laughing as they skipped to school. Comfortable now with his being there, clanging and seething with the greed and desperation re-enactors never reached for with their good intentions, Riga Village came to life, just as Trow was doing. He saw trees fall and other buildings sprout—shacks along the lakefront, other large homes, the forges, and the boarding house. Horse manure piled in the streets and the stink of human waste joined a chemical miasma as distinctive as the constant light. He heard heartfelt cries and unplanned conversations, things he hadn't read of, hadn't imagined. A man wearing a pirate's kerchief walked into the post office; cows and chickens strolled the streets; finely dressed women glided in and out of the store while ragged toddlers stood beside the entrance. A beautiful woman under an oak tree played a psaltery. He had crossed into Riga Village as it had once been. The Riga Village he remembered, where his true life was . . .

Something scraped the ground near the farm, as if a heavy object had been pushed. Then it stopped. Steven turned to the schoolhouse, expecting Mrs. Melton to have a light on, but there was none, and he had a sense that someone was there, watching him. He brought the pretend gun up to his waist, leveling it menacingly even as he realized how silly he must look. Birds whipped about and sang, yet their voices seemed complicit with the silence, a cheery front for something else.

"Mrs. Melton?" Steven called out. No answer. "Mrs. Melton?" He turned his mind back to Riga Village, but it had gone. Only the ghost town remained.

He quickly hung up his uniform in the barn and went searching for the pit. Near the easternmost building of the farm he found it; in a small clearing next to the cemetery, hundreds of four-foot-high pieces of wood stood on end, like a crop waiting to be harvested. A tight circle had been pushed together in the middle around a tall, bare pole. Obviously someone had started work.

A branch snapped behind him. Steven gasped and swiveled around against his will. Murray Lummer nearly dropped his coffee cup at Steven's panicked expression. "Virgin Mary, what's wrong!"

"Oh, Christ, Murray. You scared me."

"Scared me, too, for chrissakes." He wiped some coffee off his shirt, a loud green plaid. "Jesus." He sounded sincerely annoyed.

Steven gestured to Lummer's shirt. "Sorry about that. Is that your Durango out there?"

"No. Mrs. Melton's. You started?" Lummer asked, pointing to the wood.

"No. Maybe *she* did."

"Yeah, I was gonna say you've never done this before, so you probably ought to let me and Joe do most of the heavy lifting. We did last year's."

Steven nodded. They were not off to a good start. "Well, want to get going? We got a lot to do." Better to work with this dick than talk to him.

Lummer held up his cup to show he still had some coffee to finish, which he fully intended to do before lifting a thing. The way the old man had tied off his pants high above his navel made him appear particularly dumpy. "We have a new priest over at Saint Mary's. Reminds me of you." He took a sip.

"Yeah?"

Lummer nodded, loudly sucked a tooth. "Lots of energy. Always running around."

"Is that good or bad?"

"Depends. He wants to cut out the Knights of Columbus, which is very bad, if you ask me." Lummer peered at Steven as he sipped again.

Was anyone else coming? Steven looked around hopefully, though he had to admit that he preferred the old man's presence to being there alone. Maybe whatever was watching them would kill Lummer first. "Well, I'm all in favor of the Knights of Columbus."

"You Catholic?"

"No, but they're the guys with the swords, right?"

Lummer smiled. "Yeah, that's right. I'm Fourth Degree. I'm a lay minister, too. I take the sacrament to the sick and infirm."

"That's great."

Down the hill by the furnace, in the field, Steven saw Joe Swan stop to stub out a cigarette with his shoe. Steven waved to him for rescue, and minutes later Mrs. Melton appeared, in a simple long brown skirt and a high-necked white blouse. She would not be climbing on the woodpile today, but Swan, with no intention of breaking a toe for the sake of realism, had dressed for action, his large and highly anachronistic Timberlands protruding from beneath his green tweed high waters. Mrs. Melton greeted each man in turn, as unreadable as ever under her bonnet, and said to Steven, "I see you've started already."

He shrugged his shoulders. "Wasn't us. We thought *you* did."

Mrs. Melton did not appear concerned that no one wanted to own the labor. "Then it was the delivery men," she said. The four inspected the beginnings of the mound, the tight first layers of the chimney, and the well-chosen pole. "Let's hope Mr. Dawes, Mr. Frote, and Mr. Trow can continue the work as nicely." Mrs. Melton instructed them to sweep the circle clear of anything that wasn't a log, then set them to work on creating the chimney around the pole, or fagan, by laying thinner pieces of wood horizontally on top of each other in a rising triangle. The men moved quickly and without much chatter. Once they'd stacked the chimney as high as Mrs. Melton, she directed them to start leaning the pieces of wood, called billets, against it. By seven-thirty they'd finished the first level, a circle maybe twenty feet across, sloping at a sharp angle by the end. Judging them well on schedule, Mrs. Melton told Swan to take over.

Swan's first directive was to take a break. With the rising sun it became clear that the day would be overcast. Gray clouds pressed hard on the mountain, and a somber light pitched both towns, the real Salisbury below and the re-created Riga Village, to a higher level of industry. The insistent wind nipped at those not yet infected with a sense of purpose for the coming winter. Some sheep bleated in the barn, along with voices and clanking iron. Sitting next to Swan, gulping a mug of cold water, Steven started to ask whether he remembered listening to Curt Gowdy describe the World Series with his French horn voice, the true voice of days like this. Lummer strode up. "Ah," he said, "a couple of niggers in the woodpile, eh, Sergeant Dawes?"

The old man snorted at his own minstrel show funny. Swan smiled indulgently. "That we are, Private Frote. That we are." As Lummer padded off, Swan leaned over to Steven. "That's not Murray. That's Peter Frote. Murray's the sweetest guy in the world. Gives out communion to sick people. Did you know that? But Frote can be a nasty son of a bitch if there are any black people around." Swan shrugged. "What are you gonna do?"

Steven watched Lummer, or Frote, whoever he was, strut away, bobbing his head forward and down at each step.

"He really gets off on that, doesn't he?"

Swan shrugged again, this time with embarrassment. "Listen, some pretty ugly things happened in the past. Frote really was a fuck, supposedly. His own brother hated him. Murray's big in the Knights of Columbus." Though Lummer was apparently the only person in the village who had chosen to re-enact some of the disagreeable realities of his character, his selectivity struck Steven as suspect. Especially when there was no audience. "Does all sorts of things for people. Mass every Sunday."

"Does he give communion to black people?"

"That's not mine to say, is it?" Swan stood up, dusted off his pants, and closed the subject.

They returned to the pit and began work on the next level of the chimney. As it rode, Steven noticed small things that needed correcting—keeping the chimney straight, switching pieces of lapwood, fixing the angle of the billets. Some of it was common sense, some of it came from the material Mrs. Melton had given him to read and the letters, but often he just *did* things—asking Lummer to send up a certain piece of wood or stamping down to set a billet—things he couldn't explain, things that seemed obvious to him. Without a word, Steven took over the operation, every thought given to an old way of being, where each billet and piece of lapwood went, how the air would play between them.

By 10:45 the second tier was finished and Steven stood on top, directing the action. Arms folded, Mrs. Melton came out to inspect their progress. Visitors milled about, watching them toss bushel after bushel of dead leaves across the mound. As Steven pointed out holes and thin coverage, Mrs. Melton fielded questions, allowing him to drift back, to focus on what was in front of him and let anything outside his vision blur. Steven kept to his task without putting words to what was happening in his brain as his thoughts slipped away to the town he'd seen under the rose light of morning. Would Lincoln win another term? He'd have to start laying in more wood for the winter. He remembered another small pit he'd made with his father, not far from this spot, that had yielded up a ton of beautiful charcoal. What was Polly doing right now? He had to finish the chair he was making for Celia. As if he were thinking in a foreign language, the effect became complete. He was there. Back. Free of all that did not live then. He stood tall, demonstrated James's throwing technique to Frote as they tossed the dust, for his fellow workers were Calamus Dawes and Peter Frote. Like Manskart into Kellogg, Nancy into his wife, Steven had transformed, the blurry double image snapped into one. He *was* John Trow, and to protect that, he dispelled any conscious realization of the fact.

All was ready. Swan laid a wooden ladder down against the side of the pile. Steven took a few hot coals into a shovel and slowly clambered up to the top rung. If he dropped them on the dry leaves, the whole thing could ignite. Holding the shovel with one hand, he reached across the top of the mound, pushed aside the top wood, and tenderly dropped the coals down the chimney, into the kindling. Within a minute, thick white smoke rose out of the hole and flames licked up the ten-foot chimney, visible to the crowd, who *ooohed* at the volcanic pile. Steven pulled himself up a little higher, off and away from the ladder, and fully on top of the mound.

Swan called up, "That's not a good idea, Steve. I mean John."

"I'm all right. Hand me up some leaves." He calmly replaced the pieces of wood on top, further sealed the hole by spreading more leaves and dust, and made his way back down.

The three stood by, waiting, tending, patching up the places where smoke came out. At some spots it seeped out like mist, and Steven sprayed dust across in a light coating; at others it shot out in a plume, which called for a shovelful right on top. Smoked out, the original crowd soon got its fill of watching a pile of wood smolder, especially when the flames died down and the potential for danger seemed to diminish. Small holes the men had opened near the bottom let wave after wave of dense smoke twist wherever the wind wanted it to go. Now and then a few people wandered by, asked a question or two of Mrs. Melton, and drifted away, unsure of whether or not they should say goodbye. The pit began to settle into the quiet of the next two weeks, the long, slow, but intense burn that would create fuel. The men stood back.

Lummer shuffled over to Steven and Swan, the liver spots very apparent on his pulled and shiny pink skin. "Anyfing ess, massa?"

Suddenly a huge jet of smoke shot out the top of mound. Steven picked up a shovel and loaded it with dust. "Hey, Frote, hold the ladder for me." Gingerly, on his toes, he stepped up the first rungs. "You know, Peter, Riga Village has had its men of color. Do you remember Allan Blunt?"

Wary of the flames, Lummer held the ladder with the tips of his fingers, wincing as he looked away. "No. Who's he?"

"Unable to place him, are you? A runaway slave. Made his home in a log cabin by the North Pond. Small fellow. Had a ship tattoo on his arm and an accent of some sort. Some folk thought he might have been a pirate." Steven made it to the top of the ladder and spread the dust, but the smoke continued. He pushed off and climbed onto the pile.

Swan yelled up, "Steve, that's not a good idea! I'm telling you again!" Mrs. Melton, with folded arms, squinted into the smoke but said nothing.

"Steve who? I'm speaking of Allan Blunt. Didn't speak much, did Allan. He hunted, did odd jobs. Still can't place him, Peter?"

Jumpy and sensing torture, Lummer said, "No, Steve. I can't" into his shoulder. "Come on down, all right?"

"The story was that he'd exchange silver and gold for notes. The mountain bank, he was. He would disappear for a week or two, then return." Crouching, Steven began to stamp on the pile as the two men loudly protested. "If you followed him into the woods, the earth would start to groan. Maybe a man of magic, was our nigger banker . . ."

The last two words jolted Steven awake and back into the present. He'd never used that word before. Never. Nor had he ever heard this story. Who the hell was Allan Blunt? Had he read about him in one of Mrs. Melton's pamphlets? If so, how could he picture Blunt's face, light skinned, probably Caribbean, with a sharp nose and full lips? Sad eyes that told of a long road to this mountain hideaway, where he was at last accorded a small peace. These weren't memories of a picture; he could hear Blunt's voice, remember his small ears. He knew too much. How was he so sure what Riga Village had really looked like?

Steven abruptly stood up. How had he learned to perform drill so well after reading *Hardee's* one time? It took people months to do that. How had he become an expert at making charcoal? Steven realized that he hadn't seen the ghost since he'd started becoming John Trow. Shocked by all this knowledge that he shouldn't have had, knowledge that seemed to belong to someone else's life, Steven saw in an instant that he'd made a terrible mistake. All the time he thought he was putting on John Trow's skin, sneaking into his life for fun and improvement, Trow was actually substituting his life for Steven's. He wasn't taking over John Trow; John Trow was taking over *him*.

His panic mounting, Steven slipped and opened the hole again. Smoke and flames reached up now and grabbed at his legs, as if he'd revealed an entrance to the underworld. He felt backward with his toes in search of the ladder, but that movement shook the ladder out of Lummer's light grasp and sent it tumbling to the ground. Stranded on top of the burning pile, Steven looked for a way off. He'd have to jump forward ten feet and down ten feet. Not an option. Or maybe his only one.

At that moment he slipped again and this time began sliding on his stomach down the mound of smoking wood. By reflex, Steven grabbed at flaming logs to gain a hold, though his hands slid off. He hit the ground hard.

While Lummer and Swan flung leaves and dust on the pile to slow the burn, Mrs. Melton picked up Steven under his arms with impressive strength and walked him the fifty yards to the schoolhouse. A small group of citizens and visitors, many assuming that this was part of the show, gathered around the door and pressed their faces against the blurry glass to watch what happened inside.

The room was too dark to grant much to the viewers. Mrs. Melton guided Steven, his head spinning, to one of the two chairs, and he sat down heavily. He closed his eyes, and when he opened them again she was there. Polly's face hovered close, concerned and lovely in the lamplight. Shadows filled the soft curves of her cheeks as she searched him for further injury. Her hair stole glints of fire from the lamp. When she pulled away, satisfied that the extent of his injuries were as Mrs. Melton had described, Steven could see her emerald dress, the one she'd worn in the Grand Union parking lot. Had she worn it once to throw snowballs?

At most, Steven's hands ached. His fall had been fast, his grasp not firm enough to burn his flesh, so the effect on his palms, a reddish puffiness, did not go past what firewalkers incur on corporate retreats. Polly sat down beside him and took his left hand in hers to examine it. They had never touched before. Steven closed his eyes at the contact. Polly leaned her head over, two locks of hair falling down and framing her gaze as she lightly ran her fingertips over the palms of his hands. He groaned, a sound that in another context may have conveyed more pleasure than pain but this morning, in this room, brought Mrs. Melton closer. "Do you think he's all right, Mrs. Kellogg?"

"I believe he'll be fine, Mrs. Melton. He's in my hands. Why don't you return to the pit? I think you're needed there even more." Mrs. Melton hesitated, so Polly became more emphatic. "The shock is most disturbing to Mr. Trow. Some peace would do him well. Will you ask those at the window to leave?" Mrs. Melton stood by the door for a reluctant second, then left.

They were alone. Polly rose and returned after a moment with a small jar. Again, she lifted his hand and placed it in her lap against the velvet. Slowly, silently, she rubbed salve onto his palm in a small circular pattern. As she worked, he focused on a pin she wore on her breast, old silver or pewter, with red plaits twined into a circle; hair jewelry of the sort Patty had tried to buy. Polly lightly spread the salve, over the flesh below the fingers, to the heel of the palm and the pad of the thumb, on to the fingers, each in its turn, smallest first. With firm, exquisite pressure she cupped her fingers around his, pulled up to the tip, released, and went back down a few times on each until the salve was absorbed. She then went to the other and treated his right hand. "How does that feel," she asked.

Still trembling from the shock of the fall and the spectral thoughts churning in his brain, from the erotic tension that now choked him, Steven could only nod. She smiled, a less than innocent smile, and Steven swallowed. He could feel an erection growing. Isn't your life better this way, he heard Trow say.

"Poor thing, clear your mind and think of something that would give you great joy," Polly advised. He did not protest and he could not, did not want to, summon up snapshots from the family album. Surely there was clinical value in what she was doing. Steven looked down at her small, high boots, their black tips. He pictured himself untying the back of her dress, opening it, and peeling it away to find her underdress and crinolines, crisp and putting up only minor resistance to his hand. They fall away, half pulled by his insistence. His hands touch her corset, slide down to her cotton stockings, white, starting at the middle of her thigh. Eyes closed, he could not stop himself from groaning again as Polly shifted in her seat, unable to get the right angle.

At last, to his relief and disappointment, she stopped rubbing and began to wrap gauze around his hands. "Do you believe in ghosts?" he asked.

"I believe in the spirit world, if that's what you mean. In our loved ones returning to pass on their love to us. Why do you ask?" With Steven's hands wrapped, she went to one of the desks and pulled out her psaltery. She began to play "When This Sad War Is Over."

How honest should he be? he wondered. How should he play this? Was he Armour or Trow now? Had he seen Trow's ghost, or had it been a hiker? Polly said she'd deny everything if Trow ever mentioned the letters, and he had gathered that their game was bound by the same unspoken rules followed by the original Polly and John, though the game seemed to be slipping into something more. But maybe that was just the letters. He needed to know more about this man he'd invited into his life; he needed to know where the letters came from. "The letters. That you send me."

Polly stared at him. "The letters?" Was she acting? Was she not sending them? She stopped playing and touched his cheek. "Stay here and rest. You are still confused."

The room was quiet. Steven opened his mouth a few times to speak, but nothing seemed worth saying, and Trow's voice had gone silent. She put a hand on his. "I don't need your words. Sit here with me for a time." She unclasped the pin from her breast. "Take this," she said. "I make such things nowadays. Take it. Give it to the woman you love and think of me when she wears it."

She placed the brooch in his hand. He closed his bandaged fingers around the pin and her hand as well, both slick with ointment. He pulled her closer, his other hand reaching toward her corsetted waist, and she leaned toward him.

The door burst open. "Time for drill!" Bobby Osselin yelled into the room.

Swan stepped in with more circumspection. "Mrs. Melton said you were okay, thank God. Kellogg wants to see you right now." There was time for only the most polite thank you and good wishes, and some guidance from Polly as to the proper care for his hands. Keep them moist with salve, she recommended.

Outside, Swan asked, "Is she being good to you?"

How did he know? Was what was happening between them that transparent? "No more or less than to any other man, I'm sure," Steven replied.

"How can you say that? She's yours." The thought swelled in Steven's heart—she was his. It was so obvious that even Joe Swan could see it. "Take some time to rub down her wood. I'm telling you, she's thirsty. Especially with that boiler. Sucks all the moisture out of the place. I was planning to go electric. You should think about that."

CHAPTER

18

"Men, I have a great pleasure today."

A bank of slate clouds massed over the tops of the trees. As usual at the beginning of a drill session, Kellogg seemed to boil with preemptive anger despite his words. He paused as a great gust of wind turned the branches into a storm-struck ocean of leaves, pushed apart, twisted, and rejoined, yellow and red spray covering the field.

"On this day one of our number becomes a fully mustered soldier of the Second Connecticut Heavy Artillery." He held his chin high, and his chest and formidable stomach swayed as he paced the line, carrying a long thin rifle topped with a bayonet. Some ventured to turn their heads slightly under Kellogg's uplifted gaze to offer Steven winks and nods.

"In his brief time with our regiment, this man has demonstrated the commitment and ability we expect in this unit, and so I present . . ."

Kellogg finally looked at Steven. Pompous bastard, Steven thought; not a new idea for him, but this afternoon it did not pass. A black hate started burning in Steven's stomach, twitched in his arms and legs at each of Kellogg's waddling steps, every smug pursing of Kellogg's fat lips, at the pointless brutality, the image of *his* ring on Polly's finger. What had previously been an out-of-proportion annoyance with his son's eighth-grade teacher Steven now recognized as the heating anger of John Trow toward his rival, and he also realized that he'd lost whatever control he'd had over it just as he was losing control of himself. Hadn't he minutes before nearly kissed another woman?

". . . Private John Trow with his new wife. Long may she save him." His teeth gritted, Steven shook hands with Kellogg and took the rifle.

Swan called out, "Three cheers and a tiger!" The men let out three loud *huzzahs* while Kucharsky rolled his eyes.

As soon as all ten pounds of wood-and-steel rifle landed in his hands,

Steven wondered how he had ever lived without it. Nearly four feet long, weight perfectly calibrated to hold its ground yet still heed firm commands, the gun felt alive in his grasp, like a large, sleek hunting dog that would rip the guts out of a grouse if you wanted it to, then curl up next to you by a fire. While Steven had imagined ornate nineteenth-century decoration for his weapon, the simple wooden stock, shiny barrel, and foot-long bayonet did not disappoint. The prominent hammer curled as it leaped forward toward the nipple, thumb guide jutting like the fin on a breaching fish. Steven squinted with a pained Dirty Harry look, feeling a heavy set of potentials on his shoulders as he hefted it; though a replica, it was still a gun. He could ram a bullet down its barrel and kill a man with it as effectively as he could with a Magnum.

This is as it should be.

The words burst loudly and firmly into his head. Their certitude, their force, defined them as Trow's words, now commandeering Steven's voice.

This is the way you should be, it continued. Steven wondered what would happen if he closed his eyes and let go of the wheel.

This is how the world *wants* you to be. Your wife. Your children. They want you to be powerful.

After Kellogg had inspected all the weapons for safety, the drill began. Maneuvers like support arms had been designed for ten pounds of wood and steel, not a length of pine, so the gun fell into place, and the odd positions in which he'd sometimes been forced to hold his arms and hands now made sense. Trow's hands seemed to be in Steven's, anchored to this living plane by contact with the gun. Steven grinned. Kellogg roared at him from the left. "What in hell are you smiling at, Private Trow?" Steven could hear him stomping closer across the grass and leaves, and in a second his meaty postlunch breath was in Steven's face. "A gun doesn't make you a man, sir!"

Your boss wants you this way, said Trow. Control your world.

The anger built in Steven the way the gusts of wind did over the trees, pulling all the air out of the field and blowing it back in larger and larger waves, the storm slowly nearing them. As the men moved through drill and on to bayonet practice it continued to brew, and Steven's life below splashed into it. His marriage, his family, his job; all of these concentrated with Trow's bitter anger at Kellogg into a paste rising in his throat.

Kellogg called, "Cartridge boxes to front!"—the sign that they were about to start shooting. Steven pulled the small leather case around from the back of his belt to the front of his hip. The skies had thickened into a rich bluish gray that set off the oranges and yellows splendidly. Another vast billow of wind rushed over the mountaintop.

Your father wants you this way, came Trow's voice. You must be strong enough to care for him.

The static of a coming storm, the anticipation of rain and thunder, sent jitters through the village. Calls to children echoed across the town as the residents of Riga closed windows and shutters. The chill dug into all the men on line, their shoulders hunching. Lummer's teeth began to chatter.

Kellogg called the men to rest as a thick barrel of thunder rolled in the distance. "Review loading in nine times!" Burney and Bobby Osselin stamped their feet like skittish horses, but Kellogg seemed oblivious of the impending downpour. "Private Trow! Step forward!" Steven moved reluctantly out of the line. Kellogg stuck his hands in the small of his own back and pushed his stomach forward. "Load!"

Singled out, Steven hesitated. With guns in play, the small bunch of visitors huddling together in their fleece vests grew larger.

Becky wants you this way, Trow whispered. She wants to remember a powerful man.

"I said, *load!*"

Planting the rifle butt between his feet, Steven put his right hand on his cartridge box, unable turn his attentions from Trow's voice.

Polly wants you this way. This is the man she wants. She wants *me.*

"Handle. *Cartridge!*" howled Kellogg. Steven fished out a cartridge, the paper cylinder about two inches long and half an inch wide. "Tear. *Cartridge!*" He tore off the end with his teeth. A few grains of the gunpowder's sharp razor taste clung to his tongue, a sour, not wholly unpleasant taste that he instantly recognized. It was the taste he'd had while reading about Cold Harbor earlier in the week.

I am the person you want to be, Trow said.

Steven looked up. Off in the distance stood Polly Kellogg, on the outer fringes of the swaying trees, where the white-capped clouds surged and collided. The colonel could not see her, but Steven could. The wind whipped the trees, and her hair swirled about her face, yet she did not take her hands from her sides; instead, she let the red flow across her features and obscure them.

I am the person you want to be.

Tasting that sourness brought back the other night's smell of rotting leaves and dust, and suddenly Steven saw himself not on Mt. Riga on this chill September day but someplace warm and sunny, standing slightly downhill from some lines of trees. A few hundred yards in the distance a long thatch of bushes or what may have been branches jumbled together up high on the left. Details washed over him. He was in a ravine, a swampy bottom surrounding a small run. In front stood Kellogg, his saber raised over his head, pointing up toward an opening in the thick patch of underbrush. Anger, anticipation, and fear of the most basic kind swirled around and through him. Somehow what was about to happen had everything to do with his survival, his existence, and he was not in control of himself.

The vision began to move. He felt himself marching closer to the trees, covering the soft ground with the regiment as he squeezed his rifle harder. The men veered left up the rise. Kellogg's face tensed, and Steven could see fear in it.

Shoot! The word filled Steven's mind. Shoot now!

Steven lodged the stock on his left shoulder, as he had that first day, a position that felt perfect, and put the man who stole his wife into the cup of his sights. While the colonel and the other men began to yell, he drew back the hammer with his thumb, the round bone of his first knuckle playing on the trigger. He pulled.

The blast in his ear, the jolt against his shoulder like a dark slap of the paddle; the explosion was everything Steven had wanted it to be. With this one shot, the jitters and anger dissipated like the smoke, and exquisite feelings of strength and dominion sent him deeper into a world where he mattered again. When he focused, he saw that the other field had scattered with the shot, leaving him back on Mt. Riga—and yet part of him had not returned.

Colonel Kellogg crumbled and Walter Manskart stepped out. "What the hell do you think you're doing! You could have fucking killed me!" The other men stood their places, in shock, but Steven gave Manskart no ground or apology. "What the fuck is on your mind?"

Steven glared back. He'd never felt this way before and it was heady. He looked for Polly across the field, but she had disappeared.

This is the way you should be, said Trow.

As he lifted the rifle and began to give it back to Manskart, the teacher held up a hand, his voice low and threatening. "That was your one chance to fuck up. Do you hear me?" Steven didn't particularly want to speak at this moment, but Manskart demanded it. "I didn't hear you. This is never to happen again. Correct?"

❧ PART THREE ❧

CHAPTER

19

DESPITE THE MASS AND OMINOUS COLOR of the clouds, the thunder and lightning, only a few minutes of downpour ensued, followed by another ten of steady drizzle. New leaves freshened the blotchy mat of those already fallen, and they shone during the sun's brief appearance, before it slipped away down the New York side of the mountain. By closing time, all that remained at Riga Village was the storm's chill. Exhausted, Steven climbed up into the Navigator, but because he'd left the lights on all day, turning the key did nothing. When he looked around the lot, the only person he knew was Kucharsky, three cars away, polishing off another Pall Mall outside his minivan.

Steven coughed to catch his eye. "Hey, uh . . ." Now that he had his attention, he wondered whether to call him Kucharsky or Hyte. "My battery's dead. Any chance you can give me a jump, or maybe a ride down?"

Kucharsky sniffed. "Yeah, sure. It's not a problem for me," he said in a defensive tone, as if Steven had doubted that he would, which Steven most certainly had.

Inside, the car reeked of smoke. A Big Bird shade hung by suction cups off a back window, and cassettes of various New Country artists lay on the floor and in the door pouches. Steven figured him for insurance or some other kind of borderline paper-shuffling or sales. The stormy day had quickly turned to night, and the green glow of the dashboard illuminated Kucharsky's tightly packed features. "So where did you go to college?" he asked.

One of the few questions about his life Steven was relatively proud to answer. "I went to Northwestern."

Kucharsky digested that in silence, the slight freeze showing that he'd expected something more in the community college vein. When he spoke again, his tone had slipped into complicity; hardcore progressive or not, he considered his passenger a fellow college man. "You live in Swan's house, right?"

Steven did like to think of it as *his* house. "Well, yeah. I mean it's—"

"He still have all his little self-help books around?" Kucharsky's vampiric eye teeth slid down as he sniggered. "You wouldn't believe some of the shit that went on at those regimental barbecues he used to have."

At *his* house? "Like what?" Visions of Scobeck vomiting in his living room danced in his brain; an orgiastic tableau in his bedroom featuring Burney and Jerry Sears . . .

"His wife made people play Scrabble with him. To help improve Joey's mind, she'd say." He hissed derisively, licked the rim of his mustache. "Everybody shitfaced, and there's Swan trying to fucking spell."

Steven all too easily imagined the scene, and a month ago he might have laughed too but Swan was now his pard. Trow's pard. Kucharsky made him feel dirty, and Trow wasn't sitting still for it. He sent a warning shot. "Joe Swan's a good man, Mr. Hyte." When was the last time he'd snapped at someone like that? Steven wondered. Of course, he'd pointed a gun at Kellogg today . . .

"I didn't say he *wasn't* a good man. I said he's a *stupid* man. Mr. *Trow*," the name said with a sarcastic edge. "No one said *huzzah* in eighteen sixty-four. They said *hooray* or *hoorah* like people do now. And if you call a fuckin' tiger with it, you're supposed to growl. He *buys* shit, but he doesn't *know* shit. You golf?"

"No. Not my game."

The cemetery and Town Hall finally ahead to their left, Kucharsky pulled over. "You in the market?"

Steven's stomach throbbed whenever this topic came up. He shrugged nonchalantly. "Some mutual funds." "Some" being exactly $716. They'd paid for the house and the two cars and the furniture with the rest. Steven grabbed his gun and tried to make a hasty retreat.

"Well, sell it. Buy Qualcomm."

"That's a good one?" Steven tried to look sincere. "I'll definitely look it up. See you next week?"

"Yeah. Whatever. Hey, wait a second." As Steven opened the door, Kucharsky reached across and popped open the glove compartment. He stuck his hand into a small box marked CAUTION—LIVE AMMUNITION and handed the escaping Steven three cartridges, which sat heavily in his palm.

"Next time shoot the fucker," said the corporal.

Steven stared at the cartridges, each festooned with a large twist on one end that made it look like a miniature Christmas cracker.

"Just kidding," he said, sounding a little disappointed. "You know what they are, don't you?" Steven bobbed his head noncommittally. "Fittmann makes a mean little minie." Kucharsky grinned. "Have fun. Don't kill anybody."

He peeled out and onto Route 44 before Steven could thank him. After sticking the bullets in his pocket, Steven called Patty from a pay phone and spent a few minutes dawdling in front of the Outdoors Shop and the Liquor Store until the Saab rolled up. Rather than some bust-hugging sweater, Patty wore one of his ratty Northwestern sweatshirts, and she'd stuck her dirty hair under a black Tully, Davenport & Ates cap, one of the few signs of beneficence her firm had shown her. "What the hell is that?" she asked, pointing through her open window at the rifle.

"My rifle. Could you pop the trunk?"

She pulled her head back in surprise. "No, I will not pop the trunk. I will not have that thing in my car. And you are not bringing it into my home."

Under the buzzing street lamp, across the alley from where he'd first seen Trow, her angry words had all the substance of windblown leaves, deserving of attention, but not worth pulling over for. He remembered that he had a set of her keys on his own key chain, so he opened the trunk, empty save for a ripped Saks bag and two umbrellas, and gently laid the gun down. Patty made a show of pulling the keys from the ignition as he got in. "I'm not going anywhere until you take that weapon out of my car."

"Patty, I'm never shooting it. It's just for show."

"Then why does it smell like sulfur in here?"

Steven rolled his eyes.

"What? Am I crazy for not wanting a gun in my house? Is that so crazy?"

Tenderized by the day, Steven had no interest in a battle. Instead of his usual path of least resistance, though, he sat up straight in his bucket seat and let John Trow take over again. "I *will* do this! I am an adult! I know how to maintain a gun! I have no bullets, for godsakes!" Well, he did, but they didn't count. He didn't *mean* to have them. "Do you understand? It is a *showpiece*."

"You don't have to snap at me!" She turned away, hurt, drummed her fingers on the wheel.

Shouting back had sent a pulse of clean energy through him like the storm on the mountaintop or the blast of his rifle. Trow wasn't putting up with her shit either, and now, without the resentment that usually fogged his vision during Patty's outbursts, Steven saw the situation more clearly, received the vibe that this had not been a great day for her, and put aside his meager triumph. She hadn't made herself up, so the pores around her nose seemed larger than ever, and her eyes, usually bright and forward, had retreated and made her seem to squint. Steven always found something enchanting about any woman he saw in a movie. What, he wondered, would he think if he saw Patty on a movie screen, twenty feet high, the focus of attention in every scene?

Her father, Larry Bilmanet, had been an "executive" at a billboard company in Melrose Park, which meant, as far as Steven had gleaned, that he didn't actually make the signs and had worn a tie to work. That first night in her dorm room, "Outlandos d'Amour" on her boom box, red scarf over the desk lamp, just before Steven had made love to her, she'd told him how, on Saturday evenings, her father would take the whole family for frozen custard and then drive around Chicago to find his newest sign. Stopped next to the Edens Expressway or in a desolate Blue Island industrial park, they'd then pile out of the car, custard in hand, to admire his handiwork on behalf of Vienna Hot Dogs or some Buick dealership. The scene had sounded sweet and good to Steven—Phillip used to hoot at the television whenever any of his own ads came on the air—but she had looked so embarrassed about the smudges on her father's white collar that he couldn't help consoling her, kissing her, for a childhood that she viewed as Dickensian, compared with the Lakefront wealth of her Northwestern friends. Larry had been able to squeeze out the money for school, but he couldn't afford the trips to Stowe or the zippy Beamers that her deb pals had. Patty had hoped to climb up the next few rungs and pull the Bilmanets up behind her, at a comfortable distance, treat them to caviar and *Eine Kleine Nachtmusik* on WFMT as they visited her Lake Shore Drive apartment, but she'd accomplished neither one. Since college she had never stopped trying to reach that next level. Steven had once loved that striving, so different from his father's opting out.

They drove on, past the White Hart, and the familiar curves of the road began to calm them both. Sensitive now to Trow's increasingly direct dictates, Steven saw that kindness was called for here, so he mulled over possible openers for a conciliatory discussion. As he stole glances at his wife, he decided that if she were a movie star, he'd think she had a tremendous body, find her dark eyes mysterious, be amazed by her energy.

Patty caught him staring at her. "What?" Her eyes flicked back to the road, then back to him. "What are you looking at?"

She looked more tired than he had ever seen her, more than she'd looked in the hospital after giving birth. The sweatshirt had a big stain and a shredded collar. It looked as if Patty was ready to quit the race, ready to settle into the middle-class nightmare of rising no farther than where one began. How could he make up for his role in that, his general failure?

"Just looking at my wife." He smiled at her. How could he make up for the fact that he'd spent the afternoon daydreaming of sleeping with another woman, would have kissed her if Bobby Osselin hadn't walked in? What would John Trow do? "Want to go to the movies tonight? Get a baby-sitter?" It was a start.

She glanced over again, suspicious. "I can't. I have two contracts to finish. Plus, the asshole who lives next to the mall parcel is being a dick, so that's all for shit." Still, Patty seemed disarmed by his interest and maybe a bit puzzled by this sudden foot forward. The thought of seeing a movie hung in the air, not entirely chased by her rejection. "What would we see?"

"I don't know. *Sixth Sense?*" A ghost movie might be appropriate tonight. What he didn't want to see was *American Beauty*. Like he needed to pay money to watch an unhappy husband have a midlife crisis.

Patty shook her head. "We're the only people in the world who haven't seen *American Beauty*. Annette Bening plays a real estate agent. As if."

He shrugged. If the larger goal of complete happiness was impossible, he would do anything tonight to cheer her up. "It's in Great Barrington if you want to do it . . ."

For a quarter of a mile the possibility of spontaneous action warmed the car's interior. Each imagined a dinner someplace nice, a drink or two, no clean-up. Reality woke Patty up first. "I just don't think we can get a sitter this fast," she said. "And I have that work to do."

Steven had no answers. Deflated, they drove in silence until they got close to the house, when Patty said, "Your father called. He was talking about moving in with us. Do you know about this?"

Mumbling that he would talk to him, Steven settled into a numbed impatience, as if they'd passed their exit and now had to drive an unknown distance before the next one. Suddenly he popped up with a cry. Something had jabbed him in the leg. "What's the matter?"

"Nothing. Something in my pocket poked me." As he shoved Polly's pin aside, the near kiss, the letters that may or may not be in his knapsack, sprang into his mind. He was suddenly very happy that they weren't going out tonight.

CHAPTER

2 0

NEARLY FINISHED WITH DINNER THAT EVENING, Emily speared a flaky chunk of salmon, then froze. Sensitive by now to the rhythms of their meals, Patty, Steven, and Nate all looked to Emily as soon as they noticed her absence from the regular ring and clatter of silverware. Fork lolling in her hand, she stared past Nate, who reached across the table for the couscous.

Steven glowered. "What happened to manners, chief?"

"Oh. Sorry." Nate put the bowl down.

At times the silences Emily created sent Steven into a testy mood, the kind of jumpy impatience one gets from repeatedly hitting red lights. The family had a hard time flowing. Nate rubbed his nose with the palm of his hand and, when his father offered no further correction, spooned more couscous on his plate. Steven rolled a wooden stalk of off-season asparagus between his fingers, then bit its tip. He'd found another packet of letters in his knapsack. As soon as dinner was over he'd mosey up to his office to read the letters and clean his gun as instructed by Kellogg, to make sense of the day. Or he'd teach Emily how to play checkers, something he'd been meaning to do for a long time.

Nate scraped his chair back across the wide-beamed wood floor. "Where the hell are you going?" Popping the chunk of salmon into her mouth, Emily took a big sip from an apple juice box, eagerly watching as if she'd just come back for the good part.

The boy looked busted, eyes flicking from side to side. "Uh. I'm done."

Patty had the softer voice tonight. "Come on, Nate. You know better."

In a mood to throw basketballs at his son's head for no valid reason, Steven tried to defuse the short temper he'd brought down from the mountain. Nate sat again, but the boy's T-shirt—"It's Your Amerika!"—

did not help Steven's calm. Wearing the uniform for a few weeks and regularly saluting the flag, reading about lives offered in sacrifice to the dream of what this nation could become, had made him more patriotic than he'd ever been, even more than when he'd worked for the Anderson campaign in college. "That shirt is unacceptable."

"I spilled Mountain Dew on myself at Paul's so his brother gave me a shirt." Nate looked chagrined. "I know. It's weird."

John Trow had offered his life for this country; he would not let it rest. "Was that the *only* shirt he had?"

The boy's embarrassment turned to injury, and he flushed. "Yes! He handed it to me! I thought I was being polite!"

Steven penciled in another black check next to Paul's name. "I was thinking about going on a hike to Sage's Ravine next week. You want to come?"

Once upon a time his son would have jumped at the chance. "I don't know," said Nate. He sulked in his chair until Patty excused him.

Emily stared at Steven as if he were a visitor. "Yes?" he asked. Instead of answering, she hopped off her chair and ran up to her room. How did Trow deal with Daniel, Steven wondered. Even though he hadn't had crystal meth to worry about, the principles of good parenting didn't change.

After loading the dishwasher, Steven locked the office door and lit one of the fat beeswax candles he'd bought from Mrs. Kurlander earlier in the day. He pulled the pin out of his pocket and placed it with great care on his desktop for examination next to the bullets. Generous amounts of red hair had been twined tightly together into a three-inch length, capped with silver at each end and then joined at the top to form a circle. A silver heart hung into the center from this point of meeting. Soft, but firmly bound in their circle, the strands of Polly's hair caught the candlelight just as they had in the schoolhouse. Steven cradled the gun in his lap, then opened up the first letter, drifting back as he saw the old-fashioned handwriting.

May 5, 1863

Dearest Friend,

Shame seemingly must precede triumph in this war. We must hope this is true, for all the wagons filled with dying boys from Chancellorville are proof of our greatest shame yet, worse than Fredericksburg. I am sorry to open with such dark words after my absence, but I am all full of darkness and clotting thoughts that make my heart beat slowly. Leaving was not my choice—the colonel commanded and the wife obeyed. (I have learned, too late, the protocols of marriage.) Had I any power to decide this for myself, I would surely have remained, but many days he does not hear reason and especially so when he is stung. I give you for your consolation the sight of him stumbling forward in leg irons upon his arrest at our home. It will be small, for Wessells fails in his health and indicates that Elisha shall soon have what he wants. We have been told that charges will be forwarded as a formal matter, but no interest exists for pursuit of the case. I pray the colonelcy will restore him to the kindness that in the past let me forget his flaws.

And so if Elisha receives his reward after such behavior, and the Army still hopes to win after such a litany of defeat and embarrassment, I too can live for redemption and joy after my shame. Never think, dearest friend, that I did not love you, before and even after I had left Riga. Though I was no Juliet and did not kiss you until I was eighteen, I had loved you every moment of those years. To kiss was almost unnecessary, we were so truly joined. You were indeed my dearest friend. Oh, how two words so weak apart, so broad and lazy in their individual intent, become unique together. Husband, lover—these are ranks, positions men hold. But you were my dearest friend, one who knew my soul yet never needed to consume it. I told you secrets, did not tell them about you. I was won not by the fire of your sun, but by your warmth, and when we did first kiss it came as a crowning bloom on what we had cultivated together.

Did you doubt my love that night? The furnace fire burned brightly, and we had wandered after dinner to the far shore, so that when we looked back, the lake reflected the entire town. The flame shot high and sent sparks dancing into the evening sky, over the lit houses. Dusk lapsed into an indigo blue, the yellow light sparkled in the low ripples of Forge Pond, and I thought I was Lady Hamilton herself in the arms of Nelson as they watched Vesuvius burn. Friendship does not mean that we know all that can be known of our friends; it is that in loving them, trusting them, we welcome every surprise they bring to us, even when that surprise is a kiss. And that we each had carried one there . . .

Elisha tells me that soon some companies will be sent to Fort Ellsworth. I shall wear a piece of red ribbon at review so that you will know where my true thoughts lie. Adieu,

Polly

The phone rang. A man's voice, midrange, fast and distracted, asked for Steven. It was Jay Porter.

"Steve. God, I'm so glad you're there. I thought you'd be asleep. Whew!"

Usually unflappable, as level as Nebraska itself, tonight Jay had a panicked twinge in his voice, as if he'd met with Omaha's cocaine dealer earlier in the day. Jay was, in fact, not a likely candidate for drugs, but he did have that tightly wound air of concealed gender questioning often seen on young spokesmen for right-wing Christian organizations. "Jay, are you all right?"

"Oh, the boys in Bern are pretty serious. *Prit*-tee serious." Drunk, or at least darn tippy, Jay drew a messy word picture of the corporate offices, leaving Steven to imagine exactly how badly the meetings there went. "Dylan's flying back home in a few days because they want to get into e-commerce." Jay affected a Sergeant Shultz accent. " 'Brick und mortar ist dead!' One of them said that. I don't remember which one. They had these great suede raincoats."

"Yeah?"

Jay's buzzing plane began to sputter. "I'll be honest with you, because you've always been a straight-shooter. You've been really really great and you've been working twenty-four–seven for me and I know that. I really do. See, the problem is that Dylan wants some ideas on this e-commerce thing, and I don't have shit. They do like Food Wizard, though. Well, Bristine does." Steven could hear a heavy draw on a cigarette. "Thank God." Out came the smoke. Jay smoked? "But do you know this guy Howard? Howard Case? The kid designing it? You ever heard of him? Because the little fuck is *not returning my calls!*" Steven had had no clue that Jay thought enough of him to self-immolate in his presence. His new boss sighed. "I'm supposed to have a show-and-tell in four days, and I have nothing. Which is why I don't have anything in my brain for Petro. Petro, Petro, Petro," he said in a tripping little voice, and then, "Aw, shit."

In a business sense, Jay had just pulled down his trousers. Steven leaned back in his chair and steepled his fingers, let him stew and smoke for a couple of seconds. "Christ, Jay. I don't know what to tell you." Not only had it happened, but it had happened so soon; still, Steven's grin didn't stretch as far as he'd imagined it would when he dreamed of this moment. Though Jay had been a weasel much of the time he'd known him, Steven did not want Jay's blood on his hands, and offering his boss up, letting him split his head open on his own limitations, would not necessarily mean that Steven would get the position once Jay left to explore new employment possibilities.

Jay whimpered on the other end of the line. Steven had to make a snap decision on this, but political skills had hardly proven to be his strong suit. Before he could ask, in a casual fashion, what John Trow would do, the answer came loud and clear: Do not let people die between the lines.

"Jay? You there? Take a deep breath, okay? First, call Stan Privinger in Kosher and Hallal. He's worked with Howard and knows his father from Baruch, so the kid won't be able to hide." For the next forty-five minutes, Steven tossed out a dozen ideas, mostly marginal ones, but he could see himself pitching Gerda's Kitchen proudly to *die Schweiz*—click the freezer for frozen products, the oven for baked goods, and so on. If they decided to go into lifestyles, they could expand into Gerda's Living Room or Gerda's Yard or—sick thought—Gerda's Bedroom.

As he hung up, Steven realized that nothing could stop Jay from claiming every word they'd just spoken as his own idea. But after smarting about his ineptitude, he realized if Jay was this bad off now, it wasn't about to get better. The honorable thing done, Steven returned to the letters and heard Trow's voice read them.

May 14, 1863
Dearest Polly,

> *I am better with you here, as I am always better where you are: Tho I may have been less tortured by what I cannot touch, I cannot touch the sun but need it all the same. My hard words to you remain, but my love for you—I must say what has become so plain to me in your absence—is no less for them. If there is still love between us, it is of a rocky sort, & that it cannot be sunlit would only take us back to where it began . . .*

Trow went on to recount a day in 1847, the day the furnace went cold. The day that changed their lives. That morning Riga Village had been churning along as usual until Trow, doing a repair on the Fenners' porch, noticed that the spike of fire always visible from the top of the furnace had gone out. He heard a low commotion grow louder, wild voices become more panicked, the sound of metal clanging about faster and faster until things seemed to be thrown; the voices louder, shouting until the bell, always a crisp, regular peal that called men to the tapping just as Schoolmaster Fenner's bell called in the children for their studies, began to clang madly. Men emerged from the furnace building, some walking with hunched shoulders, others running to the townspeople who had come out from their homes. The news was screamed and murmured and wept. The furnace had gone cold. A batch of iron had coagulated and hardened in the hearth. In the time Trow had been watching, the furnace had become useless and, with it, all of Riga Village. The bell continued to toll, and people stumbled about as they realized the future had disappeared. Darkness fell over a desperate town.

> . . . *What were we looking for in the black? Already some had packed up their carts in admission that no hope remained, while hot meetings were held in homes by candlelight. You & I stole away to the woods into the night & I showed you stars you had never seen through the glow of the furnace. We took advantage of the darkness & the disturbance to find our comfort in each other, to find our future, the one we'd been looking toward for years.*
>
> *I must see you—alone. Tell me how I can. You must not leave me again.*
>
> John

Steven ran his hands along the gun and crept back slowly into the present. What would his father say if he knew how much he loved this gun? He probably wouldn't care all that much, thought Steven. He would care about Polly, though. He would care that his son had seriously contemplated adultery all day, and as much as it surprised Steven too, in retrospect, it amazed him that it hadn't happened sooner. At some point, Steven's faithfulness had become a weapon, a noble stance he had never abandoned so as to have something to hold up against her. The role of cuckold, with all its righteous pain, always felt so much more natural to him than that of the adulterer. Truth and suffering were on your side. But here he was, falling in love with another woman.

He slipped his finger into the circle of the pin, then picked up the *carte de visite*. Was he *really* falling in love with Polly, though? Wasn't it John Trow who was in love? The ghost. The man in the letters. The grim, proud face staring back at Steven, who existed now not as a shadowy sense of presence but as something inside him. Whether Trow was a ghost or a historical re-creation run amok, something he'd whipped up out of the letters and Mrs. Melton's pamphlets, did not matter in the face of the slight turn for the better in Steven's life these past weeks, all attributable to Trow. The guilt and the thrill of the new urges Trow brought with him, the urge to shoot guns, to cheat on his wife, twisted around one another in the guttering candlelight. His pastime had become his passion.

"You like this," Steven whispered to himself. He looked at his organized desk, the neat piles of papers. The history books stacked up around his office, books he was reading, not merely collecting, books on which he was taking copious and orderly notes, more than he'd done in college. No ionic waves of static flowing through the halls. The kids were in their rooms, winding down. Patty was listening to her Dixie Chicks downstairs, a sign that she was trying to relax. "This is how you should be."

If some of what he'd done had not been entirely his choice, since when had he ever made good choices? Surrendering to fate, to Trow, made as much sense as marrying Patty or working for Dilly-Perkins. And so far, as unnerving as the experience had been at moments, the sensation of having every thought and action measured by the standards of another was exactly the way he'd feel about himself if he were John Trow.

"You should be John Trow," he said softly. Then again, louder, with the joy of a revelation: "I *should* be John Trow." Steven stowed the pin, the bullets, and the photo back in the desk drawer and then grabbed the rifle so that he could hide it in the basement. If he hurried, he'd still have enough time for a game of checkers with Emily.

CHAPTER

2 1

STEVEN LEANED BACK INTO THE STRONG ARMS of the past, into the romantic and principled life of John Trow. As comfortable as he found receding from headlines and football scores to be, though, sharing the tiller with Trow demanded great activity. Extending the sensation produced by his weekly periods of complete immersion at Riga Village required that Steven select from fewer options. Beyond trying to use candle, fire, or sun for lighting, he wrote letters instead of calling or sending e-mails, stopped buying Minute Rice and instant pudding, washed the dishes by hand. As with his uniform, so it was with Trow's lifestyle; each was a construction of details, made real only by the volume of its truth. Yet continuing these moments involved great calculation and preparation, and he found himself living faster and harder in a slower paced world, a profound change for a man of relative leisure in a time speeding beyond all limits. He entered into a near-constant state of industry toward the goal of peace and quiet, like an Orthodox Jew rushing home to get ready for the Sabbath, or a Shaker doing the hard work of simple living.

On an everyday level, Steven accomplished his DP tasks quietly, efficiently, and without emotion. Over the years he had tried to convince himself that he could somehow save the world through presliced lunchmeat combinations and other highly packaged assemblages of prefab food that not only offered value but liberated working moms and dads to spend quality time with their kids. Sometimes he imagined millions of SnaxBoxes showering over the hungry plains of India, little Hindu children fixing tiny cheese-and-cracker sandwiches with the contents and, with stomachs full, finally able to create a future for their troubled land. John Trow's more practical mind disabused him of this. The brutal real-

ity that Dilly-Perkins was his job—nothing more and nothing less—
and unworthy of any time beyond its most basic needs kept him atten-
tive and reduced his urge to kick back with *Judge Judy* in the middle of
the day.

With his time freed up by good work habits and the attendant absence of guilt and procrastination, Steven rekindled small flames that
he'd thought had gone cold and continued to stoke others. He ordered a
vintage seed catalog from *Parade* magazine for an often discussed, yet
never initiated garden, and bought a field guide to trees, with which he
began a program of dendrological study. To make your home amid
forests and not be able to read them now struck him as idiotic, as if he'd
moved to a foreign country without intending to learn the language. A
nice set of old buttons turned up in a Sheffield junk shop and replaced
the originals on his jacket by the middle of the next week. He bought an
odd-sized can of stewed tomatoes and some twine with which to make a
coffee cup, an authentically amateur and leaky creation that allowed him
to clank along with everyone else in the 2nd. Cautiously, he went on-line
and surfed again through re-enacting Web sites, noting tips and standards
and the most esteemed vendors for blankets, shirts, and anything else a
traveler to the past might require. Flush with petty cash created by the
complete elimination of fast food from his diet, he ordered a plain Federal shirt, made of white wool in a period pattern, and some woolen
socks. Trow's picture offered hints as to how better to re-create him,
how to crush the front of his kepi down and where to start trimming his
nascent beard. A fairly itchy affair by late in the week, its intended path
would follow low along the line of his jaw, leaving neck and cheeks
clean-shaven, with as full a mustache as his upper lip could muster. Patty
seemed bemused, Emily uncertain, and Nate had not, as far as Steven
could tell, noticed the facial hair, consumed as he was by the onset of his
own puberty.

Though the voice that had once hollered "Kiss my arse" in Steven's
mind did not replace his usual mental processes, Trow made his requirements and opinions clearly known. Unlike his own thoughts, which
tended to come in to the fire like a wet dog from the rain, a bit jumpy
and uncertain as to whether they belonged there at all, the thoughts
Steven attributed to Trow arrived fully formed and with certitude.
Where once he might have asked himself what John Trow would do in
such-and-such a situation, he began to *know*, not unlike his unearned

knowledge of drill. The old messages he'd often received pre-Riga, those clinging statements of weaknesses, the prophecies of failure he could never quite scrape off, Trow exchanged for regular news of possibilities, better answers delivered with righteousness and charitable expectation. Sometimes he pictured the tall and brooding Trow, his guardian and guide, nodding approval or pointing out directions; other times he felt inhabited. Either way, life improved with Trow sharing the driving.

To Patty he presented a more solicitous face, eager to hear about arcane points of property law and always mindful to compliment basic changes in her appearance. If this, along with an increasingly proactive position on daily life, did not solve the problems of their marriage, it did decrease her ammunition against him, and a renewed sense of tolerance grew between them. He considered going so far as inviting her parents, Larry and Lois, for the holidays, but in the end that seemed an action more drastic than even Trow would demand.

Once in a while the old Steven Armour felt the need to push back, but the thoughts and urges that rose up in resistance, things like driving to Hartford to find a White Castle or downloading Led Zeppelin cuts on his MP3, struck him as so unworthy that he banished them from his mind as fast as indigents were once cast out of Connecticut towns. Such wallowing, such relaxation, he knew, would inevitably take him back to the edge of the precipice where he'd so recently been camped. Still, the surviving impulse they represented balanced Trow's stern presence and Steven's temper, which had remained much hotter and quicker to boil than before. His whole life seemed to be rising to a boil, fired by John Trow and in ways Steven did not always understand. For example, as annoyed as he was with Nate for how he, like almost every other teen or teen-in-training, regularly brought sloth, greed, gluttony, and the four other deadly sins to life, he found himself irritated beyond what he knew was reasonable. That Nate continued to refuse his planned hike to Sage's Ravine sent him gnashing to his office to wonder at his son's shocking attitude at the same time that he thought back to that sweet and awful moment on Route 41 when they'd hugged each other after he'd nearly killed them both.

Putting on the kepi or the jacket, picking up one of the letters, was enough to bring Trow forward, but the letters also made Steven question where they were from. He assumed that Nancy Manskart passed them along, but how they'd come to her hands, how they'd survived the centuries, stirred his curiosity. The hunger that Trow roused in Steven extended to history; an insatiable need for detail drove him to do more and more reading about the Heavies, the War, and the times, as if Trow had to be fed with facts to continue existing. While he knew that perfect knowledge was impossible, Steven invested it with a Grail-like aura, the sacred mission of every re-enactor, the hard facts that legitimated their dreaming. Boxes from Amazon.com and B&N.com began to arrive regularly at the Armour home, and Steven traveled the bookstores of the area as well, reading late into the night, past Patty's bedtime, until the candles sank low.

One chilly morning, parkas already on the streets of Salisbury, Steven headed off to the Scoville Library to read the regimental history of the 2nd Connecticut in lieu of dishing out $200 to a dealer in Cornwall for his own. On Library Street, across from the Congregationalist Church, the Richardsonian gray Romanesque stone building maintained a hushed expectation of the considered life befitting the town's legacy of thriving, educated men. Walking in at a precise, military pace, Steven encountered no perky posters exhorting him to read, no excuses for harboring books in this computer era. Instead, a woman of indeterminate age, not unlike Mrs. Melton, looked him over from behind the desk. It had been years since Steven entered a library, living, as he had, among massive bookstores. Aside from the intellectual bouncer at the desk, no one turned from his or her reading to case him, no one nursed a double half caff latte, and he found the threat of an enforcing librarian both refreshing and purposeful. Though it appeared to be a solid block when seen from the street, Scoville Library had three wings: children's to the left, books straight back, and the card catalog, magazines, and local history collection in the common room to the right as you entered. Gentle murmuring voices came from two old men in the magazine section. Farther back, pages fluttered and occasionally one made a crisp snap as it was turned. The low sounds and minor movements around the room had the natural pace of leaves sighing around a small brook.

Without grades or papers weighing on him, Steven felt a rush of pleasure on opening the door to the two small rooms of the local history collection. The back room belonged to Mrs. Melton, who, as town historian, had an office there. He intended to visit before he left. The front had a long table on one side and a few desks on the other, where the books and folios were shelved. Old maps and photos of the town hung on the walls. Steven had allotted himself two hours, and unlike his quickie approach to research in college, he was in no hurry today. Lightly slipping pamphlets and crumbling books off the shelves, he savored the touch and smell of the old paper, the fading inks, the stiff folios that had to be carefully pulled apart with a delicate touch before they shyly yielded their words. Rubbing his hands, he sat down in a large and creaky wooden chair to read the regimental history.

Written by a man with some sense of style and irony, Theodore Vaill's *The History of the 2nd Connecticut Heavy Artillery* held Steven's attention as he turned the pages respectfully at their corners. At the end, in the regimental roster and underlined in thick pencil, was the name he'd been looking for: John Trow, Salisbury. Steven tapped his teeth in triumph. Something *was* odd, though. Why was Trow's the only name to have heavy pencil underlining? Unlike the other old margin notes penciled in over the decades, this mark appeared fresh; it even had tiny crumbs of graphite around the edges.

Steven found Vaill's one other mention of Trow in a paragraph indicting eighteen Mt. Riga men in the theft of a cow during their extended service in northern Virginia, the theft Trow had passionately disavowed in his letter. Among a list of Frinks and Ostranders, there was Trow, marked in the margin with the same sort of heavy graphite; not a simple swipe in the margin to aid a researcher's eye but an exclamation of sorts, a sign of excitement and almost, it seemed, a message to anyone who followed down this path of investigation.

Steven plowed up nothing else about Trow. He had obviously made it through the War; Steven knew that from the tombstone. Other pamphlets and registers from the period had no mention of him or any member of his family. The Trows must have drifted out of the running currents of the world and into an odd tidal eddy on the mountain, concerned only with their own survival. They became Raggies, swallowed up by the trees growing back on this northern stretch of the Appalachians. Skimming again through the regimental history, this time for more information on Kellogg, Steven came across another bold slash on the page alongside a mention of Kellogg's wife. Although she was unnamed in the book, Vaill placed her in Birmingham, Connecticut, for the duration of the War, nowhere near Alexandria, nowhere near the regiment. Nowhere near John Trow. And again, the thick line.

He sat back in the old wooden chair. Who was lying? Had history been rewritten to hide something unpleasant? Or was this no more than a bit of acceptable historical inexactitude, similar to his wearing a Civil War uniform in Riga Village? And who had made the marks? It had to be Nancy Manskart.

Steven picked up a history of Connecticut during the Civil War. In his hands, the book flipped open to the photo insert, from which a familiar face stared out at him; so familiar that Steven brought the book closer to his eyes to make sure that it was or, as the case might be, was not Kellogg. With his *oompah* band mustache, his saber and high boots, the real Elisha Kellogg stood, belly out, chest back, before a decorative background, bearing a remarkable likeness in face and stature to Walter Manskart playing the part. Whatever he thought of him, Steven had to admire the exactitude of Manskart's impression, down to the lugheaded, brutal stare and the curls under the kepi. Manskart had set a high standard. It was unnatural. Had Kellogg taken over Manskart in the same way Trow was taking over him?

Mrs. Melton sat in her office amid tall gray metal filing cabinets labeled with their contents, more old photos of the area, a large iron pot, and a stuffed fox. She greeted him without looking up. "Hello, Mr. Armour," she said, licking her index finger as she counted a pile of papers.

"Mrs. Melton. I started researching my person. You know, John Trow?"

Mrs. Melton continued flipping through the pages. "Umm-hmm?"

"Well, I'm not having much luck. The only place I've seen anything is in Vaill's book." Could she be more rude? he wondered. After she'd written a few lines of notes on a yellow legal pad, none of which seemed to have anything to do with him, Steven forced the issue. "I've heard you're the person to speak to about genealogy."

She nodded, then stopped. "How are your hands? I was quite concerned."

Steven held them up and waved them about some. "They're fine. Thank you for asking. That was a——"

"What did Mrs. Armour say?" Mrs. Melton's expression did not change, but its intensity did.

She'd been in the schoolhouse with him and Polly, and though his memory of the afternoon was inexact, anyone would have noticed the spark between them. A small and stupid lie here could grow into something deadly. "You know, I didn't even really mention it to her. I didn't want to upset her."

Parried for now, she moved on. "I'll send a request to the National Archives for military and pension records. That should tell us something." Mrs. Melton did not brighten at the prospect or at his thanks. "You never know what you'll find."

CHAPTER

2 2

WEIGHT LOSS ALSO BECAME AN ISSUE FOR STEVEN. Wary of growing larger than a fighting man of the period, he now snacked exclusively on fresh fruit and vegetables, and it was while he munched a stalk of celery one afternoon, stitching new bone buttons on his pants in the proper X pattern of the time, that the phone rang in his office, a distant sound, muffled by his mood. That the stitches needed to resemble the work of some 1861 German immigrant girl in a rush to finish her day's quota of pants had sent him into a deep and tranquil concentration, tightening some stitches, leaving others slack, making certain the X's weren't perfectly aligned. The third ring finally reached him, and he heard a woman's voice, sharp and brittle, when he tucked the receiver on his shoulder. "Steven Armour, please."

The third button on the fly had strayed too far left. He'd have to do it over, thought Steven. All said, though, the buttons looked good.

"Is this Mr. Armour? I have Dylan Petro and Amanda Telestratta for him."

If she had lived in the past, Dorothy would have been stoned as a witch. Steven squinted, forced himself out of the dream and back into the present. "Yes, Dorothy, it's me. I'm sorry." Draping his pants over the neat piles of paper and the growing stack of unread *BrandWeeks* on his desk, Steven leaned forward. It crossed his mind that he was about to get fired. He waited for the angina to start.

Dylan's hello came first, manly and heartfelt as all Australian things must be, then Amanda's, as frizzy and full of static energy as her curly hair. Such pep could only mean bad news. Instead of letting his head bang off the table, though, Steven, Trow's face hovering in his brain, sat up straight. He took a deep breath. While trembling might have made sense at that moment, Steven felt a warm certitude that life would go on. He could get a job. Doing something. Somewhere.

Dylan bounded on like a wallaby with a thousand clear miles of outback ahead. "How *ahhh* you, Mr. Armour? We've been thinking of you."

"You never write; you never call." Amanda laughed at her own joke.

Were they making fun of him? Dylan sounded very far away. "Are you in New York, Dylan?"

"I'm in Sydney. It's morning here. Amanda's in Omaha."

"Great."

"I have some contacts with the Olympics, so DP's taking a leadership role with on-line sponsorship. We're underwriting fifteen miles of the torch, and we're going to stream it live on the Your Life site."

"Wow."

Amanda waved her pompoms. "Isn't that amazing?"

But there was more. "The runner's an aboriginal. Very pretty, very Evonne Goolagong, if you know what I mean." Steven did; it meant she looked white. "She's going to wear a minnie-atour camera on her head." Dylan sounded very satisfied with himself.

"That's so great," said Amanda. "Torchcam."

Steven had trouble getting his corporate engine to turn over. He made slight sounds of interest until a big "Excellent!" finally burst out, but then the engine flooded. With no angina seemingly forthcoming, Steven realized at that moment just how sick he was of these people. Of course he'd been sick of them for a long time, yet until this moment envy and a perverse admiration had tinted his dislike, and he'd known that what he was most sick of was that he wasn't one of them. Now the insipid business trivia Petro prated helped to stiffen his spine. Could Dylan even lift a Springfield, let alone perform drill? Did Amanda have any concept of the causal web of political and economic factors that had led to the greatest crisis in American history, factors that still very much existed in the current climate? Probably not. Could they go into the past? Become another person? "How's all that IOC corruption business falling out?"

After a pause, Dylan said, "Fine. It'll all be fine," his voice less buoyant.

"Where's Jay?" Steven asked.

More silence on the line. Over the thousands of miles, Dylan and Amanda tried to exchange meaningful glances. Amanda went first. "Well, we wanted to let you know how much Bern liked Gerda's Kitchen." Even with Trow in his veins, Steven sagged a little in relief.

"Yes," said Dylan. "They're ready for a *total* redo on Gerda, and this is a fant*a*stic way to start. I mean, the bleeding Wall is down, mate. Time to get *Euro*. Was it your idea? Jay said you'd had a hand."

At least he'd tipped him *some* credit. Hemming and hawing, Steven scooted over, on his now annoyingly modern Aeron chair, to the kepi hanging close by off the doorknob and stuck it on his head. Why were the homecoming king and queen being so nice today? "You know, we put our heads together for a while."

Amanda continued. "How do you like it out there?"

"I love it."

"Dale's in-laws live out there somewhere. Litchfield. Does that sound right?"

"Yeah. Very close by."

The cyberprophet jumped back in. "You're living in the future. Ten years from now the whole *planet* will be doing what you're doing." It had been at least two years since most people saw that line for the utter bull-shit it was; the power would always remain at the office. Next, Dylan would be talking about implanting chips in people's brains. So what the hell did they want? Dylan's voice became serious. "Steve, how do you feel it's working with Jay?"

Amanda took over. "Are you happy with the communication? We'd love to hear more from you about things."

"Is Jay coming to you as a resource?"

The two had finally gotten their rhythm down. "That's sooo impor-tant. I saw your first memo, and you were right on target, especially the Smurf part. God, I loved the Smurfs, didn't you?" Amanda had to be only thirty-two or thirty-three to care that much about the Smurfs.

Dylan ignored her animated reverie. "How do you think the process on Food Wizard has gone? Been rocky, has it?"

Clearly they were tying a noose for Jay, and Steven was being asked to hold one end, or at least hand them some rope. More sour memories of that Taste Report returned, Jay's frantic, hissy e-mails. A little casual bitching could send him into the cornfields, and Steven couldn't resist. He was more sick of Jay than any of them, and it was time for him to go. But as he opened his mouth to seal his boss's fate, an image of Trow in uniform at the head of a long conference table, all suits turned toward him, flashed into Steven's mind. He drew out "Well, you know . . ." as long as he could. John Trow had no interest in office politics. Though by no means on Jay's side, Steven didn't want his job anymore, either. The bottom line was that, because of his hurt feelings over a Web site devoted to TV dinners, he was about to get someone canned, as pathetic and catty as that someone was. He imagined Jay sniffling on the floor of his fussy bachelor apartment, alone among his free weights, and decided he couldn't live with that. Not anymore. Caligula and his sister could get him a better title, but they couldn't get him into heaven. Be honest, he thought, and let the dust settle itself.

Without his usual calculation as to the effect of his words, Steven pulled the brim of his cap down low over his eyes, plopped his feet up on the desk, and let Trow speak. "I must be fair and state that Mr. Porter has devoted himself to Food Wizard with a constancy and drive no man among us can match. Yes, he was a hard case to start, and rough where a lighter touch might have produced the same, yet I blame his courage. I do. His courage. With such a long and difficult list of duties, I say that I myself could not have performed as he has. He has given every moment of his being to this task, and DP is the star by which he guides his ship."

Dylan and Amanda remained silent. Steven could tell it wasn't what they had expected to hear, but he felt clean, as if he'd spoken as an adult to other adults. If they wanted to lynch Jay, they'd have to do it without John Trow.

"Well." Dylan cleared his throat. "You've certainly had your coffee today."

"Really," said Amanda. "How did that go? The star by which . . . ?"

Steven picked up his pants from the desk. "This will all work out," he said, and began to rip the stitches out on the unruly button. "The right things will happen *this* time."

CHAPTER

23

SALISBURY ENTERED RECORDED HISTORY IN 1676, when a group of soldiers fell upon a band of Native Americans resting on the banks of the Housatonic River in what is now the northeastern section of the town, a spot called Weatogue. Fugitives from King Philip's War, the Indians were fleeing westward, but not quickly enough. The slaughter resulting from this sad encounter left anywhere from forty-five to nearly two hundred of them dead; no one knows the true tally. It is fitting that Salisbury announced itself with this massacre, its first entry in the annals of American blood and death. Indeed, this pleasant region, often compared with England's Lake Country or parts of Switzerland, not only existed but thrived for two hundred years, with its small towns devoted to the needs of war.

Now the site of a health club and an interior decorator's office, the Lakeville Furnace on Lake Wononscopomuc supplied a large percentage of the cannons used by the Continental Army as well as some of the links in a defensive chain once intended to be drawn across the Hudson River. The Green Mountain Boys, conquerors of Fort Ticonderoga, boasted a number of Salisbury men among their ranks, foremost their leader, Ethan Allen, one-time owner of the furnace. After their Minutemen, Salisbury's most famous unit in this war was Major Sheldon's Horse, a flashy unit of dragoons that drained town funds with its continual requests for fodder. The return on Salisbury's patriotic investment here, though, was questionable. Putting aside Sheldon's naïve, albeit innocent, use by Benedict Arnold as a messenger, and his court-martial for poor leadership and diverting funds, the fact remains that his unit's one notable engagement ended in a rout at the hooves of a severely undermanned regiment of English cavalry at Pound Ridge. Decades later, the War of 1812 brought more prosperity than casualties to Salisbury and especially to Riga Village, as the forge on the mountain produced the anchors for the *Constitution* and the *Constellation*, along with their chains, cannons, and other iron fittings.

Going on, it could be said that Litchfield County created the Civil War, birthplace as it was to John Brown and Harriet Beecher Stowe. While Salisbury bore no such direct responsibility, the town responded to the call and delivered hundreds of men. Newly forged cannons again rolled out of Salisbury by the hundreds, and the money rolled in, but local minds also busily devised new and imaginative ways of killing throughout the War years. The company Hotchkiss and Sons moved entirely into the arms business and created a shell that not only found extensive use in the Civil War, but served as a model for many of the shells that rained over battlefields for the next century and a half. To the west and just over the river in Falls Village, the Ames Iron Works invented a weapon that Saddam Hussein would have been proud of, a supergun that could launch a 56-pound shell five miles. The war ended before it could be deployed. Both companies tested their weapons against area hills, Hotchkiss on the very one that would later host the school funded by the family's wartime profits. For years, farmers and builders dug up unexploded shells. Blood bought acres of Salisbury's green grass and many of its oldest and seemingly most gentle flower beds.

This long and sometimes off-beat list of military involvement must also register the 2nd Connecticut's doomed charge at Cold Harbor, and that Saturday Walter Manskart had his troops before him, ready to tell the story. A brassy sun threw down a sharp, late afternoon light. While the men stood at rest, Manskart had slipped out of Colonel Kellogg in order to deliver his lecture on the events of June 1, 1864. In two ranks, the men grinned as if on a field trip, relieved from the niggling ardors of drill.

Manskart placed his hands at the small of his back. "Has anyone not read Vaill's account of the battle? No? All right then. As we know, Grant and Lee have encountered each other at the Wilderness, Spottsylvania, the North Anna River, and at a few other spots as the Union Army makes its way south. The Second has been called down from Washington and is now part of the Sixth Corps. On the thirty-first of May, the Second marches ten miles from Mechanicsville to a shabby collection of houses that locals call . . . Private Truby?" He pointed a stubby finger.

"Cold Harbor, sir!" shouted Bobby.

"Correct. Cold Harbor. Thank you, Private. Custer and Merritt are trying to hold on against Hoke with their cavalry at Old Cold Harbor. Warren's Fifth is to the north, facing Early. The Sixth relieves the cavalry and digs in. Next morning the Eighteenth Corps under Smith is sent to bridge Warren and Wright and face Anderson. The assault is called for two P.M. . . ."

Manskart let a dramatic moment fly by. Though fairly familiar by now with the details of the battle, Steven was addled by names and numbers. He sighed, focusing instead on the small red ribbon fluttering on Polly's coat. Today she had taken the field with them, and now stood a few paces behind her husband. Stomach rounder, head pitched forward, Manskart failed to capture attention the way Kellogg did, and a few pairs of visitors wandered away, having realized that no one was about to start shooting. Around the field, some pines and, it seemed, mostly birch to Steven's new treespotting abilities shook gently, and all of Riga Village felt full and warm. Trow had seamlessly come forward today; almost the moment Steven had locked the car doors, his mind had slipped to thoughts of the charcoal's progress, anticipated the tang of gunpowder on his tongue. Earlier, Polly had stopped by the charcoal pit and asked if he thought her ribbon fetching. Leaning on a shovel, Calamus had watched the whole thing, otherwise Trow would have surely made his feelings plain, but as it was he simply tipped his cap and offered an unsuspicious compliment. If they had been alone they probably would have kissed, and today no rush of guilt attended the thought.

"The regiment falls in at noon," continued Manskart. "At one, Upton's brigade hooks around to the left, between Truex and Eustis. Three battalions of the Second gather. The charge will now be at five P.M. Somewhere closer to six P.M., the regiment proceeds along a river bottom between Hoke and Kershaw that neither general has covered." His voice sped up, rising to a suitably heroic volume, the award-winning instructor now in action lifted his arm to wave a pretend saber. "Kellogg leads the Second *directly* into Clingman's position, enters a path through an abatis created by the Confederates, and approaches the Rebel breastworks! The first volley misses them." He hunched slightly, as if something had zipped by. "Then . . ." Manskart lowered his voice, shaking his head sadly. "Then a second volley comes from the flank and destroys the first battalion." He paused. Most of the men had closed their eyes, their chins set on their chests in reflection. His voice was near a whisper now. "Two hundred and fifty men shot in one minute."

After a moment of reflection, Manskart said, "This spring, our Company C shall represent the entire regiment." Suddenly, Kellogg took over, sucking up Manskart's gut. Eyebrows twitching, thick lips working under his mustache, he surveyed the men to determine, it appeared, whether they were ready to engage the enemy. Shouting out names, he broke the unit into four groups, representing a company of two hundred, then moved them so that they were one line. "Facing me, on the left! Wadhams's Company A, then Lewis's Company B, Spencer's Company K and Skinner's E on the right! Battalion, attention!"

The sudden shifting of bodies and Kellogg's random method for doing it left a few men confused, boyishly darting their eyes about while their spotless uniforms beamed in the sun. Burney half raised his hand. "Colonel? Sir? Are we still who we are? I mean, am I still Private Richardson?"

Kellogg's eyes widened. "Get back in line, you goddamned Jonah!" Burney slunk back to his place. "Battalion, attention!" He took a few long strides up the line, and stopped in front of Burney, Kucharsky, and Bobby. "Company A! At the left oblique . . . March!"

Despite the day's chill, Steven felt sweat trickling off his brow and down his back. He'd hardly had to move during Kellogg's maneuverings, so it wasn't effort that caused it, but he'd never had a fever come over him so quickly, had no sense of his body battling off some viral assault. Instead, it was an external heat beating on him, a choking heat, dry and full of dust, making his whole uniform heavy. Only moments earlier he had been full of energy, but now fatigue pulled at Steven, pulled at his arms and legs, and he slumped, his eyelids following, plunging him down toward the outlands of sleep. Had he eaten a bad pickle, he wondered. Caught the flu? Yet as the colonel moved the men around, the smell of dead leaves rose in his nose, the same smell he recalled from the day he got his rifle, the night he saw Trow's face the first time, and he realized in the darkness of his closed eyes that something else was happening.

When he opened them, Steven saw a summer's day, Kellogg at the front, saber raised and pointed at a distant line of trees. And yet these were not the birches of Riga. They were oaks, surrounding a different yet familiar field. He recognized the same battle scene, knew the men around him, knew immediately where he was. Knew immediately where he was about to go. It was Cold Harbor. Trow had led him back here, to this moment that he now understood was from Trow's life.

Trow pushed him forward, and before Steven could think to stop him, said loudly, "You are quite mistaken, *sir.*"

Kellogg blinked in amazement. "And how is that, Private Trow? How *exactly* is that? Enlighten us, please, you Raggie bastard."

"Company A hugs the left side, but those men do not form a curve as you describe; the line is straight." Steven stared into the distant trees as the words rolled out, Trow describing the scene coming fully to life, fear and anger rising, as they had before. "A few men of Company D creep back, but Lieutenant Hosford shows them courage at the end of his bayonet. That sets them." Burney and Bobby made small moves that straightened their short line while Steven wiped his face with a rough gingham handkerchief, the sweat still pouring off him. "A hot day. Eighties, I would say. Dawes?"

Everyone looked at Swan, who shrugged.

"Would you agree? Eighties? Damn curse of flies, too. We are dead from marching. Dust coats the trees, our clothing. The air reeks of it. Dust and dead leaves. Our parlor uniforms have taken a pasting, and I suppose I am glad of it."

Steven turned back to Kellogg, who from the look on his face was too surprised, too fascinated, to stop him. His voice took on a bitter edge. "In a typical show of jauntiness, you, sir, sport a straw hat into the theater of battle." Kellogg did not react. "A burial detachment dispatched some Rebels to Hades, but mostly what we've done all day is stand asleep on our feet. By five the minies were crashing into the trees, the branches flying down upon us. Some boys rallied then, like you Frotes. You two wept on each other's shoulders." Both Lummer and Jerry shuffled their feet and avoided their brother. "Until we are called." The words hung in the silent air. Steven could feel Trow pulling him somewhere deeper and farther away than Cold Harbor, to a dark place he did not want to visit. This was supposed to be fun, wasn't it?

"The colonel takes a branch and scribes our battle plan in the dirt. We are put into our battalions, then his speech. Oh, he is Henry on St. Crispin's day, he is! John Paul Jones!" His voice dropped into an exaggerated imitation of Kellogg's bluster, as he pointed in turn at Scobeck, Kucharsky, and Swan. " 'Every man in this army thinks you're nothing but bandbox soldiers! *Toy* soldiers! *Parlor* soldiers!' The devil himself has come to lead us to Hell, I think. 'Now we are called on to show what we can do at fighting!' you say. 'I shall be with you! Do not shoot until you are in the Rebel works!' " Steven could not hide his disgust. "Unfortunately you did not reconsider that." Kellogg puckered his lips.

"On we go, hungry, barely awake, forward out of the old works, across a field, and into new works dug by some other sorry regiment that's come before us. 'Knapsacks off,' you order. So knapsacks off it is. They are everything we are; our letters and likenesses, crumbs of food. We are mere bodies without them, and we are edgy, well knowing that. Sergeant Hyte bites the head off anyone who approaches. Colley, you stand your ground. Good man, you help Truby write his name on a piece of paper and pin it to his jacket."

But this had never really been about fun, had it? Steven wanted to stop for the day, wanted to be Steven Armour again. Shaking his head, he tried to find Emily in his mind, Patty and Nate, but all he could see was the battle. He looked at Swan. "Cal, I shook your hand for the last time . . ." Some of the men worked their eyes and nose, struggling to hold back tears. "My good friend. 'See you over there,' you say. Kellogg raises his sword and we go through a thin line of pines, across another field, a hundred and fifty yards, I'd measure, then more pines. That we are fighting at last—not playing at drill—thrills some for the pride of it. I know I smile when the sight of our clean blue uniforms clears the first pit of Rebels and again when our lines hold. We'd always suspected that we were fine soldiers. Not a Jonah in the boat." As much as he begged, Trow would not release him. With a twitch, he winked at Burney, and the soldiers of Riga stood taller, nodding to themselves.

"But this is not parade." The general blackness of fear opened, began to consume Steven in a way that victory or survival could not solve. "The minies start to fly." The words now rushed out of his mouth. "A bullet skims the colonel's arm. By God, you do not stop. You most resemble, with the colonel's permission, a goddamned ox. You bull ahead. The men understand what's happened and it fires them. They fight for *you* now."

He was nearly breathless as his panic merged with Trow's. "We head down a slope and splash along a thin stream. Thickets sit up on the slopes of both sides, underbrush or felled trees. The lines are fifteen or twenty yards beyond. It's about to happen. You point us toward an opening in the underbrush, and the men pour in. A Confederate says, 'Aim low and aim well.' "

Though he tried to turn away, Steven saw what came next, saw it even when he closed his eyes. "Then the world explodes. The Rebel line bursts into flame as if the seals had been broken and we go down. A moment passes, and we realize to a man that we've not been hit! The volley missed us! Kellogg, you rouse us to our feet and aim this mass of good men back toward the Rebel works. Then . . ."

Before the despair became total, it broke apart in Steven's eyes, collapsed into a shower of jagged images, an atonal blast of screams and thunder, with none of the regular drumbeats of march. Tears began to slide down his cheeks. He would see a face for a second, frozen in anger or awe at the sight of death, hear a voice quietly ask for its mother, nothing longer than a beat, coming from all sides, and he tried to describe them, reporting an event only he could see. "Colley, your head exploded like a watermelon." Scobeck winced. "Truby . . ." Everyone looked at Bobby. "Three in the stomach, but that did not stop the Rebels from shooting apart your body. You Frotes are to be commended for nearing the line, but . . ." Steven shook his head. Now Burney pointed to himself. "Richardson? A shot in the leg. They hit you as you were crawling back. Hyte, Qualls, no one could determine which minie took your life. You both went quickly; for that be grateful." He turned to Swan. "Calamus, good friend, part of your skull was shot off. Yet death had too many tasks to claim you with any haste. You ran forward, splashing blood as you went. The Rebels pumped bullets into the fallen to ensure their work."

And then he came to Kellogg, who stared at him as fiercely as the man staring at him in his vision. "You have your arm in your grasp when you turn back toward the Rebels. Then the minies shred you." They'd been looking at each other when it happened, when Kellogg went down, but he said nothing about that. Polly hid her face behind her fan. "Your wife is now a widow. I venture you'd dreamed of this moment since you first saw us on Litchfield green. Of course, you have yourself to blame. You volunteered us for this charge. Do you recall that, sir?"

For a few minutes no one said a word, until Kellogg growled, "Get back in line before I have you taken away from here." It was not clear whether he was speaking to Trow or to Armour, nor did it seem to matter anymore.

CHAPTER

2 4

PATTY OPENED THE LID OF HER COMPOSTING CONTAINER and dropped in the remains of Emily's french toast. She did so carefully, at arm's length, praying that nothing got on her silk blouse or the leather skirt because if it did she'd have to shoot herself with a gun and then change, which she did not have time to do because she had a conference call in fifteen minutes and it took ten minutes to get to the office, nor did she want to change, because this was her confidence outfit and they were meeting people from Home Depot today about the minimall. Since she hadn't been able to get to the dry cleaner this week, the wardrobe took a long step down after this.

At any given moment of the day, Patty Armour considered her life completely out of control, and while she might have enjoyed having the time to chew over the career blunders and personal failings of her spouse and herself, the day-to-day process of staying afloat consumed her more than regrets. Bailing out the lifeboat was more important than worrying about the sinking ship, and leaving clothes unwashed and papers unfiled struck her as traitorous, especially during the ten minutes before any departure. With so much flapping loose in the breeze of passing days, she constantly scrambled about, trying to tie a few things down so that it all didn't fly away, so that when she returned, it wouldn't be to a house filled with proof of her inability to maintain control.

She scattered some apple peels across the top of the filled bucket, tamped them down with a wooden spoon, and washed her hands, examining her nails and wondering when she'd be able to get a manicure. The last few weeks, Steven had taken to emptying the container every morning, along with the garbage, but today he'd been too busy barking at Nate for not finishing his math homework. Since his mountain playdate last Saturday, he'd been in a foul mood, sulking and claiming to be sick, though she could hear him shuffling papers in his office. On the other hand, she'd had to dash around the whole house looking for something to straighten, put away, or clean until she finally found this garbage situation in the kitchen. Steven had dealt with most of the pressing issues—Emily's permission slip to go to the Millbrook Zoo, calling Swan for another round on the second-floor lights, cleaning out the gutters, driving the kids to school.

Tugging the Hefty bag out of the garbage, Patty could feel the skirt on the backs of her thighs. Was it too short? she wondered. She always got around to asking herself that when she wore this skirt, gray leather, from Bendel's. It was getting old, but she could still pull it off, and not everyone could. When she wore it behind a desk or conference table, Emily, Nate, and Steven became her perfect family, the happy unit she described to business associates, this creaky house transformed into a lovely farm cottage, while all their attendant issues hid behind the façade of her capability, of being the person she'd meant to be. If some guy got thrown by it or thought she was a pushover, then the joke was on him. And with these boots? Amazing. As she tied up the bag, Patty decided that she absolutely *had* to get a manicure at lunchtime. How was she supposed to walk into a meeting feeling like she could be in charge of a multimillion-dollar real estate transaction with the evidence that she couldn't keep her own self in shape staring up at her from her hands?

She plopped the bag next to the door. There was always too much to do. How unfair was it that no one gave a shit what Steven looked like? And there she was with circles growing under her eyes, darker every day since they'd moved out here to hit bottom in relative privacy. At least his face had tightened recently, displayed some knowledge of their diminishing position. He no longer seemed a permanent liquid, poured over whatever chair, sofa, or pillow he was lying on. Since Saturday he'd been sleeping badly, too, lying in bed awake, perfectly still. Totally annoying. Sleep apnea? A bad sign if it was; heart disease. He needed more exercise.

Only the newspapers were left. As she stacked them up, one of Steven's catalogs fell on the floor, a Xeroxed thing, stapled and folded, from some place called Curtsy & Co. A line drawing, or more likely a tracing, of a woman in a hoop skirt holding a fan decorated the front. How could her husband be involved in this moronic hobby? Although it had not escaped her that Steven's new attitude began around the same time he started trekking up to the top of that mountain. This weekend even his voice struck her as changed, more definite somehow; the sentences turned down instead of rising querulously at the end. She flipped through the pages of smudged illustrations of antique clothing, copied over so many times that they'd lost their sharpness, coy and corny descriptions that made her nostalgic for the J. Peterman catalog. This thing had the painful look of a menu from an imitation Gay '90s soda fountain. Ankle boots, dress patterns, paste jewelry, corsets.

Four or five pages, in fact, of corsets. The drawings here were small and old, the women topped with large tresses of black hair and carrying, so it seemed, a few more pounds than one would think of a model having nowadays. Their waists looked as if someone were pinching them together, sending the extra flesh up to their stout necks and out to their arms. Halfway to purdah, she thought, scanning through the rest of the foundations. Halfway to not having to pay the bills and think about the mortgage. All of these corsets expressed a silent desire to be controlled, taken care of, provided for. Swept away. As she stood there next to the big Hefty bag, now dangerously late for her call, trembling with the usual imploding tension that would in a minute or two explode and fling her out the door, the idea struck Patty that being swept away once in a while might be a good thing. Not forever; just for an hour or two. Unfortunately, it had been a while since the sight of Steven had made her feel all that runny. There'd been a stir, though, the day they'd fought about the gun. He'd been wearing that asinine uniform. What was that all about? Maybe it was because he'd stood his ground for once.

She took one last look at the corsets—the Elise and the Heather, all loved and provided for and safe—then dragged the whole mess of garbage and newspapers out to the driveway.

CHAPTER

2 5

A MASSIVE STORM SWELLED THE HOUSATONIC the next few days and turned the trickle at Falls Village back into the wild torrent that once drew nineteenth-century tourists. Up on the mountain, as Hurricane Floyd finally moved on, Steven, Swan, Lummer, and Japhet Beck made an emergency effort to preserve what remained of the sputtering, smoking mound. Joe Swan shoveled open a vent in the hope of drying out the saturated wood.

"You got a lot of guys thinking hard," Joe said. "Like maybe we're re-enacting the wrong part of the story. I mean, by that battle, the Second was in artillery reds, but Kellogg has us in infantry blues. That's basic shit we need to think about. He volunteered us, huh?"

Finally released by Trow, Steven nodded but did not speak. He tossed more dry leaves onto the mound. After his performance, he'd gone straight to bed with a phantom sore throat, exhausted from the experience and disappointed that no letters on creamy thick paper had greeted him when he opened his knapsack. His acceptance of Trow—whatever "Trow" was—lost part of its sunny, self-improvement quality, and a cloud settled over him as he wondered that night, lying in bed, where it had all come from. Had he stitched together the dozens of accounts he'd read, decorated them with some local color, or was he really channeling another kind of being? As the days passed and the battle's sad residue did not, he asked himself whether he'd gone too far.

"Listen, John," said Swan, "is there any way I can talk you up here for one night? Beck's starting to bitch about having to do it all by himself. I'll lend you a liner, blankets, whatever else you need. Whaddya say? Riga needs you, John."

As if knowing he'd nearly pushed his host too far, Trow had largely left Steven to his own devices after the vision of Cold Harbor, yet Swan's appeal roused Trow to fling words like *commitment* and *responsibility* through Steven's mind. "How cold does it get up here?"

Swan smiled. "Not so bad. Beck usually packs some antifreeze."

A few days later, with Patty free and the kids not going anywhere, Steven packed his courage into his knapsack and rolled up Swan's liner to camp out for a night with Japhet Beck next to the charcoal pile. After seeing the battle of Cold Harbor, virtually experiencing it, Steven found himself unable to abide the starched blue of his uniform, so he decided to wear it to the mountain for some seasoning. For the hell of it, he threw in his gun and thought about the three live bullets, too; after all, people had been seeing bears in the area, but he dumped them back in the drawer, to be disposed of as soon as he got back.

Weekdays were slow at Riga Village. Although the park was open seven days a week, few people showed up between Monday and Friday, and once again Steven had the lot to himself as he drove up in the dusk. His coffee can banged against his cartridge box as he searched for Kim Bevins, a.k.a. Japhet Beck. A burly, bearded man in his early thirties, Beck and his attitudinal, club-footed impression provided a highlight for many Riga Village visitors, none of whom realized that he was not doing an impression at all. At first Steven had blamed his father for the bad Labor Day experience with Beck, but he had seen many more like it in the weeks that followed. Beck wore the costume and answered to the name; every other duty he performed as the staff anthropologist, paid by the Park Service. Though he tried to dodge any one-on-one interactions, kids especially clung to the idea that he was a real-life blacksmith, not a museum display, and his bristling retorts to their questions only sparked more interest. All the volunteers, Steven included, gave him wide berth; rumor had it that Beck drank, and the one person who'd ever complained about it had had her quilting demonstration shut down by OSHA.

Firelight poured out from the furnace building, and Steven, reassured by all the light, found Beck there, in an arched alcove in the furnace shaped like the entrance to a cathedral, around the corner from the hearth door. Each of the three sides that did not open onto the hearth had one of these shallow brick niches, and here sat Beck, in a wooden chair, eating a cold pork chop as he read *Lingua Franca* by the light of a candle, snug inside his recess. The alcove, seven feet high at its opening, graded down quickly to a two-foot arch at the back that reminded Steven of the little door in *Alice in Wonderland*. Still learning his options for facial hair hygiene, he took note of how Beck rubbed his beard on his shoulder and upper arm as he rose, then wiped his greasy hand on his shirt. An industrious and furry mammal all ready for the winter, Beck patted the wall. "Nice and warm," he said. "Feel it."

In no hurry to go outside, Steven encouraged the founder to finish his dinner, but Beck hid away his tin foil and his empty bottle of Fresh Samantha, and the two plunged into the darkness of Mt. Riga, aiming at the large black smoking mass a few dozen yards away and the healthy campfire beside it. The rain had caused the mound to burn unevenly, but there'd be enough charcoal for the Harvest Festival if they took good care of it the next few nights. As they walked, a three-quarter moon popped out of the clouds to throw silver on the pile and everything around it, casting the stark black outlines of trees against the lighter sky. Halloween was coming, thought Steven. Emily would want to be Barbie; Nate had probably worn his last costume. He couldn't see his breath, but the chill cut into his uniform. Beck, who had slipped on an orange down vest, stared at Steven's outfit.

"You gonna be warm enough?"

"I think so. Just want to bang it all up a little. Make it real, you know?" Steven walked the perimeter of the pit, sniffing at the white smoke as it danced into the sky. The rich smell made him think of the days his father had raked up a massive pile of leaves, then burned it in the street while he read him stories about Indians or the Chicago fire. Those days were so long gone; he would never be nine again, never be a boy again. As Steven watched more lines of smoke gutter up from the circle of charred wood, he and Beck exchanged nods that all looked fine and retired to the campfire.

Beck landed with a thud and, once settled, reached into his vest pocket. "Do you ever have a sip?" he asked as he cracked open the top of a new pint of Canadian Club.

"I will, thanks." Steven took the inaugural pull, then rolled Swan's liner out across the damp ground.

After a drink and a long, wordless expression of pleasure, Beck said, "I have a doctorate in anthropology from Fairfield." He picked a shred of pork from between his teeth.

"Really?"

"Yup. Did my thesis on fuel production in Iron Age Denmark. Spent a year on a bog re-creating an Iron Age settlement." Between the limp and the pork chop grease on his thick features, now glowing in the flames, Steven definitely detected Neolithic in his companion. "Made this place look like New York City."

They each had another sip and settled into the crackling coming from the campfire, the glassy sounds of the wood shifting in the pit, the constant rush of water from the wheel at the forge. The comings and goings of the moon made the smoke appear suddenly, then disappear again into the darkness as the quiet sank on Steven, along with the sense of malevolence he'd had up here that first day with the family. Many times he'd joined his brother, Jerry, and probably even his father in the family game of peering over the edge of the existential abyss, contemplating that vast, sucking maw of nothingness. Yet the disquiet he now felt had intention, dragging Steven to a point of darkness the way he'd been dragged to Cold Harbor the Saturday before. He was not feeling particularly Trow-like; it was as if Trow had sent him up here alone. Or maybe the pit brought back sour memories of lonely nights with James that Trow himself had hidden. Most of the stars were hidden behind passing clouds. Vulnerable to whatever hid in the trees and the darkness, he leaned forward into the warmth of the fire.

"Jesus, it's dark up here."

Steven felt as if something might happen to him tonight, not by empty chance, but because he was who he was. He considered whether he was being pushed around now by Trow instead of by Patty or Petro, and though he dismissed the thought as ungrateful, his inability to shed Trow the other day had scared him, almost as much as Trow's absence unnerved him right now.

Beck laughed. "Have another drink. I don't think the Raggies liked it much either. They were all either drunk or stoked on opium most of the time." Steven kept looking toward the furnace, where the fires had begun to dim. He tossed on another piece of wood and sparks flew up. Beck lit a cheap cigar. "This is a terrible place. Did you know that?"

Fearing a long night of on-the-job complaints, at a time when he'd be happy never to say the name *Dilly-Perkins* again, Steven came to Riga's defense. "I don't know. I like it up here. I think you Park Service guys have done a great job."

Cigar smoke merged with the other smoke. "That's not what I mean. I mean this is a terrible place. Like terrible things have happened here."

This was not what Steven wanted to hear. "You mean Baby Rock?"

The whiskey splashed again in the bottle. Steven had planned to stop once he felt more fuzzy than scared, but Beck was going for all the gusto. "Oh, man, there's more than Baby Rock. You could do a fucking dissertation on it. I've heard that at least two of the houses up here are haunted. That one by the store, for one. The bedsheets come down by themselves."

Oh my, thought Steven, how very scary that must be. Did the ghost leave mints, too? "Well, that's not so terrible."

"Heard of the Ancram Screechers? All the land on the New York side all the way to the Hudson once belonged to a guy named Livingston. Anybody who squatted on his land or couldn't pay their rent, he had a private army hunt 'em all down, burn 'em inside their homes. Raggies said that a good, strong north wind brought the screams of the families murdered by Livingston's men across the top of the mountain."

Beck let that hang there for a minute as an errant current of wind sent the smoke wavering, then kept going. "There's another story about a girl who's baby-sitting for a bunch of kids up here while the parents are off, I don't know, taking opium or something. Anyhow, she's watching the kids, and suddenly she sees a little girl running through the yard with a huge bloody cut on the side of her head. The kid runs to the graveyard right over there"—Steven had been trying to put the cemetery's prox-imity out of mind—"and the baby-sitter chases after her, thinking that it's one of the kids, right? So she sees the kid jump over this huge open grave. When she lands, a little one opens up and swallows the kid up. And it wasn't one of the kids she was watching. Whaddya think of that?" Beck asked as he offered the bottle again.

Steven took another shot in the hope of bringing on the fuzziness sooner. "So, do you watch football? Did you see the Giants game last week?" He hadn't, but he felt an urge to cuddle up with the remote and a bag of Tostitos.

"There *has* to be something fucked up with this place." Beck's head wobbled as he stared into the fire. The Canadian Club had definitely loosened him up. "I mean, at most a couple of hundred people lived up here at any time, and they created all these disgusting stories. All these stories about dead kids. Listen to this one . . ."

"They need a quarterback," Steven told Beck. "Simms at least had a fucking head on his shoulders even if his arm sucked."

". . . Some orphaned kid gets sent to work for this guy with a bad temper. One day the kid pisses the guy off, so the guy whacks the kid on the head with a chain." At this detail, Beck began to laugh. "He fucking *whacks* the kid with a chain and kills him."

Steven wanted this to be over. "Yeah?"

"Nice guy, right? So he's got this dead body on his hands. He buries it in a corner of his farm. After a while the dogs find it, dig it up. They're dragging bones around and shit, and now all the people on the mountain know about it. So one day the guy's riding his wagon and the ghost of the kid jumps out into the road, scares the shit out of the horse. The horse flips the wagon and kills the guy."

"Maybe somebody threw a rock at the horse or something."

Beck took a couple of puffs. "Maybe. Maybe not. There's another version of this one. I read it in a book by the guy who owns the bookstore in town. The orphaned kid still works for those people, but the kid has a fight with the other boy, the real son, over oatmeal or some stupid shit like that, and the real son throws the hot oatmeal in the kid's face and kills him."

"How do you kill somebody with hot oatmeal?"

"I don't know. Burn 'em or something. But wait. They bury the kid, and then a few weeks later they dig him up and turns out he wasn't really dead. You know how they know?"

Steven could see Beck's teeth as he grinned. "I don't know. How?"

"Because the kid had eaten off his own shoulder."

Having reached a sort of Grand Guignol climax, they both laughed. "That's fucking disgusting," Steven said as he continued to laugh. The smoke guttered and twisted in the moonlight. As soon as he stopped, the woods became very quiet. He'd seen a ghost once. He wondered if he should tell that story.

"And there was a ghost that used to stand on the side of the road down near the parking lot," continued Beck. "He'd hold his own chopped-off head in one hand and in the other he had a letter and he'd ask people to mail it. Or with Baby Rock, some people said that the babies the guy killed are actually buried underneath it." The tips of long shadows from tombstones in the cemetery reached where they sat. Beck stuck the cigar into the mud. "I think it was probably this phosphorescent moss they used to have. That and the opium and all the smoke. It looks weird in the moonlight." The anthropologist stretched out in the grass. "Hey, do you mind taking the first shift? Until twelve? Wake me if the smoke thins out too much." Before he closed his eyes, he handed Steven the flask. "Here. Kill it."

As much as Steven wanted to keep the blacksmith up, Beck's snores signaled that it was too late for that. Steven sat up straight and listened to the sounds in the woods, saw the clouds slide over the moon and take the mountaintop into black. He sang a mixed bag of Elvis Costello and Rolling Stones numbers, finished off the last inch of whiskey, and then he was alone. He forced thoughts into his mind—Walter Payton high-stepping; watching Northwestern win the Rose Bowl with Little Nat under his arm; Mike Royko getting drunk and telling stories at one of his parents' cocktail parties; his mother, who loved the fall so much— yet the darkness quickly took them all, and he wondered in a blurry way which was worse, being able to see the shadows or not being able to see them. Nothingness soon bent a steely fear around him, and he shivered, the cold conducting the sense of personal menace directly into his bones. Was he being watched? Frozen prey, the shivers now coming in waves, Steven Armour felt he was draining into the ground, hollowing with fear, with his helplessness in the face of not just this, but of every-thing. At least at Cold Harbor he hadn't been alone. But tonight Trow was nowhere to be found.

As he wiggled his toes on the edge of major depression, Steven re-membered that his rifle was in the car. His wife. If he had that in his hands, he thought, huddling closer to the fire, he could blow the shit out of all this scared-of-the-dark nihilism. Hell, even without the bullets he could shoot a fucking bear if one came through; black powder could do enough damage to seriously maim it.

As he got on his haunches and considered dashing to his car, he looked into the smoke and saw on the other side of the gray curtain a long shape not torn apart or billowed by the air: a face. A long, bearded face, with eyes looking right at him.

Heart pounding, muttering curses over and over to himself, Steven grabbed about for something to hold.

You don't exist without me, Trow said. Any good in you right now is because of me.

Putting a hand on the whiskey bottle, Steven grasped it by the neck and raised it level with his ear like a hatchet. He squinted into the dark again. The face was gone. It had been Trow. If it had been anything at all.

CHAPTER

26

"Armour! Wake up! Wake up *now!*"

Morning light seeped through Steven's eyelids as he tried to ignore Beck's voice. He sounded pissed. Whether he'd fainted, passed out from the whiskey, or had fallen asleep, Steven didn't know, but he realized he'd never woken Beck up. The world had gone black after the face disappeared.

"Armour! Get up! Your daughter's just had some kind of seizure! They're taking her to the emergency room in Sharon right now! Get the fuck up!"

The doors swung open, and Steven charged into the emergency room. Two strides in, his hard-soled shoes cracked across the hum of brave chatter and consultations. Every head in the room turned to him and he stopped, the puzzled looks rebuffing his advance, Steven's puzzlement as deep as those who stared at him. His eyes flew to all the corners of the room. Where was Emily? Was she alive? Which one of those people was her doctor? Fear blocked his words.

A woman screamed. "He's got a gun! Oh, Christ! He's got a gun!"

With ginger steps, a portly male nurse in white leather clogs and a head of newly seeded hair plugs edged toward Steven. Seemingly thrilled to put his crisis intervention skills and hours of *ER* watching into practice, he held up one hand in surrender and pointed to Steven's rifle with the other. "Sir! Put down your weapon! You must put down your weapon!"

The dramatic, demanding tone drew a sneer from Steven; he hadn't even realized he had the rifle in his hand until the nurse pointed it out, so panicked had he been since Beck had woke him up. He'd raced here to

Sharon entirely numb, had driven without thinking, his brain throbbing with possibilities from a dead child to crushing hospital bills, none of which he was prepared to handle. He could not handle this. The woman screamed again at Steven's expression, and Nurse Hero, after an angry glance at the hysteric, announced that everyone must remain calm. Using a softer, more careful tone, one reserved for the dangerous, he turned back to Steven. "Sir. Please. Put down your weapon."

A monitor gave off a regular beep. The lights of computers and phones and machines blinked on and off. An incubator with a neon orange sticker verifying its Y2K compliance sat empty outside a door, and Steven imagined a baby in there on New Year's Day, still alive amid blackouts and chaos. Was the world really about to end? He stood there, helpless and dirty before all this technology, all this science that he had no understanding of in the twentieth century, let alone in the nineteenth, technology over which he had no control. He did nothing of value with his life. He could not save his own daughter, could not even speak. Where was Emily?

"Sir. If you do not put down the weapon, I will call security."

But the words did not come. He'd been pitched down that dark cliff of helplessness, he knew it, and he was dragging Emily behind him. Then a sincere groan of pain—sexless, ageless—came from a room to his left. It began high, full of hope that someone could do something, a call for attention, and quickly slid into a low surrender to despair. Such a private sound made so publicly, it unnerved Steven further. The image of a large tent sprang to his mind. Its canvas flaps spread open to reveal dozens of screaming, weeping men; blood-splattered doctors; soldiers groaning into their deaths. Trow walked among them, calling out names in search of men he knew, anyone, any face from home. Was there no one left? Had he been the only man to survive? He *had* to find someone else from the 2nd. Leaning his gun against a wall, Steven let the words burst out of his mouth, "Emily Armour! Where is Emily Armour! I'm the father of Emily Armour!"

Another nurse, this one an elderly woman in an aquamarine smock, lunettes hanging around her neck from a summer-camp lanyard, walked in front of Nurse Hero, already wiping his brow and accepting congratulations, and guided Steven to a desk. "Yes. She's fine now. She's sleeping," the woman said. "We just need you to fill out a couple of forms first. Your wife was too . . ." She smiled in a consoling way. "Insurance, you know. We're out of network for you."

"I must see her."

"Yes, of course, but this is most important now."

He took a deep breath, scribbled his name and address half a dozen times, and followed her down a short corridor to the room. Emily appeared tiny, lying in the hospital bed. Eyes closed, breathing through her open mouth, she looked dead, and Steven would have thought she was had Patty not been beside her, softly brushing damp coils of hair off her forehead. A tall metal stand full of spokes stood next to the bed, a medical Christmas tree, its one ornament a large IV bag connected to his daughter by a long piece of tube. Steven winced inwardly when he saw how they'd taped her hand to a board, the needle in the back of her hand. A doctor in light blue scrubs and blond anchorman hair, considerably younger than Steven and Patty, checked the IV bag, looked back at his clipboard. He had a banana in one of his pockets. "Mr. Armour?"

Patty looked up as soon as the doctor spoke, and though her eyes widened when she noticed the uniform and the clanking bits of military hardware, she went straight to her husband and began babbling. "Oh, Jesus, Steven. I was making eggs and Emily was in the living room watching that fucking *Pokémon* show and everything was fine. And then the next thing Nate's yelling for me—" she imitated his voice with a falsetto, as if Nate was still a little boy—" 'Mommy! Mommy! Something's wrong with Emmy!' " Patty must have been half dressed for work; she wore a bulky wool skiing sweater with a pair of crisply pleated black slacks, makeup done, but hair uncombed. "I went in and she was on the rug, having some kind of convulsion."

Steven put his arm around Patty. "Are you our doctor?"

"I'm Dr. Turner."

"That is not the question I asked you. My question to you is whether or not you are *our* doctor. If you are the doctor in charge of this child."

Dr. Turner folded his arms across his chest and ran his tongue along his teeth. "Yes. I am the doctor on duty right now in the emergency room."

"Are you a *real* doctor or a resident?"

Turner closed his eyes in a deliberate show of patience. "I'm a resident, but I assure you that—"

"When will an actual doctor attend to us?"

As Steven spoke, the doctor had registered his uniform and, still harvesting tales for that book he was sure he'd just *have* to write someday, he lost his defensive edge in the interests of good material. "Dr. Primati from pediatric neurology administered the EEG"—he pointed out the door—"that we just came back from. He will decide whether your daughter will require overnight observation. Right now she's sleeping."

"Has she been given any medication?"

"Dr. Primati prescribed Dilantin, which is an anticonvulsant, and Valium."

"Has anyone ventured a diagnosis?"

"It seems at this point that your daughter had a grand mal seizure of some sort. It's interesting that she was watching *Pokémon*, because there was an incident in Japan when thousands of children went into seizures during a certain episode." Dr. Turner's eyes grazed once again over Steven and his uniform, then past him, toward the interesting story he'd have for dinner tonight. "Are you an actor? Or—?"

"No, I'm not." Steven gave no further explanation. "With all due respect, *Doctor*," he said, with a sarcastic stress on the word, "*Pokémon* doesn't appear to be the entire problem, does it? Have the results from the EEG arrived yet? Are there any more tests?" Patty stood slightly behind Steven, not commenting on his brusque manner.

"There was some activity in the frontal lobe, yes."

"And that signifies . . . ?"

"Well, let me ask you both a few questions." Dr. Turner snapped a pen, happy to turn the tables for a minute until he could enjoy his snack banana. "Does your daughter have problems concentrating? Does she ever seem to freeze for a minute or two?"

Steven and Patty looked at each other and answered *yes* simultaneously.

The doctor nodded gravely. "That may point to your daughter having experienced a long series of petit mal seizures. An odd stimulus like that television show could have sparked a full-blown grand mal like the one she had this morning." He paused. "My guess is that she has an epileptic condition, but let's wait for Dr. Primati to make that decision."

As Patty's face crumbled, the older nurse came in. "Mr. Trow?"

Steven turned. "Yes?"

"You forgot your daughter's date of birth here."

Steven took the form, then said to Turner, "I must see Dr. Primati. As soon as possible."

Patty looked up at him, straight and bearded, determined not to take no for an answer. She ran her hand up and down his back, finally lacing her fingers in his, and buried her face on Steven's shoulder. "Why weren't you there?" she cried.

It wouldn't have mattered if I had been there, thought Steven. It only mattered if John Trow was. He's the one in charge now.

CHAPTER

27

LATE FRIDAY AFTERNOON, THE SUN GOING DOWN, Steven sat on the front
steps with Emily under the paper pumpkins and ghosts taped to the
screen door, blowing bubbles into the dark swiftly approaching from the
east. The day had been calm on the surface, as they all must be from now
on, he told himself. He watched Emily as she dipped the wand and raised
it to her lips. She crossed her eyes a little and blew a crop of small bubbles off into the sky. A few larger ones hung and bounced briefly in the
air, before sinking to the grass. The one thing Steven remembered from
Professor Fosgarn's senior seminar in European history came back to
him now: revolutions usually take place once things begin to improve.
Emily looked up at him. "Where are the turkeys, Daddy?"

Steven shrugged. What is it like when you disappear, he wanted to
ask her. Where do you go? "Maybe they're hiding because they know
Thanksgiving's coming soon."

They'd been doing this for twenty minutes; dozens of resilient bubbles had collected on the plants along the house, atop the brown glaze of
pine needles that had collected in drifts, and shimmered now in the last
flares of the sun. The soapy sheen of less successful ones darkened a
patch of grass before them. He patted his shirt pocket, felt the small envelope that had arrived that morning, that he'd carried with him all day.

After a night in the hospital, Emily had come home with a prescription for Ethosuximide, which made her a little dizzy and tired, and a
new no-television rule that she was a little too dizzy and tired to care
about. Patty had hit on the bubbles, an old favorite of Emily's, as a low-
impact diversion. Dr. Primati, a tall, elegant man with slicked-back hair
and the manners of an Italian courtier, advised that the whole family
simply resume their normal lives, a recommendation that depressed
Steven. Their normal lives were what had caused Emily's problem, and

Nate's and Patty's and his. Their normal lives were what he had been desperately trying to escape. Since their return home, they'd coddled Emily every moment, and rightly so, but Steven and Patty now moved thickly through their "normal life" as if they were under water or staggered by heavyweight blows. Nothing was as important as Emily's condition, yet since it was the cure, they performed every trivial aspect of "normal life" with the seriousness of a Japanese tea ceremony. Only two days in, what was left of Steven was suffocating.

Eager to read the note again, he slipped two fingers into his pocket as Emily dipped her wand, took an extra deep breath, and produced three perfect bubbles, which rode away quickly, making their escape. She popped up to dash after them, waving her arms in the manic fashion Steven was accustomed to from her. From the door behind him Patty's voice nearly shrieked out, "Honey, slow down! Take it easy! Don't get excited!"

His hand shot back to his side. He hadn't even known Patty was there. As soporific as the bubbles were, they had a meditative quality, and his wife had jolted the scene with electricity. The screen door squeaked open and Patty sat down beside him, the same place she'd been every moment of the last few days, as if Dr. Primati had chained her to him. While slowing down, Emily continued skipping and blew a few more bubbles as she went, like a piper up on toe. Steven could feel Patty shaking. She couldn't stop herself. "Emmy, honey. The doctor said to relax, right?"

Emily stopped and put her hands on her hips. "Mommy, he didn't say I couldn't move."

The mature bearing, her daughter's attempt to stake out some ground, stopped Patty, who mumbled for her to slow down because dinner would be ready soon. She spoke softly into Steven's ear. "Why did this happen? How long has this been going on and we haven't done anything about it? This kills me." As large and soul-searching as the questions were, Patty had been asking them constantly for two days and was no nearer to an answer. Had it happened when Emily had chicken pox that time, when he was working on that goddamned Alte Zeit report? Some other moment of less than full parental attention? He was losing interest in the cause. Whichever room he wandered off into, Patty would find her way there and ask the questions again, haunt him with his inability to answer her, to change anything. He would hold her, and she would calm down for a moment as he held his breath, as if he was bearing up both their weights.

Most of all, Steven wanted to run up to his office and read once more the note burning in his pocket. Written by Polly to John Trow, all it said was, *"When I see you next, it shall be to give myself to you. I shall close the wound."* He wanted to hide among the books and articles piled up in the room, imagine Polly comforting him as he comforted Patty. He wanted to do it right now as he felt himself collapsing into his own thoughts and body, his shoulders hunching as he remembered how he had frozen in the emergency room, had found himself without words or action in the face of his daughter's condition. Only John Trow had saved him, saved all of them, with the appearance of strength, if nothing else. And Steven had to continue smiling and consoling; Trow allowed nothing less, and more than once Steven had felt himself shrinking while Trow assumed his duties. He had a physical need to be in Riga Village as soon as possible. To sink into Trow's life and receive the comfort meant for him.

Emily came back to the steps. "Where's my Barbie costume?"

The Harvest Festival was tomorrow. Patty grimaced. "Well, honey, I don't know. I don't think we should go." She turned to Steven. "You, too. I don't think you should go tomorrow."

Both father and daughter reared back, and tears began to fall from Emily's eyes. He had to get up to Riga tomorrow. He had to see Polly, had to live the letter. "The doctor said she'd be fine. That there was every chance she'd never have another . . ." His voice trailed off. Which sounded better: convulsion, fit, or seizure? Though Emily had experienced it, Patty and Steven could not bring themselves to say any of the three before her. "We're supposed to do whatever we would normally do, and we would normally go to the Harvest Festival. When's Nate coming home?" Nate was off with Paul and Paul's brother; a car crash waiting to happen.

Irritated, Patty snapped back. "I don't know. Whenever." She bit her nails as Emily stomped off, wailing now, her tears wavering between sincere and stagey. "I think it's crazy to go."

Like the bubbles, the sound of Emily's sobs floated off into the hills to be heard everywhere. "I wanna be Barbie! Mommy won't let me be Barbie!"

Patty jumped off the steps, her voice rising. "Honey, stop it. Daddy and I are talking about it." But Emily would not stop and Patty's temper rose, too, and in a moment Patty had yelled at her to please shut up and Emily had screamed a scream that would have attracted a child welfare agency in a more densely populated area, and both stood now in the grass, inconsolably weeping.

A light breeze ripped bunches of golden leaves off a thicket of five sweet birch trees Steven had been watching for the last few weeks. Their leaves did not simply drop; they flittered about like butterflies nearing a field, dancing and turning until the pretense of life left them, and they fell into a bright stain across the road. Two days ago the trees had been rounded bursts of gold; now their thick black trunks and spiny branches had begun to show.

His jaw resting in his hands, Steven swiveled away from the scene of Patty trying to embrace their sobbing child, toward the door, where a face met his. In one of the glass panes surrounding the door was a bearded man, sad and angry. ". . . *it shall be to give myself to you.*" Ready for action. It was John Trow.

This time, though, the face did not disappear in the fading light. Steven stared more closely into the glass and realized he was looking at himself.

CHAPTER

2 8

ATOP MT. RIGA, THE FOREST BLAZED into so many shades and shapes and combinations that broad words such as *beautiful* and *magnificent* expressed nothing; indeed, the only way to capture the thousands of discrete instances of wonder in any satisfying manner before they slipped away into vague memories of *beauty* and *magnificence* was to speak their details, to remark how that silver maple, half blood red and half citrus orange, seemed to explode from the ground, how the yellow leaves shooting off the top of that tall slippery elm looked like sparks off a lick of fire, to hear the dissonant cries of a hundred Canadian geese swirling overhead as if one were sitting in a concert hall.

Mrs. Melton tied off a final stalk of corn alongside the schoolhouse door and rearranged into a more pleasing display the three yellow and green gourds at its foot. A lifelong New Englander, she knew how to enhance these precise and achingly transitory moments of fall with small human details— the carved pumpkins, the smell of a baking pie, the assemblage of Indian corn—that showed how man can make practical use of passing beauty. Such relative measures, such framings, and the town's snowy white buildings seen against the wild colors of the trees emphasized for her man's place amid all of God's glory.

Plus it drew visitors in droves. Thousands were expected today for the Harvest Festival, and a considerable amount of money necessary for the upkeep of Riga Village came from it. That they would continue to come for autumns indefinite was Mrs. Melton's goal as she walked through the town reviewing preparations. Japhet Beck swore as he hauled large wooden benches into the furnace for the tapping demonstration he'd be giving at twelve-thirty. The ladies manning the children's crafts tent lined up bottles of Elmer's Glue and cups full of sequins for the decoration of a wide variety of gourds and pumpkins.

Outside the store, she inspected the table piled with centerpieces and autumnal wreaths for sale, checked the apple cider situation, because last year they'd run out, said hello to the owner of the mediocre local restaurant who would be judging the small bake-off of breads, pies, and other cold weather goodies. The big horses brought up especially to pull the haywagon seemed at home and calm; good news, since, against her better judgment, she had signed the insurance waiver demanded by their appallingly aggressive Millbrook owner.

As the other residents of Riga Village made their way up, Mrs. Melton looked each of them over in turn, retying a flaccid bonnet bow, mussing the hair of a supposed street urchin. The men of the regiment showed up, some not as perfectly blue and polished as she'd seen them in the past, a slight historical blot she could live with, but Mr. Armour's rumpled uniform, the stains on the pants, actually startled her, as did his beard, a mass of unruly clumps that appeared uncombed. She folded her arms and took a stand on the bridge, intending to say something to him when he passed. The Harvest Festival demands attention, was how she would start. As a newcomer to Salisbury he may not know that, or care, but those who have lived here for their whole life do.

When he reached her, Mrs. Melton looked up at him with a frown, but his eyes stopped her before she launched into her speech. He made no sign of recognizing her, seemed entirely unself-conscious as he touched the brim of his cap in greeting. Without enthusiasm, he turned his hollow eyes toward whatever was coming. Among all the people playing parts, Armour looked incredibly real, a man heading, bored and apprehensive, into another day of life, the life of John Trow. She let him pass with no comment and went off to double check the necessaries.

After walking by Mrs. Melton, Steven returned to sniffing his beard. Usually a pungent mass of hair that smelled the way his scalp did at any given moment, he had taken extra measures that morning to drown it in vanilla shampoo, John Trow be damned. Yet vanilla was not the scent rising to his nose, and this annoyed him. He was already exhausted. Getting out of the house had been a scene from the fall of Saigon, Patty nearly tugging at his arm with questions about where and when to meet that afternoon in the village, where to park, what to do if Emily had a you-know-what. Sensing high anxiety, the kids rose with Patty's tide and were soon both howling and Steven thought at that moment that if he didn't escape they would tear him apart. He needed to see Polly, needed to continue their history. He needed her to touch him.

Since the first time Steven had seen Polly, he'd imagined himself intimate with her in all meanings of that word. Miraculously, they had converged these months, less through his effort than hers, he told himself, convinced as he was that he'd truly not pursued her. Fantasy had slowly crystallized into the sincere consideration that lit his post–emergency room days. Only the decision remained, and now, as stunned and muddled as Emily, he accepted the situation. This affair could happen without fear of divorce court, without trickery, because it would not exist in time; it could not compromise the life of Steven Armour, for Steven Armour would not be having it. And if Steven *did* involve his twentieth-century self, he could find the purity in his motivation; he needed the light and air of someone else to go on with his familial duties.

The wait to see her was mercifully short. As he crossed over the bridge, he saw Polly walking toward the schoolhouse with a tray of baked goods in her hands, red hair pulled back and clipped low so that its fullness and color, still unmatched in Steven's mind by any of the changing trees, were both very much in display. Like everyone else in the village right then she was scrambling in the last minutes before the park's opening, and Kellogg, in full splendor today, boots shined and mustache waxed, stomped along a half-step behind her with a fresh apple-cider donut hanging out of his mouth. Talking constantly, bits of donut flying, the faithful, pestering Colonel worked to keep up, while Polly, seeming impatient, never turned in her husband's direction, never indicated that she heard what he said through his mouth full of food.

Knowing that she was there calmed Steven. The vision he'd carried since Wednesday of a needle stuck into the back of Emily's hand, the whole thing taped to a board, drifted away. Now the concerns of John Trow stepped forward, pushed through Patty's neediness and his sense that somehow he'd caused Emily's condition. Enveloped by the past, pleased to be on familiar ground, he remembered that he would have to check with Beck on the quality of the charcoal.

A hand gripped his elbow; a voice said, "You're beautifully turned out today, Private Trow." Mr. Guston, in a tight suit of bold check, positioned himself in front of Steven and looked him over with the haughty scowl of a dog-show judge. Steven waited for the signature sniff, but none was forthcoming. "So rugged . . ."

"Thank you, Mr. Guston." Over the postmaster's shoulder, Steven watched as Kellogg fixed his fists to his hips and lifted his chin in the martinet posture that most boiled Trow's blood. Polly looked the short distance to the bridge. Her eyebrows arched, her lips moved, and while she did not smile, she made it plain to Steven that she had seen him and was glad.

"Have you added something new?"

"Not really, no." She wore the black skirt and velvet striped blouse she had worn the day of their first encounter, the red diamond at her stomach, the velvet stripes making the differences clear between firm, corseted lines and soft curves. She had worn it for him, he felt certain. "Though I'm looking forward to the arrival of a new woolen shirt."

Mr. Guston put a hand on his heart and nodded gravely, as if a wish had been granted. "Perfect. It will be *perfect*."

Steven imagined touching the velvet of her blouse, pushing up the back of her skirt as she bent forward, her red hair partly obscuring her face, but not her eyes. He waved away whatever doubts he had about the letters. John and Polly would become lovers again, become man and wife again. The meeting today was inevitable. Polly had closed the wound once before. He took a step past Guston. "If you'll excuse me, friend."

Kellogg appeared before the regiment with the crumbs of another donut in his mustache, the *il Duce* mannerisms portending a long day of drill. The regiment had three exhibitions: morning drill, shooting from eleven-thirty to twelve-thirty, and afternoon drill at two. Given the special events of the day, especially the three o'clock contest for best costume, many families of the 2nd had come up and gathered in the field by the time Steven arrived. A small and belligerent Buzz Lightyear lasered Kucharsky and Mrs. Kucharsky, the latter a blonde with a Junior League hairdo and a suspiciously high-end conservative sweater set instead of a costume. More pinched than browbeaten, her obvious distaste for the surroundings indicated possible friend material for Patty. Since the Scobecks had no hope of reaching their father's standard for period re-enacting, they came as chubby versions of various sports figures and teen singers, Mrs. S leading the way as a Rubensesque Stevie Nicks, bedecked in layers of black chiffon.

Joe Swan stepped into Steven's path. "Oh! Hey! Look who's here, honey!" He reached behind and gingerly pushed his wife forward in Steven's direction. "It's Steven Armour! You remember Steve, honey!"

Her husband's cheery reintroduction could not defrost Barbara Swan, who offered a stiff hand and a terse hello. She'd come in the long black dress and peaked hat of a witch, but before Steven had to stop himself from comment, Jerry produced Mrs. Sears, whose youth clearly mattered more to Jerry than her large jaw. He beamed as he presented her. "John Trow, I want you to meet my wife, Kerilynn."

She was huge, a full foot taller than Jerry, and even Steven had to look up to meet her eyes. Her vaguely nineteenth-century dress made her resemble a cheese hostess. Kerilynn had a husky voice. "I'm so *pleased* to meet you!" she said, each word enunciated specifically and with relish. Mrs. Sears offered a huge hand, which Steven stole a look at as they shook, concluding, with relief, that it was indeed a woman's. "How *is* your daughter? When Jerry told me I just . . ."

Steven nodded gratefully. "My family is well and happy, thank you so much," he said with a brave smile that expressed his desire, if it was all the same to them, to move on to a new topic. Patty and the kids would be coming up at one o'clock, in time for the pumpkin-carving and best-costume contests. He had until then to see Polly. He had until one to be Trow. When he'd left that morning, Emily had been sitting with the plastic bag of her costume in her lap, shoes next to her on the couch, staring at the blank TV.

Visitors began to pour in, so Manskart dismissed the families to the side to let the invading twentieth-century army mingle among the men. For an hour, Steven searched without luck for Polly among the passing faces, which became increasingly strange to his nineteenth-century mind. Cowboys and spacemen and Pokémon wove among those clothed in modern garb, and soon only the years of Riga Village meant much to Steven, Trow's ignorance of what constituted a good Britney Spears costume providing great relief to a mind that would have once thought hard on that question. Among his comrades, Jerry, Lummer, and David Burney all had a slightly scruffier look today, as if they'd forgone the dry cleaner that week in a first step toward authentic campaign uniforms for Cold Harbor. Steven figured they were the men Swan had referred to earlier in the week as "thinking hard" about Manskart's approach. Throughout the hour, these three hung around Steven, and together they affected a world-weary, battle-hardened air that contrasted with the Marine guard polish of the others. Kellogg said nothing, but Swan looked over at them with what seemed to Steven a kind of longing.

A boy of six or seven shook Lummer's canteen, as if everything in sight were for sale. The old man leaned over. "You know, son, slavery wasn't really the cause of the Civil War; it was states' rights. No one cared about slavery; the men of the Second fought to preserve the Union. They don't teach that nowadays."

Steven's stomach turned. As much as the men of the 2nd knew about their weapons, the history of the regiment, and the War in general, the lives of soldiers and the movements of the War, so too did many profoundly misread the larger movements of history. He walked over. "Son, I for one am completely in favor of emancipation of the African." He crouched down to the boy's level, then looked up at his parents, well-scrubbed people in crew-neck wool sweaters and khakis. "Our neighbor Mrs. Stowe of Litchfield has done this nation a great service by exposing the evils of slavery with her book *Uncle Tom's Cabin*. As a Christian, a man bound by the New Covenant with Christ, how can I pick words from the Old to bolster some beliefs, then cast away those I do not like? I do not choose to be a slave, and so I cannot force others to suffer the same."

Many around Steven had gone quiet during his short homily, and the silence held as the boy stared at him, reached a tentative finger toward the buttons on Steven's jacket. "Mommy?" he asked. "When can we leave?"

"Right now, Sugar Bear," said Mommy, and the three walked away without another word.

Steven kept to himself through the rest of the field display. Afterward came drill and a release for a short break. Steven waded back into the crowds and the strollers rumbling across the rocky paths of Riga Village, in search of Polly. Showers of leaves fell over the town, all growing things had been harvested, and a satisfying sense of completion reigned. Ignoring queries from curious visitors, Steven worked his way through the paths, the mobs of Ninjas, pirates, and Backstreet Boys, knowing she was among them somewhere, but increasingly worried. Five minutes before he had to return to the field, he discovered the object of his quest. At the end of a long picnic table in the crafts area, she sat beaming, the center of a tableau of children, villagers, some costumed visitors, others in Old Navy polar fleece, carving toothy grins out of their pumpkins. He reminded himself that she had been this way with her twin brothers, with his parents that day in the snow; there had always been such sweetness with her fire.

Polly looked up. Her forehead tilted a bit, so hair slipped over her eye. The smile had a slyness to it, and yet as lusty as she may have seemed to him, she appeared to everyone else as simply being happy to be among the children. He could hardly breathe. She wanted him, not what he did for her. The lace of her blouse played at her long neck, and he saw himself kissing her there, under her jaw, behind her ear, at her nape. A tug at her sleeve from a junior carver brought her back to the table, and as he walked past her she turned her head and said only, "Twelve-thirty at the furnace." He realized he was sweating.

Under Kellogg's command, the men fired round after round of black powder, crackling volleys that sent clouds of smoke up to the blue sky. The crowd applauded, asked questions of the colonel once he presented himself, while all through the demonstration Steven wondered why they were meeting in the furnace. Beck was scheduled to be there then. Would they finally kiss there? The first night he'd kissed Patty, they made love; she'd never been big on just making out.

When Kellogg finally dismissed them, Steven asked Swan the time. "Just about twelve-thirty," said Swan. "Hey, see your family yet?"

Steven looked around in a panic. "Why? Did you see them?"

"No. I was just wondering if they were coming up. Be nice to see Emily here with all these kids, I bet."

He patted Swan's arm as he extricated his own. "Absolutely. Yeah. They're coming around one, I think. Listen, I gotta run an errand real quick. I'll see you then. Okay?" Steven dashed off toward the furnace.

While visitors filed in through the main double doors before the hearth, Steven crept quietly through the entrance by the water wheel, a back door that took him to the other side of the brick furnace; backstage, as it were, for Japhet Beck's demonstration. The sound of the falling water covered his steps. Peeking around the side of the structure, though, Steven could not see Polly anywhere among the crowd. All hundred-odd faces focused on Beck and his skinny assistant, Gary, rapt as the founder described the details of nineteenth-century ironmaking and how those who worked at the furnace lived; information they'd never wondered about before they'd come up, information they'd probably forget within five minutes of walking out.

Steven looked to the right for her, along the back of the furnace, his eyes adjusting to the darkness of the room. Staring harder into the black, he finally saw something sticking out from near the bottom of Beck's dining alcove and jouncing slightly—the small toe of Polly's black boot. She was sitting on Beck's stool with her legs crossed, but as soon as she saw Steven, she stood up, pressed her hand against his mouth to guarantee his silence, then replaced it with her lips. The two kissed hard. Steven heard an elderly man ask a question in an accusing tone. "Now the Bessemer process. That was perfected by Mr. Holley of Salisbury, if I'm not mistaken. What does that have to do with what you're presenting?"

Turning around in his arms, Polly pulled away and placed her foot on the stool so that Steven could see her black shoe, fastened with a dozen buttons across her arch, and the first inch of her white stocking.

Beck growled, "Well, that's not really what we do here. Any other questions before we start?"

Was he *really* about to do this? Yet even as he asked the question, all he wanted to do was push forward, push forward to Polly. Over and over he told himself that he wasn't cheating, that he couldn't marry a woman from the past. That this wasn't real; it didn't count somehow. It was, well, virtual and hence something that could happen. It *had* to happen. Steven placed the hand he had burned on the leather of her ankle, and let it rise slowly up her leg as he moved behind her, his fingers tracing up. The images he'd conjured while reading the letters flooded his head, their years at her house, walks in the Riga woods, their stroll along the lake shore, that first kiss under the light of the furnace, what happened when he had burned his hands.

"This furnace would burn at approximately three thousand degrees Fahrenheit, fifteen thousand degrees Celsius," said Beck. "As the fillers dropped the rocks into the hole at the tunnel head, the top, the intense heat inside the bosh would melt the different stones into a big broth of white-hot liquid. Like lava, if you've ever seen that."

His hand became lost underneath the layers of cotton and silk, and now he relied wholly on touch, fingertips sensitive to every thread of the stockings, the firmness of her thigh, the gentle push she made into his hand. Their silence focused all their senses, made his fingers burn, his tongue remember her breath, smell her own scent mixed with the powder she'd put on earlier. Though there was the same interval between each splash of the wheel, the same splash over and over, the sound grew louder in Steven's ears, faster and with more power. With his other hand, he felt the hardness of the corset and lushness of the velvet, then scooped under her and lightly cupped her breast, increasing the pressure, then releasing.

"We've had some cooking in here for a while. Gary, could you hand me that rod? And we're about to take a look, do what was called tapping the hearth, which means letting the pure iron out of the hearth and into these channels dug here in the sand."

All Steven could see was her face looking back to him over her shoulder, an innocence melting away in the heat of the furnace wall before them and his touch, exactly as he had imagined it. Her lids dropped and her eyes fluttered as he reached the top of her stocking. Red hair loosed from its restraint fell over her face as she sucked on her lower lip, the movements of her body all familiar, all accepting, as if they'd done this dozens of times before. This was his wife, he told himself.

"The melted limestone attracts the impurities in the molten ore and creates what's called slag, which rises to the top of the pure iron like a kind of crust. The founders would skim it off the top with these. Look like rakes or something, right? Here, pass this around. That's an actual piece of slag."

From the stocking, his hand went to the cotton of her undergarments. He rubbed his palm across her as if to spank, grabbed as much as he could take into his hand, and she pushed back again, letting out a little gasp from her mouth. Reaching forward between her legs, he expected fabric, but her pants were split, completely open to his hand. Startled, Steven stopped.

"I'm gonna open this door, and the molten iron will flow into these channels. Many men were burned or injured when this took place. It's a very dangerous operation. Let's do it, Gary."

Polly continued to push down onto his fingers, moving herself back and forth in tight, concentrated circles that grew increasingly firm and fast. "It is the custom of our time," she whispered. "Easier with the hoop skirts."

The door of the hearth creaked open. As Beck barked directions to his assistant, Steven unbuttoned his trousers. Patty, he thought. But he had already crossed the line; his guilt, if there was any, would be no greater if he went on. He pictured Becky.

This is the right thing to do, came Trow's inescapable voice. This is who you should be.

Steven took a deep breath, then lost himself inside Polly.

The audience chattered excitedly and cameras snapped as John Trow and Mrs. Kellogg consummated their love.

Despite her desire to go, Emily seemed sluggish. Patty, dressed in a cheap wig of long black hair, a purple jersey minidress, and white boots all meant to add up to Tina Turner, eagerly dabbed glue on a baby pumpkin in order to rouse Emily. Nate hung out on the fringes of things in his Sid Vicious costume, hair dyed, ripped T-shirt, safety pins, and Doc Martens he'd borrowed from Paul's brother. Steven watched him cast menacing looks at toddlers around the hayride wagon, obviously interested in going on one, but unsure of how seemly it was. Such a painful moment, thought Steven, when you're ripped out of childhood. No wonder teenagers were so surly.

He slid onto the picnic bench next to Emily, who, though dressed very much like Patty, was indeed the Barbie she had hoped to be. "Hi, honey. How ya feeling? Having fun?"

Emily nodded but remained quiet. "Let's do our pumpkin, okay?" He heard the desperate perkiness in his voice, knew Emily could hear it too.

"Okay, Daddy."

Patty sidled up beside him; he could feel the pressure of her body against his. He kept up a running narrative about what he was doing with the pumpkin just so there'd be some sound, just so Emily would keep talking. Whenever she didn't answer, Steven would stop for an instant and watch for one of those harmless, dreamy moments when her eyes began to roll up and she fell silent, her own brief moments of escape that Steven told himself he had had a hand in creating. Why couldn't he take any of this suffering, trade hearts with her? It was possible, even likely, that she would never have another grand mal seizure, yet he knew they would spend whatever good moments remained in their lives waiting for that one bad one.

As Steven the Civil War soldier sat with Barbie and Tina and Sid Vicious, Riga Villagers came by to say hello and extend their good wishes. Mrs. Scobeck turned out to be a physical therapist at one of the many special schools in the area and suggested people for them to consult about Emily. It dawned on Steven that as long as he sat with his family, his uniform, his vehicle for defeating time, looked like nothing more than a very good Halloween costume.

❧ PART FOUR ❧

CHAPTER

29

Joe Swan held up a copy of *Layla* he'd dug out of one of the boxes. "You sure you want to throw this out?"

Steven didn't bother looking up. "If you want it, take it. I've learned you can't be afraid to throw things away." Grunting, he heaved another box of albums into the back of the Navigator, which now held three boxes of records, two of old clothes—all the ratty Northwestern crap he'd shredded up over the last couple decades, the paint-smeared khakis, the torn deck shoes—and two of books. He hadn't read Kierkegaard in college, and every day that passed decreased the odds that he'd read it in the future. He and Swan would see to it that some Millerton thrift shop became the lucky beneficiary of all this, and then they'd make their way to the hardware store to pick out new fixtures for the chronically ill second floor.

Swan, his nimble fingers flipping through the records, tugged out some Springsteen, some Neil Young, Talking Heads, and laid them on the front passenger seat. "You sure?"

"I never listen to them anymore." Swan shrugged and pulled himself up into the car as Steven started it, eager to get away before Patty popped out of a window with another errand. In order to assuage his guilt and the odd pity he'd developed for her in the three weeks since he and Polly had first made love, he told himself that despite what appeared at times a sincere interest, her sole concern was that he function properly. It made things easier.

Swan flipped to the back of a Neil Young album. "Didn't he just die?"

"Nobody dies anymore; didn't you know that?" Steven pulled onto Route 44. "They just get upgraded. Nothing ends. Twenty-four hours of cable television; no 'This is the end of our broadcasting day.' Nothing.

You could spend your whole life now in an Ayn Rand chat room if you wanted."

He looked over at Swan, who, with no apparent interest in his lecture, was carefully running his index finger along the liner notes as he read. Steven yawned; he'd woken up at six-thirty with Trow's voice in his head, going point by point down a checklist of what needed to be done today, and he resented the intrusion. Yet whenever Steven remembered that dark night on the mountain or the bright lights of the emergency room, he buckled down.

They slowed, approaching Salisbury proper. "Did you know that huge elms once formed a canopy over this stretch?" Swan made a little snort of interest. "Big shady elms. Yep. Dutch elm wiped them out."

Still focused on *After the Gold Rush*, the electrician shook his head in minor disbelief, a sign to Steven that his mind was free to wander to Polly and her mass of orange and red hair, one of the major benefits of being John Trow. Before Emily could launch her usual Sunday morning invasion of their bed, he had sneaked into the office to put in some time on the portrait he'd started the day before. After they'd made love on the rocky trail to Ball's Peak, a hurried but passionate joining, he'd started sketching Polly, using a small set of pastels he'd bought at the store. "Made in China" the box said on the bottom, though it looked authentic enough. Unaccustomed to posing, she'd sat stiffly against the rocks, very much the prim Victorian, as the wind spun around them, lifted and dropped strands of her hair behind her like jumping flames. He'd never been any kind of artist, but he *was* in love, wasn't he? Rather than thinking about what she was supposed to look like, Steven had drawn lines on the paper where they existed in real life, and the result had been something entirely respectable to his eyes. He imagined tossing off swift pastoral sketches while he strolled through the forest and capturing the expressions of colorful Riga townspeople, all without benefit of Nikon.

Resisting the urge to take a right on Washinee Street and head up the mountain, Steven continued toward Millerton, comfortable enough with Swan to preserve their silence. Swan, though, cracked a few knuckles and asked Steven if he planned to watch the Giants game. He didn't sound as if he really cared about the answer.

"I haven't been following this year." Once sloppy, lazy days spent avoiding homework, Sundays were now booked solid with home repair and family activities. "No, Jerry and David are coming by. You know I've been reading about the uniform, and I have to say our linings are, to a man, completely wrong."

"Oh?"

"Definitely. So they're visiting. I believe we'll be relining our jackets, possibly look through some of the other materials I've turned up for the other men." He had six or seven separate research projects going, stacks of books and index cards mounting around the office, full of details on aspects of the War and the regiment. That Swan said nothing did not surprise him. Like Manskart, Swan had surely noticed the increasingly rough shape of the Heavies' uniforms as more men decided to play the fighting 2nd, not the bandbox 2nd. The one blind spot in his research was John Trow himself. Mrs. Melton had to his knowledge made no progress, and given that the letters were the kind of thing a man hunted for years to find on his impression, Steven didn't see the point of more work in that area. What would a pension record tell him that Trow's presence in his mind couldn't, even if the voice *was* supernatural? Or neurotic. He asked himself again whether the colonel knew about him and Polly. They'd been cautious so far, but Steven had learned quickly that a regular paranoia attended adultery.

Weaving along the curving road, they passed Lakeville, seeing slices of the lake off to their right. So far, he'd counted three staghorn sumacs and a scarlet hawthorn. Swan offered a barbed comment: "Well, you got Kellogg going."

Steven immediately shot back, "Because It's Right Dammit! You said it, not me!" Then, just as quickly, he regretted it. Such outbursts made up another normal feature of life under Trow's rule. Feeling contrite, he said, "I didn't invent history."

Swan rolled his eyes. "Yeah, well. Listen, you want to know the god's honest truth? The fact is, I like the fancy uniform. I do. That uniform is the nicest suit of clothing I own. I mean, I got over being pissed at you for all you got hanging in your closet, because that's just how it is, but now you're asking me to shit up the one thing in my life that makes me look good." Steven shoved the mat on the floor around with his toe, not looking up. "You're right about a lot of this, but it's hard for me to take, you know? Besides, if my wife saw me getting that outfit dirty, she'd fucking annihilate me." He finally caught Steven's eye. "Is that the right word? Annihilate?"

"Yeah, probably." Steven shrugged. "It's too bad. You'd enjoy it." He didn't like arguing with Swan. Yet aside from Trow's taste for brussels sprouts and his mounting dislike of Nate, things were, as Steven often reminded himself, generally perfect this way. "You see that lake over to the right?"

Swan turned his head a little. "Yeah?"

"Used to be Ore Hill. That was a mountain once. All the Riga ore came from that spot." As usual, he slowed out of respect as he passed.

"Yeah." Swan exhaled and leaned back on the rest. "I know."

As they entered Millerton, for a few seconds Steven had an image of making love to Polly, though that was hardly the sum of their activities. They talked about the War, too; about their past together, about the village and the trees. They made each other laugh, said only good things. Sometimes she would bring her psaltery to give it all a glow. A small leatherbound edition of Shakespeare's sonnets he'd found on eBay was on its way. In public, they gave each other polite, appropriate greetings and hoped the charcoal sheds and nestling outcrops of rock would keep their secret. It was always 1864 for him and Polly, a year preserved forever. They had no future, no other place to be. Steven would never have to choose . . .

"Here we are. You wanna do this first since we're here?" Swan pointed to the right, where an empty parking lot and Jerry's Millerton Tru-Value, a long one-story shed, waited for them. Steven swerved in. "I didn't even know he was open this early until you called me."

Steven couldn't tell whether he was happy with that information or not, but he didn't care. Other things had settled in his mind as he locked the car. For one, what would he and Polly do when there were no Saturdays? Already the weather had sharpened; winter hung just off the western side of the mountain. The park closed in December. He tried not to remember that there hadn't been a letter since the note that brought them back together, almost a month ago.

The automatic doors whisked open. On the radio, two men with Long Island accents loudly discussed the waning prospects of Notre Dame football. Swan stalked the deserted aisles until he found a small middle-aged man, thin, but highly muscled under his short-sleeved green jumpsuit, stocking a display of drill bits. He had a bushy throw of brown hair, a thick mustache, and looked as if he ate cigarettes. Steven had spent thousands of dollars here during the house renovation, dreading every visit, resenting every penny paid to this hostile local. He prepared for the worst. "Hey, Jerry." Jerry nodded. "You know Steven Armour . . ."

A squint; then Jerry raised his eyebrows apologetically. "I can't say I . . ."

"Sure you do—he's John Trow."

Jerry's face lit up. "Oh, jeez, sure. How ya doin'? You let my boy hold your gun last time we were up. Oh, jeez, did he love that." He continued pumping Steven's hand. "Whaddya need? Lights? Back to the left." As they headed that way, Jerry hollered, "If you like anything, take off ten percent!"

CHAPTER

30

A FEW DAYS LATER, WHILE STANDING IN LINE at the Salisbury post office, Steven felt a finger poke his shoulder, like a test for doneness as much as a request for attention. Turning slowly, he caught Mrs. Melton ready to apply another, deeper, poke. Her navy cloth coat, unadorned and not very thick, exuded purposeful self-abnegation amid all the puffy, particolored ski wear.

"Oh, Mrs. Melton! It's you. How are you?" he said quickly, pulling away to prevent any further prodding.

"Mr. Armour?"

"Yes, of course." She eyed him suspiciously, poking finger still in the air but now pointing at him. Did *she* know what was going on with Polly? She had to at least suspect. The woman at the counter had two oversized packages going to some exotic destination; no way he could avoid conversation. "Of course it's me. Can I do something for you, Mrs. Melton?"

She relented finally, dropped her arm. "Have you ever heard of a magazine called *The Lure of the Litchfield Hills*?"

"No, I haven't. Is it new?" He pictured one of those *Arizona Highways* magazines his father used to get, spread after spread of four-color autumnal vistas meant to entice the senior auto tourist into a fuel-burning search for natural beauty.

"No. It's *old*," she said with savor, drawing out *old* to make the word itself something well rounded and mellow. "They don't publish it anymore. Mostly historical articles, pictures and such." He raised his eyebrows. "I've found something, a little something, about"—the rest came reluctantly—"Trow."

"Oh."

"It's in a small article about Civil War veterans in the area. Circa nineteen twenty." He nodded as Mrs. Melton refocused to stare past him, toward the counter. Now that she'd opened her mouth, she seemed to regret it, and for a moment appeared to ignore him.

"Please, what did it say?"

"Well, the only mention of him, and it's very brief, I must tell you, the only mention refers to the quote tragedy of John Trow end quote. That was it." She did not make quote marks in the air as she spoke. "I haven't gotten anything back yet from the National Archives, but as I've thought more, I do remember some talk of him when I was a girl. You know, I grew up here in Salisbury."

The "tragedy" of John Trow? Steven hated that word. Tragedy. "Of course you did."

"There'd been a terrible illness, a long hospitalization, as I recall. Something not quite right. His son died young, too."

"Yes, the tombstone says eighteen." A hard life in the woods, deprivation, war. Tuberculosis made sense, too. That was pretty tragic, wasn't it? Tragic enough for him, at least.

By now Mrs. Melton's eyes had glazed over as she pulled more out of her memory. "The old people used to say that neither one of them belonged in sanctified ground."

Despite all of Trow's good qualities, the order and responsibility he'd bred back into him, this struck Steven as entirely believable. Even while he enjoyed the benefits of being John Trow, he had to admit that at times he resented and feared what was happening to him, as well as the man who was behind it. At home his anger with Nate galloped along at a disconcerting pace, and whenever he yelled at his son he felt the hopeless rotting inside that he'd felt that night on the mountain and during that enervating vision of Cold Harbor. The memory of that day seemed to feed Trow with horror and sadness, the way dead leaves feed the trees they fall from. Steven regularly prayed that Trow would not urge him back to those darker places.

He and Mrs. Melton had both fallen silent. The woman ahead moved on, and Steven retrieved his parcel, the woolen shirt he'd been desperate for on these increasingly frigid days on the mountain. Though he tried to pass by her unmolested, Mrs. Melton suddenly shot out a hand and grabbed his forearm, a disturbed, frightened look on her face. "Why don't we stop here, Mr. Armour? Not everyone has to know everything about the subject of their impression."

Steven looked down at the box. "Mrs. Melton, I like John Trow. I want to honor him by knowing all that I can. Good or bad." He pulled his arm away gently and moved ahead. The Web site would go up for its first test at three o'clock, and he had to be home for that. "Please do send me that article? I'd be grateful."

Preening before the bathroom mirror later that afternoon, Steven set his jaw over the woolen shirt's collar and fluffed out his beard. It fit well, the restrained blue check a handsome match with the rest of the uniform, but the beard still annoyed him. Though he was more accustomed to its smell, its uneven coverage disturbed him; bare skin peeked through in some spots, often next to dense patches of long, entwined strands. So far, managing his facial hair was more like cultivating a bonsai garden than a style choice. Every time he moved his head down, he had to lift his chin and beard up and over to clear the collar. From the corner of his eye he caught himself doing it in the mirror, and his resemblance to Kellogg appalled him. Did the colonel do that out of necessity, not vanity? Steven hated to entertain charitable thoughts about Kellogg, but this did seem possible and certainly preferable to any notion that involved Steven becoming more like *him*. Becoming Trow was quite enough. As he took a final look, deciding that the buttons on this shirt would need replacing too, he heard the mail truck pull away.

An American Girl catalog and *Nickelodeon* magazine for Emily; Harry & David, Smith & Hawken, Swan's fattening though discounted bill, a bundle of letters on the behalf of a bundle of worthy causes, and the one thing Steven wanted: the next letter.

There was only one in the manila envelope, and it was from Polly.

May 8, 1864
John,

I write in great haste. Elisha has just shared with me the news that the 2nd may be called up at any moment. Any parting we make now may be our last. You and I have parted too often because of me, and if we do so now it will be the fault of Grant, not you. I live for your constancy, how I have never left your heart. A pretty butcher is our Grant, but he is changing worlds. He makes things inevitable, makes even the weakest of us ask true questions about ourselves. He is judgment come and our lives shall all be weighed as he waves his sword southward. Even now I am examining my conscience.

You, I fear, shall be marching behind Grant, and there are things I must tell you before you take up your sword, things that I have not wanted to visit again now that we have found each other in the present. When we kissed first here, as secretive and urgent as our first on Mt. Riga, you said you no longer needed to know why I left, but somehow the mere fact of our reunion made time secondary, and so it has been since. Yet we have spent enough hours together to make me think of the future, of us, of this war. To do that, the past must be settled.

My evil doubt that we would never speak to each other again flew off when we met the morning after the furnace died. I had awakened in a panic, as did everyone else on the mountain, yet knowing that you were already involved in a mining venture sweeping through town gave me hope that we would all survive, and that I was right to trust you. I must admit, however, to my fears. Fate had come with a different hand from that which we had expected, but it had indeed come and cast itself upon us with a finality that my spirit told me could not be dispelled by faith and hard work. That I made the choice I did soon after, in the face of my misgivings about the possibility of a future on Mt. Riga, must tell you how much I loved you.

Two months later, Polly discovered she was pregnant, and Trow, as he'd always intended to do, proposed. Her father, for all his warm feelings toward John, was not pleased. Bearing a bastard, in St. John Fenner's mind, cast less shame on the family name than did marriage to a Raggie. He offered Polly a choice: stay and be Trow's wife alone, or bear the child and leave with the Fenners, who planned their departure from the mountain. Polly stayed with John Trow.

The sun shone the morning I gave birth to Daniel. Weeds had already begun to grow over the sides of buildings and cluster along the paths, ready to reclaim the abandoned. As few of us as remained did make a merry group, and the comfort they gave did soothe some the sharp pain of my family's leaving. Tilly and Ruth visited the night before they parted, the yellow house already silent.

The mining scheme Trow engaged in happened to be orchestrated by P. T. Barnum, a detail that lent confidence at the time. Was he not a man of means and influence? In short order, everyone who'd signed on learned at first hand how Barnum got rich. The plan collapsed, and the only man not to lose a dollar was Barnum, leaving this young couple to make meals out of wishes for their baby son and paper their shack on the mountain with pages from her father's old schoolbooks. Winter pushed on. Too late for farming, the slow months arrived, and what forge work could be had in the area was taken.

By no fault of yours, you could not provide, and as the days passed and I received more generous baskets of barely edible food from our moun-tain companions I could not find it in me to be a wife and a mother. I loved, I suckled, but moreso I still craved both myself. I had remained a child, a girl who until the day she walked out of her parents' home had had her every need filled without effort. I had dreamed of the love of the sonnets and found too quickly the hard and unpoetic requirements daily life places on it.

Mrs. Frink handed me a letter one day as I returned from a wasted journey to the barren apple trees. In it, Tilly and Ruth begged me to come to Winchester. A small orphanage had engaged Father as headmaster, and but for my absence, life was happy there, full of new and pleasant com-pany. I remember looking at my hands, which were red and broken, and laundry remained to be done that morning. Clouds hung down so low that it seemed the snow would not fall so much as be placed on the mountain-top. Daniel began to cry. He probably felt my being stiffen to him, a drowning girl faced with a terrible choice.

I bundled him up, put on my coat, so oddly elegant and out of place now amid the faltering buildings, and took him next door. I asked Mrs. Frink to look after Daniel for a few minutes as I ran to the old house. I'd scavenged a few odds and ends there, since the family had left and been generous with my findings, so she was happy to do it. Did she remark later at how long I kissed him? I will be back as soon as I can, I said. I will hurry. And I began running, running toward the old house. But before I reached it, I turned down the road and began running faster, knowing I had only a few hours before the sun would begin to set.

I am to begin packing now for my return to Connecticut. This cam-paign will have no wives, no diversions from finishing the bloody task. How simpler it would be if Elisha could find the glory he desperately wants among the angels and I could find again the earthly happiness I once had. The happiness I had with you. Oh John, come back alive and we will be a family once more! I am strong enough now to care for you and our son. I am strong enough to desire a certain life, no matter its chal-

lenge, but I do not have the power to change certain circumstances, ones that Grant or his army, or a particular soldier in his army, may alter in the course of war. Simply, if the colonel comes home, I will have to remain his wife. Yet if only you return, I will be yours at last, and forever.

John, act on our love.

I am your
Polly

The phone rang. "Hi ho, Steverino."

"How you doing, Dad?" He realized he had never spoken to Patty about his father's moving in.

"Who gives a shit? How's Emmy?"

Steven smiled. "Good. She's good."

"Aw, that's great to hear. I've been sick about her. Listen, I got my flights. The Mustang's on blocks for a while. You got a pencil? I can't wait to see her."

Flights? "You're coming in?"

"Thanksgiving's in a couple weeks, yes? Parade? Lions game?" Phillip's voice dropped. "Unless . . ."

"No. Yes! Of course you're coming! Emily will be thrilled." Steven took down the information, promised to send a check for the tickets that day.

"How's it look out they-uh?" asked Phillip, taking another shot at a New England accent. "Good col-uh on the trees?"

Steven looked out the window and hoped that a few leaves would last until his father arrived. "It's beautiful. Mom would have loved it."

"Oh, Christ, she loved autumn. You know, I walked down Michigan Avenue a couple weeks ago, by the old office? Full of goddamned German tourists fighting to get into Crate and Barrel." Phillip blamed it all on Michael Jordan. They talked for a few more minutes, long enough for Steven to admit that he was looking forward to seeing his father, even if Trow didn't like him that much.

At three-fifteen, Steven went to www.dillyperkinsfood.com and clicked on a blue, pointy wizard's hat with yellow food shapes in place of stars. Instead of the Castle of Goode Eating, though, up came "Site Under Construction," the sign of disaster. Its implications left unexplained, Steven tucked the latest letter into the file and dialed Jay.

*   *   *

That night around eleven, Patty knocked on his office door. "Come to bed." Immersed in a large tome about American ironmaking, Steven called back that he'd be in later. "No. Come to bed *now*. You have to."

As freely as she offered her presence, forced it on him, in fact, Patty could not be generous with good words, whereas Polly spoke them constantly. Slipping a marker next to a brief history of the Saugus Ironworks, he went to her with the sense of duty one has when attending the sick. Quietly they went about their prebed checklist, flossed, brushed, removed makeup, and, still without speaking, pulled the blankets up to their chins. Steven lay there in the silence for a few minutes, but he wasn't tired, didn't turn out the light. "I have one question," he said, his voice loud in the absence of sound.

Patty hadn't fallen asleep either. "What?"

"Why do I want to sleep with someone who doesn't like me? I mean, I know we're married and you love me, but you don't *like* me anymore."

"Well, of course I like you. Don't be an asshole."

"That's what you say to people you *like*? You call them assholes? Face it, Patty, you don't like me anymore." He paused before he said the next sentence, bold enough now to peer over the edge. "Do you really want to spend the rest of your life with someone you can't even pretend to like?" Steven turned off the light, both of them surprised by where he'd taken them.

CHAPTER

3 1

PAUL WANTED TO NAME THEIR BAND FORESKIN, that being one of his favorite words to say, but Nate vetoed it, feeling, but not admitting, that he wanted a name that he could say to his mother. Then Paul suggested they use the number four as part of it, hence 4skin, but Nate hung tough. Paul's other favorite word, *diaphragm,* reminded Paul's brother of geometry class, so that was out too. Nate could have gone with Mime in Hell, a creation of Paul's brother, yet its alterna-wit eluded Paul, and Nate was thrown back to the phrase that kept running through his mind, something he'd read in a magazine in his mother's bathroom—Fruit Acid Peel. Stone Temple Pilots, Blue Oyster Cult, Fruit Acid Peel. It just worked for him, and the enthusiasm of Paul's brother, an actual sophomore in high school, got him fairly stoked. Overriding Paul's objections, Nate immediately got to work on the logo, but Paul's brother pointed out that their drummer still didn't have a drum set. Not to worry, though. He had an idea, if they were up for it.

Patty kept pace with Steven as he took long strides toward the front doors of Salisbury Central School. "Steven, he was in the back seat holding a snare drum. Just remember that. He did not actually break into the school. Paul and his brother broke into the school. *He* did not."

Steven flared his nostrils, unable to even look at her as he bored ahead. "He was an accomplice. He's got no excuse."

"No one thinks he's starting a life of crime, Steven. He's confused and . . ."

They'd reached the door by now. "Confused, my ass. If you ask me, robbing the school band room is a terrific way to start fucking up your life. It's two days before Thanksgiving. Do you have time for this shit? I don't. My father's coming, I have a Web site falling apart before my eyes . . ." The fact that Manskart would be present at this meeting smelled funny to him. "He's destroying our lives, Patty!" said Steven, without knowing whether he meant Nate or Manskart. In the past week, rather than simplifying his life, going up to Riga Village had begun to create in Steven a sense of tightening complication. On Saturday, in honor of what he termed "the new interest in campaigning"—a glaring jibe at Steven—Kellogg had led the regiment on an unscheduled hike that left Scobeck heaving up Ding-Dongs on the side of the road. Even worse, the hike hadn't allowed Steven time for a rendezvous with Polly, so for the first time in weeks the lovers had not met somewhere in the woods, nor were there any letters in his pack. Without the reassurance of their regular tryst, Steven found himself pining for her. Did Kellogg know? Was she drifting? What was supposed to happen next?

Kids streamed past them into the school, none higher than their shoulders. Patty peered down at them as if she were wading across a quickly rising river. Clenching her teeth, she hissed out in lower tones, "Oh come on, Steven. He's never been in trouble before. Don't make a goddamn scene!" She looked around to make sure she hadn't permanently corrupted a passing third-grader.

"Scene? *I* don't want to make a scene. *They* want a scene." Steven ran a finger around the inside of his collar, looser now. Pulled out of hiding from the back of a closet, his blue pinstripe Brooks Brothers suit had always been cut large but now he staged his arms into vertical positions to keep the cuffs off his hands, puffed out his chest so that the jacket would stay on his shoulders. With his uncropped beard and shaggy hair, what he'd seen in the mirror this morning was a farmer in his Sunday best.

"What makes you say that?" Fewer children pushed past them now, but those who did came faster, until a bell hammered away loudly over Steven and Patty's heads, and the latecomers raced past them.

"Well, why's Manskart have to be there?"

"What's wrong with that? I thought he was your big re-enacting buddy." He rolled his eyes. How little she knew about his life, thought Steven. Surely the teacher had orchestrated all of this as revenge, weaseled his way into a meeting that he had no business being in. Patty continued. "Besides, Nate really likes him. He's doing great in his class. And I think it's great that he has some other male role models." Steven gave her a poisonous look as they went inside.

Unless you were homeschooled or raised by wolves, the smell of a

grammar school elicits a wave of acute memories in adults, the particular blend of chalk, finger paint, and vomit absorbent acting as powerfully
on a tender part of the brain as musk does on another. Heading toward
the principal's office, familiar after a few meetings on the subject of
Emily, a moment from his past appeared with such force and immediacy
that Steven had to slow down amid the stream of students, a few of
whom stared at him as they went by. He had cried the first day of school,
he remembered; begged for his sister, Barbara. Though plied with
crayons and clay by the impatient Miss Stein, he'd wept for hours. Lock-
ers slammed randomly around him, kids scrambled to their rooms before second bell, and Steven came to a complete halt, leaning against a
bulletin board stapled full of Pilgrim hats and bonnets. Miss Stein had
never revised her opinion of him after that. He'd been good at kickball,
fascinated by Woodland Indians, played Joseph in the Christmas pageant,
though downgraded to shepherd the year after. Was his life flashing before his eyes? Miss Donedio, Mrs. Porter, Mrs. Andes, Miss Frykowski;
the doughy, tired face of teacher after teacher shoved into his mind as if
desperate to be recognized. Were they trying to save him, or were they
jumping off the ship before it sank?

Patty had stopped next to him. "What's the matter?"

"I just . . . You know, the smell is so . . ."

"I thought you were having a heart attack or something. You're not,
are you? Honey?" She touched his arm, actually concerned, it seemed.

"No."

"Good." His wife forged onward towards Bob Daluisa's office, but
Steven still couldn't move. From far away, he heard Patty say, "Yes, he's
coming. He's just down the hall." When he looked up, he saw the last five
inches of Manskart's rear end going through Principal Daluisa's doorway
and Patty standing with her arms crossed, smiling a sickly smile and tapping one spectator pump in the rhythm with which she hoped he'd get
his own rear end over there. He trotted to catch up, and together they
entered the office, where Bob Daluisa sat behind his desk, fingers
steepled, while Manskart rearranged the chairs.

The tweed jacket, the rep tie, the reading glasses perched sportingly
up on his thinning hair fooled no one; as much as Principal Daluisa
draped his teamster's body in the patrician style of the surrounding private schools, he still looked as willing to administer a broken leg as a de-
merit. More Atlantic City than Rugby College, Daluisa eyeballed Steven
and Patty as they took their seats.

Steven had not seen Manskart since Saturday, and though the sight of him scraping a chair across the floor stirred up Trow's bile, this was a different man. In Wallabys today, with a brown-and-yellow checked shirt and a brown sport jacket so stiff that it could have been made out of cardboard, this Manskart was the waddling, fact-filled geek who'd given him his introductory tour. After a crisp nod at Steven halfway to a salute, he ducked his head and gave a cautious look in Daluisa's direction.

"How's that for you, Bob?" Manskart asked, his usual deep, stagey tone meant to convey equality with the principal, an equality that did not exist. Daluisa waved an annoyed hand for him to stop. No broad scan of the field here, thought Steven with pleasure. Though he detected no sign of knowing cuckoldom on Manskart's face, he could feel Trow bristle.

All three sat down. Daluisa forced his top lip down over his square teeth, erasing the permanent smile. "One of the responsibilities we have as educators is to know a cry for help when we hear one. These boys did not, god forbid, walk in here and create any kind of Columbine situa—"

Patty gasped. "Jesus Christ."

Daluisa held up his hands. "Let me finish, please, Mrs. Armour. I am saying they did not do that. I am saying it is important we do *not* overreact. Which is not to say that I am willing to see this handled with a slap on the wrist." He slid his glasses down to his eyes, assumed a concerned, professorial expression, as if commenting on camera, and cleared his throat. "We want to find ways to provide these boys with what they were really asking for when they performed this rash and dee-structive act." Steven sighed dramatically. Sometimes stealing a drum set is just stealing a drum set.

Manskart held up a finger while Patty and Daluisa stared at Steven. "If I may, Bob, I'd like to say one thing here. I have—"

Daluisa shook his head. "In a minute."

Manskart's head sank into his shoulders in deference. "Of course, Bob. Of course."

What a loser this Manskart was, thought Steven, this king of Riga Village. Every inch of him knew every minute of the day that he would be teaching eighth grade until he died. As Daluisa launched into a discourse on "Tolerating Who You Are," the school's new values program, Steven looked with pity at the man he'd horned, noting the bent neck and pilling pants, finding himself even forgiving some of the churlish brutality on the mountain.

"Mr. Armour." Daluisa's voice. Steven blinked. "Mr. Armour? Have you noticed any differences in Nate's behavior?"

Steven coughed to buy time. The truth was that recently he didn't notice much about Nate aside from how much the boy annoyed him. He wore those repellent skater pants. He'd stopped listening to KISS. He liked bands Steven had never heard of. He didn't want to go hiking. Steven had made the effort, checked homework, and assigned character-building chores; Nate was the one not paying attention. More than once, Steven had fought the impulse to slap Nate hard, to scare him, to force his respect in a manner he knew was wrong but for which he'd lately developed a strong taste. Yet in the end he was helpless with Nate, had no answer except Trow's anger. He was about to say something innocuous about how the boy kept to himself when Trow leaped into the breach and said, "I am profoundly disappointed in him."

Daluisa raised an eyebrow, as did Patty, who quickly dove in. "Do you think it's possible that the situation with our daughter caused him to act out? Emily's consumed so much of our time recently."

"If I may ask," said Manskart. "How is your daughter? Nate talks a lot about her. He's very concerned."

Patty smiled valiantly. "I know. The medication is doing a lot for her. Most kids just grow out of it."

The principal nodded. "That is certainly something we should factor in here. Let me ask this: what do you think is special about Nate? Mr. Armour?"

Steven folded his arms and madly sifted through his mind for something to block Trow's intervention in his son's life, some proof of love and paternal focus. The silence swelled painfully. All he could think of were things he'd said at parent-teacher conferences past: Nat loved reading chapter books; Nat was a cheerful, helpful child. "He's always, uh . . . he . . ."

Sensing panic, Patty grabbed the wheel. "He has a terrific relationship with his sister. Really nurturing and positive. And he loves music." She led Steven with a broad nod. "Don't you think? He really loves music."

The principal turned to Manskart. "Wally, tell us your impressions of the boy. Mr. and Mrs. Armour, you may find this enlightening."

Manskart lifted his chin; a Kellogg move. "Well, quite frankly, Nate is an exceptional student. Exceptional. As you say, Mrs. Armour, he has a definite aptitude for the musical arts, particularly drumming." The teacher turned to Steven with the smile of a man about to spring a trap. "Do you know, Mr. Armour, who his favorite drummer is?"

Not this Socratic method shit again, thought Steven. "Peter Criss?"

No one registered the name. "Gene Krupa."

All save Steven made appreciative sounds, and Manskart's smile grew larger, his admiration of Nate as unmistakable as Steven's embarrassment. "He says Krupa had the sharpest technique, and Mickey Hart has the deepest soul. Do you see what I mean? From a twelve-year-old. Exceptional."

Patty slumped in her chair, relieved that her son had not only redeeming qualities, but even a few superior ones, and Daluisa let his capped teeth beam forward to show that all was not lost.

Manskart, though, pressed his advantage. "The boy did a report for me on Japanese taiko drumming. Do you know what taiko drumming is?" Manskart wasn't asking Steven, he was testing him, and Steven squeezed a *no* through his clenched teeth. "Japanese ritual drumming. They use those huge drums. The finest report I've seen in my years here. Look at it."

Taller in his chair now, Manskart stared down his nose at Steven as he handed a plastic folder to Patty, gloating that he knew Nate better than his own father did. He'd turned into Kellogg; Steven was sure of it. "Every once in a while a student like this comes along, one with real talents that you want to help blast out of his orbit. What happened to make him do this, that's what I wonder."

Go fuck yourself, said Trow. I've been inside your wife.

Steven had to clamp his jaw to keep the words from flying out. Wide-eyed, Patty passed on the report, twenty pages of perfect spelling, exclamation marks in the margins, musical notation, even some stabs at calligraphy, all produced by the belching, gawky Nate of the big arms. Who was this child, Steven wondered. Had he ever been his? His memories of Little Nat had become perilously thin recently. "What is it you're saying? That the fault is mine? I'd assumed we were called here to punish Nate, not me. Yes?"

Patty put a hand on his. "Steven, I don't think Mr. Manskart . . ."

Peering over the top of his glasses, Daluisa said slowly, "Mr. Armour, we are not here to punish anyone. We are here to find strategies to help Nate."

Manskart again felt free to speak. "Everyone gets another chance, Steve."

Daluisa let Steven's sneer pass without comment. "Wally has an idea. It satisfies my requirements, and I think it may improve the situation. Wally?"

"Nate's other great interest is, of course, history." Of course, thought Steven, biting his lip. "So why don't you bring Nate up to Riga Village? We would be honored to have him as our drummer boy." A pressure welled up inside Steven, pushed against his skin.

He must die, said Trow. He must die.

Falling back in his chair, Steven suddenly knew what had to happen next, where Polly's letter was leading him.

He must die, said Trow.

Steven was supposed to kill Kellogg.

Polly had asked Trow to kill him, to shoot her husband in the heat of battle. Steven's vision of Cold Harbor—Trow's memory—stopped before Kellogg's death, so he couldn't entirely disprove the possibility that Trow had indeed shot his rival at Cold Harbor. Murder on the battlefield made a perfect end to the story of Polly and Trow, this brambled little trail of facts that ran alongside the well-paved road of history. It would certainly explain Mrs. Melton's tragedy.

The teacher smiled sweetly. "You'd have him up there at your side every minute of the day."

And yet Kellogg was really Walter Manskart, his son's eighth-grade teacher. A living person.

You must pay the price of a perfect life, said John Trow.

Patty squeezed Steven's hand. "I like what Wally says. What about you?"

"I hate it." Though he'd never put a hand to his son, right now he wanted to drive straight home and slap him. Or Trow wanted to. At this moment anything seemed possible, even necessary. "You think you know my son better than I do. Am I correct, Mr. Manskart? Do you?"

"No, of course not, but—"

"Do you? Because you most certainly do *not*, sir. What that boy needs is a sound lashing, not a damned hobby!"

Patty squinted into his face as if trying to recognize the man she was sitting next to. "What are you talking about?"

Steven recalled the day Kellogg had presented him with his rifle. Against every notion of what he then considered possible for himself, he'd lined up the colonel in his sights and pulled the trigger. While the memory of his rash disregard for Kellogg's life caused him to flinch now, at the same time he couldn't help noticing how the knot between his shoulders released even as he thought about it.

"Beating him up would only send him the wrong way, Steve." Manskart glanced to make sure Daluisa knew exactly where he stood on that. "You won't be compromising. Bobby was an inch away from juvenile prison before Hube got him up there with us."

Steven pictured Cold Harbor, imagined how it would feel. Through the smoke, he saw Kellogg clutching one arm, pointing toward the enemy line. A buck against his chest and then a blossom of red blood exploding on the colonel. Steven muttered to Trow, "You can't do that."

Daluisa spread both his hands flat on his desk. "In fact I *can*, Mr. Armour. I am afraid Mr. Manskart is being too polite. The reality is that *you* have no choice here. Well, you do. Would you like to hear it?" Steven nodded. The principal looked at his fingernails as he spoke. "Nate can either join you on Mt. Riga, or I *will* press charges. That's your choice."

Steven said nothing. Framed photos of the extended Daluisa family sat on the shelf behind the principal, along with an electric pencil sharpener, a Mr. Coffee, large piles of papers, and a picture of Daluisa shaking hands with Phil Rizzuto. He had no other plan to offer for Nate. But how would he see Polly? How would he have John Trow's life? And how would he keep him from killing Manskart?

"That is what I thought." Daluisa abruptly rose to signal the end of the meeting. "Good to see you both. Thank you for coming."

Killing Manskart was too high a price to pay, he told himself. It wouldn't happen, especially with Nate up there; Trow had to realize that. Yet as Steven tried to shake the shocking, satisfying image of Manskart's dead body, his own hand holding the gun, it would not leave.

CHAPTER

32

THANKSGIVING DAY AND AL ROKER'S I'm-happier-than-you'll-ever-be
voice bubbled up from the living room. "Uh-oh, Katie. Here he comes.
That little German boy in the lederhosen that I know you love so well."

"Oh, yes, Al. He's one of the oldest . . ."

Emily came running into the kitchen in her pink nightshirt, the
medi-bracelet tinkling on her wrist like the bell on a cat. "Daddy! Come
in! It's Little Klaus! It's your balloon!" Given the holiday, he and Patty
had decided that the Macy's Thanksgiving Day Parade presented no clear
health risk to their daughter, though seeing Little Klaus, a sixty-three-
foot floating replica of Happy Gerda's gluttonous son, promised to make
Steven sick to his stomach. And if that didn't do it, then the large pile of
chopped onions before him would. It was just the beginning of the day's
cooking. He'd unearthed this authentic nineteenth-century game dress-
ing recipe in the course of his research. Tears blinded him, and he wiped
his sniffling nose on his sleeve as Emily's small, insistent hands tugged
him into the living room.

On the couch, his father opened his arms wide. "Come on, Emmy,"
he said, and she skipped over to snuggle up to her grandfather, where
she'd spent most of the eighteen hours since his arrival. "You okay?"
Steven nodded, wiped his eyes some more as Phillip sniffed the air like
an old bloodhound, his long ear lobes trembling as he followed the
scent. "You eating an onion bagel?"

"No. Chopping onions."

On the other side, Nate sprawled across the couch, eyes closed, still
profoundly in the doghouse despite his abject and tearful apologies. Only
his big hands keeping time with Little Klaus's introductory marching
band proved that he was awake; Steven could detect the slight darkening
where police house ink had stained the pads of his fingers. Squinting, in

the hope of bringing his son into some kind of focus, he wondered at this being on his couch, a person of talents and desires he had nothing to do with, a person threatening to ruin his life on Mt. Riga. Steven leaned toward the kitchen, eager to make stuffing, to legally wield a knife and chop away some of Trow's choking anger toward Nate and Kellogg. When he'd awakened the morning after the meeting, he did not feel like a killer, nor, to his relief, did he the morning after or the one after that, and while the gulf between thought and action remained wide, the idea of murder warmed him too well these colder November days.

Phillip clucked. "Looks like Little Klaus could use a face lift." The big blue feather on Klaus's cap drooped, and large patches could be seen on his pudgy, spaetzle-chomping face whenever the wind gusting through Herald Square pulled him upright. Phillip sniffed again. "Stevie, go wash your hands."

Steven ignored his father. "He's as long as a city bus," said Katie Couric. "And each of his boots could hold a ton of Dilly-Perkins egg noodles, all buttered up, just the way Little Klaus likes them." Katie sounded anguished speaking these words, her strained shilling for DP embarrassing to Steven, not just because it was *his* company she could barely bring herself to name, but also because of his complicity in this circus of commercialism. In years past he'd honored this appalling tradition of family inertia, but what exactly did a Rugrats balloon have to do with Lincoln's order to the American people to solemnly, reverently, and gratefully acknowledge God's grace with one heart and one voice?

He folded his arms as Little Klaus turned into the homestretch. "An abomination of the intent," he muttered. "His son Willie had recently passed over when Lincoln proclaimed a day of Thanksgiving. He meant this for a silent day of religious observance and—"

Patty yelled out from the kitchen. "Oh Jesus, Steven! Stop it! Are you going to do the stuffing?"

The three on the couch showed no sign they'd heard anything other than the television.

Thanksgiving's end-of-the-year warning was hitting Steven hard today. Christmas was coming, the new millennium; time was tumbling at top speed into who knew what, and there was no turning back, no denying that the end was near once Santa showed up. Only three more Saturdays with Polly. He had to see her, thought Steven, he had to know her thoughts, her heart. Did *she* really want Manskart dead, too? He stopped, realizing that once again he'd actually been considering murder.

Katie passed the buck. "Takes you back, doesn't it, Al?"

Emily waved at the TV. "Hi, Klaus."

"Sure does, Katie. You know, Little Klaus always wants one more helping of noodles, so they'd better keep him away from the next float. It's Noodleland, sponsored by Dilly-Perkins! Thirty-two feet long, it's a magical trip through the world of dumplings and pasta. And who's that on top? It's Lou Bega!"

Unable to watch any longer, Steven turned away and saw Emily in the throes of a petit mal seizure, staring blankly at a wall.

Although she did nothing different from what she had always done in this state, sat perfectly still like a doll put aside, now her brief departure signaled crisis, and Steven took a fast step forward. Phillip held up a hand, warned him back with a shake of the head and some distracting chatter. "Nice coup for you guys, getting Bega. 'A little bit of kugel.' Is that what he's singing?"

"I don't know, Dad." From the corner of his eye, he saw a circle of large rotini doing the mambo around the zoot-suited Bega. Emily still hadn't moved. Nate had opened his eyes at the changed tone of their voices and now looked from father to grandfather and back.

"You know I did some business with Willard Scott once. He was the first Ronald McDonald. This is going back, oh, what, forty years?"

Had she had her medicine today? Steven vaguely remembered hearing the snap of a cap being opened, Patty saying, "Here you go." In his mind he drove the route to the Sharon hospital. He was in modern clothes today. Dr. Primati wouldn't be around, but Steven would be ready. Or at least Trow would be ready, Trow, who'd now set his mind racing, ready to force action out of him like some twisted personal trainer of the soul. His dad could stay with Nate, he thought, and Patty would—

Before Steven had to work through any more logistics, Emily broke her spell with a yawn. Stroking her forehead, Phillip asked what Steven had always been afraid to. "What does that feel like, Emmy? When you do that?"

She shrugged, eyes back to the TV. "I forget what Emily is. And then I'm Emily again and I'm happy." She was not upset.

Bouncing on his toes like a golden retriever, Steven reached for the remote, concerned that the bizarre sight of dancing pasta had triggered this episode. The end of Emily's seizure—no longer something dreamy or voluntary, no sign of genius, just an electrical disturbance in her brain—did not relax him. John Trow may have been the man he should be, but, Steven wondered, was the humorless Trow still the man he *wanted* to be? Though he had no interest in returning to the old Steven and his passivity, he'd savored Thanksgiving Day once, and part of him missed that normal, stupid excitement about the passing parade. "Some air would do us all good," he said. The stuffing could wait half an hour. "Dad? Nate? Anyone for a football match? Emily? Bubbles?"

Noodleland had moved on, followed by the ticking cadence of a massive drum-and-bugle corps from South Carolina about to launch into the theme from *Titanic*. Phillip pointed to the set and was about to deliver a defense of the parade's sedative value when the sound of live gobbling came from the front lawn.

Emily sprang to the window. "Daddy! It's the turkeys! It's the turkeys!"

Despite the charms of Emily's bubble dance, this was their first appearance in two months, and she jumped up and down at the sill, the bracelet ringing like jingle bells. "Hi, turkeys! Gobble gobble!" Only twenty yards away, a group of three males and six or seven females wandered across the field in their staccato motion. Feet and heads took one position, were held, then took the next, as if frames had been cut out of the film. Phillip began to gobble and Emily ran to get her shoes.

Patty called out from the kitchen. "Steven? Did you hear me? What's going on with the stuffing here? Do I have to finish it?"

With rubber boots on and her parka, Emily took tiny steps out the door and toward the turkeys. Suddenly one, a male, stopped. He turned to the rest of the assembled fowl and unfurled his archway of feathery splendor, an earthbound rainbow shimmering at the other awestruck turkeys. It would have been beautiful if he'd quit there, brought a slice of Americana to life, but the big tom then shook his feathers with the sound of dry leaves rattling in the wind. It was a showy, arrogant move calculated to win respect, fear, and hens. This, thought Steven, was the Wally Manskart of Turkeydom.

Kill him, said Trow.

A taste for blood surged through Steven, as sudden as Trow's voice. He had dissected a few members of lower fauna in high school, bagged a couple of sunnies in the lake, and even that had made him feel slightly ashamed. Yet as loudly as he told himself that this was dangerous and stupid and probably illegal, Steven felt the urge to kill something immediately.

Everything dies, said Trow.

Steven could not deny that death was certain, even good in its way. Learning how the soldiers died was helping his regiment get real; Emily's close call had forced him and Patty to move her back into the land of the living.

Some must kill and some are killed, said Trow. Cain and Abel. Abraham and Isaac.

Driven by the same nameless propulsion that had worked on him that first day of drill, Steven ran upstairs to his office. He shoved on his brogans, popped his kepi on, opened the top drawer of his desk and dug around in back until his fingers hit them. Grabbing the white paper cartridges, with their decorative little twists, always heavier than he expected, because of the knuckle-sized bullets, he stuffed them into his pants pockets. It was Thanksgiving, wasn't it? The day to kill turkeys.

Dashing into the kitchen, he ignored Patty, grabbed the keys off the hook by the door, and clomped downstairs to the cabinet holding the rifle. An inch away from the stock, though, his hand froze.

This isn't the kind of thing you do, thought Steven.

But who *are* you, exactly, came the reply from Trow. You're nothing.

Steven's hand shot forward to the gun. He raced back up before he could think again, unlaced brogans flapping at each step.

Out the front door, kepi low over his eyes, he charged past Emily. The turkeys plodded away from the house, wise enough to sense danger in the commotion. In nine times, thought Steven, as he stood the rifle between his feet. With precise, almost delicate, movements, he took out a cartridge, tore it open, poured the powder down the muzzle, dropped in the ball, rammed it, primed the cap. He took aim with the butt of the rifle on his left shoulder the way Trow liked it.

"Daddy!" screamed Emily.

As Steven raised the barrel, the big annoying tom slid into the cup of his sight. Steven's left index finger, unused to the pressure, squeezed harder and harder. This is insane, he told himself.

Sometimes you *must kill*, said Trow. To be right.

Steven squeezed a little bit more, and a bit more, until his series of small movements finally overcame the resistance.

At the blast, the gun pulled left wildly, the bullet spinning through the puff of smoke and out into the field, ten yards away from any turkey flesh, tossing up a few leaves where it landed. The shot echoed off the side of the mountain.

Hauled inside by her grandfather, Emily cried loudly from the doorway. "Don't kill them, Daddy! They're my friends!"

All the birds gobbled anxiously and picked up the pace of their escape.

Phillip hollered out the door as Steven loaded again. "What the hell ya doin', Stevie? Don't you need a license or something?"

Steven capped and took aim at the big one, which had only moved ten feet or so since the last shot. He held the gun more tightly and fired again, missing even farther to the left this time, the turkeys now sprinting out of his range. The second shot echoed like the first, off the side of the mountain and away into the clouds.

"Oh, shit, Dad! I mean, oh man, Dad! That's excellent! When did you get a hunting rifle?" Nate had raced out of the house at the first shot and was dancing around Steven's left shoulder. "Can I try?" Nate grabbed at the rifle barrel.

This was the closest he'd stood to his son in months, the first smile he'd seen his face in as long. "No! Are you crazy?" Steven ripped the gun away. As he did, he took stock of what he'd just done, of what John Trow had just done. Something good about Steven Armour was gone forever; he could feel it dying in the clouds amid the echoes.

HER HUSBAND'S STRANGE HOBBY HAD BENEFITS; Patty admitted that. Through Betty Scobeck she'd met a Birkenstock-wearing but entirely serviceable neurologist for Emily. The asshole owner of the property next to the minimall turned out to be the same Jerry Sears Steven knew, and she got 25 percent off her meat from that good-looking older guy, Hube or Hugh. Wally Manskart liked her son, thank God, and after hearing Steven mention some guy putting every penny into Qualcomm, she'd picked up a little with some money she'd stashed aside. And so, in the end, while hardly suitable friends with a capital F, the men Steven played with up on Mt. Riga were undeniably good people.

Which brought her to Joe Swan. Patty had dealt with enough losers, men aggrieved that a woman was beating them up instead of another man, and they didn't bother her. In fact, she enjoyed watching them wear themselves down against a level of resolve only twenty-six hours of labor (seventeen with Emily) can create. But goaded by his miserable, dry-skinned wife, who clearly confused envy with ambition, Swan had whimpered and canceled and backed out of so much in the process of selling this house that Patty had fully expected to leave the closing empty-handed, which they very nearly did once the Swans had begun to cry. No matter how many times Steven now tried to push him on her as a changed man, she still rued the day she told Steven to call him. She'd had it in her head that it remained Swan's responsibility, an idea that his monthly bill had dispelled. As she flushed the toilet and opened the bathroom door, there he was, on a ladder, staring down at her, nipping a wire.

"You know, if you're having trouble with that one, I can get you one of those three-gallon numbers from Canada." He motioned meekly toward the toilet. "We always meant to get rid of those one-sixes. They just don't do the job. Know what I mean?" Patty furrowed her brow.

Could he fathom how much she didn't want to have this conversation with him? He motioned again. "I mean the toilet. The threes are illegal but I—"

"How are we doing? Almost done here?" Patty chose to pretend he'd never spoken. "Think we'll be done today?" Usually Steven had the great pleasure of chatting wattage with his pal, but this day after Thanksgiving he had to run some errands with Phillip and the kids, and she did not like being here alone with Swan. She'd greeted him in her most raggedy sweats to keep any "Dear Penthouse Forum You'll Never Believe" thoughts out of his head.

Swan climbed down from the ladder, wiped his hands with a rag tucked into his work belt. "All I need now is to get inside the office. I think that might be some of the problem." Swan pointed at the door-knob. "Do you mind?"

"Be my guest." He turned the knob, but Steven had locked it, another surprise, as if the turkey thing and the tough-guy show at school hadn't been enough for the week. Yet just as surprising as his recent behavior was her increasing desire for him. He no longer looked like the man she'd married. Sometimes when she saw the unfamiliar face and beard, her heart started, positive for a few beats that Steven was some dark in-truder. If not exactly a good thing, it certainly was different, and differ-ent *was* good at this stage in a marriage.

"Hold on a second," Patty said. Though she was all in favor of privacy, she personally had nothing to hide, and she hoped that Steven didn't ei-ther. She went in search of a paper clip. Up until the turkey thing, for which he'd apologized copiously and attractively, she'd figured all his personality twists for some form of midlife crisis, though in her experi-ence such things usually resulted in people falling apart, not getting their shit together. It was still not clear to her which way he was heading, but it was time for some answers. Clip untwisted, she slipped it into the knob and popped the door open.

As she entered, she whispered, "He's gone fucking insane." She didn't mean to say it out loud, but there it was, as undeniable as the bizarreness of this room. On the floor, a dozen piles of books, three rows of four, each shin high, stood in perfectly straight lines like soldiers at attention, their spines aligned on one side, Post-its of many colors hanging out the other at exactly the same length. A bent card with one word, such as "Colley" or "Qualls" printed in precise block lettering, topped most piles; a few others had "Home Life" or "Cold Harbor" or "Weapons."

Patty had taken Steven's new mania for organization as a sign of matura-
tion, so when he bit her ear off for putting the 2 percent in the wrong
row or not sharpening a blunt pencil, she could excuse the attitude. But
the order imposed here had a desperate air, a depth of control that be-
spoke obsession. To the right side of the computer, on his desk, sat a
small metal file box and his office equipment laid out by category along
the top: first, black pencils, in ascending length; then reds, then blues,
then the pen selection and a box of old pastels. Every object knew its
place, each file card and sheet of paper was aligned with its neighbor; the
overall effect a silent scream warning the rest of the world to stay away
from the one place that made sense to its inhabitant. The only break
among the right angles and straight lines were the white stumps of half-
burned candles poking up from most of the level surfaces like a field of
waxy young plants bursting through the ground.

With small steps, Patty edged farther into the room. A single sheet of
white paper sat on the desk. *Your Duties For Nov. 28th*, it said along the
top, with a series of tasks neatly printed below, some home and job related, others having to do with Mt. Riga, almost as if a higher authority
had laid them out for him. Did he do this every morning? Over his desk
he had taped a map; it said, "Cold Harbor, June 1, 1864, 12:00 P.M. to
6:00 P.M." On it, flags and heavy blue arrows swooped toward a spot he
had circled with energy; red dotted lines pointed away. Drawings of
wasp-waisted nineteenth-century women surrounded it, torn from
those ludicrous catalogs she'd seen around.

Though his low whistle annoyed her quite enough, she could hear
Swan shuffling behind her, trying to stay out of the way. Some papers
bearing the reassuring logo of Dilly-Perkins, proof that he still had a job,
sat in a bin on the far side of the computer next to CDs with titles such
as *The Sounds of the Civil War, Captain Teddy's Old Tyme Fife and Drum Band
Presents a Carolina Cavalcade*, and *A Pageant of Psaltery*. Other pages in the
bin he'd scrawled dark with notes and page references to Civil War
books, index cards with even more notes clipped to them. Atop the
monitor a plastic soldier guarded the room.

She turned from the desk. On the floor a sewing box, once hers,
rested on a stool, with a pair of boxers made out of some rough fabric
folded neatly on top of it. Period underpants? That seemed too weird,
even given his wacko hobby. Behind the door, in a garment bag, hung his
uniform, shoes just to the left. The rest of the floor beyond the little regiment of books had been given over to green and red and orange leaves,

sorted, she guessed, by species, each taped to a piece of poster board bearing the tree's Latin name. The family photos and the framed page of his one interview in *Advertising Age* had come down from the walls, with only one thing in their stead—a pastel portrait sketched on heavy brownish stock. It was of a woman, the lines shaggy in an amateur's attempt to be artistic, topped with a mass of deep red hair. The face looked familiar to Patty. She'd seen this woman before . . .

"What the fuck?" she whispered. It was Becky Padden. Not exactly, of course, but considering the poor quality, close enough to connect. Did Steven still carry a torch for her? Swan continued to rustle behind her. Having him see this made her feel exposed. "You know, Joe . . . could you come back later in the week?" With a peep of assent, Swan scooted out and down the stairs.

Patty quietly stared at the portrait even as Swan pulled away; she reserved her tantrums for broken nails and secretaries. Since when did he draw? she wondered. Plopping down on the creaky old wooden chair that had apparently replaced the Aeron, she scooped up the underpants; for some reason, he'd stitched new buttons on, though a bit out of line. She could have done a better job. Why hadn't he asked her?

The rigid, nearly compulsive order of the office reminded Patty of his college dorm room. About this size, with a bed in one corner, it wouldn't look all that different from this—neat and crisp, almost prissy. Bed made, desk in order, not *that* in order, but in order. He'd always taped odd photos and quotes and postcards to his walls then. She'd thought it proof of his intelligence and drive. Then. Becky Padden's face stared at her, with all its affected innocence. He'd been so in love with Becky that Patty had never said a word to him about how she felt, not until that winter weekend when Becky was off in Baltimore, supposedly visiting an aunt. Patty knew enough people in common with the regal Becky to know that she was in fact down in Baltimore fucking some other boyfriend. Patty never told him that, though. He never needed to know that.

She had a craving for a cigarette right now, but she satisfied herself with the calming effect of picking her cuticles. Of course she still liked him, she thought. What had made him ask such a silly thing? He'd been wallowing there for a while, but she'd been no happier with herself. Was *she* a partner at some big firm? Was *she* a fashion model or Martha Stewart? Of course she liked him, Patty thought. She liked him the way she liked herself, loved him the way she loved herself. So what if she was an impatient, demanding bitch? She was as impatient and demanding of herself as she was of him. In her mind, they'd become one person with two names and clothing sizes. When their marriage had lost its tautness, she'd accepted it with the same annoyed resignation she had when the veins on her thighs got spidery, something permanent and probably irredeemable without invasive surgery. Lately, though, he seemed almost on fire, the way he'd once been. Anger never bothered her as much as passivity did. After losing the promotion, after Emily, thank God he *was* angry; he deserved to be. He finally seemed angry enough for both of them, which let her finally relax.

Yet as she scanned the walls again, it became clear to her that he'd created another world in there, and as far as she could tell, she did not have a part in it. Unlike her own combined vision, he had his own life, twisted though it might be. She imagined him having an idiotic affair with someone he didn't really love, some Becky Padden lookalike; the ugly, seething divorce. He'd move back to New York and *she'd* be the one stuck here. Every night Emily would ask where her daddy was and Nate would sit in his room blowing pot smoke out the window. She heard their crabbed discussions about schools and visitation, pictured strained meetings at graduations and weddings. He would have another family by then. And she'd be alone.

Such things happened every day. A deep breath caught in her throat. On this gray afternoon, in this tiny office, she decided that she wanted Steven to be with her by choice. How unhappy he must be, to have created a room like this. Damp cold seeped through the panes as she pulled her legs up to her chin, wrapped her arms around them. Though it meant she was on her own, she also realized that she was happier this way, with both of them trying. Folding up the shorts, Patty resolved to have this stranger, her husband, back at her side. She would have to win him away from Becky Padden one more time.

Atop the radiator sat a catalog full of hoop skirts and parasols. And corsets. Patty picked it up and paged through. Checking once to make sure the room did not look disturbed, she locked the door behind her and headed downstairs, catalog in hand.

CHAPTER

34

THE MOST SPECTACULAR CHRISTMAS SEASON in all of human history had begun. Money flowed through the streets, into superstores, over phone lines, as the New Economy spread its digital largess across North America, a cornucopia tipped over by charging bulls. Yet the question seemed not to be whether there would ever be another one like it, but whether there'd be another one at all. Packages were wrapped to songs pondering the end of the world, and sales were rung on computers that had suddenly taken an ominous cast, like slaves who'd been overheard trading whispers of uprising. Was consumer confidence driving it all or consumer fear? Whenever confronted with gaudy silver and gold celebrations of the millennium or Furby lines, Steven recalled an image from a movie that had always depressed him. As alien spaceships approach, a boy and his dog gorge themselves on the contents of an ice cream truck overturned in the panic, blissfully unmindful of the fact that they are soon to be incinerated. Or maybe they *did* know? Even as a child, he'd always thought the boy's parents had to be insane with grief. Out of time, on its mountaintop over the clouds, Christmastime Riga Village bore no such peril, though. Mrs. Melton and the other ladies of the town had replaced corn stalks with pine boughs, pumpkins with red ribbons, and, suffused with the knowledge that they had another hundred and fifty or so Christmases to go, the citizens walked the paths with a calmer joy, happy to forget that technology had once killed this village, too.

With no time to prepare, Steven had had to improvise a costume for his son consisting of a cut-down pair of old corduroys, a flannel shirt, and his pea coat, which, to his dismay, fit Nate well. The effect was more turn-of-the-century newsboy than Steven had hoped, and, like a popular child stuck with a tagalong sibling, he stepped away whenever he introduced his anachronistic young companion. While Steven expected Nate to return the hospitality with sullen, teenager grunts, instead he lunged at every person in period garb and thrust out his hand with brio, the fingerless gloves and verve lending him an Artful Dodger air. He wondered what Polly would make of him.

By now the last remaining stands of brilliant leaves had fallen, and browns and blacks had stepped forward in their absence, lit by an occasional thatch of tan or what could be generously called dirty orange. Bare trunks showed, and those trees that held their foliage to themselves made brittle sounds as the withered leaves shivered in the wind. Though full, these trees seemed more dead than those that had given in to the inevitable, seemed frozen in place and undignified for not letting go. The pines, on the other hand, stood wise and prepared. Their needles, as out of place in July as a bulky sweater, were exactly the right thing for this weather, and their unremarkable green the only lively color in the woods. There was little to do now but wait for the first snow.

Nate trotted a few paces ahead toward Mr. Guston, who leaned against the school door frame, eyes half shut, as if drawing what heat he could out of the pale sun. Steven held his breath. That morning Mrs. Melton, with a rare smile, had explained first person to Nate, but Steven could only hope for mercy from Riga's Mr. Blackwell.

Before Steven could offer a warning, the boy had made his approach. In seconds he had the imperious Mr. Guston not only engaged in pleasant conversation, but also curving one eyebrow up in an unnerving display of interest. Steven immediately trotted over. The talent to connect had skipped over him, and while he'd never imagined Nate a gladhanding businessman or a taiko drummer, he could no longer presume anything about his son's future. Nor could he about Emily's, he decided. Even if you knew all the details of their lives, what they ate every day and the exact toy every stray part belonged to, you would have no clue as to what they were thinking.

His lips curved with amusement, Mr. Guston extended a cool hand to Steven. He scanned Nate again as if about to ask Steven for a price. "My thanks, Mr. Trow, for bringing your fine son to our village. He tells me you passed Mr. Lincoln's day of thanksgiving in search of fowl . . ."

Phillip's presence and the growing détente between him and Patty had compensated a little for what had rushed out of him on Thanksgiving morning. Feeling as bad as if he'd slapped his wife and daughter, Steven had talked away the tears in the house after the turkey incident, and Patty had later discussed Phillip's coming to live there with surprising openness. And yet his father's pleasant visit couldn't shove the idea of killing a man out of his brain. Trow had made it all so palatable, so understandable. Now that he'd seen it happen in his head, shot a bullet, felt the hopeless black anger that was a prequisite for murder, Steven had none of the disquieting questions as to the nature of the experience that might otherwise dissuade a reasonable man from such an impetuous act. Killing a man dangerously approached experience in Steven's mind; like heart surgery or filing for bankruptcy, it was becoming something awful and unconsidered until necessary, yet fathomable all the same.

Still, he regretted this ability to understand murder, and right after shooting the gun, he'd shoved the remaining cartridge far back in the drawer, explained to Nate that he could not clean, carry, load, or otherwise touch his rifle, requested that he not say anything about the incident. And now this. "Well, I . . ."

Nate jumped in. "Aye! We made it clear to Bear Mountain the two of us without a bird till Father finally spotted a party and took the fattest. Did we not eat well that day, Father? And Mother's mince pie? The finest!"

"Indeed. Indeed." Steven felt as if he'd been dropped into an episode of *Masterpiece Theater,* his transforming uniform just a costume, as he'd feared Nate's presence would make it. "Well, friend. Cold enough for snow, is it not?"

"That it is, John. That it is. And it's a true pleasure to make your acquaintance, Daniel," said Mr. Guston, who put one hand on his hip and the other on Nate's shoulder. He had such a trim waist that Steven wondered if Guston himself wore a corset. Dandies of the 1840s did, and Guston certainly was a dandy. "We are glad to have you here in Riga Village," the postmaster said to the boy.

"Aye, I do like it here. 'Tis a fine village."

'Tis? Steven rolled his eyes, but a grinning Mr. Guston nodded. "Thank you. I'm certain a fine young man such as yourself will help us make it even finer. Especially if you follow the words of your father. He's a good man and he does much here of importance. He may be mayor of Riga Village someday." Nate beamed up at his father's face with a look of admiration. Steven could not remember when his son had last looked at him that way. "Will you be making any more charcoal, John?" It was long before the day he'd nearly killed them both with his eye-closing business. "John?"

And now Trow had made him forget his own name. "I do apologize, Mr. Guston. My mind's wandering today. Too much turkey, I'm afraid. No, we'll not be doing another pit."

A few moments later Mr. Guston excused himself without a sniff and they moved on, Nate occasionally turning to Steven with that hopeful expression, searching for a sign that he was doing well. The boy's complexion had cleared; he was red-cheeked as he smiled. This might have been easier if he didn't fit in, thought Steven. Nate would have hung around in dark corners, sneaking cigarettes, while he got on the business of his real life. But now he'd have Nate at his side always, just as Manskart had said. The distance between father and son widened a bit, and Steven watched as two dowdy women struck up a conversation with the boy. When Nate pointed back in his direction, grinning proudly, Steven could hear him say, "I do not know this Steven Armour of whom you speak. Here is my father. John Trow." Steven couldn't decide whether he was shattered or relieved.

A little while later, while Nate was feeding the cows under Mrs. Melton's eye, Steven caught up with Swan outside the store and treated him to a pickle. "So, friend," asked Steven. "Explain if you will the scene in March. Cold Harbor. I've not attended this type of event. For instance, how many people do you guess will be present?" Trow needed to know. Nothing strange about him asking his friend Cal.

"Oh, hell. Fifteen, twenty thousand?" Swan stubbed out a cigarette and took a bite of the pickle. "They usually have 'em in the middle of nowhere. In a forest or in some farms or something nearby the actual thing." Swan described what he'd seen in the past, the two camps for each army and their civilians, the sutler alley. "You know, everybody's walking around in uniform, and I gotta tell you, that feeling you and me were talking about, how you just go back in time? Man, it can really hit you at one of these. Like you can totally turn into your impression."

"Any officers of the law in attendance?"

"Cops, you mean? Yeah? Never seen it. Most I ever seen a cop do at one of these is direct traffic." Swan regarded the pickle with the one bite out of the top, then looked back to Steven. "Man, you can totally lose it out there." He checked his pocket watch. "We better get going. The colonel's gonna chew our asses off."

With great effort, Steven thinned a torrent of Trow's profanity into a simple "Fuck him." They gathered Nate and headed over to the field. Stranded here in the land of predestination, Steven wondered as they approached whether or not he could still reject John Trow's tragic fate, a fate the letters pointed to as much as Trow's urging. Yet as the regiment mustered, Manskart and his wife could be seen on the fringe fifty or so yards away having an obviously difficult moment. Bobby Osselin tugged at Steven's arm. "Steve! Hey! John!" Kellogg leaned forward and said something with vehemence into Polly's face, now hiding in her hands. He knew. What else could it be? Please stop making me hate you, thought Steven. He bit at a fingernail. Thick strands of red hair swayed from Polly's head like Spanish moss, as if she'd torn at it or her head had been violently jostled. "Hey, come on!" said Bobby. "I wanna show you something!"

Over the holiday, the Osselins had apparently come over to his side of the regiment. Great blotches of grease stained their once pristine jackets, and a layer of gray dirt almost blurred their sympathies. The disarray of Hube, who'd been especially striking before in his perfect bandbox uniform, made their unwashed hair and unshaven faces seem almost a pity to Steven. "Wow!" he said. "You guys look great!"

Bobby bounced up and down. "You really think so?"

"Absolutely. Meet my son, um, Daniel." Steven's eyes skidded over the Osselins' shoulders. The colonel had broken away from Polly, and she continued weeping as he bore down on the men with decisive, ill-tempered strides. The thought of never seeing Polly again hardened in Steven's stomach, presently larger and more sour than any thought of losing his family.

Kellogg came to a stop next to a tall drum about two feet high, with shiny crimson rims around top and bottom and a folk art painting of an eagle grasping a shield in its beak, arrows in each claw, in the middle. Now in the minority, the colonel, with his lustrous blue coat, gleaming buttons, and snowy white gloves, stood out among his largely grubby men. He paced up and down the line as the men held their silence, then settled in front of Bobby and Hube, scratching his beard with a gloved hand as he took in the new defectors.

"Well, you *campaigners* may be disappointed that we shall not have another march such as we had last week." The colonel smirked, though the men had the good sense not to groan, object, or cheer. "Instead, we welcome a new man to our ranks," he said, waving Nate forward with his fingertips. "Private Trow, I welcome you to our ranks," and as he shook the boy's hand, "We will expect much."

Though desperate to speak with her, to touch her, to find out what Manskart knew and whether he needed to listen to Trow and her letters, Steven resisted the urge to signal Polly even as he watched her from the corner of his eye. The risk was too great. She would tell him everything after drill, he told himself. They would make love. Reaching inside her reticule, green velvet, rimmed with some dense fur, she pulled out a handkerchief, dabbed at her nose.

"Gentlemen, I personally vouch for the quality of this drummer," the colonel continued. "And I would like to present him with his tools." After a salute, Nate accepted the drum and sticks from Kellogg, who glowed with the look of a parent pulling a gift from behind the tree.

Look at him, Steven told Trow, praying the message got through to wherever it had to go. He's not worth killing.

Trow had no interest in discussion. You must act, came the reply.

Details and reasons, wearying by now, once again paraded through Steven's mind as his anger mounted. Yet however much he had the urge to push back against Trow, he found less of himself to summon, as if he were waiting for someone to haul the rest of the old Steven away.

Nate strapped on the drum. For a moment he stood alone in front of the men, unsure of his next move. Finally he looked at Kellogg, who gave him an encouraging nod. With a deep breath, Nate snapped off a few very crisp, very tight rolls to break the ice. The men, who'd started to trade nervous looks, began nodding instead. Then, with no direction from his commander, the boy segued into a military marching rhythm. After a few seconds of that, Nate's big elbows angled up, flinging his hands skyward, and when they came down, the marching beat broke into a crackling dance step full of backbeat, a multilayered pattern of rhythms straight out of a Grambling half-time show.

The entire regiment bobbed and laughed as Nate's knees pumped. He marched with wild, exaggerated movements, his body swaying with the beats, arms flying high. He strutted figure eights around Kellogg, shifted effortlessly into a samba, and then back into the half-time show. Nate's face illuminated the field. Nearly ecstatic, he let his head roll where it wanted, his lips working silently, eyes rolling back at times, focusing only at moments when he tried to catch his father's eye. Hardly masters of rhythms, the others moved as best a group of middle-aged men could move, nodding their approval to Steven. Manskart grinned as Nate drummed on.

Kill him, said Trow.

Steven realized his boy was showing him what he loved best, the thing he did best, what was good about him, and he panicked, the way he had with Daluisa. Repeating his own name in his mind, Steven rummaged about for some part of the old Steven, the man who'd attended every Little League game and school musical presentation, for some dried bits of affection and identity to stand in for current interest. He closed his eyes and tried to fall back into his old life, but as he did so he had the sense that no one stood behind him, that even if Trow released him, he'd have nowhere to return to. All he really wanted right now was for Nate to stop. He *wanted* to be proud, and a part of Steven did want the boy up there with him, wanted to do all the things a father should want to do. And yet he could only guess now at what the boy wanted and needed, and the effort to learn hardly seemed worth the effort when he still had so much to learn about Polly.

Nate's eyes always came back to him. Steven had been so eager to give away who he was, to replace the trivia of his life for the trivia of history, that there seemed to be nothing left to surrender. Hadn't Nate denied his name just minutes earlier? And yet as much as he wanted to blame it all on Trow, be it spectral or psychological, he asked himself whether the Steven who'd enjoyed football hadn't died a long time before, along with the person who listened to new kinds of music, who laughed out loud at TV shows, who played with the kids, took hours of home movies. The man who knew his children and wife. If not *that* man, Trow had indeed brought someone back to life. The night before, at bedtime, Emily had said, "I love you, Mr. Trow," and went on to ask if he was their daddy now, as if Patty had been suddenly widowed and he was the charming new man in their lives.

Only Polly stood completely still like Steven, as if stricken by the show. With every beat from his drum, Nate's intrusion shredded their world more and more. Finally Steven met one of his son's looks with a dark stare, and though the soldiers and all the spectators who had gathered could have listened for a few more minutes, the boy downshifted the rhythm back to the military tempo with which he'd started. He came to rest, bowed, and doffed his cap, and the field burst into applause.

*   *   *

After the morning session, Steven checked to see if anyone was nearby, then pulled Nate aside near a farm building with a violent tug on his lapel. "You cannot do that! You *must* stay in the time period. You *must* stay in first person."

Confused, Nate flushed and looked around for help. "What did I do, Father? I thought—"

"Don't call me 'Father'! I'm your dad!"

"But you just said—"

"What the hell were you thinking? It's not from the time period. All right? That sort of drumming . . ." Steven sputtered. How was he supposed to reprimand him for being too talented? "It's unheard of. You know, it's . . . it's the devil's work." Did he really just say that? Nate squinted at him. "Oh Jesus. You know what I mean."

At that moment, Polly's green velvet appeared a few yards behind Nate and stopped there. Steven affected a Great Dad voice, bluff and rolling like Kellogg's. "Good job out there, son. Fine job. Could you go fetch me a coffee? I'm freezing." Puzzled by the swift change in his father's attitude, Nate turned around. He didn't move, curious as to why his father needed to have a private discussion with this woman. "Black," said Steven as he handed him his tin cup. "No milk. No sugar."

Nate stared her up and down, and finally agreed. "Bobby said he was going to show me how to bloat, anyway."

Once Nate disappeared into the store, the two looked at each other, and before Steven could speak, Polly said, "My God, I've missed you." Slipping around the corner and inside the empty farm building, they pressed into each other's arms, Steven's hand rubbing all over her back and sides where the corset held her, down to where it stopped and she softened. She gasped as he touched her, as she had when they'd made love the first time, and she wrapped the name *John* within her heavy breaths. All of Trow's anger went into his embrace, into the force of his hands as they slid back up her sides, onto her breasts and farther up, along her cheeks, until only his index fingers traced her face and they stopped for a moment. "Polly, does he know?"

"No, I don't think so."

He exhaled and smiled. Set free from fear, perhaps even from murder, Steven ran his hand through her hair, held her head at its back so that he could force his mouth further onto hers.

You love this, said Trow.

Do I love *her*? asked Steven. He thrust his face into her neck, kissed her in the small cup where it met her shoulder as she stroked his head. "Darling, what's wrong?"

He held her closer, then heard Trow whisper in her ear, "Soon you will be free again. After Cold Harbor. Free forever."

Startled, she cut him off, put her fingers over his mouth, stuck them in. "Shhhh. Please be quiet. Please," she said.

He began to suck on her fingers, his tongue lingering over some places, flicking at others. She reached for the front of his pants with her other hand, and he pulled up the front of her skirt. They moved in a slow rhythm until she pulled him in toward her and he could feel himself against her body. She shivered at the contact, and he pressed forward leaning to kiss her as she pushed back at him. As he slid into her, they fell into motion, his movements short and hard, hers wilting, a giving over. Polly let her head go loose, the hair fall forward, but suddenly stiffened at a sound.

"Dad?" Nate crunched in the dry grass outside the barn. Pulling herself off him, Polly shoved her skirt down and, with a final hard kiss, ran out, tears falling again. Steven stood shrinking in the cold, with only one weekend left before Riga Village went into hibernation. "Dad? I got your coffee."

Embarrassed, Steven shoved himself back into his trousers. The strong scent of Polly clung to him, and he relished it as much as he wanted to get clean.

Kill him, Trow said. Accept your responsibilities.

As Nate handed him his coffee, Steven decided that he had to make an effort to find the man he'd once been. If he couldn't, he thought, he might as well be a killer.

CHAPTER

35

SUNDAY MORNING STEVEN EXPLAINED in forceful terms that he was not to be called "John Trow" around the house, an edict Nate skirted all day by calling him "Father" in an only semi-ironic fashion as he hovered, asking questions about the rifle and Riga Village. Once the place cleared out on Monday, Steven turned the satellite dish inward in search of signs of the old Steven. Five hundred channels beamed into their television; surely somewhere among them a rockumentary or a replay of the Ice Bowl or an episode of *Taffy's Time* on TV Land would speak directly to him, stir a pulse of amusement, a nostalgic tug. He molded himself to the couch and began clicking, image after image flying past, but for all his hopes, by Channel 263 he felt as if he were standing in front of a Korean deli steam table, fascinated by the possibilities of the pepper steak, the fatty allure of the macs and cheese, yet equally revolted and wary, too. A feeling of disgust came over him as he realized he was still in his pajamas, unshowered, watching television at ten o'clock on Monday morning. He considered pulling out the photo albums, but the message came clear and strong from Trow not to bother.

He's gone, said Trow.

Steven Armour's gone. And after the last wasted hour or two, Steven couldn't mourn him. This was the best defense Steven Armour could offer? Even if he *could* fight back, the cause seemed terrible.

A little while later Dylan called. "Mr. Armour! A pleasant turkey day?"

"Yes, thank you."

"Good. There's a situation you should know about. Let me bring in Dale."

"Steven!" Dale's voice blew Steven's ear away from the phone. "Good holiday?" He didn't wait for an answer. "So here's what. Sometimes you gotta let the kids take a shot. I believe that. But it got tricky here, and we know who kept it together as much as you can call this whole *fucking mess* 'together.' "

Dylan hopped in with a reminder of who the scapegoat was. "Jay's gone on. Going to work with some beef *pay*-ple back in Omaha. Beef Consumers' Union, they call themselves, yes? K through eight outreach."

"E-mail about *E. coli.*" Dale snorted after he said it, paused for a beat, then said, "Well, Food Wizard's dead." After a second of quiet mourning, Dale continued. "Alte Zeit was all over the magic thing, anyhow. Meat Monsters, they came up with. Characters. Some kind of devil pig called Hell Pork. What the fuck is that? Hell Pork."

"We're still sorting through the pieces," said Petro, "but we'd like to hear your thoughts on something."

Looking out into the hallway from his office, Steven noticed a small pile of light blue fabric lying on the runner. After a moment he recognized it as Nate's dreadful Amerika T-shirt. Not only had the boy worn it against his expressed wishes, but he'd dropped it on the floor afterward like a shit on the rug. A wave of anger swelled in his chest and, with it, Trow, rising and expanding; a purely emotional tempest not to be reasoned with, intent only on pushing Steven to that darkest shore. He dug into the drawer and pulled out the cartridge, rolled it between his fingers, felt the ball under the paper. "Shoot."

Both Dale and Petro laughed. "You've become quite a lone wolf out there, haven't you," said Petro. "A *ray*-gular Ned Kelly." Detecting a puzzled silence, Dylan quickly gathered himself. "We think you did the right thing with Jay."

Steven couldn't take his eyes off the T-shirt. Disgust with Nate, with Dylan's yapping bullshit, rode on the top of Trow's wave. Before he knew what he was saying, "You mean dingo, don't you?" came out.

"What?"

"Not lone wolf. You don't have them in Australia. You mean dingo."

"Well, I guess. They're more like a coyote, but . . ."

As much as he generally admired Trow's high level of gamesmanship with the DP crowd, dissing his boss in front of one of the big boys did not strike Steven as smart play. But still his stomach churned, and the T-shirt remained on the floor, just out of his reach.

Dale did not seem to register the affront to Dylan. "Okay, Marlin Perkins, here's the challenge. We've been marketing the piss out of women, moms, kids, families, even pets, for chrissakes, but if I may say this, since I'm with friends, everybody's fucking forgotten about men, with all this politically correct bullshit. Whatever happened to food for men? Men's food. Big stews, meat, potatoes. Traditional family values food."

Petro chimed in. "Comfort food."

"Nope," Dale rumbled. "That sounds kind of lesbian to me. Like that Fried Tomatoes movie. Anyhow, the agency has fucked this up royally, and it's our big push for next year. We got a whole line of men's food coming and we're thinking of letting new media get into the mix on driving this. It's where things are going. Lots of men on computers nowadays; it's the new garage. Guys fucking around with their machines, turbocharging 'em, talking about RAM like they used to talk about horsepower."

"The Swiss were com-*plate*-ly happy with Gerda's Kitchen—Allan and Mark both *loved* it—and I'm sure that was all your doing. So can you wrap your head around this one, mate? Get us some thoughts for tomorrow?"

Oh, "mate" it was now, was it? From Dylan, who'd been so disappointed in him. They'd be renting *Gallipoli* together soon, Steven thought bitterly.

"I will do what is possible," Trow said firmly. Steven's eyes widened when he realized what he'd just said instead of the expected *yes, you betcha*. Was Trow trying to get him fired, trying to blackmail him into murder? "But it is short notice. I'm struck by the fact that we're *all* in this situation together. Dylan, you should prepare some thoughts as well, and we'll speak again in the morning." Trow clearly did not care how Steven would have handled this; he was playing to Dale now, making the play Steven should have made years ago. Before Dylan—or Steven—could interrupt, Trow continued. "Dale, does that seem like a provident strategy?"

Dale cut off Dylan. "Ready to eat chairs today, huh, buddy? Yeah, I think that definitely sounds like a . . ." he lowered his voice for dramatic emphasis ". . . provident strategy. Dylan, let's all do our homework tonight, okay? Now, Steven, I hear you live in Salisbury, right?" Done with business, Dale shifted into Mr. Hospitality Suite, the man beloved by Sales, downer of poolside margaritas at Amanda Telestratta's.

Steven had never had any sort of social conversation with Dale, but Trow had no fear, no hesitation. "Correct. And your wife's family resides in Litchfield?"

"That they do. Cammie's parents. Great people. Don't drink. We're coming out this weekend, and we're gonna need a place to get a decent meal."

The pickings were indeed slim, but Steven and Patty had made the rounds in their first months, deluding themselves that they'd be taking regular breaks from the kids for casual but sophisticated cuisine free of New York attitude. Steven passed along a couple recommendations; then Trow said, "Dale, why don't you and Cammie drop by for a drink some night while you're up here? I'd love for you to meet my wife. Maybe that Saturday?"

Crumpled and wincing in his chair, as cast aside as Nate's T-shirt, Steven closed his eyes and hoped that Dale would gracefully decline.

"You know, let's do that," Dale said. He sounded genuinely pleased. "I think it's time you and me got to know each other better."

CHAPTER

36

ALTHOUGH SO OUT OF KEEPING WITH HER otherwise unsentimental nature, Patty did come by her Christmas obsession fairly. A member of the display and signage community, her father, Larry Bilmanet, had received as one of his few perks unlimited access to outdoor electric lights, which, on the day after Thanksgiving, he would drape and staple to every available surface of their Rogers Park bungalow. So liberal was he in his decorating that the Bilmanet home became a site of local pilgrimage. Patty had often told Steven of the cars driving slowly past while she stood at the window, waving to those who honked their horns as proof of their connoisseurship. This vignette explained much to Steven. At any time now, he knew, he could walk in on such unnerving scenes as her sucking egg yolks out of their shells with a tiny cocktail straw, or hunched over the kitchen table dicing small bits of candied fruit, eyes nearly crossed with a diamond cutter's concentration, for a *stollen* so dense as to have it own gravity. Cheap decorative objects made of porcelain or resin, often incorporating the word *Noel* or winsome mice that Patty would have stomped with a high heel during any other month, suddenly appeared on mantels, shelves, and tabletops.

This year the tree received special focus. While she had always insisted on large trees, now that they had ten-foot-high ceilings Patty demanded something taller, wider, and shaggier than ever, and she found it at a nursery on the way toward Great Barrington, a massive, vaguely Teutonic spruce with sagging branches that swooped up at the ends like spectral arms. Once in the house, it defied their efforts at erection for the better part of an hour, until at last they got it teetering in a corner of the living room. Victory achieved, Patty dispatched both children to bed and disappeared to wash sap off her hands, leaving Steven alone with the tree.

As much as he tried to ignore it, the intimidating presence in the corner only grew in the silence as he looked for the lights. At last he turned to face the naked mass of Norway spruce and said, "Hello, *Picea abies,*" just to clarify that he was not your everyday Christmas tree owner. After speaking the tree's Latin name, Steven imagined nasty forest spirits seeping out of it, while the family slept, instead of sugar plum fairies, recalling the dreary evergreens deep in the back corner of the cemetery and the boughs that rocked over John Trow's grave. Though Trow clearly did not like this tree, puzzled by its purpose, Steven set to the task of taming it with lights and their collection of insanely expensive Polish ornaments, which Patty touted daily as a smart investment.

When she returned for the official tree lighting in jeans and a silk blouse, freshly showered, she bore some presents, including Emily's gift to them. Wrapped in green construction paper and covered with red stickers, its completion had been a triumph for their daughter, according to Miss Trainey. Emily had already informed Patty that she would never guess it was a painted tile. She set down the packages, left once more, and returned with two glasses of merlot. The first cut of some anesthetizing "cool jazz" Christmas CD started.

Steven could feel Patty's fantasy begin to drag him in, a posed catalog scene that, for all its canned whimsy, part of him longed to inhabit right now.

But Trow elbowed in first. "I trust these are all the gifts we need. The Lord himself received only three."

In spite of himself, Steven continued splashing cold water on her mood as he rounded the tree, clipping lights to the branches while he added bits of his own research to Trow's bleak mood. "Christmas wasn't celebrated this way during the War. The Pilgrims banned Christmas. Did you know that? Santa was an advertising gimmick invented in New York, the way Rudoph the Red-nosed Reindeer was a Goldblatt's promotion."

Until then, Patty had been welcoming back a turquoise glass angel, dangling the ornament before her eyes, but suddenly she wrapped her hand around it. "Shall I throw out Emily's gift?" she snapped. "Nate's a little late on his shopping, what with nearly being expelled from school and all. Of course, any tips you could possibly give him on how to please you would be most helpful."

For a moment Steven thought she might pop the angel. She hadn't come out with this sort of thing in a while, but after $85 and a near hernia hauling in this tree, John Trow did not accept sass. James Trow's rough face, smeared with dirt and charcoal, came to mind, sneering. "My father would have beaten any woman who spoke to him like that," he barked.

"Your father? Are we sure we're talking about *Phil*, your father? *Taffy Time* Phil? Whose life are *you* remembering?"

Steven fell silent, unable to answer that question.

Patty boosted her courage with a gulp of wine. "What exactly are you doing up there, Steven?"

"Nothing interesting." Nonchalant, he shrugged as he wound the lights around the boughs of the last tier. "You can come up anytime and see."

"And hang out with that crew? The turban guy? No thank you. I get enough of Joe Swan right here."

She'd put down the ornament and folded her arms. Steven could tell she wanted to take this someplace he didn't want to go.

"I've got nothing to hide, Patty. All we do is——"

"Like hell you've got nothing to hide."

Steven froze while a soprano sax cover of "Have Yourself a Merry Little Christmas," more snake charmer than Bing Crosby, whined around the room and through their silence. So this is what it felt like to be caught, he told himself. The cold knife in the chest, the air rushing out. Even if Kellogg hadn't known, Patty was too smart to be wronged forever. What happened next, he wondered; would it all disappear?

And he suddenly realized that this was his chance to escape. More than anything now, Steven wanted to rest. Trow had ridden him too fast and too hard. If he came clean, there might still be a chance to save it all. He'd have to stop being Trow. Stop seeing Polly. They'd come up with something for Nate . . .

Patty took a breath, worked her jaw as she stared off toward the fireplace and the silver-framed picture of her turtlenecked parents waving back from the shores of Lake Wautosa. There were many ways this could go now; they both knew that. Her arms had slid down into a hug around her waist, as if she were cold. She looked particularly thin and delicate and breakable, still that vulnerable college student he'd fallen for, who'd left nothing to fate with her loud declarations of love. "I know about her, Steven. I saw her picture in your office."

"What were you——"

"Swan had to get in there."

He wondered whether Celia ever found out. Trow may have killed Kellogg, but what had happened to *her*? Did Trow even know what to do here? A riled up Patty would match up pretty well against John Trow, a thought that amused him. Nothing was said for too many beats; neither moved until Steven knelt down beside the outlet, plug in hand. It was time to tell the truth. A hopefulness came over him, the optimism of one about to confess. "It's not as if *I'm* in love with her." At that, he stuck the plug into the socket, and hundreds of small bulbs threw a measured, comfortable glow into the room that reminded Steven of candlelight.

Patty made an effort to restrain her sarcasm—physically, it seemed— as she continued to hug herself. She looked ill. "Well, then, who *is?*"

Should he say that he was possessed? That he'd gone a little mad? "Some other part of me, I guess. Something from the past that's come for me." Every word he spoke sounded lame to him. Should he tell her about the ghost? The letters? How he felt as if the Steven she knew, had married, had essentially disappeared? Evicted from his own life by a man from another time? Steven held up his hands in surrender, the music's mock sophistication wearing him down. "That sounds stupid, doesn't it. It sounds stupid." He shook his head, disgusted with himself, eager to ex- plain but unable to find the words.

"Well, you did break up with her, what, thirteen, fourteen years ago."

What? Still repentant, staring down at the floor, Steven cast his eyes about as he tried to figure out what she meant.

"I mean, this goes beyond carrying a torch. You're carrying the fuck- ing Olympic flame here, pal."

It was Becky. She was talking about Becky Padden.

And then the lights went out. Not just the second floor, not just the tree, but the entire house. The stereo died, and with the golden light gone, the moon's silver filled the living room. Patty could not see the disappointment on Steven's face. She sighed angrily. "Would you please get a *real* electrician instead of that idiot? All he does is walk around talk- ing to the walls. I feel like he wants to date our house." They both laughed and for an instant Steven felt back in this world. "This isn't what I wanted to happen. I didn't want to fight."

His eyes adjusted to the pallid light. "Patty, I'm not in love with Becky Padden."

"Well, I know you're not having an affair, because I would fucking clean you out," she said with as much affection as could be applied to such a threat. That was not what he wanted to hear, the sound of his es- cape hatch slamming shut. Apparently the truth would *not* set him free. He tried not to swallow or betray any emotion other than a general

mournfulness, but the reality was that the small flame of Steven was quietly getting smaller and smaller, waiting for the passing breeze that
would finally snuff it out. The kids, DP, even he had picked Trow. Patty
was his last chance to still exist as Steven Armour. He'd keep fighting if
she still wanted him. She stepped closer, so they were now both standing
beside the tree, at the fireplace. "Maybe we were too young to get married. But after Nate came I always felt it was worth it. I really did love
you. I still do."

Bouncing between worlds and time, Steven could barely mouth the
words "I love you too."

Patty touched his cheek. "I know I'm a bitch. And I know you've run
up there to hide from me. Nate said you're a real mover and shaker up
there." She looked at him with a soft expression. Years of bitter lips and
glaring eyes had disappeared from her face in the moonlight; her deep
eyes held more than shadows. "I like you this way. It's like I don't quite
know you again. I feel like we should forget the last twenty years. Just
meet each other fresh."

Steven felt the last bit of air in the room go. He lit one of the squat
holiday candles sitting on the mantel amid sprays of pine. "Do you want
me to go downstairs and see what I can do?" he asked.

"No." She folded her arms again. "I'm starting to like all the candles."
Then, lowering her voice, she said, "I didn't want to argue with you
tonight." She paused importantly, then pulled one of his hands toward
her, put it on her waist. Through the cotton he felt an unusual firmness,
a bound straightening that he'd never felt on her before. Only on Polly.
So much hope in her eyes, thought Steven. Just like that night in her
dorm room. The look of someone falling in love. "I want to be with you.
John. Whoever you are, John Trow, I love you." She kissed him, a strong,
slow kiss, then reached for a candle, pulled out of his arms, and walked
toward the stairs, grabbing her wine as she passed it. "Meet me upstairs."
After a few steps, she turned and said over her shoulder, "And bring
more candles."

On his way to the bedroom, Steven stopped in the office. Patty's kiss had
gently blown the old Steven out. All that remained was life as John Trow.
Taking the piece of hair jewelry out of the drawer and a piece of wrap-
ping paper from the little stash he kept in the desk, he looked around at
the perfect stacks of books, the drawing of Polly. He had a wonderful life

full of devoted family and purpose, he reminded himself. Hard work and commitment. The benefits were immense and obvious: he was back in play at DP, his wife liked him again, his kids listened to him, he was accepted in his community and even admired by some. So what if he'd handed over his soul?

CHAPTER
37

AFTER THREATENING ALL WEEK, a dense, wet snow finally fell across northwestern Connecticut on Friday night, edging even the thinnest of branches with a fine white line and covering the dank litter of leaves. Though sure to last only a day, snowflakes sparkled under the white sun and the blue sky, giving the world the illusion of the long rest that winter once was, before rest was eliminated. The end of Riga Village's season had come as well. Consumed by the unique duties of this millennial holiday season, the shopping, the baking, the stockpiling of cash and toilet paper, few visitors trekked up to the top of snowy Mt. Riga, leaving the village largely to its residents to store their friendships and enmities with their candle works and iron casts, to prepare for the return of the ghosts. The same men and women who would see each other frequently in Salisbury and Canaan during the months to come exchanged valedictory holiday wishes with the dry cleaner they'd visit on Monday, tearfully hugged the neighbor they were driving to the mall in White Plains next week as they packed away their Riga lives.

Yet unlike the rest of the citizens, whose sad sense that it was time to go home hushed the town as much as the snow, Steven did not accept this fate with equanimity. In the last few days, he had accepted the notion that this cluster of re-created buildings was his true home and everything below an illusion. He was Trow now. Walking through the town, Daniel at his side, trading pleasantries and kind inquiries with each passerby, he couldn't stand to leave, feeling a searing pain matched only by his urge to see Polly. In the breast pocket of his jacket sat the book of sonnets, wrapped in tissue paper; the bullet in his right pocket, bouncing against him like a talisman, a reminder of who he was, what he would eventually have to do to guarantee a future for him and Polly. Today he would pledge his faithfulness to her through their separation, assure her that no one would ever come between them again. They would make love one last time before the winter, and then it would flower again in March. John Trow would have her then. Forever.

Nate struck a quick drum roll to get his father's attention. "Dad!" Through the wonders of overnight shipping, the boy wore his jacket, pants, and kepi, though he still had on his Timberlands. Steven couldn't stand to look at them. "Dad! What's up with the guys?"

In the field ahead, all the men of the 2nd were exchanging the uncoordinated high fives and backslaps of a victorious softball team. David Burney saw them first, waved happily, and soon the group swallowed father and son into the festivities, though Steven did his best to avoid the splayed palms waved in front of him; people in the nineteenth century did not "give each other skin." Despite his recent and despised boot camp attitude, Kellogg, too, hugged and laughed among them, all seemingly forgiven at this odd moment. Lummer went so far as to pat the colonel on the stomach, while the colonel in turn pinched the cheek of Kucharsky, who stood in the center of it all, receiving the lion's share of affection. Steven had read about strange pre–Santa Claus Yuletide revels featuring such rowdiness and role reversals and figured this for a similar tradition of the Heavies, like Swan's barbecues.

Jerry Sears waded over and pumped Steven's hand. "So how'd you do?"

"How'd I do?"

"Yeah! With your Qualcomm! How'd you do? Fucking Scobeck made sixty-eight thousand dollars! I'm just sorry I didn't put more in. Kerilynn nearly killed me for being such a chicken, but I'm on Social Security, for chrissakes! How'd you do?"

Visions of a drum set dancing in his head, Nate looked up at Steven. "Yeah, Dad? How'd we do?"

Unfortunately, one of the few traits shared by John Trow and Steven was their lack of business acumen. Steven's stomach sank heavily; and if alone he would have retched. Instead, he mustered a wink and said, "We did okay," with an oblique, knowing look meant to convey both satisfaction and modesty. He waited for the consoling thought that Trow was above all of this, but Trow had his own regrets in this area and it did not come.

Jerry whacked him hard on the arm, shaking his kepi loose. "I bet you did, you smart sonofabitch!" He pointed toward Kucharsky, fangs fully revealed as he grinned the grin of one redeemed. "Go shake hands with the millionaire! I'll say this, we owe that man. This is the richest regiment in the Union Army!"

A cell phone rang. Kucharsky dug into his uniform and plucked out a tiny receiver, stuck a finger in his unoccupied ear, and professed his preference for leather upholstery over anything involving kilim. Steven closed his eyes, took long, deep breaths while Nate drummed a polka beat.

Kellogg called the men to order, for once saving Steven. Kucharsky snapped his phone shut. "Gentlemen, I believe these inclement conditions are in no way conducive to proper execution of drill, so we shall not drill today." A great cheer went up from the men, and after a moment of gloating in their secondhand gratitude, the colonel waved them down. "Instead, in celebration of a fine year, and a fine millennium, and the recent good fortune bestowed upon us—" another cheer—"let's burn some powder!" The men cheered once more as they fell in to Nate's peppy marching beat and began a half-hour of shooting that expressed each man's happiness and new power in a loud, swaggering way that words could not approach. It was an act of will for Steven not to pull out the cartridge and start shooting right there. Kellogg finally dismissed them so they could help close up the town. "See you at Cold Harbor!" he said.

The field emptied. Nate chased after Bobby, who, while not many notches up the social scale from Paul's brother, did have a clear path to a prison-free life. With his son now in the care of Japhet Beck for a while, Steven stood in the trampled snow, a circle of brown slush amid the white on the trees and the untouched edges of the field. The sonnets felt small in his pocket, the bullet heavy. He turned back toward town, toward Polly.

Three months earlier he had seen Riga Village burst alive before his eyes, saw the streets filled with people as it had been at its peak, but today a different town presented itself to him, a place drained by partings. Where he'd once seen buildings sprout from the ground, today they sank back into the ground as men and women pulled out their boxes and bags and shut the doors without a final sweeping. He watched the streets empty, a few uncoralled cows chewing their cud where once crowds and trains of horses would have shooed them aside. No smoke, no heat from the cold furnace, and with the creek freezing into a trickle, the water wheel would not move again until the spring. The store and the post of-fice, the homes, remained unlit, schoolbooks torn apart to line the drafty shacks of those staying. Plants began to swallow the outlines of the roads, mounted the timbers of abandoned houses until they collapsed. In this vision, Riga Village died before his eyes, covered by the snow, a blan-ket pulled over this mad town so that it could rest. This was Trow's Riga, the dying place he had lived in after the furnace went cold and Polly left.

Suddenly desperate, as desperate as Trow must have been when he realized Polly had left him, Steven began searching building after build-ing, most empty by now, with afternoon getting on. She was not among the shop clerks stowing the inventory into rummaged boxes from Ames, nor was she in the post office or in any of the farm buildings, preparing animals for their winter quarters in barns down below. Fi-nally, just as he admitted the possibility that she wasn't there at all, he heard the icy shimmering of a psaltery from one of the small houses past the main intersection, closer to where the Fenners had once lived. Immediately calmed, he wondered if she had gotten him a gift. The building was an out-of-the-way, less-visited place, a perfect choice, and he imagined a longer-than-usual meeting. He could not go back now. He was glad of that.

As Steven came to the doorway, he realized that he was humming the melody, if it could be called that, lacking the regular beat of most of her sacred songs. No one would ever march to heaven on this loose wave of notes, each executed with a vibrato that extended the sound long past any beauty. As much as he recognized this haunting, and annoying, song, he recognized it as one that he hated. Maybe it wasn't Polly. Steven ducked his head around, and at the moment he positively identified the woman sitting on a large crate, psaltery in her lap, as Polly, he also placed the song. It was the theme from *The Bodyguard*.

The hair rose on his neck. Like an arching cat, he hesitated to go for-ward, sensing something wrong inside this small shack. Polly put down the instrument. Though she wore the brown work outfit of their first walk along the lake, a purple Scrunchy held her hair into an off-kilter spray too vertical to be classified as a ponytail. And while Polly always sat erect, chin raised, palms up in a prim and erotically charged position of submission, this woman hunched over as she watched him walk in. This was Nancy Manskart.

He got to within three feet, arms opened in the hope that she would snap back into Polly, before she stopped him. "Stop. We have to . . . Oh,

John." She abruptly stood up. "I mean Steven. Listen to me—John. It *is*
Steven, right? *Steven*—" she said with emphasis, so there'd be no confu-
sion—"before you say anything, we have to break this off." Her face softened and even with the Scrunchy he could find Polly in there, in the
kindness. "This has been really amazing, but . . . I mean your son is up
here—"

"I'm going to deal with that as soon—"

She held up her hands. "Oh, that's not the only thing. I'm pregnant."
She shrugged her shoulders—there was nothing she could do. Steven's
eyes widened. Nancy had a lower, less breathy voice than Polly, with
none of her crisp diction, but she had a real voice all the same. "Don't
worry; it's not yours. It's Wally's. As far as I know he doesn't know about
us." He made a move to protest that she waved off. "No, Steven, it's time
to end this. It's getting too scary. I've gone too far—that letter about
killing Kellogg? Over the top. I don't know what I was thinking. I mean,
I do. I've had a wonderful time." Now she came closer, touched his hand.
"You are a very special guy. Did you know that?" Steven fought for
breath. "This was exactly what I needed. Every minute has been so special. But I *am* pregnant." Nancy dropped his hand and pressed her fingertips to her temples as she walked away. "That's what upset me so much, I
think. Wally, too. That's why we've been fighting. He thinks I haven't
been taking care of myself enough. And I'm such a cry baby. I didn't
know if I was ready yet to have a baby, so I was probably pushing it too
much. But I think I'm ready now. I need to settle down. If he ever found
out, it would kill him."

"But the letters." Would he have to beg? "This is Fate. We're meant
to—"

She laughed, not meanly, as she pulled a cigarette out of a small velvet
bag. "If you ask me, fate is what happens when you don't have a better
idea." She couldn't hide her pride, rubbing her hands together, finally able
to fully appreciate her work with him. "Did you like the handwriting? I'd
been practicing with other scripts for a while. The paper came from
some guy in Baltimore. He does all this replica stationery. Looks real,
don't you think? I did the first one on an actual piece of period paper I
bought at Gettysburg." She shrugged. "I figured, what the hey. You looked
like you'd be worth it. And you were." She bumped him with her shoulder, still pals.

That was all it had taken to fool him—some fake paper and the wish to
be fooled? "But what about the affair? They really did have an affair . . ."

"Oh, no, honey; I don't think so. I think Kellogg's wife was here the whole time." Somehow that reality had stopped mattering to him. "That was part of the fun, making it all up. I couldn't figure out any way to squeeze her in there, so I fudged it. God, you were *so* great." She had that Becky look, the head pulled back in estimation. "Mr. John Trow," she said with admiration. "You really got into it. I hope my story didn't wreck it for you. I learned *so* much about Polly. You know, I was a lit major about a hundred years ago."

"But he killed Kellogg, didn't he?" She was so much smarter than he was.

Slowly Nancy drew up a hand to cover her mouth. "Oh. My. God. Omigod. You thought they were real, didn't you?" She laughed, but stopped at the sight of his injured expression. "Jesus, Steven, how could Trow have written those letters? Those Raggies could barely speak. How could he write letters like that?" Steven sagged under the weight of his uniform, his pack. "God, I'm so sorry. I thought we were just getting each other through a rough spot, having a little fun . . ." Nancy's face suddenly reddened, verged somewhere near tears, yet the absence of immediate forgiveness from him transformed her sadness into defensiveness. "I've been trying to steer clear of you, but you weren't getting the hint. I'm *married*. I just can't do it anymore."

"So is that really Trow's picture?"

"I don't know. I bought it at an antique store in Egremont." She lit her cigarette with a lime green Bic. "It had the name on it. The guy said it was real."

"So who was the man in the uniform that day at the cemetery?"

"What man?"

"And the tragedy? Mrs. Melton told me Trow had had a tragedy."

Nancy chewed on her lip for a moment, thought hard, then shook her head. "I mean, there could be. I just don't know any more than you do about the real John Trow. I made the rest up." She looked at him. "I made *you* up."

And that quickly, John Trow went silent.

CHAPTER

3 8

PETRIFIED AND BEREFT IN THIS DRAFTY HOUSE, Steven watched Polly silently slip on her silver space boots, the matching parka, and shuffle past him. His perfect dream of comfort and lust lugged a duffle out the door and through the snow, etching a trail of brown behind her.

For the rest of the day, he staggered through the streets of Riga Village with a vacant expression, pitching in where needed to lock, close, and store, unwilling to leave, as if he were one of its ghosts. Finally only the schoolhouse cast light onto the town. Inside, Mrs. Melton put the lid back on a jar of spice cookies as Nate took a bite from the one he'd picked. They both looked up. Mrs. Melton folded her arms.

"This is a good boy, Mr. Armour," she said. "A fine young man." She shook a finger. "You must take good care of him."

Steven promised that he would, and then the three stood silently for a few seconds. More than anything, he wanted to be the last person out of Riga Village tonight, but Mrs. Melton seemed to read his mind.

"It is my job to shut out the lights, Mr. Armour," she said with more kindness than he ever remembered from her. "Go home to your family."

As he pulled up to the house a few minutes later, having left any sense of what he wanted, what he liked, who he loved, up in the dark of the mountain, Steven noticed a black BMW in the driveway. Had Swan shot his money on a car? With Nate alongside, Steven grabbed his gun and meandered to the house.

He fumbled with his keys until the door opened on a large man in gray flannel slacks, ocher turtleneck, and a tan plaid jacket, tumbler in one hand, the other wrapped around the waist of a busty woman wearing her own pair of gray slacks below a bright red twinset. Both were well-tanned and combed out like show dogs in their silk and wool, flecks of diamond and gold glinting from rings and watches and buckles and

the ornamental logos on their driving mocs; overall, a breathtaking combination of soft fabrics and precious metal.

"Welcome home, honey," said Dale with a rolling voice and a wicked
smile. "Seems you forgot a little something." Steven had never seen him
outside a convention hall. His presence filled all the corners of the living
room, and though only a few inches shorter, Steven felt that he had to
look up to him as Dale wrapped a mitt around his hand in greeting and
with a sweeping gesture welcomed him into his own home. "Come on
in. If your wife'll let you," Dale chuckled, delivering a commiserating
swat to Steven's shoulder. His head ducked tentatively forward, Steven
entered and found Patty standing in a corner, a thin, shell-shocked smile
on her face, fury at being caught unawares visible under the hastily applied layer of powder, the red slash of lipstick.

"You've met Cammie," Dale said, stating what to him was obvious.

"Well, no, I haven't," replied Steven. "It's a pleasure."

Cammie stretched out a long-fingered hand. "We really appreciate
this," she said, perfect teeth beaming like so many bulbs in a Vegas sign.

With the hobnails of his brogans clattering on the floor, Steven
rushed into a flurry of service-oriented motions punctuated with
phrases like "I'm so sorry"; "How long have you . . . ?"; and "Can I get
you . . . ?" to prove his embarrassment.

Dale held up his tumbler. "Listen, we're in great shape. Patty here's
poured us drinks, put together this nice cheese plate." He pointed to a
tray hosting a few blocks of blessedly DP Havarti and cheddar while
Cammie turned her shell of blond hair toward Patty, exposing her teeth
again, and applauded with the tips of her fingers. "This is exactly what
we were looking for."

Cammie nodded hard, though this had no effect on her hair. "No matter how much you love your parents, and I do a *lot*, you can only take so
much." She turned to Nate. "And you forget I just said that, young man."
Everyone laughed. "Nate, right? Your sister is adorable! I was telling your
mother what a lovely tree this is. Did you help . . . ?" Whether she'd
been an anchorwoman in a small market or an exotic dancer Steven
could not tell, but wherever she'd learned it, Cammie exuded charm
and good manners, golf outings with the girls, and athletic sex with her
husband. It had been a long road to Big Dale's side, and she was clearly
committed to making it her last stop.

Unlike Patty, neither Dale nor Cammie seemed to mind Steven's
tardy arrival. The big Scotches in their hands, the cheese scoured out of

the back of the bin, and the fact that they were not at her mother's house had them quite happy. Dale strolled to the bar for another round. Steven followed with the heavy steps of a new walker. Wavering between numbness and sharp pain, his entire body felt like a sleeping arm or leg coming awake, struggling to tingle its way back to life but still unusable. Though the stakes were clear, his mind refused to help. "So, you found your way here," he said, uttering anything he could think of.

"Absolutely no problem. Great place, Steve. Real New England." Dale fished around in the ice bucket, didn't look at Steven as he spoke the next words. "A secret life, eh, soldier?"

"Well, on weekends Nate and I go up on Mt. Riga. We're re-enactors. We, uh, we play historical figures who lived there in the town." He tried to dismiss the practice with a wave of the hand. "Kind of a father-and-son thing, you know? Basically an educational program." He wondered if Dale could see the panic.

"Wild. Really wild. You wanna drink?"

"Not quite yet." Steven tugged a lapel. "You know, if you don't mind, let me get out of this real quick." Frantic to reconnect with Steven Armour or John Trow or anyone who could save his job, he glanced feverishly around the house, prayed that a normal shirt and a pair of corduroys would gain him back some ground. "Nate, why don't you go up and change? We'll be right . . ."

Cammie squinted at Steven and Nate as they clanked toward the stairs. "Steve, could you wait a second? Nate, you too. Dale? Take a look at those two."

Again seated, Dale had begun focusing his square head toward the cheese plate when his wife called. He looked up, knife in hand. Despite Cammie's request, Steven continued to edge toward the stairs, shoving Nate ahead.

"No, just stand there. Both of you," said Dale. Steven grabbed Nate and stood caught in Dale's headlights. Big Dale rubbed his chin, the huge class ring glimmering in the light of the tree. A wry smile started on one corner of his mouth. "Is this some sort of *Bewitched* thing?" Steven's eyes cruised the room, looking for some clue as to what Dale was talking about. "It's like that old Minuteman, but it's got family. Father and son in uniform. Men's food! Fuck Happy Gerda! Oh, excuse me, Patty; forget I said that, kid. What's his name?"

Patty said, "Nate."

"Nate. Your dad's a genius. Did you know that?"

Steven winced a little when Nate didn't hesitate. "Well, yeah."

"He just came up with the new brand image for Dilly-Perkins's line of men's food; you know, chili, sloppy joes, stuff like that."

"I guess."

Big Dale waved Steven to his side. "I hate to cut right to the chase, because I do want to spend some time here as just folks, but let's get the work out of the way. I think Petro's whole cyber thing isn't for you." He made himself another Triscuit-and-Havarti sandwich. "You and me are old school. And the problem is that they boarded up the old school." Dale smirked at his joke and bit into his appetizer. Too exhausted and empty to think about what he meant, Steven had only the strength to imagine himself unemployed. Big Dale whisked a chunk of Havarti out of his teeth with his tongue and leaned in close. "Steve, have you thought about brand imaging?"

Because he had no idea what it was, Steven had never thought about brand imaging, though he'd heard the phrase bruited about the way *synergy* had once been. "Well," Steven ventured, "I know a lot's going on there."

"We're pulling ours in-house. I'd like to see you over there. You *get* DP. You know what DP means." He drained his tumbler and set it on the coffee table. "What's the name of this guy you play?"

Reeling, a bit sick to his stomach, Steven answered, "Trow. I am John Trow."

"Do I have to buy rights?"

❧ PART FIVE ❧

CHAPTER

39

THOUGH ONLY ONE DAY REMAINED until New Year's Eve, Steven noticed that his was the only cart in the Grand Union piled high with toilet paper and Parmalat. He had noticed this every day this week. Did no one else care that the world might be plunged into chaos in a matter of hours? Or had everyone else finished shopping already?

Emily held a can of DP ready-to-heat Dino-ghetti up to him as he wondered how much bottled water he could get away with buying today. "Daddy, you bought too much of this. I don't like this."

It may be all you have to eat soon, and then you'll be damn happy you have it, thought Steven. "It's for me. I'll eat it."

"You never eat this stuff."

Five gallons? Ten? He'd squirreled away $5000 in cash, in case all the ATMs went down or the entire banking system imploded. But without potable water, all that cash wouldn't mean much. If Sydney went black at nine o'clock EST the next morning, the lines here at the old Grand Union would be suddenly long indeed.

"I just got a taste for it."

Emily stared at the cart, then looked up at him. "There's a lot in there."

"I know. I know. Here." He handed her some shrink-wrapped mini bottles. Bizarre a circumstance as Y2K was, Steven found comfort in the sudden paranoia and hoard mentality it engendered. As he cast about for some sense of who he was now after the disappearances of both John Trow and the old Steven Armour, the constant talk of global disaster gave him flashbacks to fallout shelters and all the other dark images of imminent nuclear destruction found among the snips and snails and puppy dog tails of that generation of boys. Preparing for the end was

something he could do, something he could make sense of, something
he'd been doing his whole life.

"Can I have candy?"

Such a sweet little plea in Emily's voice. Rolling down the aisle,
Steven remembered that boy and his dog chomping away at ice cream as
the aliens approached. He came to a stop. She should have joy. Steven
tossed in five pounds of assorted Twizzlers and Milky Ways, enough for
two Halloweens.

"Wow," said Emily.

"But it's not for right now," Steven warned.

She shrugged. "OK."

Though he felt justified in his mass purchases, Steven was glad that
neither Bobby nor Hube was around to see him check out. Word was
that they had taken the whole family to Disney World for the holidays.
The thought of where Polly was right now floated across his mind.

Out the door and into the cold, he headed the cart toward the car.
Then something in the store window caught his eye. He stopped. It was
a face. Clouds of breath rising in front of him, he stared back at it. Intel-
lectually he knew it was his, knew that some portion of his self-worth
was tied to those nondescript features, yet he could no longer attach
himself to the man staring at him with the blank expression. At home,
he'd been avoiding mirrors because of the sinking feeling they caused,
the long and puzzled examination he would perform on the image facing
him, on the color of the eyes, the thinness of the lips, the beard he'd
kept at Patty's request, as if he were seeing an alien for the first time. But
now, like Narcissus, he could barely pull himself away, though befuddle-
ment more than love held him.

"What are you looking at?" Emily jumped up in an attempt to see
what entranced Steven, untying her cap in the process.

Steven had lost himself before. Three years earlier he had been staring out the conference room window at the Chrysler Building while giving blood, distracting himself from what felt like the large hose stuck
into his arm, when suddenly he had no clue as to where or who he was.
Everything, including Steven, lost its name and its purpose as he lay on
that blue vinyl mat. Merely unusual at first, the sensation soon turned
unpleasant, the blood dripping down into the bag, and he flayed out
wildly, grunting phonemes, until he fainted in a doctor's arms. Later,
over juice and cookies, he recalled hearing himself ask who he was, or
being asked, one or the other. Only a general sentience had existed in his

mind at those moments; no personality, no time. While a Buddhist may have found this experience a connection to the Great Mind, it had scared the hell out of Steven.

"Mommy said to get champagne," she reminded him. Steven shook himself free of his own gaze, but nothing raced in to fill the empty place in his mind. "And film." Nodding all the way to the car, he buckled in Emily over her thick coat, handed her one of the six Barbies she'd scored at Christmas. His sense of the future rendered as unreal as the rest of the planet's, Steven had sleepwalked into the millennial party after Nancy's announcement. He'd sent out the cards, attended the carol sing on the Salisbury Green, counted down the top ten moments of the last thousand years, and piled gifts around the tree. Right now, Nate was at home playing on his brand-new drum set. The precious leather edition of *Shakespeare's Sonnets* he'd given to Patty, a signal of their new, more imaginative start, sat proudly on the mantel. Though Steven had expected Civil War objects and other reminders of his hobby gone wrong, when he opened up the KISS CD from Nate, he'd nearly burst into tears. A trowel from Emily and a Smith & Hawken gift certificate from Patty. Phillip, a last-minute invitee for the holidays, had given him a complete set of *Taffy's Time* videos, recently reissued by some Belgian outfit. Maybe they hadn't all been so enamored of John Trow after all.

"I can try champagne tomorrow," stated Emily. "Mommy said."

"Oh, really?" He couldn't think of anything else to say. He made a right on to 44. Emily pulled out another Barbie from under the seat, and the two Barbies chatted about a recent ski vacation.

And yet the gifts weren't exactly right for the man driving this car either. As much as he wanted to wake up and find himself Steven Armour again, Frank Capra happy to be toasty in his bed next to Donna Reed, the Steven Armour he had known was most definitely gone, the tastes and passions of forty years exchanged for those of a fiction. Morning after morning he continued to open his eyes, hoping to be attached to his surroundings, the pictures in the frames, his face in the mirror, but only an empty mind remained to sift through the few true facts of Trow's birth and death, to acknowledge the guilt of adultery and contemplated murder.

"Oh, no," said one Barbie in Emily's falsetto. "We're not going out. We're going to watch the end of the world at home."

"On Fox Five?" asked the other Barbie.

"No, *Dateline* with Stone Phillips."

The world was about to end, thought Steven, and things remained to be said.

"Hey, anybody back there want a piece of candy?"

The rest of the day passed slowly. Steven paced and puttered, while Phillip entertained Emily and Nate drummed in the basement. More than once he and Patty ended up side by side, and he would tremble then, wondering whether he should say something about what he'd done, fess up before Judgment Day.

"Christ, that's a lot of toilet paper, Steven," she said when she opened the linen closet.

"Well, if nothing happens, then we're set for the year," said Steven, without a smile.

Patty took a step closer to him. "Are you okay? You seem very nervous."

Was this the moment? Should he end his own world pre-emptively and admit the affair? "No. I mean I'm stressed, but not about the Y2K thing. I think that might just be a pain in the ass for a few days."

He managed a smile, and the day went on, normal in all respects save for its possible finality. When Steven put the kids to bed, he did so with long hugs and many kisses so that there would be memories of good days before whatever was about to happen happened. Fidgety the rest of the night, he couldn't tell whether he was rooting against the end of civilization or for it.

At seven A.M. Steven was up and sipping coffee as the entire staff of CNN tried to read the future. Fiji went off without a hitch, but Steven figured that no one in Fiji even had a goddamned computer, and that seemed to be the prevailing attitude of every major news organization. Sydney was the test.

As nine approached, Steven wanted everyone in the same room with him. The news would spread like wildfire; things would start happening immediately. "Hey, Nate! It's almost midnight in Sydney!"

A few seconds later he heard a distant voice say, "Yeah?"

"So come in and watch! Emily, come on!" Reluctantly, his children gathered on the couch. Steven bit at his nails and described the fireworks show they were about to see, the most amazing in Australian history. With only seconds to spare, Patty and Phillip wandered through the room. Steven took a deep breath.

And then, at nine A.M., EST, twelve A.M. in Sydney, nothing happened. An enormous fireworks show burst off the side of the bridge in Sydney Harbor, but no planes fell from the air, no seizing-up of global financial systems. Australian blenders and jeeps functioned as before. All was right with the world.

For a moment Steven felt dizzy, almost nauseated, but as he watched Australia celebrate without incident, a tremendous sense of relief swept through him—the world they knew, the modern world, would continue on.

What struck him the most, though, was that he seemed to be happy about it.

CHAPTER

4 0

THE KIDS BOTH ASLEEP, PATTY POPPED THE TAPE into the VCR and clambered into bed beside Steven, throwing a casual leg over his as an electronic melody only slightly less louche than the score of a porn film began, the intro music for *Staying Together—Forever!*

"Millions of couples worldwide have learned Dr. Mervin Pang's secrets for marital success," said the announcer. "Millions of couples like *you!*" At this, a studio audience burst into applause and the lights went up on a stage outfitted with couches, coffee tables, and false window frames, all giving off a reassuring sense of domesticity. "Meet Dr. Mervin *Pang!*" An energetic man in a pullover bounded onto centerstage.

Steven sniggered, but not in any way that would make Patty think he wasn't taking Dr. Pang's valid points to heart. One unmistakable change in Steven's post-Trow existence could be found in the Armour boudoire; since Christmas, he and Patty had returned to a second-year-of-marriage schedule—making love twice, sometimes three times a week, with the corset reserved for special occasions. Even more surprising than the increased quantity of their lovemaking was its quality: happy, intense, and often terribly, terribly naughty, much more so, he thought, than his hurried couplings with Polly. As much as his meetings with Polly had been illicit, they'd also been essentially performances, acts of escape.

Dr. Pang rubbed his hands together. "Tonight brings us to the hardest part of our journey . . ."

Steven tried to keep an open mind about Dr. Pang, or at least the appearance of one, so he straightened up in the bed, the better to hear. Though in some ways Steven still missed the old Steven Armour, that genial working dog of a man who'd often needed to be poked awake and out of his warm spot in the sun before he'd do anything, a little action obviously went a long way. Patty leaned against his shoulder, rubbed a hand lazily over the beard she now insisted on.

"Let me start by asking every one of you a question." Pang's bulging eyes twinkled with mischief. "Do you have any secrets from your spouse?" The audience tittered. "Hmmm?"

Small beads of sweat popped up under the front hairs of Steven's brow.

"Are there things you've done—while you've been married—that you've never told your husband or wife?"

He felt an elbow in the ribs. "What sort of secret things were you doing up there, anyway? I think it's time to confess."

Suddenly strangling, Steven couldn't help himself, though he knew she was joking. "I told you! Nothing!" It came out more forcefully than he'd intended.

"Lighten up, big boy. I'm kidding."

After a second, he said, "I know."

"It's Becky Padden I'm worried about."

"Oh Christ! I'm not in love with Becky Padden!"

"You have a thing for red hair." She grabbed him playfully by the beard. "You do. Listen, you better *not* have done anything secret up there, mister. You'd be in *big* trouble." A serious warning ran underneath the last sentence.

"Turn to your spouse right now and ask them," demanded Dr. Pang. "Complete honesty is the fundamental aspect of every solid marriage. Let's take a moment right now and do this. Ask them, 'Do you have any secrets?' Ask them right now."

As the studio audience began its soul-searching, Patty turned and stared at him very hard. Steven took a deep breath. She closed her eyes once, slowly, thinking about her question, then just as slowly opened them. "Did you call about Emily's cake?"

"Yes, I did," Steven said. "All twelve are coming. I got the last RSVP today."

"Thank God." Patty paused the tape and began shifting around in the blankets, distracted now by other details of daily life. "I think she's going to have a great time. Did you reschedule Nate's drum lesson?"

"Yes." Steven began to breathe again.

"I'll buy the loot bags tomorrow. We can give them each a can of Dino-ghetti and a roll of toilet paper."

"Oh, it's so easy to laugh now." Wasn't it, thought Steven.

Patty stopped shifting around. "What if she has a seizure at the party?"

"Why would she?" They were going very low key—games in the basement, manicures, expensive cake. While still beset with intermittent seizures, Emily continued to react well to her medication, and Miss Trainey had reported enough solid progress to warrant an end to their weekly conferences.

"Too excited? I don't know. Too bad your father can't move in sooner. Emmy would love to have him here for that." Declawed and docile, Phillip had shown himself to be a threat to no one. He would be moving to Salisbury in March. After Cold Harbor.

But Steven couldn't think about that, skipped over Cold Harbor whenever he came to it. "He'd come in a minute," Steven replied, "but I think we have to get everything worked out first. I'm looking forward to it."

Whether a matter of evolution or mutation, Providence or just good luck, he could sense the shell hardening on this new species of Steven. He grabbed the Smith & Hawken catalog off the night table and began flipping through, all the lillies of the valley and violets calling to him. How, he wondered, would he look in Japanese gardener pants? Was that something he could get away with now? *Fort Bluff Monthly* had been thrown out earlier in the day, unread.

"Really, Steve. Did anything weird happen up there? Wasn't somebody playing your wife or girlfriend or something?"

Could he trust her? he wondered. Or would the truth send them crashing back to earth?

"No." He couldn't do it. Not yet. "I told you, there is *nothing* going on."

Patty regarded him with a finger on the remote, *Vogue* in the other hand. "OK. Just asking. Do you want to watch any more of this?"

Steven nodded. "Why don't we fast forward a little and see if it gets any better?" A risky move, but better cover, and his willingness would most definitely be rewarded.

His wife's leg thrown back over his, Steven placed a hand on top of her knee and the two watched Dr. Pang work the room.

CHAPTER

41

THE WORDS SLID OUT OF MARK SOLOTOW'S MOUTH, greased with his superior and slightly exasperated tone. "Well, Steven. What do *you* think?" He had butler manners, one of the reasons why Big Dale had muscled ahead of him in the line behind Allan Bristine.

Sitting one chair away from Mark at the head of the table, Steven looked up from the focus report on which he'd already doodled some seasonal motifs—a grinning George Washington head, a shamrock—and saw a five-foot-high die-cut stand-alone John Trow staring down at him. The eyes pinned Steven, whose heart beat a little faster. The art people had done a tremendous job; the uniform, the weapon, the material, every bit they'd reviewed with him to capture the essence of John Trow. The face was craggy and prettier than the photo; after all, this *was* a brand image, not history. Still, he had a hard time looking at it.

Two off-the-shelf young creatives named Max and Hannah, each sporting the same small black rectangular eyewear, actually leaned forward to hear what Steven had to say, as did a few of the executives sitting around the long conference table. It was, after all, *his* meeting. Steven doled out his words slowly for effect. "I like it." Pause. "A lot." Then he sat back, squinted hard at it, and sighed. "What do people think about the cap?"

Max flinched. "What? What about the cap? Is it the color? We did a test—"

"No, the color's fine. It's just . . . I don't know. He looks . . ."

Dale caught his eye, winked, and nodded approval. The shift over to Brand Imaging had offered a respectable if not eye-popping raise but no "Senior" to go with his VP. Still, Steven did have the light back on him, and Dale had let out a lot of rope. Though he had recently misplaced his own identity, Steven Armour was now paid to understand the identity of

a multinational food conglomerate and, out of that understanding, produce images that expressed what DP wanted people to express about
how they felt about DP, thus making people more likely to express that
feeling when asked. In essence, he did the company's makeup. Sentences
combining "core values" and "mission" with "string cheese" and "child-
directed family snack" fell out of his mouth with relative ease. So absurd
was this world, at once so cynical and starry-eyed, that Steven could be
as ironic or earnest as he felt at any given moment and have his ideas received with equal interest and favor. This life of free-association agreed
with the wanderer Steven's mind had become.

By now Mark had assumed the same assessing squint as Steven. "He
looks Republican. You're absolutely right. It's the cap. It's very low, very
Clint Eastwood. Do we want that message for DP?"

Dale said, from the other end of the table, "What the hell's wrong
with being a Republican?"

With her long, straight black hair and all-black outfit, Hannah looked
as if she belonged at Sarah Lawrence smoking clove cigarettes thirty
years ago. "Maybe this is useful: ninety-three percent of the males eighteen to fifty-four surveyed at nine different enclosed malls one Saturday
in January responded that they would buy a product featuring a Civil
War soldier on the package."

Steven broke away from Trow's cardboard stare and returned to his
doodling. With virtually nothing factual to work with, the copy department had told John Trow's story as one of simple, solid family joy.
Happy husband, father of a large brood, John Trow returned from the
Civil War to start a restaurant in a small Connecticut town. That restaurant no longer existed, of course, but its tradition lived on: "Together,
with Family Man brand foods."

Max's voice quivered. "We'd like to show the alternate uses. He did
really good on cured meats and canned stews. They really like the head
shot." He fumbled with some papers, muttering a little as he did.

Steven tried to steal a look at Trow, but turned away quickly. For
large chunks of time now—the whole drive down to New York this
morning, for example—the autumn's events and turns of fortune felt to
Steven like things that had once happened to him, and he reminded himself of that now. A man named John Trow had indeed once lived on Mt.
Riga, but the character Steven had been playing was exactly that, a character, his occupier, hero, and ultimate possessor just as imaginary as this
two-dimensional figure glaring at him from across the table with its

oddly penetrating eyes. Aside from the photo, he had no clue to what the real Trow had been like.

The lights dimmed slightly as Hannah pulled the pointer away from Max. She began the PowerPoint demonstration. RELIABLE—FILLING—HAS TASTE read the first image. He wanted to confront Trow head on, stare him down, and prove that he no longer had any power over him. He looked up and met Trow's eyes. Instead of dominance, though, suddenly he felt accused.

Hannah cleared her throat. "These are the key qualities men have identi—"

Whatever is looking at you is false, Steven told himself. John Trow was a fictional being, a brand image no more real than the Jolly Green Giant or the Pets.com Sock Puppet. Steven had done that, trapped him in a logo, locked him away in the land of TV trivia along with Taffy, so that he could move on.

Mark leaned over to Steven and whispered, "Did you get my memo on the new Gerda?" Steven shook his head no. "Well, I think we should go with Hingis. I know Dale likes Graf, but the nose is a problem for me. Maybe Graf with a nose job." Shrugging, Steven turned his attention back to Hannah and her idiotic correlations. All of this marketing blather seemed unworthy of John Trow.

A large package of bacon appeared on the screen. "As mentioned, John Trow scored extremely well here, in cured meats. The numbers spike with bacon, but all pork products seem a perfect match with our John."

And then Steven heard a voice, a familiar voice that only he could hear.

Kill him, it said.

He flinched, shocked not only but by the words, but the voice, supposedly gone, that spoke them. He whispered, "What did you say?" to Mark, who clearly hadn't said a thing. Nor had anyone else in the room other than Hannah; Steven knew that. He recognized the voice too well. The table, his hands, the screen—Steven looked at anything other than the cutout across from him. In the thick air of this sealed conference room, a dreadful possibility had become manifest. Maybe his life had not really changed. Maybe John Trow had only been hiding, and Steven's own particular darkness still thickened outside the pale light of his recent happiness.

A bar graph replaced the bacon. "What was a total surprise was the success of Family Man resealable carrots and prepared salads." Steven watched Max slouch farther down in his corner, push his glasses back up the bridge of his nose. "The only difference from the entire Crisp Time packaging set was a change in logos and type and . . ." Steven sat up very straight in his chair.

Though he did not hear Trow's voice again the rest of the day, he listened for it through the oldies and sports talk he cranked the entire drive home. Coming in the door at eight, he found the mail on the dining room table: an insurance bill, *Elle*, two offers to switch his long distance carrier, and a thick envelope postmarked Riga Village.

Steven dropped his briefcase. Was Polly coming back too? He tore open the envelope and found a form letter with his name penned into the salutation.

Dear Private Trow,

The time for action is nigh! The 2nd Connecticut Heavy Artillery has been called to the front by Father Abraham to rightly serve the cause of the Union! You are ordered to report to Cold Harbor on March 23, 2000, with rations for two night's stay on the fields of Virginia. Enclosed is information regarding the area, a map, and a list of materials required. Car pooling will be arranged.

Steven realized that Phillip was moving in that same weekend.

Do your family, your state, and your nation proud!
Huzzah!
Colonel Elisha Kellogg

Below, in Manskart's boyish script, was a personal note.

SA—Remember that you and Nate MUST attend as required by your son's probation. You must also attend the opening of Riga Village on April 1. WM

Kill him, said John Trow.

CHAPTER

42

HAVING PAID FOR EMILY'S PRESCRIPTION, Steven reviewed the Salisbury Pharmacy's extensive selection of homeopathic remedies and considered which his symptoms qualified him for. *Aconite: Good for anxiety, arrhythmia, shock. Ferrum phosphoricus: Good for nosebleeds, vomiting, incontinence.* Since moving here full time, Steven had regarded the pharmacy as the heart of Salisbury, largely because the people who worked there had been the first to greet him with local familiarity every morning when he picked up his *Times*. Even though the months on Riga had turned him into a known commodity, wandering the aisles to browse the tick nippers and imported shaving brushes still gave him a sense of comfort. *Mercurius vivus: Good for backache, abscess, earache with discharge of pus.* Other small bottles offered relief from stage fright, joint pain, and hard, dry stools.

Steven idly rattled the bag of Euthosuximide. *Ignacia: Good for tension headaches, irritable bowel syndrome, hemorrhoids, depression, grief.* He lifted the bottle out of its rack, and as he asked himself why he was lifting it, what exactly he was grieving, the bells of the front door rang. When he looked up, Steven saw the new customer: a man, standing at the counter in a light-blue-and-white striped vest from the Snack Shack, a putt-putt golf place on the way to Great Barringon. Tall, bearded, and lanky, the man—for he was most certainly a man, not John Trow's ghost—slapped a *New York Post* and tin of Altoids down on the counter. Sighing angrily at the lack of immediate attention, he tossed some balled-up dollar bills onto the Kodak blotter and stomped off toward the door.

Should he do this? Steven thought for a second, half-expecting Trow, this man's double, to answer, but Trow remained silent. It was up to him, so Steven dropped the ignacia and dashed after the fading bells of the other man's exit. Out the door with no clear intent aside from not losing him, he saw the last of a heel and a hand swinging around the corner of the pharmacy, down the walkway toward the gourmet supermarket and the parking lot. For this first Thursday in March, a sunny day trying hard to reach the fifties, Steven had dressed optimistically, and shivered now in his flannel shirt and light jacket, rubbed his hands, blew on them as he counted to three, then took long, casual strides to get the man back in his sights. Lagging behind all the way to the lot, Steven quickly slipped into his car.

Hidden behind the smoked glass, he watched him open the door of a LeSabre, butterscotch and pocked with rust holes. "Who is this guy?" he asked the Navigator. Why was he following him? Before he could answer either question, the Buick pulled out onto the side street that led to Route 44. Through the many curves and switchbacks around Salisbury's hills, Steven followed as close as he dared, his stomach tightening. What were his questions, he wondered, aside from Who are you? How much more did he want to know about John Trow? Only the ice scraper on the floor offered itself as a weapon if this man objected to his inquiries.

Steven listened for Trow's voice, but didn't hear it.

"It's over," Steven said out loud. "Don't you get it? I'm happy! Everything's fine now! Leave me alone! You're a fucking figment of my imagination!"

But there were things that he'd chosen to forget, details he'd been happy to let Nancy Manskart's confession explain away. While this man driving ahead of him, identical to the one in the photo, offered another explanation for Trow's ghost on that dank day in September, small things about John Trow began to jut out as the comforting forgetfulness of this winter melted a little. There were sides of Trow that she hadn't known, he reminded himself, details that bore no relation to her fake letters. She'd never heard of the black banker Allan Blunt, for example; she didn't know that Trow loved checkers and those damned brussels sprouts he'd eaten all those months. Nancy had written nothing about Cold Harbor, yet he'd had a vision of that day so vivid that its colors had only recently begun to fade. He hadn't made all of that up, had he? And who was this guy up ahead?

Ten minutes from Salisbury, past Canaan center, the Snack Shack appeared on the right, the last thing of interest before the Massachusetts line. During the summer Nate and Emily clamored to be taken here for pee-wee golf, batting cages, and better than expected road food doled out from a faux log cabin. Apparently based on some of the more impressive PGA desert venues, the landscaping of the golf course boasted an unusual range of plants and beautifully kept greens, all ribboned with streams and fountains spouting water tinted the same atomic blue as Windex. Today it was empty. Mounds of dirty snow remained through-out the vacant lot as the red, white, and blue OPEN flag snapped in the sharp breeze. Steven parked near the batting cages, a few cars down from the LeSabre, and stared from behind his windows until he spotted Trow inside the equipment hut.

The Navigator's engine ticked. Operating on pure impulse up to this point, Steven reached down and slipped the scraper into his pocket as he considered just how good an idea this was. Only the truth could settle things, he decided. To bury Trow once and for all he needed to know who Trow was.

With a deep breath, Steven opened the door, hitching up his pants as he strolled over to the hut. A good six inches taller, the man stooped over the Astroturf counter, polishing junior clubs as a wall of pinball ma-chines flashed and whooped behind him. His nametag said "Len Trow." Clearly once dashing and bearded in a biker sort of way, Len had begun the descent from the glory days of *la vie bohème*. The gray hairs ran even with the brown, and old age loomed like the floor coming up on a knocked-out boxer. As Steven stepped forward, Len's knobby hand gripped a club and raised it a very quiet, very menacing few inches.

"What the fuck are you following me for?" growled Len. His beard and hair had seen only a cursory tug of a comb, his expression was more scared than tough as he made small circles in the air with the head of the putter.

Steven held up his hands in a posture of surrender. "Listen, I'm sorry. I'm not trying to mess with you. But I work up at Riga Village, you know? And you look a lot like someone I'm doing some research on." Without waiting for a response, he pressed forward. "This sounds crazy, but do you have an ancestor named John Trow? Or Daniel Trow?"

Len scowled and looked his visitor up and down. "What the fuck business is that of yours?" he said brusquely, though the resistance in his voice had to weakened at the news that Steven had no law-enforcement affiliation.

"Well, we're trying to learn as much as we can about the people who lived up in Riga Village around Civil War times. I do an impression of a guy named John Trow, and I think, from all I know, that you look a hel-luva lot like him. You have the same name and all, so I was just wondering if there was any relation. Some families let us read letters and diaries and stuff like that, if they have 'em."

Trow did not speak for a moment, and his expression did not change, until he said, "Did you know he was a crazy ass motherfucker?"

For some reason this did not surprise Steven. "No, I didn't."

"Yeah, he died in a fucking mental institution." Len dropped the club onto the Astroturf. He smiled now, baring teeth stained tan by tobacco. "You really run around pretending you're my relative?"

"Well, it's like an educational thing, you know?" Len continued grinning, pleased to meet someone possibly more out of whack than he was. "I'm sorry I was trailing you around, but I wanted to see if you knew anything about him."

Len picked up a little putter, held it close to his eyes for a brief inspection, and started hitting his palm with it. "Okay, *Grandpa*." Len snorted. "Here's what I know. He was my great-great-great-grandfather, I think. A fucking maniac partyer. If they had 'em, he would've been an Angel, you know?" Though he seemed like the kind of guy who'd have been proud of having a Hell's Angel ancestor, Len became serious as he tucked the putter into his armpit and scratched at his beard. "So he gets back from that war, right? He was no citizen before, but he was a decent guy, I guess. He'd buy you a beer and shit. But now he's a total fuck. You know, like a *punk*." Shaking his head, Len put down the club and began wiping Day-Glo golf balls with a rag. "So the thing is, while he was gone, his son, Daniel, my great-great-grandfather, knocks up some chick. He doesn't say anything right away, because his father is so obviously fucked in the head, but the girl finally comes by so he's gotta tell him." A veteran bar stool storyteller, Len let Steven hang there while he put the balls in their proper hoppers. "When the girl takes off, whaddya think he does?" More Socratic method. Steven shrugged. "He gets a fucking hoe and kills his own kid with it." Len pointed to Steven as he saw his face fall. "See, I told you. Crazy ass motherfucker. Nobody saw him do it, but everybody knew. Told everybody it was an accident. Went nuts right after that. They said it was grief, but that's bullshit." Len gave him a nasty smile. "That's who you are, dude."

Steven held on to the counter, stared at the leering aliens on the *Mars Attacks* pinball machine glowing over Len's right shoulder. Rather than feeling a stone settling over Trow's grave, Steven sensed a rumbling, as if Trow had been lying dormant, asleep inside him, waiting for a signal to burst forth and execute a destiny still at large, one stronger and more

real than any of Nancy Manskart's whims. Whatever nascent contentment Steven had experienced these months had been a false spring. The
real Trow, the one who'd crawled inside Steven's head, had been an evil
lunatic.

And the voice hadn't been telling him to kill just Manskart. It had
been telling him to kill Nate, too.

"By any chance, do you have a Civil War uniform?"

Len rolled a batting cage token through his fingers. "Yeah. So what?"

"Do you remember if you were wearing it one day back in September? It was raining—?"

"How the fuck would I remember that? I mean I had my picture taken
in it once. I don't know; I wear it sometimes." He tossed Steven the
token. "Here. Hit some balls." After a minute without Steven's moving,
he said, "So you wanna buy the uniform?"

CHAPTER

4 3

ALL THE TIME STEVEN THOUGHT HE WAS CHANGING himself for the better by imitating the imaginary Trow, the real one had been seeping into him like poison trailings. The murderous voice he had heard was that of a man who had killed his own son. That was Trow's fate, he thought, standing at the Snack Shack pay phone. Nate's fate. Something inexplicable and evil was trying to make it happen to him, something faceless, now that Len Trow had claimed back the image in the photo. He dug through his wallet, searching for the tattered photo of his boy as he waited for Information to answer.

"What city?"

"I don't know. The name is Melton. Probably in Sharon or Salisbury. Number and address."

Through the operator's reproving silence, the clicking keys, Steven crammed happy memories of Nate into his head, pretended he could remember the Picture Day that had produced this photo. Nate had lost both of his top front teeth the day before. Hadn't he?

"Falls Village. Please hold for the—"

"What's the address?"

He hung up without taking the phone number and drove to an immaculately kept two-story Victorian just outside the short and vacant main drag of Falls Village. The building's pristine condition, its crisp gray-and-white paint job, the gingerbread scrollwork lacing all the eaves, seemed more the result of responsibility than joy. He wondered if Mr. Melton was still alive, pictured a straw-hatted duffer puttering across the lawn on his riding mower, stray blades stuck to his pearly shins and leather slippers.

As he made his way up to the porch, a white curtain moved in the window to the right. Steven folded his arms and tapped his nervous foot while he waited for her to come to the door; maybe she needed to get a robe. After a count of fifty, he rang the bell, to no avail. With light steps that creaked the old porch wood, he went to the window and peeked in. Despite his expectations of toile and Hummels, the room had a modern feeling, full of midcentury furniture, all chrome and leather, and scrolls of Japanese calligraphy.

"Mr. Armour?"

He jumped. Mrs. Melton had only half-opened the gray door and leaned out into the cool afternoon. "I wasn't sure you were home."

"Well, I am." She said nothing more, made no move to invite him in. Instead, she gave her maroon cardigan a defiant tug, as if hoping that he would ask his question and leave.

Steven came toward her quickly. "May I come in? I've found something out about John Trow and I really have to talk to you." Mrs. Melton pursed her lips. Beneath her usual stony expression, Steven could see caution, maybe because he was acting strangely; maybe because it was *him*, the tragic John Trow. "It's very important. Please." At last she held open the door.

Steven declined the offer of tea and took a seat on the couch. Every chair, every lamp appeared to rest exactly where Mrs. Melton had placed it when she had decorated sometime back in the 1950s. The lozenge coffee table, the James Jones and Norman Mailer on the shelves, spoke to an intelligent woman of her time, even if that time had passed. A black-and-white photograph, vintage late '60s, of a sharp-faced, middle-aged man hung on a narrow wall near the door. No pictures of children, though. He pointed at the portrait. "Mr. Melton?"

"Yes." She did not wish to expound, nor did she wish to sit; instead, she stood in the arch to the dining room. "How can I be of help, Mr. Armour?"

"Well, I just met a man who claims to be John Trow's descendent. Great-great-great-grandson, I guess. Three greats. Len Trow. Have you ever met him?" Mrs. Melton shook her head. "Well, he told me that Trow killed his son Daniel. That he was committed for hacking his son to death with a hoe. That's his tragic ending. I just wanted to let you know . . ."

What he really wanted was for her to make it go away, to tell him that Len had lied. To tell him that John Trow hadn't come back to possess him. But Mrs. Melton did not move.

"You knew." The unpleasantness of that fact dawned on him. "You *knew?* You picked *me* to be the insane child murderer?"

Steven slumped as if shot. With a wounded man before her, Mrs. Melton could not maintain her defense. Head bent, sadder than usually allowed by her Yankee aplomb, she took a place next to him.

"I had no idea that first day. That *is* the truth." Fussing with her buttons, she continued. "Now I must tell you that I'd heard things as a child—I've said as much to you—but in those days, well . . . Trow was a mysterious name to us. A bogeyman. But nothing as horrifying as this. You struck me as a man who might benefit from mystery. I'm so very sorry."

"When did you know? Did you know at the post office?"

She nodded. "I did. I found some papers in the Town Hall. John died in a state hospital for the insane in 1899. And it was my duty to tell you, but so many . . . No, I shouldn't say."

"What? Shouldn't say what?"

She paused for a moment, rearranged herself inside her blouse. "There are people who, in my opinion, go too far with this. I shall not name names, but I'd hoped you would not fall in with them. Some even begin to believe they are actually the people whose impression they're performing. They blur what's real and what's not real." She softened, offering him a chance for forgiveness. "I once saw a man become an alcoholic in one week after he found out his corporal died of cirrhosis. I've seen people who I'd say, if I didn't know any better, had been taken over by their subject. Of course, no one we know has ever gone that far, but can you imagine such a thing?"

Steven stood up and took a few steps toward the door. "You'd have to be insane."

CHAPTER

44

AT FIRST HE SAW ONLY THE TOP OF NANCY'S HEAD through the plate glass window of Diane's Amenia Hallmark, a dash of red amid the wide assortment of party goods, fine collectibles, and the Mylar balloon concession, which added sparkle from a back corner. With her face obscured by a rack of greeting cards and a purple-and-green sign that read CHICK OUT EASTER!—APRIL 22, Steven focused on the hair, pulled back into a taut shine and fastened with a sedate barrette, the way she wore it at Riga Village. No Scrunchy today. For a second he forgot himself and thought maybe Polly had returned. From the tilt of her head, he assumed that she was concentrating on something, as she did when playing the psaltery, before they would kiss . . .

He opened the door. After the tinkle of wind chimes, he heard some quasi-operatic singing, more *Les Miz* than Bellini, and went to her on the other side of the rack. Nancy's uncorseted stomach bulged gently under her cinnamon stretch pants and smock, today's simple hairstyle indicative more of a lack of initiative than of classicism. She looked tired, and her puffy fingers, once tendril thin as they twined through his hair, into his clothing, flipped sluggishly through the piles of Easter cards splayed across the gray plastic cart beside her. Polly was buried under the burdens of being Nancy Manskart. In fact, only the red hair reminded him of her, and he could hardly believe that he had made love to this woman whose smock boasted four large Easter egg pins, along with her name tag.

"John Trow was a madman," he said, with no other greeting, only the immediate intimacy of two people who'd once made love. In truth, he'd spoken to this woman Nancy Manskart only once before, knew nothing about her, though he'd been prepared to kill a man to have her. In this world, he would never have noticed her, maybe not even twenty feet high on a movie screen. The thought made him blink hard. "He killed his son and then he went crazy."

She ignored him, didn't move, save for tucking in sixes of bright yellow *For My Mommy* and *From a Special Nephew* cards. Bits of glitter had rubbed off onto her flaking manicure.

"I said, he was crazy. He murdered Daniel. Did you know that?"

A smiling chick bursting out of a striped egg announced Baby's First Easter and slid in beside two properly submissive children, with teardrop-shaped heads and outsized blue eyes, who asked, *Grandma, Do You Know What Easter Means to Me?* She was not happy to see him.

"He was a crazy fuck. Do you understand that? And I think he wants to take me over. It's not an act. He's trying to possess me or something."

Steven got close to her face and was about to shake a reaction out of her when she spoke, softly and with no sympathy, as she sorted through five styles of Snoopy and Woodstock. "Our pasts catch up with us, Steve. We shouldn't go back to the past."

"Look who's talking! Your husband's the one who drafted me! I would've been happy to go home that day and watch the goddamn Giants game!"

Dusting off her fingers on the smock, she finally faced him, her proud expression making it clear that she was merely deigning to speak. "No. You weren't happy. You know that. You were looking for something that had nothing to do with who you were. I think we wear costumes to express who we really want to be." She looked up at him with red eyes. Either she'd been crying a lot or smoking pot. "I told Wally about us."

He swiveled around to see if anyone else was in the store, saw a young woman with stringy hair inflating the Mylar balloons. Her T-shirt featured a cutesy drawing of a blonde saying, "I Don't Care If That's How You Do It in New York." Their eyes met, and in the loud silence everyone realized that the music had ended. Still looking at Steven, the woman said, "What do you want to hear next, Nan?"

Nancy tried to sound cheery. "I don't know, Kee. How about those Spanish guitar guys."

The woman scratched her head. "Oh, we have them *too*? What are they called again?"

Steven snapped, "Oh, for chrissakes, the *Gypsy* Kings."

"Don't be pissy," Nancy said to him. As the woman retreated to the back room, Nancy shrugged. "She's new."

"What the hell did you tell Walter?"

She lifted her jaw, proud of what she'd done. "The truth."

"Why did you tell him? What's the point? Tell me!"

A keening came over the speakers, accompanied by the plucking of unnamable instruments, causing Nancy to toss down the Snoopys in exasperation. "Why did she put on Enya? I told her I *hate* Enya." She fished around in her smock pouch and pulled out a pack of Marlboro Lights. "Hey, Keeanna? I'm going out to have a cigarette."

They walked out, setting off the wind chimes again, and moved to the side of the breezeway, where they hid from Nancy's co-worker behind the window display, a tall set of shelves hosting sculptural replicas of Norman Rockwell paintings and an assemblage of porcelain rabbits. Nancy lit up, took a long, mind-clearing drag. "Wally and I needed a fresh start, you know?" she said in a pinched voice, holding in the smoke as if it were from a joint. "We saw Swan last week. He told me he thought your wife was going to divorce you. Don't look so surprised." She took another drag. "He was there when she went into your office." Nancy shook her head in disgust. "I had to tell him. Just to be clean."

Steven's jaw dropped. "Swan doesn't know shit, and by the way, my wife's not divorcing me!" He could feel it all slipping out of his hands. "Why don't you people get real lives and stop fucking with me!"

Nancy let the cigarette fall from her fingers. Ignoring his tantrum, distracted by something else, she leaned toward the window and traced something on the glass. "I lost the baby, Steve. I had a miscarriage."

The mounting sadness of all this, the rising count of dead children, left him numb. Such a sad place, Mt. Riga.

"We've been trying forever and the fact is I can never have children. That's what the doctor said. Wally's very unhappy. He wants you to be unhappy, too." She turned to him. "He wants to tell your wife."

Limp, and craving one of Nancy's Marlboros, he leaned back against the glass. He'd seen what a reasonable life could be, begun to will a better self out of pieces of his past, and now the ground was shifting. Len Trow buffing putters as he described the family stain; Enya-hating Nancy Manskart currently picking nail polish off her thumb. It was all too absurd. What could a man count on, he wondered. Even if you changed, you could still change back, be dragged into the sorry place you'd been. And in that instant, as he contemplated the constant uncertainty of the self, the beauty of allowing Providence to decide such things blossomed in his mind like a black rose.

For the first time in months, Steven closed his eyes and imagined the big, overstuffed Kellogg plodding ahead of his men at Cold Harbor, the lead turkey ruffling his tail feathers. The inevitability of it all calmed him more than any cigarette could.

Keeanna's voice floated over the sounds of battle. "Nancy? Phone call."

Manskart turns back in shock at the reality of his wound; he turns back into a minie straight into his heart . . .

No one will find you, Trow said to Steven. You have been wronged.

A new image took shape in Steven's mind: Trow standing in a Riga field, hands flecked red with blood sprayed from his son.

Kill him, said Trow.

As Nancy walked past him, she held out her hands as if to display her world. "Do you think this was all I ever wanted? Cards?" She stopped at the door, opened her mouth to say more, but decided not to.

Somewhere in Lakeville, around Emily's school, Steven pulled over to the side of the road and rested his head on the steering wheel for a very long time.

CHAPTER

45

"GET YOUR ASS DOWN HERE, NATE! NOW!" Steven jangled the keys. "You're going to be late for school!"

As Nate thumped down the stairs and into the car, Steven scanned the charged skies, painted in putrid greens and yellows. Back in Chicago, March and April were tornado season. Though moving East had let him shed his childhood fear of tornadoes, the stillness of the air, the imminent storm, made him remember the excruciating hours he had spent next to the basement door, counting down the minutes remaining in tornado warnings.

Emily gnawed on a frozen waffle in the backseat. "Jesus, Emmy, why the hell don't you cook them?"

Day by day the snows had melted, Cold Harbor drew closer, and Trow continued to make his presence known. Yesterday he'd snapped at Big Dale; trivial enough, but still requiring some quick fawning, and now here was Emily, wincing at his unchecked annoyance. Trow could be a mean bastard.

"I like 'em this way," she said in a meek voice, offering up the last few bites if he wanted to take it away from her.

Cool down, Steven told himself. Daluisa would not let him get out of Cold Harbor if he behaved like a madman.

"It's okay, honey. Finish it. I just think they taste better cooked."

Higher and higher the clouds boiled as they drove; the air took on a jaundiced cast. For miles, the inside of the car stayed as silent as the land outside, the children made tense by the storm, by his unpredictable temper. They passed Town Hall and the library. Back at home, boxes from outfitters filled with rubber liners, tents, and Nate's new shoes were heaped up in Steven's office. No matter what Patty said, what Daluisa said, he could not take his son to Cold Harbor. Not while Trow stalked his mind. Not while Manskart was around and eager to tell all. Why hadn't he yet, Steven wondered. The tension was killing him. Phillip's things would begin to arrive tomorrow. His marriage and relatively happy new life threatened, an inexplicable urge to kill—these things swirled together into daily attacks of panic, and Steven felt his heart beat faster now as the clouds stacked over the early crocuses, his skin bristling with static.

Steven slammed a fist on the dashboard. "Jesus H. Christ, would it just start to goddamn rain!" He heard both the children freeze in place.

You are not this kind of person, he told himself. You are a different person now.

"I'm sorry, guys. I really am. I'm just, you know, stressed."

"It's okay, Dad," said Nate. "Just don't start beating on us. All right?"

Steven turned around, aghast. "Nate! You know I would never—"

"Dad! Jesus, turn around and drive! I was *joking*!"

Big raindrops splattered on the windshield as he double-parked in front of the school and kissed his children goodbye. Once he lost them in the crowd, he looked around for Manskart. Steven often considered talking to him man to man in the selfless, moral, bittersweet way of a Graham Greene character, but those men always had less to lose. Besides, Manskart didn't have much of the chummy English gentleman about him. For hours Steven would think about telling Patty, but he still couldn't gauge where that news would take them. However much he wanted to wish it away, that moment when Steven would meet eyes with Manskart loomed as inescapable, its result a subject of endless speculation.

Steven parked the car in the visitors' lot and jogged in before the rain got worse. Daluisa's secretary let him sit in the principal's office to wait and wonder how he could explain that he was no longer fully possessed by the spirit of a dead Union soldier and was doing his best to hold him at bay. Scanning the photos of Daluisa shaking hands with some U Conn basketball player, holding up a plaque surrounded by a passel of teens, Steven sensed Trow's dislike simmering. As he heard Daluisa's door swing open, he forced the same smile he'd had to force more and more often these days.

The principal entered with a hand extended. "Mr. Armour. Good to see you."

"Thank you for seeing me, Mr. Daluisa. I know you're a busy man."

Daluisa accepted this fact with a nod.

"Let me get straight to the point. I don't believe that Nate and I need to attend the re-enactment at Cold Harbor. A lot has changed since Nate's . . ." Steven looked for a neutral word. ". . . run-in, and I honestly don't think it's necessary."

By now Daluisa had leaned back in his chair, toying with a rubber band, which he put down once Steven stopped. "The terms of Nate's probation are very clear and, I think, quite lenient. Don't you agree?"

Steven bowed his head and held up his hands in a broad show of supplication. "I completely agree. But I think the circumstances have changed. The last time I was here, I was under extreme pressure at my job, and that has totally cleared up. Our daughter has stabilized. My wife and I have entered therapy . . ." All right, that was a lie. "Nate and I have been getting along great. *Nate's* been great. Ask him yourself."

Daluisa took up the rubber band again, glanced at the clock behind Steven's head. He looked dubious. "If I recall, in our prior meeting you had made some strong statements about physically—"

"I know, and I'm sorry for that. I don't know what I was thinking. But please know that I hear you. I understand what Nate needs, and I am more than willing to provide it. I just don't feel that attending the re-enactment of a battle is the way to do that. My father, his grandfather, is moving in with us, too, and I think that will also be great for him."

The clock ticked. The principal's face softened slightly as he considered Steven's case.

"I guess I don't understand your reluctance. Our school has a policy of zero tolerance for the kind of behavior Nate displayed, and we've already extended ourselves by allowing him to remain in class, based on the terms of the probation. This is a simple enough thing, Mr. Armour, to prevent more serious problems."

With a roar of thunder, the clouds emptied, shook the panes in a blinding wash of rain. For a moment both men stared out the window without comment. Steven flashed upright, hit with a sudden idea.

"What if it's dangerous for Nate to be there? How would *that* help him? If he were in danger?"

Daluisa pulled back his head; professional demeanor could not hide his dismay. "Like what? Who's going to hurt him?"

Me, thought Steven. "It's, uh, it's a very dangerous pasttime. You have to understand that. Gunpowder is in play and—"

"Understand this, Mr. Armour—that's why *you're* there. To learn how to take care of your son. To teach him how to be a man. I can understand that you may not want to go, but people don't want to go to prison either. Do you see? I'm trying to be honest here. And helpful. But you have no other options. The story is laid out. You and Nate do what has to happen and it will all be over with." Daluisa stood up, unwilling to listen to any more arguments from Steven. "All right?" He guided Steven to the door. "I'll assume that everything will take place as planned, then."

When he got home, drenched by his walk to the car, Steven sifted through the mail in search of the letter from Manskart to Patty that he'd been expecting to come now every day for weeks: Williams-Sonoma, PC Mall, and a dentist's bill. He collapsed on a dining room chair, regarded the table, the light fixture, the peach tone of the walls. The house was silent, and for a moment the farmhouse on Route 44 seemed like a normal, happy home. He squeezed his hands against his ears to keep out the sound of Trow's voice.

CHAPTER

46

THURSDAY NIGHT, THE NIGHT BEFORE THEY LEFT, Steven shoved his gear and uniform into the car. He hadn't touched them since that last day on the mountain in December, and now he had trouble remembering that he'd ever worn them in public, let alone preened in them. Something would happen tomorrow; that much was clear. He'd tried everything he could think to get out of this, short of shooting himself in the foot, but Trow and circumstances were too strong. He had to play this through, had to placate Manskart and save his son at the same time. If he could keep Trow in control at the re-enactment, things would be fine. They'd drive in with Scobeck and Burney, do their thing and be out by Saturday afternoon, latest. Stop worrying, stop worrying, he repeated to himself over and over, a constant noise he made to block any sign of Trow.

Steven came down to the kitchen the next morning to the smell of strong coffee. Nate, in his uniform, sat at the table, eating a plateful of toaster waffles. The thrill of an officially approved day off from school had shot him out of bed an hour earlier than usual. "Made you coffee, Dad."

"So I see." Pitch black, it reeked all the way up from the counter. "Thanks. Wow. Good and strong. You didn't have any of this, did you?" he asked, concerned.

Nate stuffed half a waffle in his mouth. "I don't drink coffee."

"No. No you don't. You might want to try this, though. It'll put some . . ."

Patty walked in with Emily. "Nate, you look terrific!"

"The private made us coffee, dear." Fearing that her brother had eaten all the waffles, Emily demanded a full accounting. Patty began to pull out a pan for eggs. As he sipped from his mug, Steven became aware of a curdling in his stomach that could have been the coffee or the thought that if Manskart so chose, if the phone rang right now, this insignificant twenty-minute breakfast would be their last as a family.

Emily licked milk off the down on her lip. "Where's your uniform?"

"I'll put it on when we get there." Gone were the days of worshipful respect for the wool. Given all the bother of checking a gun, he'd ruled out flying, though he did hope that Burney and Scobeck, his passengers, would be in mufti; the idea of entering a roadside McDonald's somewhere in Virginia with three companions in Union blues, one in a turban, gave him pause. "Nate, you sure you want to wear it all the way down?"

"It's perfect for the weather, Dad."

"I know, but . . ."

Patty shrugged What the Hell behind Nate's head, and Steven looked up at the clock. They had to leave. Would she instantly divorce him if he admitted what had happened? He could tell her right now, right here, the way Dr. Pang recommended, weep, and beg forgiveness.

"Don't you guys have to pick up somebody?"

Patty's voice. As he stared at the hands, he believed that he could see the second hand glide into each place on the clock, every moment now seen by him in its entirety.

"Does the light in Phillip's room work?"

He tried to take it all in, the appliances, Emily's fingers around a Little Mermaid cup, Patty's trim ankles in her boiled wool slippers, the magnets on the fridge, egg whites popping in the pan, Nate's audible chewing. He'd been so stupid to risk all of this; he couldn't stand to lose it now.

"Steven," said Patty. "Steven? Hello? You look spaced."

If he shot Manskart, he could run off into the woods and hide. That had been the plan, the insane plan, Trow had been concocting. He wondered what he would do with Nate, where he would stash the gun . . .

"Steven, have more coffee."

He slapped his cheek hard, shook his head, all in a burlesque that made Emily laugh. "No, we have to go. Come on, Nate. Let's move."

Nate sprang up and kissed his mother goodbye, poked a finger into Emily's ribs. Patty abandoned her eggs to put her arms around Steven. "I'll deal with your father; don't worry. Just take care of our son, all right?"

"I'll do my best."

*   *   *

From Salisbury, Connecticut, to Cold Harbor, Virginia, takes a good eight hours by car, less if one speeds, which was what Steven did as much as traffic allowed. Though the Navigator was a large vehicle, once Scobeck and Burney—both in uniform—had piled in with all their weaponry and clothing and coolers full of Gatorade, the car became intimate, so the sooner they arrived the better. Soon after they pulled out of Scobeck's driveway, the new passenger made it clear that he did not like music—not just Nate's throbbing wall of guitar, admittedly too grinding for eight in the morning, but music in general, from Neil Diamond to Bach.

Burney sat squarely on the side of the music lovers. "Have any Dead?"

Nate's jaw dropped. "Like the *Grateful* Dead?"

"Six hundred and forty-two concerts, my friend."

"No way."

"Only three bad trips. After Jerry died I took up re-enacting. I needed something solid to fall back on, you know?"

Thus began a low-grade argument that lasted until Burney finally found a topic that would bring them together: their still-surging Qualcomm, now nibbling at the juicy underside of 150.

"It's a beautiful thing," said Burney.

Scobeck hacked as if he had a hairball. "Won't last forever. Warren Buffett's the only one with any sense out there. You have to look for *value*."

Just hearing the words *Warren Buffett* come out of Scobeck's mouth nearly sent Steven careening over the divide.

"I mean, I gotta make this last, you know? I'm getting out, going into cyclicals. I don't think bonds'll be a bad place to be soon. Or gold."

With all his children, Scobeck clearly viewed this not so much as a windfall but as a near escape from destitution, his fevered discussion of investing the panting of a man hauled out of the ocean, still panicked and trying to catch his wind.

Burney snorted. "Gold. You gotta be fuckin' kiddin' me."

"Just you watch. If there's so much as a hiccup on the Big Board or the Nasdaq, you'll see it go crazy."

He'd be buying books for mediocre liberal arts programs with his sixty-eight grand, not browsing for luxury sedans, and this uncharitable thought calmed Steven.

"The capital gains'll kick your ass. You know that, don't you?" asked Burney. "You gotta ride it out until you get the lower rate; otherwise, you're just handin' money to the Uncle."

At the start of the Saw Mill Parkway, an hour or so out of Salisbury, the topic went to sports. Debates pitting the Yankees versus the Red Sox, the Patriots versus the Jets, the Knicks versus the Celtics continued on to the Maryland border, by which time everyone had fallen asleep. Amid the soft snoring, Steven imagined what Cold Harbor would be like, a place where twenty thousand people gathered to dispel as much reality as they could. For all of what he'd been through, the notion still had its attractions, and he wished he was one of those chippers who could just pick it up and put it back down. Instead, he slightly loosened his grip on his modern self, thought about the silence of the nineteenth century, the voices of children playing simple games, the smell of sulfur and wood smoke, ordered lines of men, women where they should be.

A bank of silver gray clouds rode across the sky. Still hours from Cold Harbor, Steven hoped it didn't bode rain and a night of soggy camping. Nate's head jounced lightly against the window as the car hit some tar lines in the highway, the boy's hands still holding two pretzel rods in his lap like drumsticks. It was getting on to one. Nate held his dazed head up for a beat, then let it fall to the left. In the mirror Steven could see the top of Burney's turban resting on Scobeck's shoulder. So far, no Trow.

Outside Washington, D.C., they hit a drive-through McDonald's, and all four munched America's Best French Fries as they watched the Lincoln Memorial and Washington Memorial pass by outside. The stretch of I-95 between the nation's capital and Richmond could qualify as a NASCAR training ground; at times Steven found himself going ninety and being passed on both sides. Yet outside, only blue skies shone above the gentle Virginia countryside. Yellow patches of dogwood bloomed on the shoulders, and the grass had already turned green. The scenery benefited from the softness and blurred edges of spring, a distinct change from the mud and the light shadings only now beginning to wreathe the Connecticut trees. Though it struck Steven as no more beautiful than any number of other states he'd been in, Scobeck and Burney both rhapsodized about the Old Dominion as they covered a month's hard marching in less than two hours.

Exiting 95, the energy in the car changed. Steven rolled down the windows to welcome the warmer air and submitted himself to the twisting roads of rural Virginia, slowing down enough to catch a whiff of history thickening around them. Signs began to appear. CIVIL WAR EVENT and CIVIL WAR, they said, with arrows pointing any passing mercenaries or visiting partisans like them in the right direction. They were in the holy land of their religion, their voices lower now as they all bounced excitedly in their seats. Coming closer and closer to the place he'd seen many times before in his mind, Steven tried to still his growing excitement and the itchy sense of familiarity, the kind he'd felt many months ago when the bus first took him up to Riga Village.

Finally, a six-foot-square sign appeared a block or so ahead, next to the two-lane county road. In tall, block lettering it announced CIVIL WAR HERE!—with the do-it-yourself marketing sense of a roadside corn stall. At three-thirty, with the sun still holding up the western sky, they made a left and pulled into the fringes of a large farm.

Scobeck sneered. "This doesn't look anything like Cold Harbor."

"It's not," said Steven. "We're about half a mile from the battle site, close to our position." Had that been Trow speaking?

Two event officials in orange windbreakers that said COLD HARBOR manned a lone card table. Steven found his name and Nate's on the list of registered participants and then read the release handed to him through the car window. He paused for a moment: Would he promise to hold no one responsible in case of injury or bodily harm?

Nate bounced in his seat. "Come on, Dad."

Steven returned the signed papers, and a young man waved them on to a parking area hidden behind a rise, out of sight of any re-enactors. When Steven looked over his shoulder, he saw all three grinning the way Nate had at Disney World, the grin of good people being ushered through the Gates of Heaven.

We're here, said Trow.

CHAPTER

47

HIDING BEHIND THE NAVIGATOR DOOR, Steven hopped into his uniform, very purposefully keeping his Jockeys on in lieu of any period underwear.

Leave me alone, thought Steven. I am here because Nate has to be here. Because I have to settle with Manskart.

As he stuck a ballpoint pen into his pants pocket, he vowed not to succumb to the trills of bird song edging this broad Southern field, to the righteous order and unexplored mysteries of that century already freshly evident in those swirling past him. Swan had warned him that the past would draw hard here at Cold Harbor; he grabbed a Bic lighter and some Tic Tacs.

The men heaved their packs onto their backs, shouldered their rifles, and joined the general movement of refugees up the gentle rise and away from the ravages of modern times. Steven gave the Navigator a door-locking cheep from his key-ring remote, startling a family of four as they wrestled tents and grocery bags out of their Taurus. The father, a scruffy Union major, packing juice boxes into a cooler, sent him a sharp look. "Gave us a fright, Private," he said, his glare melting before he was taken too seriously. The uniform conferred a basic level of acceptance similar to wearing a team jersey to a home game; if nothing else, at least you had that going for you.

"My apologies, sir," said Trow. "And to your lovely wife." Steven threw back a salute. The major's wife, mid-thirties, competent before she was pretty or nice, waved Hi from the hatchback, busy rallying her junior troops. His easy slide into John Trow unnerved Steven. He pointed at their Ohio plates. "Bengals or Browns?"

Steven hadn't crossed the line, but he'd stepped on it. The major's friendly smile froze. "Don't follow it." Dismissing Steven with a nod, he said, "See you on the field, Private," and slipped his cooler into a large, disguising wooden crate.

Ahead, Nate and his fellow Heavies had made it halfway up the low ridge. In the warm air and wool uniform, heaving fifty pounds of food and camping gear, Steven broke into a light sweat after only a few steps. His son tapped a light, encouraging beat on his drum until he crested, at which point he stopped, hands at his side, clearly amazed by what waited below, a little Moses laying eyes on the Promised Land.

Scobeck huffed, "What do you see, Private?"

Nate didn't have the words, nor did Scobeck or Burney, and when Steven reached the top, he too stood silent. At its best, Riga Village had presented a few dozen re-enactors and living historians milling about among the T-shirts and gimme caps, but here, in the final blazes of the day, an impromptu city sprawled out below them and continued to grow, like Canaan for those in exile from their time. Thousands of men and women liberated from reality went about their business in period clothes—shopping, chatting, raising new booths, carrying buckets of water down three long rows of wooden shacks and tents. The swirl of long skirts, the general tumult, made Steven think of Mecca, yet instead of a regular circle around the Ka'ba, the people here flowed about in no structured fashion, streaming past all the booths and tents. A circle of about ten men formed a rousing fife-and-drum band, which played in a clearing near the center. Nate grinned and picked up their beat. Save for a line of portable toilets off toward the back, the modern world had been cleared away so that this town could sprout in the fields of Virginia. At the far end of the village, near the Porta-Potties, the grass, already trodden into paths, converged and hooked into one wide dirt road leading into the woods. From the constant flow of men in blue and gray, Steven assumed this was the road to the camps, and when he squinted, he could see the flecks of the canvas tents white between the trees.

No sign of Manskart yet, but Steven sensed John Trow growing with every deep breath of country air. With at least a quarter-mile to go and tents to erect, fires to build before nightfall, they had a lot to do, so he waved his small detachment down into the bowl. A grayish white haze rose out of the trees beyond. Three months without smelling wood smoke made its tang exceptionally strong in Steven's nose. As he sniffed the smoke, his senses immediately sharpened, the sounds of swishing crinolines, boots crunching dry stalks on the ground, burst in his ears. The colors swirling around the makeshift village—no Soho blacks and browns down there—and the scratch of his woolen jacket on his wrists and neck produced a dizziness, an overload of pure sensation that made him fear a seizure or migraine. Even more frightening was how utterly right it all seemed once again. His few months of modern living couldn't reduce the benefits of silence, the dance of etiquette, what Union could truly mean to this nation, all the fundamental things he'd been so tightly connected to. Going down, he felt the pull of a time when every moment was savored with senses undulled.

What was Patty doing right now, he made himself wonder. He pictured her frying eggs that morning, already so long ago. Had Phillip arrived yet? The major and his family, hauling their whole campsite, passed on his left. "Need some help there, Major?" asked Steven. The theme from *WKRP in Cincinnati* floated through his head, and he vented it as a loud, perky hum. Nate looked back, puzzled. Steven pictured the major as a paramedic, maybe a drama teacher at Case Western Reserve. Smiling broad smiles that a big-city dweller might well mistake for Midwestern hospitality, the Buckeye parents shook their heads no. "Hey! Anybody want a Tic Tac?"

Burney minced down the final steps of the incline. "Pretty worked up, aren't ya, John?" He dealt Steven a big slap on the back.

"Yeah, take it easy, Dad." Nate rolled his eyes. "Don't be such a farb."

Scobeck and Burney laughed, but Steven's eyes narrowed into slits, and he grabbed one of Nate's cuffs. "Don't you speak to me like that, boy! Do you hear me?" He snapped the cuff. "I said, Do you hear me?"

Pure Trow. Nate pulled away. Steven stood still for a moment, waiting to see whether Trow would make him do anything else. He then ventured a few words to see if it was safe.

"Nate? I'm sorry." Relieved to hear himself speaking, not Trow, Steven continued. "Okay? We have a lot to do, and I guess I'm, you know . . ."

"Stressed?" Nate said sarcastically.

"Well, yeah. Stressed. I'm sorry. I know I say that a lot, but I guess I'm a pretty stressed guy. I'm sorry. Let's get our tent set up, and then we'll come back here and see if there's anything else you need, all right? I'll try to relax."

Though the hurt showed on Nate's face, he nodded and accepted his father's hand around the back of his neck as they entered the sutler alley.

Packs of rowdy soldiers clomped about, many of them straight out of the pages of *Fort Bluff Monthly*, their uniforms beaten down beautifully, every detail correct. All four Connecticut heads swiveled as a couple of young Rebs strolled by, lean and perfectly wolfish in their ragged butternuts. Though the booths and tents did not, in fact, resemble a real town, the absence of anything to break the dream gave the whole place the intensity of a fantastic outlaw village on the fringes of a foreign land. Civilians hawked their wares, armed men swaggered about with the full entitlements of their weaponry while the women deferred. Those anachronisms he saw—the shopping bags, the cassette tapes, the occasional bits of plastic—seemed the wondrous goods of adventuresome traders, like exotic spices or bolts of silk. Boys in knickers and checked shirts brandished wooden swords as they ran through the crowds. Music continued to play.

Steven's Jockeys began to feel not just constricting but immoral, and the old urge for perfection, the lust to own it all, bubbled as he passed the tent of Colby, Dakins and Co. A sharply dressed man in plaid pants and vest, either Colby or Dakins, tipped his hat and welcomed him to look at the racks of handsome uniforms inside. Steven demurred, but unable to help himself, he peeked into the next tent, Cletus Suggs Dry Goods and Novelties. Inside the greasy canvas sheltering thick shelves made of two-by-fours, he found old Woolworth's enamelware, wrong for the period, and leather objects made of rough slabs of skin that barely bent, rusty forks and knives of yard-sale quality. Off in a corner Suggs himself sat on a high stool in his loudly striped pants, twisting a handlebar mustache. Steven couldn't tell whether he was doing an impression of a sleazy purveyor of substandard goods or if that's what he was.

The shops went on and on, and Steven's eyes skipped from tent to tent, from person to person, scouting for Manskart, hoping to see him and get their unpleasant business over with. A pale blond woman, drained of color and possibly consumptive, tested the credit card imprinter at Veona Tyler Ladies Wear with an air of one who truly deserved the attentions of a slave. Instead, two pre-teens in blue pinafores served their waifish boss, skittering about the tent, arranging things. Next to The Breech Loader and its broad range of solid and well-turned-out weapons, a rare circle of mixed Union and Reb soldiers swapped stories of earlier campaigns. The ubiquitous wooden swords came from a basket near the tent flap of Rebel With a Cause, a shop that also sold Confederate playing cards—Jeff Davis the king, Varina the Queen, Lee the Ace—recorders and the Rebel flags flying everywhere. Though Steven had no interest in doing a count, he decided that his own flag would be probably outnumbered. Nate tugged his arm and showed him a small sign with an arrow pointing left toward a wide, dormant ground, the word BATTLE-FIELD painted in red; all in all a less ominous marker than Steven would have imagined for the greatest slaughter of the war. Before he went into Titus Sterming, Stationer, of Baltimore, full of morbid curiosity, Scobeck yanked at his jacket. "Come along, Private Trow. We've got to find the rest of the regiment."

"Whatever you say, Scobeck." He let the corporal lead them out of the sutlers, past the portable toilets, and toward the camps and Manskart. The Confederate camps came first. Unlike the energetic commerce of the sutler alley, the forest road swarmed lazily with people. Despite the size of the crowd, an intimacy reigned among the acres of tents and smoky fires stretching out beneath the trees; its murmuring hum became rich and deep in the forest, a single natural sound made from the voices of thousands, like swaying leaves or a thrumming hive. It was here that the past and the present met most profoundly. Steven could feel it in the dour air preceding tomorrow's massacre, could see it in the flirting of the girls with their parasols, the preacher standing on a stump, quietly pressing repentance on those who would listen, soldiers who should have been dead walking again with sad faces that expressed too much; all of them people playing their parts perfectly, no matter whether anyone watched, contributing their lives to the alluring unreality. Unattached to time, the trees seemed as pleased to host the nineteenth century as any other and to welcome the presence of these men and women nestled into their roots. If there were such things as ghosts, he thought, they could wander through this forest unquestioned. Dust had begun to coat his boots, and he scuffed up more as he walked. He needed to find Manskart soon.

Two little boys about Emily's age twisted their faces as they saw the small band of Heavies approach, and took to eagerly, angrily, waving Confederate battle flags with the rapt eyes and immodest fire of children lurking in the corners of lynching photos. The smaller one, sweet-faced, spat out, "Yankee pigs!" to the delight of some onlookers. Steven scattered them with a quick feint in their direction, though Nate continued to look wounded.

"Aren't they just adorable?" Steven asked those silently watching. "I would be so proud if those were my kids."

Hoofbeats thumped closer and closer and in an instant, with fevered snorts and creaking leather, pebbles flying off of horseshoes, a Rebel lieutenant ripped past on a dappled horse, his head tucked low, long hair streaming against the setting sun, visible through the trees, urging on his mount with his brimmed hat. All four of the Heavies stopped in their tracks, as did many others. The Lost Cause was so beautiful in the dimming light, especially with no slaves around. To the right, a uniformed doctor arranged plastic limbs on the table of his medical tent. If all these men and women hadn't been able to secede from the Union, they had been able to secede from time, sitting around their fires waiting, it seemed, not so much for tomorrow's battle as for a sign.

As he neared the Union section, fewer faces scowled. Many looked at peace, and Steven felt himself sink deeper into their world, pictured spirits riding everyone here; spirits that had found a way to ride the living, mounting them in this peculiar form of white voodoo so that they could speak again. From a distance he saw Bobby Osselin waving madly, and the round, imposing silhouette of Manskart. He pictured Polly's red hair falling on her back as she reared her head.

The time has come, Trow said.

"Dad! Come on, Dad! Let's get the tent up!" Nate's voice woke him up. "Do you need some coffee? I'll make you some. You had to drive a lot."

Steven would have to keep fighting. He barked at Nate, "Come here!" A boy once stung, Nate took only a tentative step closer. "I said, come here," said Steven, less gruffly this time. When his son was within arm's reach, he threw a light shoulder into his midsection and wrapped his arms around him, driving him forward in a small cloud of dust. Nate held his ground and the two rough-housed for a minute, each happy for the contact.

Manskart's voice pierced the quiet trees, the hum of the thousands. "Trow, get over here! You've got work to do, goddammit!"

CHAPTER

48

THE 2ND HAD ARRANGED ITSELF within a lopsided triangle of ground bounded by three massive oaks, with Manskart's big tent closest to the dusty path and the others in two crisp lines. An admirable fire sat in the center, and Hube had taken his place there, frying up steak and onions for dinner.

"Wa ho!" cried Burney. "Lafayette, we are here!"

"Wrong fucking war," said Kucharsky, leaning out of his tent, an earpiece in one ear and a small black radio in his hand.

Scobeck sneered, setting down his backpack. "Look who just invented the radio."

"How was the market?" asked Burney.

"Yeah," seconded Scobeck. "Time for the parachutes yet?"

Kucharsky shrugged and waved them off, too concerned with Bloomberg Radio to speak with his pards.

Jerry popped his head out of his tent. "Hey, buckos! Haven't seen you boys forever!" He emerged with Murray, his new tent mate, to greet the newcomers.

Giggling a little, Lummer nodded at Hube, who'd waved from the fire. "He's got my flask of schnapps, if you're interested."

Steven held up his hands. "Not quite yet, Murray." The old man dimmed, as if someone had declined an invitation to his party. "Maybe a nip after dinner."

While Steven staked out their small spot of dirt and dropped off their things, Jerry leaned close and whispered, "If you know what's good for you, stay clear of Kellogg."

Steven scratched his leg, itchy from the sweaty wool, as he tried to look nonchalant. "Why's that?"

"I don't know what the problem is, but he's got a real hard on for you

today. All he's been doing is walking around asking when you were supposed to get here, checking his watch, shit like that. You know, being
Kellogg." Jerry shrugged.

"What's with you and Murray?"

"Aw, you know the brothers were close. We figured we ought to do
this whole thing for real."

"Good idea." Steven handed Nate a pole. "Here, bud. You know how
to do the tent. Why don't you start working on that and I'll go talk to the
colonel? See what he wants." Jerry gave him a doubtful look. "Listen, I
don't feel like having him on my rear the whole time," Steven said. "I'd
rather see what the problem is and be done with it."

Warning delivered, Jerry stepped away, and Steven went to Manskart, wearing a new straw hat and standing next to one of the oak trees.
When he saw Steven, Manskart's eyes flashed and his whole body shook
as if rearranging itself. "It's about bloody time you arrived, Private!" he
bellowed.

Straight off Steven noticed something different about his face.
Though usually plastic and marked by raised eyebrows, thick pouting
lips, and jowls, today its constant motion appeared twitchy and nervous.
The magic was gone. Once again Steven saw Puss in Boots, the cuckold
in Daluisa's office. Polly had definitely told him; the eyes said it. As much
as the folds on his brows tucked down in fury, his eyes looked wild and
sad, darting about as if distracted even as he faced his former rival.

Steven could understand why he would feel desperate. He nodded,
ready to confess. "Walter, listen, we have to talk."

Manskart's large frame stiffened. His voice was loud. "Who on God's
green earth do you think you are addressing, Private?"

Hoping to salvage the encounter, Steven put himself into first person. "OK, *Colonel*. Could we take a walk? I think we have some stuff to
discuss, and I'd—"

"A walk? You, Private, are an inch from the stockade! Get your goddamned tent up and get the hell out of my sight until I ask to see you!"
Manskart glared back at Steven, who, though only a mediocre chess
player, tried to guess what moves Manskart might be lining up. Was he
simply intent on telling Patty and having nothing to do with Steven? Or
did his scheme have to do with Nate? Obviously something was afoot.
"Unless you have something further to say, you are dismissed!"

Steven returned to Nate and helped him finish putting up the tent.
The evening passed slowly, the damp and chill of early spring settled

over them as the night went on. Hube's dinner was eaten, his schnapps drunk, and with a five A.M. wakeup call coming, most of the men were happy to tuck in shortly after dinner. Life with no channel surfing meant more sleep. Nate went down quickly, but Steven lay on his liner, listening to whispers among the trees. At times he could distinguish words and phrases, like mist curling into shapes, in the drunken mumbling and laughs of those nipping at their flasks.

As the fire died outside their tent and the shadows joined forces with the night, one by one the whispers became snores, but still Steven could not sleep. He rolled about on his liner, puzzling at what Manskart had in mind, until, while lying on his stomach, he felt something hard pushing against him from inside his breast pocket.

The bullet.

It had spent the winter there, quietly waiting for him to see the light.

Trow didn't have to speak; Steven knew.

CHAPTER

49

THE OTHER BODY SHIFTED, THREW A LEG OUT that jostled Steven awake. He had no idea where he was. Back aching, neck stiff, he wanted only to find one more hour of sleep, something less thin and oily than what he'd just had.

"Up and at 'em, gentlemen. We got some coffee, tack, some nice fat belly for you boys."

He knew that voice. It was Joe Swan's. The rest came back in a not entirely pleasant rush. He was in a forest, on the ground, in Cold Harbor, Virginia. It was the year 2000 and the body next to him was his son. With no watch, he could only guess that it was around five A.M. The fire had been restoked, and he could smell Swan's coarse coffee boiling and some bacon frying, but he wasn't hungry. Nate lifted his head a couple inches off the ground, eyes barely open.

"Boy, you got just about enough time ta piss and eat and only if you do 'em at the same time!" Swan's head disappeared back out of the tent flap.

They'd be going into battle soon, the battle they'd been preparing for since the fall. Nate groaned, closed his eyes, and put his head back down. Time had begun to remold the boy's face, tug at his Adam's apple, but Steven could see the baby in Nate, lying in his crib, thumb resting on his bottom lip. Little Nat had evolved into this complicated young man whose independence felt to Steven more like a loss, a failure, than something to be proud of. He could understand now why Phillip had wanted him to stay in Evanston for college; if they stay children, you don't have to get any older, either. With a sudden sweep, Nate whipped his blanket aside, his hair a very authentic mess. "Morning, Dad."

The boy rubbed his eyes, but his father stopped him before he did anything to his hair. Steven stuck their kepis on their heads. They were not the last to answer Reveille; that honor belonged to Kucharsky, whose sense of military order had markedly diminished since the arrival of his ship. As the men spat out Swan's hardtack and pork belly, munched contraband Pop-Tarts while making final hurried visits to the Porta-Potties, Kucharsky stuck out his head from his tent, yawned, and lit his first Pall Mall.

The slaughter of the Heavies was a sort of warm-up act for the better-known charges of the battle's later days, so Manskart called them to attention in a small dirt clearing. Throughout the woods, other regiments began to fall into line, too, the noise that had been growing in the last hour quieting down as the mist burned off and the serious work of imitating war began. Commands and the pleasing sound of synchronized movement built, held down low by the canopy. Following the chilly night under the stars, every man had a hobble, a slight limp or crouch, and the bleary faces evidenced little sleep. Manskart tramped up and down the line, glaring at Kucharsky, who ambled into place. "Thank you for joining us. I trust you didn't bring your cell phone."

Amid the sniggering, Kucharsky dashed back to his tent to put away his phone, and Manskart started the weapon inspection. Though he'd done it quickly at Riga Village, here the colonel placed a ramrod down the barrel of each musket and jerked the weapon to hear it make the *ping* signifying that it was not loaded. Though slow and methodical throughout this task, the colonel was especially so with Steven and his Springfield. Manskart unsnapped the cartridge box, poked around. If he was looking for real bullets, he wouldn't find one there; Steven had kept it in his pocket. He'd considered ripping it open last night, but right now, in this field of uncertainty, it made him feel a little safer. The colonel capped Steven's musket, aimed it down at a blade of grass, and shot. Though every moment that passed increased the chances of Manskart going through with whatever scheme he had in mind, he was hardly going to chat right now about his wife sleeping around. Steven decided to wait until after the battle to approach him again.

Satisfied, Manskart handed the musket back with a disconcerting smirk, and, resuming his place at the front of the regiment, tucked his hands into the small of his back. With the men at rest, he described the day's plan.

"Gentlemen, forthwith the orders shall arrive for us to decamp." Usually deep and resonant, today his voice had a nervous edge. "We will, um. We will march about a quarter mile over a, um, over a, you know, a field and up a rise." His train of thought continued to wander as he described in halting terms how they would then wait behind a line of low bushes for the order to advance into the trees and the Rebel line, not far from the original place where the Heavies had fought. He paused. As directed by *Hardee's*, all eyes skimmed past him toward the field beyond, and he lifted his chin in the Kellogg fashion they were accustomed to. "There is nothing more I can tell you about your fate today, gentlemen. You fine soldiers, Connecticut men, you know what awaits." His voice cracked, and a few of the men crinkled their brows in spite of themselves. "Whether or not volunteering for this charge made any sense, it has now been written for you, Heavies, and I must tell you how privileged I consider myself to have been your colonel, to lead you into this battle."

Looking up and down the line, at Jerry's set jaw, Bobby's peach fuzz mustache, Steven noticed something different about Manskart.

"We have been living for this day, for this chance to defend our honor . . ."

He was wearing a pistol. He'd never worn a pistol before; only the sword.

"Now it is come and I say be brave, men of Connecticut! I shall never forget any of you . . ." No matter how paranoid Steven may have become, Manskart was definitely staring at him as he spoke, his eyes tearing up. A young runner trotted up to the colonel, who ignored him so that he could finish his speech. ". . . through whatever time I'm allowed on this earth."

The men exchanged puzzled looks as Manskart turned to receive the orders. The colonel nodded gravely and turned again to his men. "Attention!" He gave the signal, and Nate's rolling drumbeat began.

"Right face!"

The regiment turned crisply, each man hitting his mark at the right place at the right time, a most satisfying sensation. Manskart held them in this moment for a few beats, a moment of perfection, a few seconds at the crest of the roller coaster. The birds sang around them, and other units shuffled into place. Women and children camping with the soldiers hurried on toward the battlefield so that they could watch the men be gunned down with appalling speed and completeness.

To a man, the Heavies held their breath, waiting for the command to move out, and as the moment ripened, Steven glanced at the open flap of Manskart's tent, a major construction of pine and canvas complete with cot, a few hefty wooden boxes, and a camp chair. A splash of red caught his eye; large printing on a small box. In familiar modern type, it said, CAUTION—LIVE AMMUNITION. Steven recognized it as a box of cartridges, just like the one Kucharsky had had in his glove compartment.

"We are ready," Manskart said in a hoarse and dramatic whisper

The sight of the cartridges made everything snap into place: the new pistol, the nervousness: the bizarre pep talk. Manskart's scheme exploded into Steven's mind; it was the same one he'd once had.

Manskart planned to kill him during the battle.

"Regiment! Double quick! March!"

Before he could react, Steven was trotting with everyone else into the glare of the sun, doing his best to run in time with the others as Manskart and Swan ranged up and down the line, demanding an all-consuming, military attention. When they hit the line of bushes, Manskart sent them down. The Heavies hunkered next to a small, upward sloping field soon to host soybeans, but at the moment a waste of dusty rows, clods of dirt, and dried plants. Only a few hundred yards beyond it, Steven could see the tops of a band of oaks. The Rebels were that close.

Too fast, thought Steven. Any second Manskart could kill him. He needed more time.

You will have to kill, said Trow.

Under an order of silence, Steven sat on his haunches and reminded himself that he had no proof of Manskart's intentions. As sure as he was a total loser, he was not a killer. He couldn't be that insane. And suddenly he felt exhausted, ready to fall asleep right there in the dirt. His uniform became warm, and the sun started to make its presence felt on his cheeks. Pressing closer into the bushes, Steven closed his eyes and breathed the long Lamaze breaths that had done Patty no good, but that he used to practice before big meetings.

He could hear Manskart scooting from man to man. "Now we are called on to show what we can do at fighting!" he said. "I shall be with you! Do not shoot until you are in the Rebel works!"

When Steven opened his eyes he saw Manskart staring at him, one lid slowly coming down as if lining him up in his sights, thick lips working, slurping or discussing something with himself, obviously not in full control.

Trow's voice became more agitated. You must kill, he said. You must kill, you must kill, he chattered, almost as if he were reminding himself of the fact.

A cramp of fear wrenched Steven's bowels, so much so that he became dizzy, and a desperate need to write a note to Patty and the kids gripped him. He would explain everything, tell them how much he loved them and how sorry he was that his life had spun out of control in such an idiotic fashion, tell them everything that he'd ever wanted to do and say, give them a lifetime in a few minutes' words. But he had no paper, and no time, and he recalled something he'd read months ago in his tight little room, a final journal entry written by a man at this very battle as he lay bleeding in the dirt: "Today I am killed."

Someone giggled to his left. It was high-pitched, probably Bobby. Steven scanned the line. Murray Lummer chewed gum; Swan and Burney were both smiling. The rest looked businesslike, at most. For all the talk of honoring the dead, Steven concluded, few wanted to taste their fear. No one re-enacted panic, no one re-enacted fear, because that wasn't the point of re-enacting. On this field there would be no true risk, no real valor, no pain or fear, and no matter how authentic these thousands of people were, however much they could enter the lives they pretended to live, they could not enter their deaths. He was the only man facing death out here, and he didn't need the uniform to appreciate its power.

He felt in his pocket for his only chance and slipped it into his cartridge box. As he did, the scene became grainy in his eyes and the smell of dry leaves rose in his nose, the heat burned on his neck. More of what was happening around him became familiar, the curves of the ground, the aching sense of expectation; every second Trow was taking him back farther. A young man with spectacles and very red lips trotted over to Manskart, who saluted and then whispered to Nate. A strict, martial beat began. The regiment came to its feet and fell into line. "Load!" cried Manskart.

The men went through the steps of loading, yet as Steven reached back to his cartridge box, he couldn't decide what to do. His fingers played on the twist. If he took the precaution of loading the bullet, it could accidently fire and rip off an arm, blow open a head. But if he didn't, he would be defenseless, held in the palms of fate. Up ahead, Manskart stroked the handle of his pistol.

You must kill, said Trow, the words more desperate each time they ran through Steven's mind.

While he didn't know for sure whether Manskart meant to shoot him, he didn't know for sure that he didn't. Steven pulled out the cartridge and loaded the minie. He had never bargained for this—having to die, having to kill. Religion meant nothing at this moment of judgment; God meant nothing. He was abandoned. Trow was dragging him to the edge, forcing him to look over into the blackness of despair. Steven had been able to stop short the other times, but today he held his roaring bowels as tightly as he could, wondered whether there was a point to it, whether there was any difference between dying with shit in your pants and dying without it. His face puckered, only seconds from tears.

To his left and right he saw not his fellow modern Heavies, but lines of hundreds of men, scared, exhausted, determined. They were not the men he knew, though he knew them all the same, knew them as he'd known what took place here. He could see them, the real men of the 2nd Connecticut, in the last minutes before their deaths. They wore artillery uniforms still bright blue and trimmed with red. Instead of the quiet march of these ten men, Steven found himself inside the roar of a thousand, at the crest of a wave of stunned Connecticut men who'd never before seen a battle.

Manskart raised his pistol. Steven turned to Swan, who'd only wanted his house back. His punishment was that he would always be Joe Swan. "See you on the other side, friend," said Steven. He extended his hand to Calamus Dawes.

Swan shook his hand, smiled, whispered, "Still a fucking hardcore, eh?"

You must kill, you must kill, Trow's voice babbled away. Words of hopeless panic bounded, the spoutings of Babel, of one being cast down to Hell.

You must kill echoed again in Steven's mind, but now the words came slowly. No longer a command, they were heavy and terrible with the sad truth that Trow was trying to face. He would have to kill.

The voice sank to a murmur, the quiet counsel of the Devil. You will leave the world worse than you found it, Trow said. You should never have existed. No one cares that you will die. It is all meaningless.

At that moment, Steven understood that Trow was not speaking to him, Steven Armour. As the torturous emptiness of being the real John Trow swept through him, along with the sight of Manskart up ahead, he knew that at this moment on June 1, 1864, marching into this battle, John Trow had gone completely insane from despair. And yet the words of self-loathing he heard were familiar, familiar from long before he'd met John Trow. In the end, they *were* bound: two average men who'd lost all hope.

They went on through the soybeans with Nate marching ahead, through the line, drumming, until the boy was beside the colonel. The men cheered. To the beat of Nate's drum, the regiment headed forward into the trees. The Rebs were now visible, guns bristling out from behind their works.

Trow's despair spilled over into the abyss, and Steven could barely walk. In these last minutes before battle, Trow had damned himself—Steven knew that now—but Steven gripped the edge, the same edge of reason his brother and father had let go of in their own ways. They had dared to ask the point of it all, and both had come back permanently damaged. Now it was his turn to decide whether hope existed in his life.

It's about to happen, he thought; it's about to happen. The men splashed into a tiny rivulet at the bottom of a ravine, closer and closer.

"Aim low and aim well!" called a voice behind the Rebel lines.

This doesn't have to happen to me, Steven told himself in protest. I'm not John Trow.

The Confederate line blossomed in white smoke, the first shots, all of which missed the 2nd on that day in 1864. Steven could no longer tell what he was seeing, a false fog of war or the smoke of Trow's dreams, but it didn't matter. The men around him went down. Steven threw himself on the dirt, too, heard the bodies thudding all around him, and for a moment he felt saved. How could Manskart kill him here? All in a minute? Couldn't be done. He'd stay down.

Getting back to his feet, Manskart waved his pistol again and called the men forward. "Get up! Everyone up! Private Trow! *Get up!*"

Nate pounded feverishly on the drum, and all the men stared at Steven. He shoved himself up, and they moved three or four more steps forward until the second wave of shots exploded. The hundreds of images returned and multiplied in Steven's eyes, the screaming, the expressions of horror, raw fear and pain, surprise, unchecked by reason. And amid the scenes of true slaughter, he saw the men of the modern 2nd going down in their wild, balletic fashion, arms opening, bodies collapsing. Jerry fell, and Murray crawled toward him until he took a hit in the back and slumped down. Bobby took the all-time hit of his life, screaming and tugging at this throat. The smell of sulfur erupted through the field, and great bolls of smoke merged into banks of gray and white that the breeze couldn't move, so heavy was the volume of shooting.

Just as Steven was about to take his own hit and snuggle under Hube's body, Manskart jolted upright, straw hat still on his head. Grasping his arm, the arm supposedly just shot, Manskart turned and stared directly at Steven, pinned him with a dark intensity, and slowly raised the pistol, up, up, up to shoulder level. Arm trembling, eyes wild, Manskart waved the gun.

Steven had no choice. He pulled the gun to his side in Trow's unusual, uncontrollable stance.

He heard Manskart's minie whizz by him and plock into the leaves behind, felt his own gun veer left, and saw Nate's arms fling to the side, his body arch forward and fall heavily. Suddenly silent, the drum rolled off to the side.

CHAPTER

5 0

Heavies lay scattered in exaggerated postures of death, groaning, hands clutched to pretend gut wounds or lost limbs, faces frozen in horror, some men writhing for the total effect. The slaughter was complete. Scobeck cursed softly at the Cessna buzzing overhead, destroying the peace of the fallen.

Nate appeared to have fallen asleep, hands held sweetly near his face as they'd been that morning, his mouth open slightly, the only sign of violence on his face the small coating of dust created by his fall. The boy's chest was still.

"My son!" screamed Steven. "My son is dead!" On his knees, Steven scooped up the limp body and buried his face in it, thoughts imploding in the darkness he had created. This place where Trow had taken him, where he'd taken himself, had no words, the self-pity and the loathing simply sharp edges on the cliff he scraped against as he tumbled into the void. In his mind, all he could see was Nate's face breaking into a smile; over and over again, the slow action of his boy's face as he realized he was happy. Nate was dead. He had killed his son. Killed his son—the words that sealed him into the despair he had been unable to escape.

Steven rocked the boy, weeping, just as an appreciative roar went up from the spectators a hundred yards to the left and from the Confederates in the field, rewarding the Heavies for their performance.

A hand landed on Steven's shoulder. When he opened his eyes he saw Manskart standing over them, aghast, his lower lip blubbering up and down as he whispered, "Is he all right? Oh Jesus. Jesus." The cockeyed fatal duel had released whatever murderous impulse had been driving him, and he too began to crumble and weep. The evil stupidity of what they'd done was all too clear on the child's empty face. Steven's only wish was not so much to die as to disintegrate, to no longer exist, to have never existed.

Someone in the distance started a jaunty lilt on a solitary flute, and the general resurrection began. First Jerry Sears, then Lummer raised their heads from the red Virginia dirt, peering around for their first look at the afterlife. Scobeck heaved himself up, dusted off his pants, and the other followed him, replacing kepis, patting each other on the back. Rewinding his turban, which had been loosened by his fall, Burney came toward Steven and Manskart, both kneeling over Nate.

"Did he sprain something?" he asked.

Without affect, Steven said, "My son is dead. I have killed—"

Nate's eyes popped open. "Pretty good, huh, Dad? Bobby taught me."

It made no sense. In the first seconds of incomprehension Steven experienced the sensation of being torn out of something, as if some indulgent god had nullified his trip to Hades, until finally the light exploded in his head and he understood. Nate was alive. His shot had flown wildly into the forest. Steven could only weep more loudly now, his tears a kind of rain over the boy in his arms.

He had been given a second chance.

As the smoke cleared from the field, a future instantly appeared. He would have to tell Patty about the affair. Some day she'd forgive him. He was sure of that now. He was better than his actions; she knew that. That was why he loved her. He buried his face in Nate's hair.

"Take it easy, Dad." Nate shoved himself up. "It's all fake, remember? Like none of this is real? Hello? Dad?"

He imagined holding hands with Patty, watching Emily eat her waffles, looked forward to watching *Nick at Nite* with his dad, learning to ski with Nate. Becoming a senior vice president. All trivial pursuits, and revealed now to be wonders.

Steven grabbed Manskart's lapels, angered by the dumb sadness in the teacher's eyes. "Are we finished? Can we be done with this? We've each had our shot." So stunned did Manskart look, his jaw slack, rheumy eyes lacking any incisive gleam, that Steven questioned whether the man understood what had happened.

"I'm sorry, Walter. I'm sorry for what I did. It was wrong in every way. I know that and I'm sorry." He let go of Manskart's jacket, softened his tone. "I have to go home to my family, Walter. I'm gonna eat some shit and be done with all this. I'm pretty sure I still have a future."

CHAPTER

5 1

THAT EVENING, AFTER A LONG PULL OF DRIVING, Steven arrived home. It had been a hot day in Connecticut, strange for this early in the year, and along the side of the house where the lilies of the valley would go, Phil was watering the bushes. In front of him, wearing a pink bikini and getting drenched, Emily stood at attention, eyes closed, a young stalk of asparagus taking in all the light and water she could get and trying very hard to grow. "Dad, it's too early for that."

"Does anybody ever say it's too early for rain?" Phil asked. Steven couldn't answer that, so he took off his kepi, wiped his brow. "Didn't expect you back so soon," his father said. "Where's Nate?"

"Still there. I wasn't feeling well, but he was having a blast, so I let him stay with that teacher, the one he likes."

"Hey, you just missed your sister. She said she's coming through New York in a few weeks with Pierre after some conference in Ann Arbor. Wants to see everybody, so I invited her up. It's only a couple hours from LaGuardia, right?"

"Yeah. Well, about three."

"I was thinking we should get Jerry up here too. Maybe have a little Easter egg roll on the lawn. Whaddya think?" Steven smiled at the prospect of his family all together in his house. "Why don't you take off that costume and come help me water this little Emily tree before the sun goes down." The girl giggled and stamped her feet. "Don't forget to change the clocks tonight. Fall back, spring forward." Bracing himself with a deep breath of evening air, Steven turned toward the house and the conversation he was about to have with Patty. "Stevie."

He stopped. "Yeah?"

"Welcome back."

		DATE DUE	